The Seven Churches

Andrew
This may at least
be useful as a
guide to your
next trip to Prague

Robert
29/7/10

Miloš Urban

The Seven Churches

or

The Heptecclesion

A Gothic Novel of Prague

Translated from the Czech by
Robert Russell

PETER OWEN PUBLISHERS
London

PETER OWEN PUBLISHERS
73 Kenway Road, London SW5 0RE

Translated from the Czech *Sedmikostelí*

First English translation published in Great Britain 2010 by
Peter Owen Publishers

ISBN 978-0-7206-1311-7

Printed in the UK by
CPI Bookmarque, Croydon, CR0 4TD

This project has been funded with support from the European Commission. This publication reflects the views only of the author, and the Commission cannot be held responsible for any use which may be made of the information contained therein.

Education and Culture DG

Culture Programme

TRANSLATOR'S NOTE

Czech Names

Květoslav, the name that causes the hero so much embarrassment, translates roughly as 'Flower-lover'. His surname, *Švach*, is simply a Czech spelling of the German *schwach*, meaning 'weak'.

Streets are generally referred to only by a single name (usually ending in –á or –a), without the word *Ulice*, 'Street', though it has been retained in some cases for clarity.

Many Czech names have English equivalents, some of which I have used. In most cases, however, I have retained the Czech forms, thus *Václav* rather than Wenceslas, etc.

All but one of the characters in this story are imaginary, whereas all but one of the buildings are real. The institutions are, without exception, fictitious.

TO PRAGUE

THE NEW TOWN OF PRAGUE

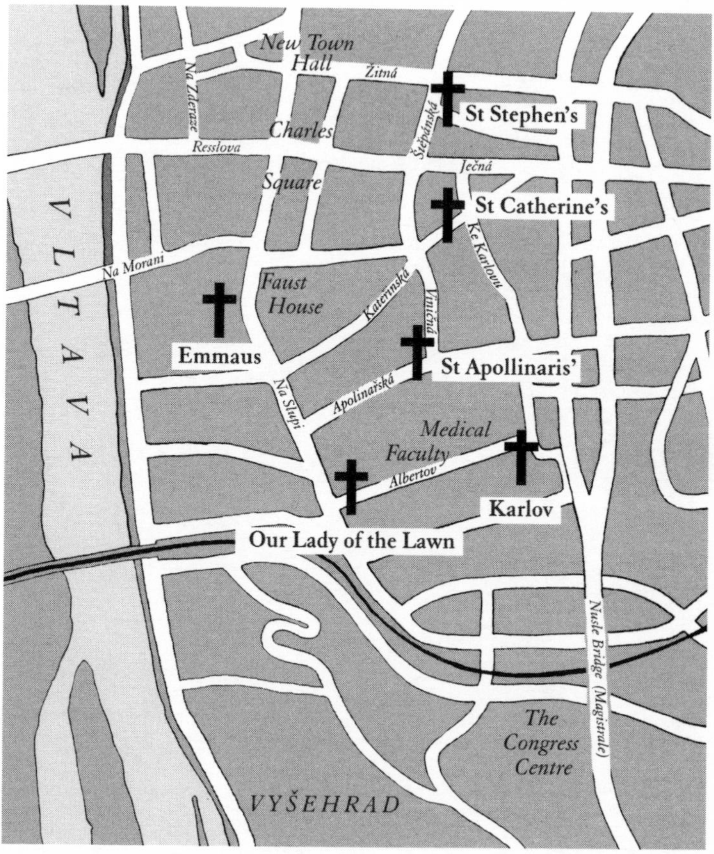

New tensions of reason and feeling, new concerns with the claim of the subjective and the psychological were generating the gothic novel . . . Not only was fiction recovering some of its origins in romance and the fantastic, but it was also debating the relations of reason and the imagination, the static and the revolutionary.

Richard Ruland and Malcolm Bradbury,
Puritanism to Postmodernism

Horror stories and narratives of historical events can be mutually illuminating and evoke an awareness and feeling for the past in readers otherwise indifferent to it.

Martin Procházka

The Romantic artist turns his sight away from himself and his own society and looks back.

Friedrich Nietzsche

1

I talk of the new season.
Spring has come in winter. Snow in the branches
Shall float sweet as blossoms.

T.S. Eliot

It was a beautiful early November morning. All through October a lingering Indian summer had kept autumn at bay until, with a flick of its wand, the first sharp frost numbed the city into immobility. Not half a year had passed since the end of the Modern Age; now the metropolis was bracing itself for the coming winter. As the days closed in and the cold crept under fingernails, factory chimneys exhaled their hot fetid breath and window-panes glistened with condensation. But they were the fumes of putrefaction, the sweat of death. For all the smart new façades and fast cars – the city's make-up and jewellery – this stark truth was best disguised by the unchanging trees in Charles Square, some a year old, some a century, some as old as the millennium itself. Yet everyone saw it coming. Many averted their eyes in dread and yielded to the onslaught of that final autumn, as the three-headed hound lunged headlong at the ancient city of Prague, its three ravenous maws devouring any living being that dared venture forth at this late hour of human history. The massacre was merciless.

That was last year, before everything changed. Then came the Age of Mercy.

*

A low, pale sun crept over the hospital wall and caught in the cobweb tops of the maples. Slowly, almost grudgingly, it warmed the icy air heavy with the smell of fallen leaves that covered the whole pavement. In Kateřinská they were no worse than in other years, but in Viničná they formed a great rustling dune all down the street, obliterating asphalt and cobblestones alike. Gone was all certainty of *terra firma*. Every step was an adventure into the unknown that left an ill-defined and vaguely ominous footprint in the russet drifts. But wading through a leaf-filled street can be dangerous – as dangerous as walking on a frozen river.

Cleaving the yellow sea and dodging the swirling showers of ochre, vermilion and umber, I made my way up Větrov Hill towards Karlov. By now the street had become a canyon, its sheer banks formed by the hospital wall on the left and the Museum of Mankind on the right. In my mind's eye I followed it over the crest of the rise, spanning the valley beyond and leading, inevitably, to the church. Here the devout pilgrim needs no guide.

An ambulance drove past, then another and, after an interval, a third. Not many really. In the old days, when I still wore a uniform and came this way not simply for pleasure, I had usually counted more. Then you could stroll up this quiet street, far from the haunts of drug-pushers and money-changers, and never meet a soul. What brought me here now? Habit perhaps, or the pleasure of a walk at dawn that promised more from the day ahead than the inevitable click of a light switch at dusk. But who would want to dash through the New Town in a wailing ambulance, disturbing the sublime peace of the morning?

Viničná Ulice is almost three hundred yards long and dead straight, affording an unobstructed view from one end to the other. I was no more than halfway up the street when I spotted a woman walking a short distance ahead of me. How had I not noticed her sooner? It gave me quite a start, as I had thought the street deserted.

The small stooping figure, though far from decrepit, seemed to be making laborious progress. She had short grey hair, a brown overcoat and – that indispensable accessory of elderly ladies – a brown shopping-bag. I slowed down so as not to startle her. This proved unnecessary: despite being knee-deep in leaves she walked surprisingly briskly.

As she waded through the gold-and-scarlet tide she kept glancing at the ochre wall on her left, as if on the look-out for a red street-sign or some other aid to orientation. She was not a local then. I noticed she was wearing large spectacles that concealed the entire upper half of her face. As I watched she turned her head, stopped and peered inside an open gate leading into a yard on her right. At that moment there appeared over the gatepost, directly above her, the massive tower of St Apollinaris with its pointed roof. It looked like a mischievous monk waiting to pounce on any hapless pilgrim to the church. I was on the point of shouting a warning when I realized that the shimmering air was playing tricks with my eyes.

The woman hesitated and walked on. And now my first hallucination gave way to a second: the rustle of her footsteps in the leaves no longer seemed to come from some way ahead but from close behind me. Though I was sure no one was following me I turned my head. The street was deserted. On the roadway tyres had traced black lines in the snow; the silence, now that the sirens had died away, was more profound than ever. A gust of wind stirred the leaves and the tracks disappeared.

Laughing at my own jumpiness I turned to continue on my way. But the small woman was nowhere to be seen. She must have turned into Apolinářská, either right towards the church or left towards the Magistrale, the freeway that bisects the city. Or had she carried straight on down the old steps to Albertov? Would she have dared?

Větrov Hill is an inhospitable place and treacherous to those foolish enough to succumb to its beauty. The wind rushes up Viničná and Apolinářská, creating where they meet a whirlwind like a small tornado. On more than one occasion it has whipped off my cap and hurled it over a fence or under a car, and the rain always caught me unawares here with nowhere to take shelter. Today those two bullies were at work elsewhere – possibly across the valley – but Větrov had another trick up its sleeve: just before I reached the junction I tripped on a hard object hidden in the leaves, scuffing my shoe and stubbing my toe painfully. I pushed aside the leaves with my foot to reveal the broken paving. The square-cut greenish stones were laid in a geometrical pattern. Many were missing. In the grey cracks fluttered a few bleached blades of grass – a pale memento of summer.

At the crossroads, where once stood the Poisoned Chalice – a notorious public house frequented by students and criminals – I turned right and, not for the first time, was astonished by the brilliant colours of the flowers in the garden of St Apollinaris' Vicarage. Perhaps they bloom in memory of the now-vanished hostelry and those generations of regulars who used to stagger out at closing time to water them through the slatted fence. I know a bit about flowers, but I have never managed – at least not with any certainty – to tell the difference between dahlias and asters. I admire both. *Tall asters, those last constellations of declining summer, grew there in bright profusion*. That morning I recalled those words and let them jog my memory. I don't know who wrote them or when I read them, but now they reminded me and dispelled all doubt. The next time you pass St Apollinaris' Vicarage, remember that those spiky heads behind the fence are asters. Names are important.

Out of habit I raised my eyes from the red and mauve flowers to the mighty walls and dark windows of the church. Approached from this side St Apollinaris' seems like an impregnable fortress, too close for comfort, and you quicken your pace as the towering mass of masonry threatens to crush you with its countless – yet precisely counted – blocks of stone. Better than this eastern aspect is the view from the south side: here you can take in the whole church, which now appears in a brighter, friendlier light. Not until you see the building from the south-east, however, can you appreciate the whole of the tower, nave and apse in all their splendour. Indeed, though the church was until recently badly neglected, you would be hard put to find its equal.

My gaze wandered up the buttresses and over the leaded windows with their pointed arches. Time had taken its toll on the walls of the apse: the ochre rendering, turning green and patched with moss near the ground, bulged where the damp had penetrated, forming fragile insect-infested pockets. Moisture glistened on the bare stone buttresses scarred with cracks, where over the years lichen, soot and decaying matter had lodged. Spiders crawled out of crevices into the warm sunlight. In the recess of one tall window sat a brown cockroach. It seemed to have just woken up and taken fright at something.

In bygone times the place had known other denizens. The buttresses that still held up the walls had once supported flimsy roofs of bundled faggots, in whose shade the destitute, in the hope of alms, had held out their leprous hands to artisans, clerks and merchants on their way to mass. They, too, had their guild and defended their miserable hovels against newcomers from the countryside who had nothing at all. Of the beggars not a trace now remained, yet the Samaritan spirit of the place lived on: not far from the church was a centre for drug addicts – the lepers of the twentieth century.

But this morning no one was out and about; no one dared venture forth into this blinding light. Apolinářská was empty and silent. No congregation flocked to the church, which was closed for repairs. All was as usual. Except for one thing: in the open space outside the ugly concrete infant school across the road, beside a statue of a kneeling girl, a second figure had appeared.

It was the woman who had been walking ahead of me. Still clutching her brown bag, she stood gazing at that stylized representation of innocent childhood. I saw her lips move. Perhaps it reminded her of something. I drew closer. The unusual sight of a person conversing with a statue was disquieting. Quite forgetting I was no longer in uniform, I quietly walked up to the woman and asked if she was in need of help.

She pointed to the statue. 'That's not possible . . .'

What was not possible? The awful building? Or the institution it housed? The nearby Poisoned Chalice, the scene of several infamous murders, had been pulled down long ago and replaced, in a more enlightened age, by – what else? – a school for infants! (But can the *genius loci* be exorcized just like that?) Yet the look of wide-eyed astonishment on the face of that woman with her spectacles and shopping bag expressed not indignation but panic. It occurred to me she might be mad. Maybe she was on her way to the doctor's or the psychiatric clinic just up the road and had forgotten where she was going. Lost in familiar memories, she had lost her way in unfamiliar streets.

Again I addressed her, as gently as I could. 'It's only a statue. If you're going to the doctor's and you've lost your way I can take you there.'

'Can't you see?' she snapped, turning on me angrily. 'Don't you know what kind of flowers those are?'

My suspicions were confirmed: the woman was raving mad. All the same I glanced at the crumbling concrete statue. All that remained of the left arm was a rusty wire. On her head, which was wet with dew and darker than her body, the maimed girl wore a crown of bright-yellow flowers – no doubt left there by some other, living girl, a girl of flesh and blood.

'They're fresh,' said the little lady with the spectacles. 'Someone picked them this morning and made them into a garland. A garland for a stone virgin. How on earth . . . ? I know for a fact these flowers only grow in the spring.'

'I expect there's a simple explanation,' I reassured her. 'There's an institute just down the hill, some kind of genetic garden that belongs to the university. They've probably developed a species that flowers in autumn.'

She looked at me as if I was the crazy one, not her. 'Oh yes? Show me who could do a thing like that and I'll go down on my knees and pray to them! That is a medicinal plant, young man, and a very rare one. Not that it means much to you, I'm sure. It only ever flowers in early spring.'

Childhood memories flashed through my mind: walking with my grandmother, picking yellow flowers; honey, cough syrup; old wives' remedies.

I took a closer look. The little lady stepped aside to make room. Carefully, I reached up and removed the garland from the girl's head. For a moment I held it in both hands, turning it this way and that. And then I sniffed it. Suddenly the name came to me: coltsfoot.

I was still gazing down at the garland when I was startled by a loud crash followed by an ugly metallic sound. It came from somewhere above me – out of the air, out of the sky. Then all was quiet again. I looked up from the flowers still dangling from my fingers. I was alone with the statue – the old lady had vanished. Again I heard the sound, clearer this time, its strange, irregular tones reverberating all around: ding DANG, ding DANG . . . Yes, there was something odd about it, something different. Up in the church tower the bell was ringing, horribly out of tune. I glanced at my watch. It was eight forty-five. My blood froze: the church was closed yet someone was ringing for mass.

I am not a hero. I went to the clinic near by and called the police from the doorman's booth. Automatically I dialled my ex-boss's number and was secretly relieved when his secretary, rather than my ex-boss himself, answered the phone. Four minutes later a patrol car arrived with two officers, both of whom I knew. The excruciating din of the bell continued unabated.

Finding a side door ajar, we entered the church. Through the dirty windows of the apse a murky light filtered into the nave – here even the daylight was in need of renovation. There was no one about. The altar was thick with dust, the organ loft a dark tangle of cobwebs. We made for the shadows below the gallery and, feeling our way and following the sound (by now the din of the bell was quite deafening), found the door that led up to the belfry. It was unlocked. Beyond the door the stairs were in pitch darkness. One of the policemen flicked on his cigarette lighter, and we took the first flight of steps three at a time. Soon the flame was redundant, paling into invisibility in the white shafts of sunlight streaming down from above.

At last we came out under the timberwork that held the big bell.

The noise was unbearable – a moment longer and all three of us would have leapt from the belfry windows just to get away from it. The air was thick with whirling dust, and what with the blinding splinters of light glancing off the walls we could at first see almost nothing. All we could make out clearly was the outline of a gigantic spider swinging to and fro on a long strand of web. Was it a ghost? Or a puppet to scare away children? The answer was much simpler. What we saw hanging there was a human being – the wretched victim of some nocturnal monster, now transformed into a monster himself. There was nothing particularly frightening about the figure, but what had been done to it was terrible. The man jerked about like a marionette, now dancing on his hands to the music of the bell, now crawling up the walls, now swinging back into empty space like a fish wriggling on a hook, hurtling this way and that with each beat of the iron clapper. One of his legs was attached to the bell by a rope.

We rushed forward, but the bell's momentum plucked him out of our reach and dashed him once more against the opposite wall of the bell-chamber. As the living pendulum swung back towards us we grabbed the poor man by the arms and held on to him until the angry clapper was finally subdued, rocking like fishermen on a choppy sea as his body gave a final lurch, first left, then right, before the bell finally came to rest. Our ears ached, our heads ached; we ached all over.

The policemen held him while I cut the rope. The bloody head lolled level with our chests, the eyes tight shut, the face ashen. The only sign of life came from the feebly groaning mouth. We laid him gently on the floor: he was unconscious. First we checked his breathing, then we felt him carefully all over and pulled up his shirt to see if there were any signs of contusion. One of his ribs looked as if it might be broken, or at least cracked, and he probably had concussion – caused by the relentless battering against the stone wall – but his condition was evidently not hopeless. One of the officers called the station on his radio and asked them to send an ambulance.

That was all we could do. It was not until I had mopped my face with my handkerchief and straightened up that I saw just how brutally the man had been turned into an involuntary bell-ringer. We had assumed the rope had been simply looped around his ankle, but to our horror we now saw it had in fact been threaded through his leg, disappearing into an ugly wound between his ankle and Achilles tendon and causing a horrible swelling in the surrounding skin and tissue. On the other side the rope came out like a thread from the eye of a needle and was secured by a double knot. There was hardly any blood, but the skin around the wound was rapidly turning purple with a few darker bluish patches.

From outside came the wail of a siren followed by a clatter of feet on the stairs, and the ambulance men appeared in their red overalls. Though clearly shocked at the sight of the man, they lifted him on to a stretcher without a word, fastened the straps and carried him down the steep steps. I told the policemen it looked as if someone had been swinging the man just before we arrived and quickly gone into hiding. He could not be far away. We searched the octagonal belfry and climbed the ladder into the conical loft above it. Then we opened the shutters to make sure no one was hiding on the ledge outside, but it sloped so steeply that only a monkey could have found a foothold on it. My suspicion remained unconfirmed, though I could not rid myself of the feeling that we were not alone in the tower. The policemen made a few notes and left. My statement could wait – after all, I was a former colleague. I searched the whole place again. The only way out of the belfry was the staircase by which we had entered. It was a total mystery – like the freshly picked coltsfoot in November.

2

Qui vive?
'Tis I, Time Past, who stand at your door,
your friend and guardian
and admonisher.

Richard Weiner

The history of my misfortunes began on the day I received my name – or, rather, the day I was born. Or was it nine months earlier? Or perhaps it all began with the birth of my father, the man whose hideous name I was later to inherit.

My parents never wanted me. For my sake they consolidated the mire of their relationship into the rock of matrimony. The excesses into which as an adult I was insidiously lured are simply the logical outcome of that misunderstanding. To my mind there is nothing so pitiful as marriage in the twentieth century, and I count myself lucky to have reached the end of that ghastly era as a bachelor. No doubt this was only because I was able to turn back in time, to escape into the past with its secret stories. Not all of them can still be told; only the worthwhile tales survive. My own story, itself now a thing of the distant past, is one of the most remarkable.

I shall begin with a memory, still vivid to this day, that encapsulates my childhood – a memory of an outing my father treated me to on my eighth birthday. At the time we lived in the town of Mladá Boleslav, in the heart of a region steeped in history – though our home was on a modern housing estate. Every year my parents took me on holiday to nearby Mácha Lake. Each time we talked about visiting the picturesque castle that lay on our route, and each time we put it off until the following year.

Until, that is, my eighth birthday and my father's surprise announcement: a trip to Bezděz. I was allowed to sit in the front of the car, where the seatbelt conferred a greater sense of importance than any general's sash. I was happy. Not even my father's grumbles about my mother, which at the time were becoming ever more frequent, could dampen my spirits. I simply ignored him, determined to let nothing spoil my day. Forgetting I was there, he gave vent to his spleen.

'Mother's just lazy. That's the real reason she lies around on the sofa all day. She should bake *me* a cake, not you – who's she trying to fool? She couldn't care less about you. You've been pestering us about that bloody castle for four years now, and who ends up taking you? Your dad, of course. The things I do for you!'

His knuckles were white as he gripped the steering-wheel and argued with my absent mother. He reached across for a cigarette and seemed surprised to see me there beside him, huddled in my seat under a seatbelt that was far too loose for me (those were the days before inertia-reel belts). With a laugh he ruffled my hair. My scalp burnt under his touch as if he'd scratched me.

When the engine started emitting strange noises his mood grew even worse. He slowed down, cocking his head to listen, then undid my belt and told me to get into the back and press my ear against the seat-back, behind which was located the engine. I heard nothing out of the ordinary – but then my mind wasn't entirely on the job, since we were at that moment passing through Běla Pod Bezděz. Between the last houses of the village, beyond fields of wheat, two olive-green hills could be glimpsed in the distance, atop the higher of which stood the white castle – a sight I had no intention of missing.

Retribution for my indifference to the workings of the engine awaited me at the car-park below the castle. My father refused to leave the car until he had found the cause of the knocking noise. As he poked about under the bonnet I ran to and fro between the car and the first stone gateway at the foot of the hill. Through it passed an ancient roughly paved track that wound steeply up to the castle. The baking-hot slabs of broken stone made me want to lie down and snuggle into the cracks between them, the way you snuggle into a duvet. Then Father could walk right past without seeing me.

He spent an hour examining the car. No fault was found, nor any means of stopping the knocking. So when my father simply smiled at me and shrugged I could hardly believe my eyes. I was so thrilled I could have hugged him – except I knew he didn't like being hugged. While he was packing up his tools the village clock struck eleven. It was oppressively hot, and we were plagued by mosquitoes. My father announced that we could now set off for the castle and took me by the hand. His fingers were covered in oil, which I suspected he wanted to wipe off on mine. Guessing my thoughts, he laughed. I let go of his hand and darted off like a hare, quivering with rage and impatience.

Father puffed his way up to the castle in the sweltering heat and arrived at the third gate exhausted. At this point one enters the castle fortifications and the forest gives way to prickly scrub; on one side, built on the bare rock, a crenellated wall leads up to the Devil's Tower. In the meantime I had been up to the ticket desk at the top gate five times and five times run back – each time disappointed at his slow progress. On the way I passed lots of people, all of them coming down, it being nearly noon. We were the only ones going up. I was delighted: we would have the castle all to ourselves. I'd always thought of it as mine.

My hopes were dashed by a man with a cigarette dangling from the corner of his evil-looking face who was hanging around by the hut that served as a ticket office. From here a wooden paling, about ten yards long and higher than a grown man, extended to the first of the beech trees at the top of the north side of the hill, closing off the area below the last gateway with its heavy oak door. To see the view you had to either retrace your steps and peer though the treetops for a glimpse of Břehyň Pond and, beyond it, Mácha Lake or, as I discovered only later, carry on to the south side of the second courtyard, from where you could see the village of Houska, with Říp Hill in the distance behind it and – perhaps once a year, in windy weather when the sky is streaked with cirrus – the spires of St Vitus' Cathedral in Prague.

I decided to slip round the paling and look north. Clinging to the splintery planks at the very edge of the drop, I had no sooner left the area designated to the public than the man with the cigarette grabbed me by the arm and shouted, 'You're not allowed there!' His voice was brusque and harsh with a foreign accent.

I turned to him with a start. His hair was slicked down with a dead-straight parting, which, along with his square-cut moustache and fake-leather belted jacket, gave him a bizarre and rather fearsome aspect. I had no idea why he was so offended.

At that moment my father appeared. I expected him to have a go at the fellow, but, instead, with a nod in my direction and a roll of his eyes, he hustled me off to the ticket office in silence. There he told me in an angry whisper not to talk to anyone. I glanced at the man with the cigarette. He was watching us, his eyes narrowed in inexplicable suspicion verging on contempt. Today I know what that look was: it was the look of the twentieth century.

Armed with our tickets, we entered the small door set into the gate and found ourselves in the first courtyard. Relaxing his grip on my shoulder, Father explained in a kindlier tone that a few miles north-east of here was an airport – a Soviet airport – and that the purpose of the paling and the guard was to prevent people from looking in that direction and taking photographs. I objected that it wasn't the airport I was interested in but Ralsko, a hill even more precipitous than Bezděz, on top of which stood a lopsided ruin that bore a chilling resemblance to a dilapidated throne. On it, as I had long known, sat an invisible giant – arms resting on the crumbling walls, legs dangling down the steep hillside – who kept watch over the ancient lands of the Berks of Dubá and thus over my own home in Boleslav. What did I care about airports and Soviets? Compared with my guard, theirs was a pathetic joke.

But my father was no longer listening. Coming down the steps from one of the castle doors was a beautiful woman – today I would call her a girl, but at the time she seemed old and unattainably adult. She greeted my father and, seeing that there were only two of us for the tour, laughed and said at least we'd soon get it over with. We hardly knew where to look first: at her long eyelashes, rosy lips and fair hair; or her slender figure clad in a short yellow skirt, green T-shirt and waist-length faded denim jacket. Sheep-like, we trailed after her through the tumbledown halls and blackened kitchens, concentrating mainly on those bare legs and feet in their loose, slapping sandals, which echoed loudly through the empty banqueting-rooms. She drew our attention to the Gothic windows with their stone tracery, the floral motifs on the capitals and corbels; but I was incapable of raising my eyes, which remained riveted on her ankles, and it was left to my father to evince any interest of an architectural nature, though he, as I was well aware, was even more smitten by our guide than I. The girl was young, totally modern and seemed quite out of place amid those grey ruins; yet she moved through the place as naturally as if she were the lady of the castle herself, bringing it to life with brilliant colour. The bulging walls and piles of masonry competed with us for her favour: wherever she stopped they fell silent and, like us, made a show of listening in rapt attention.

Despite our failure, indeed our inability, to take in what she was saying, we pretended to be knowledgeable about history, trying to outdo each other with what we hoped were interesting and occasionally witty questions and observations. Needless to say, Father won: he earned looks of appreciation, while all I got were a few indulgent glances. Furious, I tried all the harder to show off how grown-up I was, until Father was obliged to reprimand me and apologize to the girl. She, however, simply went on nibbling at a blade of cat's-tail grass, half opening her lips in a smile of amused condescension and revealing her moist white teeth. For a moment I imagined I was that lucky blade of grass, exploring her lips and tongue, and the dazzling afternoon sun was suddenly eclipsed.

Piqued, I decided to keep my distance. How dare he tell me to shut up! It was a clear abuse of adult authority. I hadn't meant to be cheeky – just witty. Spotting an old stone tub full of rain-water at the foot of a nearby wall, I began extolling the virtues of medieval plumbing and with a wink asked our guide if that was where she took her showers. It was a feeble joke, but at the time it struck me as the height of waggish sophistication. Father told me if I didn't stop being a nuisance he'd take me back to the ticket office and finish the tour without me. I was quite sure nothing would have given him greater pleasure.

I stopped listening to the guide's commentary but continued watching her from a distance. I tried to imagine her as my mother. It was a thrilling thought. How wonderful it would be to have such a beautiful, kind young mother! Instantly, however, I was overcome with shame and guilt. That would be betraying my real mother – and quite unnecessarily: the girl could equally be my sister or my aunt . . . but that was as far as my imagination went.

She and my father had obviously taken a shine to each other. Now and then she even departed from her script, explaining how she was studying history in Prague and that this was compulsory 'brigade' work, which she described as 'summer activity'. Father found the expression comical. Was she sufficiently active? Wouldn't she like to be even more active? His jokes embarrassed me – they weren't a patch on my medieval-plumbing quip. To my surprise she laughed. This maddened me, and I fell even further behind so as to keep out of their sight. When the guide pointed over the top of the paling to Houska Castle, shimmering white in the haze just below the blue line of the horizon, I could barely bring myself to look.

I cheered up a little when, as we were coming to the end of the tour, the girl suddenly suggested we have lunch together – we could improvise a picnic. Father thought it a splendid idea, and I, too, was pleased we could now spend more time with our beautiful guide than our tickets entitled us to. We sat some way apart – he at the foot of the Great Tower, I below the ruins of the oldest wing – each of us wondering where she would sit when she returned from the ticket office with her sandwiches and lemonade. Father gave me an inscrutable look, then set about cutting slices of yellow cheese, deliberately tilting the knife to catch the sun and dazzle me. Or was I imagining it? I had a knife, too, a little penknife with a British flag on the handle. But I had nothing to slice, so instead I threw it down on the turf. I was lucky: it stuck in perfectly. This did not escape Father's notice; in fact he got such a fright he dropped his cheese. At that moment the guide reappeared. She took a few steps in my direction, hesitated, then changed course towards my father who, cocking an eyebrow at me, revelled in his triumph like a Roman conqueror. I scraped up a handful of sand and tossed it in the air, covering myself in dust.

As they resumed their conversation Father became increasingly relaxed. They sat in the shade of the tower, while I was ensconced in the sun a few yards away chewing a disagreeably crunchy cheese sandwich and listening with closed eyes to the faint murmur of bees mingled with the two distant heat-baked voices. I couldn't make out the individual words and was glad of it. I stared at the parched grass sprinkled with daisies and tiny five-petalled flowers whose name escaped me.

The south-facing stone wall behind me was scorching hot, and I had the unpleasant sensation it was burning a hole in my back. I realized that Father, who was still chatting away happily, was quite unaware of this and would remain so until the old wall baked me to the bone and flames burst forth from my chest. By then, I thought, rubbing my hands in satisfaction, I would be beyond rescue.

I must have dozed off, because what I saw next – quite distinctly, on a clear, sunny afternoon – was impossible: a flash of lightning, followed by a shuddering crash of thunder. I looked up and saw something falling from the top of the tower: a large black object, with geometrical protuberances like arms and legs, hurtling down to crush the people sitting below.

Before the monster hit the ground I woke up. The guide and my father were still chatting quietly away. From a crevice in the wall behind me came the chirrup of a cricket. I was dripping sweat, my head ached, but I barely noticed: I was staring in horror at two black rods sticking out of a clump of bushes just beyond the Great Tower. I got to my feet and was on my way to investigate them when Father called me over to have a drink of water. Seeing the sweat trickling down my temples, he got up, felt my forehead and told me off for not wearing my cap. The guide tried to look concerned, but I could tell she was not sincere so decided to ignore her. Pointing to the thing in the bushes, I told them it was a triangulation. I didn't know exactly what a triangulation was but thought it was a pyramid that had once stood on top of the tower and that they were lucky it hadn't fallen right on top of them. To this day I have no idea how that strange word came into my head at that precise moment nor why I uttered it. Judging from the look on the guide's face I wasn't the only one who was surprised.

She asked if I had ever been to the castle before or read anything about it – I could read, couldn't I? – or whether I had heard about it at school. Where did I go to school? In Boleslav? I merely shook my head, inwardly rejoicing at my success. I had aroused her interest. I had impressed her. I had won! Avoiding Father's eyes, I now hung on her every word. Introducing herself as Olga (she and Father were already on first-name terms), she took me by the hand and led me over to the strange object that I had been able not only to identify but to locate correctly on the roof of the Great Tower, where indeed it had once stood. Father trailed along behind us in glum silence.

The iron pyramid was black with age and in places had rusted away completely. Its tip and what remained of its sides were buried in the ground, and all that was visible were the two projecting legs of L-section iron, about eight feet in length, that I had seen from the other side of the courtyard.

Olga, now back in her role as guide, told us how the hoisting of the pyramid on to the tower had become part of the latter-day lore of the castle. The operation began in 1824 but was interrupted by an accident: an arch had collapsed under the workmen's feet, and it was only by good luck that no one had been seriously injured. The men had remained stranded overnight at the top of the tower, huddled on a narrow ledge, until local villagers came to their rescue the next morning with hastily constructed ladders. Within a year misfortune struck again: one fine, clear afternoon a surveyor was taking readings from the tower of the Provodin Rocks when, literally out of the blue, lighting struck the triangulation pyramid and knocked it to the ground, together with the surveyor, who lost consciousness for several hours. When the unfortunate man tried to tell the castle warden what had happened, however, he could not even remember his own name. The warden recorded the incident in the castle chronicle, adding the date: 4 April 1825. The broken pyramid was dragged to the foot of the wall where it lies rusting to this day. Olga finished her account by remarking that 'the story of how Bezděz resisted the baleful march of progress' had not been included in the official commentary since before the war. She couldn't imagine where I had got hold of it.

While my head swelled with pride, Father struggled to suppress a fit of yawning.

Olga looked at her watch and said there were other visitors waiting for her outside. At the gate she held out her hand and asked me my name. I could not bring myself to tell her. It would have spoilt the whole day – especially my amazing display of erudition and her admiring response. So I said nothing. Father, with a dismissive wave of his hand, explained that I was ashamed of my name, and the instant she unlocked the gate I rushed out before she could ask me again. There were about fifteen people waiting at the ticket office. For some reason they all stared at me, except for a man leaning up against the paling. It was not the same guard as before lunch; this one wore a flat peaked cap. But he, too, peered inquisitively at the new arrivals from under his bushy eyebrows as he puffed at his cigarette, which stuck out of a huge moustache that masked his entire mouth. It took Father a suspiciously long time to say goodbye to Olga.

That evening, though it was my birthday, Father went off to work as soon as he had finished his supper. Even more surprisingly – both to my mother and myself – he took the car instead of his usual bus. I guessed where he was going but said nothing. In our contest for Olga's favour he had beaten me hollow, yet I was resolved to take it like a man. I felt let down. Worse, I felt betrayed. But I refused to betray him and looked forward to the day when he would come to appreciate my magnanimity. That day never came. Instead, I was oppressed by the certain knowledge that I had, by my complicit silence, betrayed my mother. The cake she had baked for my birthday was delicious – the best cake I had ever tasted. But there was bitterness in every bite, and it was all I could do to eat a couple of mouthfuls.

It didn't take my mother long to discover Father's infidelity, nor was it the first time. For a while the atmosphere at home was pretty unpleasant, but I learnt to anticipate these periods of silent resentment and grew accustomed to them, just as I was accustomed to my parents themselves. I learnt to overlook their weaknesses and childish whims and became reconciled to the fact that they could not, or would not, understand me. My revenge was to exclude them from my world. But the worst thing about my eighth birthday was that now, for the first time, I had become directly involved in our domestic disasters. A little pimp – that's how I saw myself. And for years to come I felt ashamed not only for my mother's sake but for my father's and my own. Now I prefer not think about it, though for years I did think about it every day. Until last autumn, when Time threw events into reverse. Don't get me wrong; I'm not complaining – quite the contrary. By then it had all become pointless anyway.

3

I wander in a land of dry stones:
if I touch them they bleed.

T.S. Eliot

My name became a problem when I started going to school. At first the children accepted it as they did all the other names: they only began sounding ridiculous when uttered by parents. I could handle that. But as we moved up the school, and the children discovered their capacity and proclivity for cruelty, the real hell began. Any kind of intimacy between pupils was inadmissible. Hatred and contempt were the order of the day, and school etiquette demanded there was always somebody who had to be systematically ignored or insulted. Friendships were out of the question: anyone who transgressed against this unwritten rule was lampooned and ostracized.

When I was born, Hitler and Stalin were long dead but Mao was still alive. My parents did not have me baptized and gave me only one first name – a name for weaklings and losers, a name single and solitary, just like me. How I longed for a different name! But you can't just go out and find a name, the same as you can't find a brother or a sister. You can find friends, yes. But where?

Olga, the perfidious Lady of the Castle, remained long in my thoughts. Above all, she remained in my dreams, which would haunt me all through the following day. For years her face was in my mind's eye and such was my naivety that I even conceived the notion of tracking the woman down and pouring out my heart to her. For a while the image of Olga was replaced by that of other girls (which meant girls at school), but my taste had already been formed and, if anything, became even more particular, largely as a result of my shyness. My ideal of beauty was unattainable beauty. The more unattainable the object of my desire, the more intense my fantasy attachment to it.

My schoolmates' directness and audacity in these matters, while I envied them, only served to inhibit me. I felt my name was a handicap, since I could not even introduce myself – after all, telling someone your name is the first step towards friendship. I began avoiding people, but since I carried so many of them around in my head it didn't bother me too much. And in time I learnt to make do with these inner companions – or at least that's what I told myself. I also read a lot.

At high school I took to calling myself K. In my first year everyone teased me about it, then they got used to the single initial and actually started addressing me by it – it was, after all, far shorter than my full name, and in their eyes one letter was about all I was worth. I was a bad student, and my poor results did little to improve the jealously guarded reputation of our science-oriented class. In fact, I was among the weakest students, and on more than one occasion it was suggested I might fare better in another school. I liked the idea of foreign languages but never managed to get into a class where they were taught, there being too much competition from others like myself who were flummoxed by the simplest equation with two unknowns. More complex matters such as logarithms, integrals and problems of descriptive geometry passed me by like a bus full of jabbering Chinamen: I saw it coming, ready to jump aboard, but as the bus approached the stop my courage failed me, and I was left standing there, watching it disappear round the corner never to return.

Every year I was in danger of failing because of my science grades. I was so hopeless that my teachers despaired of me and told me I should forget about university – assuming, that is, I passed my school-leaving examinations. The anxiety and paranoia caused by my abysmal grades, along with Father's constant jeremiads about not having entered me for the Military Academy (where anyone could get a degree), drove me into the consoling embrace of the north Bohemian countryside. It was a landscape admirably detached from the world and the brutalities of the twentieth century – though of these it had seen more than its fair share – and for that I was grateful, seeing in it a sign of grace.

While I was not indifferent to nature, I found those forests with their endless trees oppressively empty. What fascinated me about the countryside was the stone – stone once fashioned by the hands of men who had taken God's design and adapted it to their own ends. I sought refuge in the stone dwellings of long-vanished noblemen: in the silence of winter; in summer, when they resounded with the din of day-trippers; and in spring, when the melting stone revealed its mysteries. But autumn was my favourite season for exploring ruins – ruins with such poetic names as Bezděz, Kvítkov, Milštejn, Děvín, Sloup, Ronov, Berštejn and Dubá – for that is the time when stones are most communicative: all I had to do was place my hand on them and listen. This may surprise you, but to me it has always been the most natural thing in the world.

I had no wish to get involved in school activities or youth groups, not that there was much chance of my being chosen for any position of responsibility. But I did win the respect of the staff with my contributions to the school exhibitions board, and it was these that helped me scrape through to the next class. Once a year, on Independence Day, our form master diligently put together a colourful display of socialist slogans and pinned them up on the board – a job he later delegated to a 'board boy' picked from among the best students. Conscientious though he was, I remember the fellow was none too pleased at the privilege. But when the others mocked him for his unseemly zeal, his excuse was that it would count in his favour when he came to apply for university.

Though nobody asked me, I had a shot at it, too. I produced an exhibition of pen-and-ink drawings of Czech castles by the Romantic poet Karel Hynek Mácha – a task that occupied me for many a winter evening. Under each reproduction I added a caption and a brief account of the best-known legends associated with the place in question. If I couldn't think of any I would make something up or borrow stories from other castles. My inventions were always inspired by local history and invariably bloody. My modest exhibition duly appeared on the board, to the astonishment of my schoolmates, right next to the annual display commemorating the socialist victory of February 1948. When the bell went someone told me I had better take it down as it might be construed as an act of provocation. I didn't think it would.

When our form master arrived he noticed my work at once. Approaching the board, he put on his glasses and examined each picture with its accompanying text. Then, removing his glasses, he turned to the class and asked who had prepared the display and why. I stood up and said the first thing that occurred to me: I had wanted to mark the anniversary of Mácha's visit to Mladá Boleslav. The teacher at first looked doubtful, suspecting a prank. But when nobody burst out laughing he asked me why I found that so interesting. I replied that Mácha had been fascinated by the name of the rock which in those days had stood just above the town: *Hroby* or Tombs Rock. He had spent a night there and later wrote a story about it. Some years ago the local council had had the rock dynamited to make way for the new flats that now stood on the site; I had simply wanted to make sure my classmates did not forget about Tombs Rock. The teacher gave me a long, searching look and decided I was telling the truth. When at the end of the lesson he actually praised my work I was thrilled to bits. I was easily thrilled: it was the first praise I had ever received.

Our teacher mentioned my project at the next staff meeting and asked the headmaster to put it on record, in connection with some inter-school competition, as a Special Class Activity. I was asked to prepare similar thematic exhibitions on a regular basis; it was even hinted that my prospects of getting into university were not altogether hopeless after all. I might even be recommended.

My narrative displays – or 'comic strips' as they were jokingly called – soon made me a focus of attention. For my classmates I was a creep and a swot, while the teachers thought I was just sucking up to the Head. The only person who appreciated my work was our history teacher, Mr Netřesk. Once he told me that my tendency to turn to – not to say escape into – the past, however uncritical and dangerously idealizing, clearly betokened a genuine interest. Of course, I was flattered but remained secretly ashamed of the real purpose towards which all my efforts were directed. I positively devoured his lessons on ancient Greece and Rome, while my passion for the Middle Ages burnt brighter than any medieval torch. I studied three times harder than I needed to get top marks, and before long I knew almost as much as university students. Netřesk took to asking me, in front of the whole class, about Masonic guilds in the thirteenth century or medieval attitudes to original sin or the significance of the formal excesses of the Flamboyant Style or about violence and chivalry as characteristic features of the medieval mind. I was grateful for every opportunity to show my knowledge. I would eagerly deliver papers which I had sat up all night preparing, often taking over the lesson from Mr Netřesk and treating it as a kind of seminar. He meant more to me than anyone I had ever known, and I became utterly devoted to him. He gave me hope that my existence in this world was not totally pointless.

The more I learnt from books, however, the less I cared about learning from the direct testimony of the past, the testimony of stone. Perhaps that was my undoing. Today, in hindsight (the only sight I now possess), I can see how it came about: in those adolescent years I lost touch with myself; I strayed from the path Fate had ordained me. So Fate intervened to set me back on her path. Not immediately – that would have been too obvious – but in her own good time.

Netřesk betrayed me by marrying one of his former pupils, a girl three years older than me and forty years younger than himself. It was an impossible union; but it happened, and I was disconsolate. To escape the derision of petit-bourgeois gossips, as well as my own mute reproaches, he and his young wife moved to Prague, and once again I was without a friend in the whole town. Netřesk was replaced by a priest who at some point in the 1950s had renounced his faith in order to become a history teacher. He was an expert on the labour movement and showed little interest in any other history.

In my last winter at school I registered for the university entrance examinations. At that time I was preparing an exhibition for the Recreation Room – a pictorial history of education in Mladá Boleslav – accompanied by quantities of painstakingly unearthed documentary material. The school inspector commended it to all educational establishments in the county, and throughout the summer term our school became a place of pilgrimage. After that everything fell into my lap. My school-leaving results were so good that I could hardly take the entrance examinations seriously, and a month later I was accepted to study history at the Prague Faculty of Arts. I was horribly nervous but determined to make the very most of my success.

4

Day follows day. It only seems
That we are closer to the future.

Oldřich Mikulášek

I talk of the new season . . . Of the old season, only God knows. He alone knows my part in this whole affair, my frailty, my insignificance. He alone knows the difference between black and white, good and evil, truth and make-believe. I do not claim, and have never claimed, any such knowledge. I never wanted to be a part of it. It was all their doing. It was they who picked me, though not without God's knowledge, that's for sure. What I had to offer them was, after all, His gift. It therefore follows – incredible as it may seem – that their plan had His blessing.

So who was I to say no?

Winter dragged on, all mud and snow and bitter frosts, from November until March. Even now, in May, there are still mornings when you feel its icy whiplash on your fingers. The crystal blooms have long since vanished from the window-panes, but the wind that bore them away has veered back into the north. Fallen petals and now fallen leaves. Is this spring or autumn or all seasons together? Coltsfoot was flowering in November . . . and in midwinter a red poppy appeared at the foot of the New Town wall. It will be some time before nature's old order is restored. With God's help we, too, can play our part. In a week the lilac will be out. That will be a good sign.

I was discharged from the police last summer, several months before that bloody business at St Apollinaris' Church and just a few days after the tragic incident on Nusle Bridge that I am about to relate.[1] Someone I was supposed to be protecting lost their life, though to this day I have no idea what I could have done to prevent it.

The investigation lasted several weeks. The Criminal Investigation Department couldn't make up their minds whether it was murder or suicide or whether it was a case for the CID or the city police. The matter was eventually settled in the usual way – by finding a scapegoat. And that scapegoat was me. It being summer, public interest in the case was minimal; it evaporated completely that sunny morning when the bell of St Apollinaris' announced the end of the Old Era – or do I mean the end of the Modern Era? Perhaps the end, in fact, came on the day Time's pendulum first faltered in its trajectory over Prague: the day Mrs Pendelmanová died.

In mid-July I was summoned by the Superintendent of the CID, though as a regular constable I did not come under his authority. It was our first encounter and by no means our most pleasant. When I entered his office at the New Town police headquarters someone else was already in the room – a tall man standing with his back to me in front of a large oak desk. I announced myself and took up a position at his side. Ignoring me, the man carried on talking in a low voice to the Superintendent. I knew the man by sight. We had worked together briefly when I finished police college, before he moved to the CID. He had gone into the police as a young man and had already done five years' service, which may have explained why he now stood before the Superintendent with such casual self-assurance. If I had known how often I would have to put up with his rudeness in the coming days I would have excused myself and walked out there and then.

I had the awkward feeling I had interrupted the two men in a private conversation. They were obviously none too pleased to see me. The Superintendent, whom I had never seen at close quarters, looked about fifty; he was of medium build, almost bald and had a fleshy, revoltingly pock-marked face. When he at last registered my presence he raised an eyebrow and remarked with a shrug of impatience that we had better get straight to the point. Out of the corner of my eye I saw the other man grin.

'I'm sure you know my name,' began the Superintendent, producing from his jacket pocket a white handkerchief with a pearly sheen, probably silk. 'But, to avoid any misunderstandings, I'm Superintendent Olejar, and I'm in charge of this whole outfit, which gives me much less pleasure than you probably imagine. It is my hope that you will soon be working under me.' He paused, spread the handkerchief over his left palm and began to wrap it round his right index finger. Despite the oppressive silence the other man kept on grinning. 'You may have heard that four of our men have had to leave us, though the deception they've been accused of by the investigating commission has not yet been fully proven. At any rate, they've been suspended from all detective duties until the court has cleared their names.' Olejar gazed at his silk-swathed finger as if in anticipation of some signal. Then he continued, 'We've been asked to do a job – the kind of job we generally give to experienced CID chaps. But since we're a bit undermanned I asked Personnel to suggest someone who might fit the bill. The computer came up with your name, though I have to say some of my colleagues don't have a very high opinion of you.' With his left hand he picked up a file lying on the desk in front of him, waving his right, its index finger still wrapped in the handkerchief, condescendingly in my direction. 'Still, I'm willing to give you a try. One word from me and you'll be relieved. You'll be working with Junek here.' He indicated the man beside me. 'So I'd better introduce you. Sergeant Junek is soon to be promoted – he got a commendation from the Chief of Police for distinguished service. Saved a child's life, you know. Just the kind of man we need. You can learn a lot from him.'

He had barely uttered these words when a dark, treacle-like liquid began dripping out of his right ear. I started in fright but somehow managed to hold my tongue. His face a mask of stone, Olejar dabbed at the secretion with the waiting handkerchief, which he then held for some moments to his ear before poking his index finger inside.

I shot Junek a bewildered glance. Rocking gently on the balls of his feet, he was staring at some point above the Superintendent's head as if nothing had happened.

Olejar, his head tilted to the right and his finger still in his ear, nodded in my direction. 'And the constable here is our new recruit, one of the few people in our section who've been to university. Though as far as I know . . .' He paused and gave me a doubtful but surprisingly sympathetic look. I felt dreadful. Then he removed his finger from his ear, examined it, screwed up the soiled handkerchief and tossed it into the wastepaper basket. '. . . You *dropped out*!' These last words he almost screamed at me. 'And apparently you like people to call you . . . What was it he likes being called, sergeant? K? How ridiculous! Are you ashamed of your own name, constable? I admit it's not the best of names for a police officer. Have you never thought of changing it? Well, I suppose that's your business. Not that it matters much: to members of the public you're just a number, after all. Anyway, you have an arts background, and with us you've done a course in psychology. The woman you're being assigned to has delicate nerves, so we need a sensitive approach. You may not believe this – and I'm sorry to have to say it – but right now we don't have anyone better suited to the job than you. I need you, constable. I hope you won't let me down.'

'I'm afraid you've been misinformed, sir,' I said, struggling to control my shame and anger. 'I did study history but, as your enquiries have no doubt revealed, without much success. I don't feel qualified to do anything. I would like to go back to my regular duties. I like being on the beat. I need experience on the ground.'

For all my assertiveness – with which I surprised not only myself but also Sergeant Junek, who shot me a sidelong glance of profound scepticism – the Superintendent remained unconvinced. 'Oh, come on,' he said. 'I can't abide false modesty. Anyone else would jump at the chance. There's not a police constable I know who wouldn't gladly swap his uniform for civvies. Or perhaps you don't think it's a job worth doing? Well, I can assure you it's an honour for both of you.'

I nodded. My resistance had evaporated.

The Superintendent surveyed us with obvious satisfaction and began dictating instructions. Within seconds, however, his features froze in a contortion of pain, as if someone had plunged a knife into his innards. He took another silk handkerchief from his pocket and pressed it to his ear – this time the left one. Knowing what was coming I managed not to flinch.

If at that moment I had betrayed my revulsion Olejar would quite possibly have relieved me of my mission. But would I have been spared what was in store for me? I doubt it.

Mrs Pendelmanová had strong, albeit indirect, links with the former communist regime. Her husband had been a member of the Central Committee and one-time Deputy Minister of Labour and Social Affairs. In 1990, I discovered, soon after New Year, the disgraced apparatchik had devised an unusual suicide: he had driven his heavy limousine on to the frozen surface of Orlik Reservoir and steered it straight towards the outlet, where no ice had formed. The car sank without trace. The following night was bitterly cold and the reservoir froze over completely, trapping the car and its occupant beneath the ice. It was a week before they were recovered. Locals spoke of seeing soldiers cutting a huge cube of ice, like a giant glass paperweight, from the depths of the reservoir. As it was lifted out by a floating crane the assembled onlookers saw encased within it a black car and, at the window, a ghastly face. From the rigidly grinning mouth floated a trail of large and motionless bubbles.

Mrs Pendelmanová was not devastated by her husband's death. She carried on with her job at some department in the Town Hall, where she had worked all her life, and for three years resisted her colleagues' efforts to oust her. In the old days they had been afraid she would inform on them to her husband. But the fall of the regime obviated this risk, so they stopped concealing their hatred of the 'old witch', as they called her, and actively tried to get rid of her. This was not easy, as she was well versed in the law. In the end, however, she did retire – though not before she had secured a higher-than-average pension. But she had no intention of taking it easy. In his youth Pendelman had been regarded as a talented leftist poet. After the war he joined other radicals in setting up a workers' publishing cooperative and managed to publish three volumes of verse before the arts went into eclipse in 1948. He spent much of the 1950s in gaol, was rehabilitated after President Gottwald's death[2] and eventually worked his way into the top echelons of politics in the 'normalization' years of the 1970s – the clamp-down following the Prague Spring. It was at this time that he gave up writing, though until then literary periodicals had published a constant stream of his poems. His widow decided to put together a posthumous collection of his work and found a publisher.

Then, last summer, she reported that she was being followed. At first the police didn't believe her, but when someone threw a stone through her window – a smallish square cobblestone – she took it to the station and insisted they subject it to forensic tests. Still they didn't take her very seriously, though they had to admit there was something rather unusual about the whole business – unless, that is, the widow had made it all up. She lived in a fourth-floor flat in Pankrác, a modern neighbourhood far from any cobbled streets. To hit a window at that height would require considerable skill and strength – or extraordinary luck. Mrs Pendelmanová was convinced that she was the victim of political persecution: someone was settling old scores connected with her husband's past. She was taken to the CID Superintendent who decided she was entitled to personal protection and promised to assign two of his officers to the task, initially for a month. If she received any more threats in that period the police would investigate the matter thoroughly.

The forensic people examined the cobblestone for fingerprints. This was no more than a token effort, however, since it was quite clear that none would be found on the roughly hewn stone. I had a look at the photograph attached to the report. There was nothing special about it – a hard-looking stone, probably common flint. The only thing that struck me was the delicate green veining.

Junek and I worked week and week about. His turn of duty started on Saturday 20 July. Mine was due to finish four weeks later, after we had relieved each other twice. We went for a drink together – partly just to get to know each other a bit but also to agree on a plan of action in case our client received any more threats or was actually attacked. Junek talked mostly about himself, with a candour I found quite embarrassing. As we clinked glasses he said I was to call him Pavel. I didn't dare ask him to call me by my initial, so I told him my full Christian name. To my surprise his friendly manner remained unchanged, but as we said goodbye and shook hands I thought I detected a slight smirk as he spoke my name.

The widow's flat was full of strawflowers – some yellow and red but mostly mauve. Everywhere there were vases, glasses and plastic mugs full of the scentless blooms. There were strawflowers stuck behind picture frames, strawflowers poking out from books on the shelves. They had a strangely calming effect on me, but Junek found them quite infuriating.

Mrs Pendelmanová gave us a room with a small window overlooking a cluttered yard. Dark and cramped, its walls were lined with black wardrobes full of old-fashioned men's suits and outlandish ladies' attire in a variety of styles reflecting the changing fashions of the past forty years. Poking out of their pockets, buttonholes and collars were yet more strawflowers. I was reminded of the garlic used to ward off vampires. When I asked the widow about all these dried flowers she said she'd had them for years, since shortly after her husband's death when someone had sent several large wicker baskets of them to her address. They had arrived late, after the funeral, she said, and she hadn't had the heart to throw them out. So she had decorated the flat with them as a memento of her husband. She claimed they also kept the moths away. On hearing the story of the strawflowers I shuddered in revulsion. It occurred to me, even then, that the flowers had been meant for her rather than Pendelman himself, but at the time I had not yet learnt the difference between coincidence and consequence.

The wardrobes' owner suggested I help myself to any of her husband's clothes I fancied – she would be only too pleased to see someone benefit from them. I dismissed the idea. But on 10 August, having rung the doorbell and uttered the agreed password at the start of my second (and thankfully last) stint as her reluctant bodyguard, I noticed that she was carrying some garment wrapped in paper over her arm. Pavel Junek, standing in the hall behind her, was smiling to himself as he zipped up his leather jacket, which he wore over a white shirt, giving him more the appearance of a young hustler than a police office. What kind of figure did I cut next to him? Mrs Pendelmanová seemed irritated. Instead of greeting me she simply handed me the parcel, adding by way of explanation that since Pavel didn't want it (they were by now on first-name terms) I might as well have it myself. It turned out to be a white raincoat. No doubt the more able and experienced of her two bodyguards had been telling her how a proper detective should dress, and she had not realized he was pulling her leg.

They got on well together. He could talk to her on any subject, and they spent the evenings playing ludo or watching television. They understood one another and had similar political views. Junek's parents had belonged to the same privileged social group as the Pendelmans, but with the inversion of the social order after 1989 they had lost all the deference and respect they had once enjoyed. For the young man the experience was traumatic: joining the police was a response of rage. He was out for revenge – though on whom or for what he did not yet know.

Every day I accompanied Mrs Pendelmanová on her shopping trips like a well-trained dog. She insisted on cooking supper for me every evening. The food was tasty enough, but it came at the price of my privacy. After supper she would try and engage me in conversation, at which I proved quite inept, and from the outset she interpreted my silences as a sign of ideological hostility. Whenever I could I would slip off to my room to read the history books I had brought with me. Offended, she complained that things had come to a pretty pass when those entrusted with the protection of society, instead of perfecting their shooting skills, preferred to learn about the Middle Ages. More than once she told me she had never seen such a peculiar detective and how glad she was her husband was not alive to witness it. In his time, she said, policemen had been of quite a different calibre. I laughed and said they certainly had been. After that she didn't speak to me for several days, which suited me fine.

Towards the end of my 'tenancy of duty' she became more approachable. On my last evening, a Friday, we were sitting watching television. She was drinking Hungarian wine and persuaded me to join her – for one glass at least. I enjoyed it and let her top me up several times. I am not a drinker and never have been. By eleven o'clock I found myself chatting away, telling her about my favourite haunts in north Bohemia and explaining all about the castles and their history. Everything I said fascinated her. Of course, her interest was feigned – the usual fake enthusiasm of the drunk. I realized this, but in my light-headed state I didn't give a damn. I don't remember what time I went to bed.

I was awoken by the doorbell, stabbing my sleep like a splinter of broken wine bottle. I knew at once I had failed. I knew it the moment I got up, leaden-headed, from the couch in our airless little room. My feeling that I was alone in the flat was confirmed by a quick look in the adjoining bedroom, then in the kitchen. Sliding my revolver from its holster, I crept across the pitch-black hall towards the door. I snatched at the handle to pull it open, but to my surprise it was locked. Immediately the bell stopped ringing, which was some relief.

Then someone started banging on the door, shouting 'Police!' I told them who I was and explained the situation.

After a quarter of an hour, during which I alternately took gulps of water from the bathroom tap and threw up in the toilet, someone outside managed to force the lock. It was Sergeant Junek. He told me to go with him. Suddenly I felt like a petty criminal and jokingly held out my wrists for the handcuffs. Junek was not amused. Fortunately we did not have to go far.

She was dangling in thin air a little way beyond the first pillar, a clothes-line round her neck, like an old onion forgotten in a larder. Dawn was just breaking, but looking down at the streetlamps of Nusle far below it still felt like dead of night. Every now and then the bridge shook as a train rumbled beneath the roadway, and occasionally cars whizzed past behind us, the intervals becoming shorter as the sky grew lighter. The more curious drivers slowed down, only to be shooed away like bothersome flies by a constable with a lollipop-stick. The squad cars had been left at the end of the bridge so as not to obstruct the traffic. The one vehicle parked at the kerb beside the scene of the incident was an ambulance. The blue light on its roof flashed diffidently; its siren, shamed by its own superfluity, was silent.

I should count myself lucky there would be no investigation, they said, adding that if I applied for a discharge immediately it was sure to be approved. The devil's own luck, too, that there was no mention of alcohol in the report – the police couldn't afford that kind of scandal. My discharge papers were signed by Olejar himself, who advised me for my own good to keep out of his sight. Through my immediate superior I requested an interview with him but received no reply. From the start the whole business had struck me as fishy. I knew perfectly well that I could face charges for having signed an incomplete report; but I had no wish to play the hero, and anyway it would have been a poor performance. The official version, in a word, was suicide – a suicide that her protector had been unable to prevent. The protected party had locked the officer responsible for her security in her own flat while he was asleep. The keys in her handbag, found on the pavement above the scene of the incident, were cited as proof.

How the old lady climbed over the six-foot wire-mesh fence, or why she chose to hang herself with a clothes-line when she could simply have leapt to her death, remained unexplained. No one was interested. On the same day there was another tragedy at Nusle Bridge: a young woman stood clinging to the railings for several hours, giving the television crews plenty of time to set up, before jumping into the abyss. It was duly broadcast on the evening news, and the 'live death' became an instant silly-season hit. Mrs Pendelmanová's suicide lacked prime-time glamour. Had she been murdered things would have been very different. But that was a possibility the police refused to admit.

5

Be strong, my arms! Be my support
Against the day that hastens nigh
When, my life wasted, I must die.

Richard Weiner

I remember my first year of adulthood, which I spent at university, with no more pleasure than I recall my childhood. The faculty admitted me as a history student simply by virtue of my having passed the entrance examination, an embarrassingly easy affair. No doubt my smooth transition from secondary to higher education owed more than a little to my past as a diligent curator of classroom exhibitions. But I hardly let that trouble my conscience, intoxicated as I was by my success, which was marred only by the fact that I had no one to share it with.

By then my parents had long been divorced. My father had moved out and found a job in another town. Now and then he telephoned and was always scrupulous about sending my mother's modest alimony. On my eighteenth birthday he sent me a thousand crowns and a letter telling me that since I was now grown-up it was up to me to get in touch if ever I felt like a chat. Unsure what I might chat about, I never took up the offer. How long is it since I saw him, I wonder?

I disliked living in a student hostel. My roommates were young hedonists little interested in their studies, though they sailed through them easily enough. I was not used to sleeping in a room with three strangers and suffered from insomnia. They were by nature noisy and naively exuberant, which I detested. I tried changing rooms, but nowhere could I find the peace and quiet I craved. I knew nobody else who prepared methodically for every seminar, never missed a lecture and sat up three nights a weeks poring over our prescribed texts. Nobody laboured at their studies the way I did. Perhaps in the past the university had known such hard-working students. Who can tell? Initiation rites, bacchanalian revels in Old Town hostelries, illicit sorties to the Jewish Quarter of Josefov, duels with officers of the Prague Guard and romantic adventures with the fair sex – of these there are any number of historical accounts. But you'll find nothing about young men devoted to their studies, sacrificing their all in the name of education. Did they ever exist? Or was I the first?

Yet my work never bore the sweet fruits of gratification, since I could put none of what I learnt to any use. And the harder I tried to excel, the more stupid the mistakes I made. Every time I delivered a paper, the presence of girls in the class (how I wished I could have banned them!) made me so nervous that I became quite tongue-tied and couldn't remember even the simplest facts. My essays were full of bold and brilliant insights that my teachers would rubbish in a single sentence. But they could not take from me my love of the Middle Ages: that had long since grown into an obsession.

In time, however, I did learn to distinguish between different types of student. There were four main groups: good students who managed without difficulty; idlers who courted expulsion and lived the life of Riley while they could; slackers who never did a stroke unless they had to, then, as the examinations approached, mugged up just enough to scrape through; and, finally, those with special privileges who, though nominally students, only pretended to study – and got away with it. It was noticeable that this last group – mostly rather queer fish who lived in the best rooms and regularly went abroad on student exchanges – tended to support the official ideology, and though some of them purported to be reading history or philosophy it was clear their true interests lay elsewhere.

With fellow students such as these life was not easy. In fact, without even realizing it, they drove me out of the hostel. Any attempt to study while an impromptu hockey match was going on in the corridor, or when desks were pushed together for a ping-pong tournament, was quixotic to say the least. I did what I could. I even asked the Hostel Board to evict the boisterous fools. Nothing happened – except that in the canteen I overheard someone at the next table call me a killjoy.

I moved out to a housing estate in the suburb of Prosek, where a distant relative – a Mrs Frýdová, a pensioner who lived alone – sublet me a small north-facing room in her large apartment. She was, or claimed to be, very devout. On my first evening she made a point of telling me she prayed every day – Our Fathers and Hail Marys from dawn to dusk – and never missed a Sunday mass in Libeň church. I was to hear this many times – she seemed to have a notion that I should go to church with her. I told her one had to learn how to go to church, and I had never learnt.

At first I found all this talk confusing, but I got used to it. I also got used to the rather cheerless apartment – surprisingly quickly, in fact. I had been prepared for the kind of hell I had known in Boleslav, but actually it was more like living in a desert. Like Simeon Stylites atop his pillar I would sit motionless gazing out of the window. For most of the day the streets were deserted: thousands of human habitations and not a soul in sight. Unaccustomed to such silence, I found that between these concrete walls I could at last concentrate. The only sound that emanated from the prefabricated panels was the groaning of the metal girders as they cooled at the end of a hot summer's day. Then a chilling thought came to me: supposing no more people were ever born again – not in this town, not in this country, not in the whole world? The living would eke out their remaining years, and then there would be no one left.

For days and nights on end I gazed down on that geometrical grey Gobi. I could not help thinking that nothing in human history could compare with Twentieth-Century Man: the greatest dreamer and the greatest bungler of all time. And, the more I thought about it, the more I knew it was true.

I rarely went back to Mladá Boleslav. It no longer felt like home – the word had lost all meaning for me. To get through the endless weekends, when exhausted by my studies I found time on heavy my hands, I devised an amusing pastime. I would wander around the northern districts of the city discovering, with a pleasure all the greater for being unexpected, little oases of sustenance: an overgrown quarry hidden in a coppice, an abandoned shooting range, an observatory run by amateur astronomers, a water tower built just before the advent of functionalism, an old cemetery at the end of a cart track . . . There weren't many such places, but more than once they helped lift my spirits.

One bright windy day, as clumps of white cloud raced across the azure sky, I felt like venturing further afield – to Hradčany and Prague Castle. My plan was to go to the top of the Great Spire of St Vitus' Cathedral and look down on those parts of the city created in a bygone age when the builders of human habitations still revered the idea of beauty. Armed with my binoculars, I set out on the long walk. In the event I did not climb the spire that day. It was unseasonably hot, more like July weather, so after my two hours' tramp I decided to rest in the cool twilit interior of the church. I sat down on a pew towards the back of the nave and observed the foreign tourists as they wandered about, caps on heads, with that vacuity peculiar to their kind. With their craning necks and upturned heads they reminded me of so many speckled birds. Then, remembering that I, too, was a stranger in this place, I averted my attention from their petty preoccupations and gazed up into the great vaulted space above me.

What I saw was the past: stone tracery weaving wondrous shapes in stained glass; the decorated shafts of columns soaring high above my head and, branching out from them with perfect and pleasing precision, the ribbed vaulting that steadfastly supported the great ceiling and roof. Carved into them I saw the humility of medieval man, of princes, soldiers, labourers and of the builders of the cathedral themselves. I picked up my binoculars and angled them obliquely upwards. Suddenly I was looking through a child's kaleidoscope, dazzled by the brilliant flashes of colour in the tall windows that miraculously transmuted the plain white light of day beyond the church walls into rainbows of enchantment. My eye was first caught by the window in the Chapel of the Tomb of Our Lord, which depicts the laying of the foundation stone of the cathedral. I felt I should be kneeling, not sitting, in gratitude at such beauty and was so moved I had to look away. Turning to the Thun Chapel window I saw a human figure fighting for its life. The face was universal, neither male nor female, and quite unaware of my own. In it I recognized perfection, and the awful realization made me cower in my pew. When I had mustered the courage to raise my glasses for a third time, I saw a sight of awesome majesty: the Last Judgement in the huge window of the southern transept. This, too, spoke to me in a clear voice: Save yourself before it is too late. In sudden panic I again averted my eyes and, wedging my feet in the hassock, leant back in the pew and stared up at the rib-vaulting spread out above me like a skeleton: my own fragile mortality within arm's reach. By cricking my neck I let my eyes travel on over my head until they came to rest on the rose window above the west portal behind me. What I saw froze my blood. Here was the very beginning, the creation of the world – but a creation turned upside down. That inverted image, I knew at once, said more about humanity than all the books in the world.

Every weekend I would pack my binoculars in my rucksack and visit the churches of Prague in search of the most colourful stained-glass windows. Places given prominence in the guidebooks, such as Malá Strana and the Old Town, I preferred to leave to the tourists, heading instead for the New Town founded by Charles IV in the fourteenth century. In particular I was fascinated by the upper end, around the churches of St Catherine, St Apollinaris and St Charles the Great and the never completed medieval ramparts on the slopes below Karlov where not so long ago sheep had grazed and grapes had ripened. I also loved the quiet area around the old hospital – those narrow streets stalked by Death, who rarely departed empty-handed.

With the exception of the churches, the town hall and a few inaccessible cellars, hardly a building had survived the late eighteenth century's passion for 'progress' – and what Joseph II failed to destroy was swept away a century later in the great Prague Clearance, regarded by many as the city's cultural holocaust. I kept returning to the New Town, driven by a sense of sympathy for those vanished buildings and by a strange nostalgia and yearning for a bygone age that Fate had decreed I should not witness.

My growing fascination with the Middle Ages was not reflected in my academic achievements. What interested me was how ordinary people had lived: everyday things such as how often they took Holy Communion, how they brought up their children, whether they travelled or not, the clothes and food they bought, how they got on with their neighbours and their domestic animals. I searched contemporary records for clues as to how people in those days responded to beauty or ugliness. How did they feel about living in the world, in their own particular town, square or street, in a single-storey house built of wood and stone with pointed gables, a slender chimney and a narrow strip of garden?

My method of study brought me little success. I did badly in examinations and was one of those who despite their best efforts cannot get through their assignments because they are more interested in other things. Everything goes to pieces, and they have only themselves to blame. I was incapable of memorizing all the dates and events that make up conventional history, since I couldn't see the point of them. What was presented to us as history was, for me, no more than an enumeration of political decisions and their consequences, lists of ruling dynasties and statistics about the wars they waged on other families. I was looking for a different, living history, a space and time within which I could move just as surely as in my everyday life. How could all those kings and battles possibly affect my life? What did they have to do with me? Guided by such thoughts, I was looking for the kind of history whose object of study was all those who, like me, had no name. I was looking for a history of myself – a nameless and involuntary member of the human race.

Surprisingly, as soon as I realized that university had nothing more to offer me it became more bearable. I knew that by jumping through certain hoops I would complete my studies and receive a piece of paper with a rubber stamp on it. I imagined I would then get some tedious day job – after all, everyone has to work – and looked forward to pursuing my own historical interests on the side. A quiet, steady life without grand ambitions or the disappointments that inevitably follow.

And then the times changed. My sorry country became a different country, in a new Europe and a new world.

I was not quite nameless. Today it no longer matters much, but in those days surnames were an integral part of people's identity. You might have a name like Švach, for example. As I did.

6

Unlocking the House of the Siren,
or the House of Three Stags fame,
I hear a voice in a dark passage
Calling name after name.

Karel Šiktanc

Sudden freedom caught me unprepared. The chance to travel abroad, use hitherto unavailable study resources or choose new combinations of subjects – my fellow students embraced such opportunities with a glee I was unable to share. Sensing a favourable wind, they boldly and busily hoisted their sails; all it did for me was break my mast. My rented room in Prosek enabled me to concentrate on my work, though that rarely happened. Most of my time I wasted on activities of a largely non-academic nature, such as dreaming of the days before the dawn of the Modern Age when people had a fixed place in society, lived in the place where they had been born and let the course of their lives be determined by their feudal masters, by their sovereigns and by God, while their own chief concern was how to avoid sin. I had no reason to socialize with the other students. Not that I was much bothered by the constant parties thrown by the Marxist Studies crowd – I just didn't want to have anything to do with them. The dazzling sun of liberty, at first illuminating then blinding, drove me back into the comforting, cavernous darkness of the past.

One day in early spring I attended a lecture in the Great Auditorium on the meaning of the Old Testament at the start of the third millennium. It was given by a priest called Father Florian, the Vicar of the Church of the Annunciation (also called Our Lady on the Lawn), who had been illegally ordained in the West and whose breadth of knowledge, especially of medieval theology, was unrivalled in Prague. His talk, particularly his thoughts on the need to reassess key concepts such as crime and punishment, so impressed me that I signed up for his seminars on Christian ethics, in which I was soon taking an active part. Before long I was visiting Father Florian in his home, borrowing his books and having passionate discussions about them. I thought I was beginning to believe in God, convinced that only He in His mercy could have sent me this new teacher to fill the gap left by my old history master Netřesk.

That summer I stayed in Prague so as to be near Florian. I would listen to him closely, then attempt to counter his arguments – which being a wise teacher he expected of his students. He was full of praise. None of his other students asked the kind of questions I did; none was as disgusted as I at the state of the world or as determined to renounce it. He used me as an intellectual sparring partner, often defending moral positions that I, in my puritanism, regarded as too worldly. Secretly I longed for him to suggest I take up theology. I never dared mention the idea out loud, not even at home, since my mother would have thought it madness. But Florian, perceptive as always, picked it up: in the course of a conversation some weeks later he casually remarked that I might make a good priest. That was all I needed. I began reading volumes of theology and, with my mentor's help, preparing for the entrance interview. He soon discovered what I had never dared admit: I was not baptized. This had to be rectified – and quickly. We agreed that he would baptize me himself and fixed on a day: 24 September, St Jaromir's Day – my father's name day. And it was Florian himself, hoping to bring father and son back together, who asked him to the ceremony. He knew this would be the hardest and most convincing test of my resolve to enter the priesthood.

A month later, just a week before the baptism, I finally decided to write to my father. I took the letter to the post office, then went straight to Father Florian to tell him of my good deed. He was not at home. In the afternoon one of his students phoned me from the hospital on Charles Square. He told me there had been a robbery at the Church of Our Lady. Someone had tried to steal the altar painting and a carved Gothic Madonna. Happening upon the priest, who had been quietly praying in the dark, the intruder panicked and hit him with a crowbar used for barring the door, cracking his skull. The doctors said there was hope – though it would hardly have been worse had they pronounced him dead: Father Florian would live, but he would never celebrate mass again or utter a single word of sense.

I ran to the post office and asked for my letter back. I must have looked absolutely desperate because they complied without a murmur. I snatched it from the woman's hand and tore it to pieces before her astonished eyes. Thus ended my attempt to make peace with my father.

I returned to the faculty only once – to officially terminate my studies. I never finished my dissertation, nor did I put my name down for the final examinations. They insisted on noting in my study record that I had completed eight semesters, to which I simply shrugged. I left the faculty building and headed for Manes Bridge. There I breathed in the fresh air and looked up at the cathedral. Then I took my study record out of my pocket and threw it over the railings. It weighed next to nothing – a few sheets of stapled paper covered in writing and rubber stamps. Four years of study. For a few seconds it fluttered in the breeze before landing on the water. Perhaps the fish would read it.

Along with any desire to continue studying, I also lost all interest in life generally. Everything disgusted me. To escape my thoughts I took to wandering all over the city, from Těšnov to Výtoň and Bojiště to Žofín, observing through a black veil of melancholy the phenomena that defined and constituted the material of Prague: her buildings. In the New Town all the churches are old and all the secular buildings modern, the Town Hall being the exception that proves the rule. Though I had stopped going into churches, it was quite clear to me that none of the other buildings could compare with them. Without her old buildings – fragile and vulnerable collectors' items of incomparable worth – Prague would not be Prague, whereas the buildings erected in the last hundred years or so are no more than mass-produced consumer objects, indistinguishable from those you can see in any industrial town: large, functional and utterly sterile. For six centuries architects had ridden roughshod over the noble aims of the New Town's founders. I could actually feel their arrogant anger, their petty defiance of their predecessors, the vengeful spite they felt for any exceptionally talented individuals who might still be capable of creating buildings as fine as those of the fourteenth century. I had nothing but contempt for these architects of the modern era who had failed to learn from the very best teachers of their day. The Gothic master builders alone had had the courage to rebel against the dictate of classical form and create a new style that achieved the impossible: the victory of mind over matter. With all preceding and subsequent styles the reverse had been the case. It occurred to me that the world would have been spared the disaster of modernism in the apocalyptic twentieth century had we not abandoned the building style of the Middle Ages. Crime would not have become part of our daily fare (as it had certainly not been in the days of Charles IV) – a sacrament of evil dispensed to us by television newsreaders. There would have been no such thing as television. There would have been no such thing as modern architecture. There would have been no need for people like Father Florian to die at the hands of ungodly thugs.

But history had taken a different course, and we were stuck with it. I had no wish to live in the world I observed around me, but I was powerless to change it. Yet still I felt I must do something – to rebel, somehow, against an order I saw as evil, perverse and murderous. That's when I had the idea of joining the police. The thought of myself in uniform with a gun at my belt protecting all the benighted idiots who live in this unfortunate city was so absurd that I was seized by a fit of incontrollable laughter. And in this grotesque fantasy I saw a way out of the gloom that oppressed my soul. In fact I could think of nothing else. If everyone else was eagerly grasping the opportunities the new social order had brought, why shouldn't I do the same – in my own, rather different, way?

One advantage of being a policeman would be that I could avoid military service, of which I lived in constant dread. But, most importantly, I would be exposed to greater danger. Or so I imagined. I saw myself as a reckless hero of law enforcement, a zealot in police uniform – the very antithesis of the good soldier Švejk.[1] I had no wish to live, but I had neither the courage nor the resolve to put an end to my life. To put my life on the line for others, however – that would be a different matter. Suddenly I wanted to take risks, to feel the thrill of danger whatever the cost, to discover what I was truly capable of – even if it was the last thing I ever learnt. Wouldn't it be the perfect way out for someone who felt he had been born in the wrong century: to make the supreme sacrifice and die a hero?

This plan, as ingenuous as it was ingenious, induced in me a new cheerfulness. My landlady, who had not seen me in such high spirits for months, no doubt concluded I had taken leave of my senses. And it was in this exalted mood that I presented myself at the police recruitment centre for Prague's Second District. I was accepted on the spot and told when I would be starting at the Police Academy. When I confessed to the police doctor that I had recently been having a drink problem, he laughed and said the training would soon knock that out of me.

In fact it knocked more out of me than I'd bargained for. But I got through it somehow. I was not particularly good at anything. In firearms practice my hands shook so violently that the other shooters feared for their lives. I had to give up driving lessons after getting stuck on a gridlocked intersection and abandoning my vehicle in frustration. I did best in communication skills and worst in physical training and unarmed combat. I attended all the theoretical classes but avoided the practice sessions whenever I could. The proximity of sweating male bodies was not something I relished: there was an odour of brutality and blood-lust about them. The stink of my opponents alone was enough to make me retire from the ring, citing various excuses from allergies to nosebleeds. In fact I was terrified of my future colleagues and shuddered to think what they might be capable of in anger. How little it takes to silence the voice of compassion, conscience and common sense! Watching my fellow recruits, handkerchief at my nose, as they sweated it out on horsehair matting, I divided them into four categories: cocks, bulls, rams and dogs. The prospect of becoming one of them – and of my own free will at that – was suddenly not so appealing.

Once again, as so often in my life, it was my name that denied me access to the group. Before long, as I had expected, it became the butt of jokes. True, some cadets did me the favour of calling me K as I had asked them to, but even they could not conceal their contempt. My self-confidence again began to forsake me, seeping away like water through my fingers.

To make matters worse, I was given a nickname – the same one my fellow students used to call me in the dorm. It came about quite by chance, though when I think back on it now I suppose I brought it upon myself. Ever since my schooldays I had had a horror of showering *en masse*: at the sight of all those naked bodies the first thing that came into my mind was school trips to the slaughterhouse, followed immediately by scenes from documentaries about Auschwitz. But there was no getting out of it, so whenever I took a shower I kept my eyes tightly shut.

At the police academy, too, I always avoided the shower room after physical training, preferring to wash when I got home. This was not pleasant but certainly better than the sight of pale human flesh turning a hideous pink under the steaming jets of water – like some primitive artist's vision of pig carcasses being scalded. And, of course, there was the noise, the usual rowdy vulgarity of tough guys in the shower.

One day I waited until they had all gone and, looking forward to a quiet wash alone and wearing no more than a large towel, went down to the shower room in the basement. Too late I realized that I was not, in fact, by myself: three male bodies, huddled under a single shower, gleamed through the steam. As they became aware of me their sudden stillness made it clear I had caught them off-guard. In the dim orange light I could not make out from a distance what they had been up to, but I was glad that this time, at least, my own conscience – that policeman who punished *me* for the sins of others – was clear. The sight of a white-clad ghost gave the three figures in the shower quite a fright, but they quickly recovered their poise. One of them laughed and said, 'Looks like old Calvin has caught us in the act!' It was hardly an appropriate nickname. Perhaps that's why it caught on so quickly.

I sold my binoculars and stopped looking at churches – there simply wasn't time. I missed those expeditions, of course, but at the same time I realized that as a policeman I could not afford to be too eccentric: by attracting ridicule I would jeopardize my secret plan of self-destruction. Better to hide behind my uniform, go for a drink with the lads after work and feign an interest in football – and all the while wait for my chance to be tragically exceptional.

At my request I was transferred to the Upper New Town – that remarkable quarter bounded by Žitná, Sokolská, Horská and Vyšehradská. In addition, I was assigned to Charles Square and the area between Emmaus, Fügner Square on the Magistrale, Na Hrobci down at Vytoň and Karlov. My favourite haunt, however, remained Větrov Hill – perhaps because the place always gave me a mysterious and irrational frisson of fear.

In those days crime was still a stranger to those streets. That was to change after the case of the hanging man in the belfry. Or was it not until the Pendelmanová tragedy? But in those days that name still meant nothing to me, and I spent many agreeable hours roaming the sleepy streets around the hospital and in the shadow of those three Gothic churches: St Charles's, St Apollinaris' and St Catherine's. When the weather was fine I would pass the time looking at New

Town houses. Once again I saw all too clearly the paltriness of the Modern Age, its mute inability to inspire or communicate, in such stark contrast with the assured yet unassuming perfection of the old churches. And once again I was invaded by melancholy. To escape it I would retreat to the unspoiled area above Albertov which had been spared the scourge of 'development'. I saw wild vines sprouting at the foot of medieval ramparts, walked down the deserted steps to the little church on Na Slupi and gazed up at the panorama of Větrov and Karlov from the valley below.

One morning, at a spot where once stood a wayside shrine and many gruesome murders are said to have been committed, I came across a solitary vine shoot climbing up a Gothic wall. I uprooted it and transferred it to the alien environment of my own room, where I put it in a flower pot with a little lattice of wooden skewers for support. Beside my umbrella plants, crotons and azaleas it seemed oddly out of place. I tended it with the utmost care and would sit staring at it for hours on end until I eventually persuaded myself that I could see it grow. I was fascinated by how similar we were. I was determined it should survive, and when it appeared to be doing so its will to live infected me as well.

Life again became precious, and my futile wish to end it evaporated. And, the more I came to value it, the more anguish I felt at the sight of other wasted lives. But it was not so much ruined human lives that saddened me – after all, I didn't read the newspapers and never had to deal with a murder at work until last autumn. What grieved me most were the lives of buildings – those eyes and ears and tongues of the city which the Czechs, with their contempt for the past, had gouged out and mutilated. The streets I walked had been amputated from the body of memory; the new buildings I passed in silent horror were instantly and inevitably forgettable. I began seeking out any surviving traces of the city's stone inhabitants, long since cannibalized for building material. Only the names remained: Rychleby, Vokáč, Crown of Bohemia, City of Žatec, Stonetable Hall – the houses are no more. Fišpanka, too, is gone, as is Mediolan. Nor could I find

Black Dog House or Crest Cottage. You will look in vain for Pupils' Court. The list of the missing goes on: Plumbers' Yard, Poland Close, the Leaf and Stalk, Tabu's, the Sauceboat, the Three Pillows. A catalogue of brutal murders unavenged to this day. The Black House is deaf, the Golden Lion is blind, the Three Graves are mute. No light shines in Tallow House, the ovens are cold in the Golden Loaf, the presses in Apple Yard drip no more.

Lives had been lived in all these houses – lives we should never forget. And yet they were razed to the ground, consigned to oblivion and replaced by buildings that by the end of the twentieth century were no longer even inhabited. Bankers cannot tolerate having anyone higher than themselves, so they move their counting machines to the top floors. The more opulent of the new buildings are now populated by banknotes and coins; the poorer ones by filing cabinets, computers and electric kettles.

And up and down the New Town marched a tin soldier in uniform, a one-man funeral cortège for all the houses that perished.

The Golden Cross, the Golden Wedge and the Golden Wheel; Tailor's Yard and Fourteen Helpers' House; the Jackdaws, the Butts, the Wells, the Red Field; Locksmith House and Musketeer Hall; the White Ox, the White Stag and the White Rose; the Blackamoor, the Blue Crabs, the Three Swallows, the Slav Linden; Cakebaker House and Chimneysweep House and Gardiner Court. Paradise House. And Hell House.

7

Name! Your true name, you
banished rival of the Sun
that they call Shade.

Richard Weiner

A few days after the incident in St Apollinaris' belfry the police began their investigation. The man who on 3 November had been brutally beaten by an unknown assailant, then suspended by his Achilles tendon from the clapper of the church bell, was one Peter Zahir. I was summoned as a witness. This was two months after I had been quietly dismissed for gross dereliction of duty and just two months before the Zahir case was closed for good.

I got off the tram in Na Bojiště, the street where the huge police headquarters is situated. It was raining. As I waited at the traffic lights to cross the Magistrale I stamped my feet in the chill November wind. Glancing across at the pavement opposite, my eye was caught by a strange figure striding along the arcade of a modern building on the corner. The man, elegantly dressed in an old-fashioned black overcoat and hat and carrying a walking-stick, was heading in the same direction as me. In a different setting I might have paid him little attention, but here, against the flat grey façade and geometrical lines of a 1930s block, it was impossible not to notice him: a mysterious figure who had stepped out of the past; or, more likely, an actor from a nearby film set on his way to lunch. Though very tall – at least six foot four inches, I guessed – there was nothing lanky about his broad, powerful frame. His unusual bulk, the strange sheen of his coat and, above all, the immobility of his fleshy face, called to mind nothing less than an animated Egyptian mummy – apart, that is, from the hat and cane, which were more reminiscent of the nineteenth century. For some reason – perhaps simply to get a better look at the curious apparition – I felt impelled to run after him but was prevented from doing so by the heavy traffic on the freeway. Before the lights changed to green I managed to register two more things: his beard and the flower in his left hand. His stick was, in fact, a slender round-handled cane which, instead of leaning on (it would have snapped under his weight), he swung casually in time with his long energetic steps, apparently unaware of the irony, even mild absurdity, of the eccentric and constantly repeated movement – a flamboyant dandy who knew exactly the response he hoped to elicit: admiration and curiosity.

It was only then that I noticed, peeping out from behind the cover of that titanic torso, a second person walking, or rather trotting, at its side. The inconspicuous little fellow was in every way his opposite. He was surely no more than five feet tall and barely stouter than the giant's cane, though far less straight: his gait was a disjointed headlong tumble, as if his right leg were where his left should be and his left helplessly redundant. There was something rather disturbing about such total lack of coordination, something that aroused not pity but laughter – laughter of which one was immediately ashamed. Despite his physical disability the little man walked briskly, keeping up with his huge companion effortlessly and chattering excitedly all the while. He wore a grey suit and what looked like a bright-red cap. But I was so fascinated by his companion that I gave him no more than a cursory glance. By the time I finally managed to cross the road among the throng of pedestrians they had both disappeared from view. As I was soon to discover, they had not gone far.

I spent a good two hours at the police commissariat. The case had been given to Pavel Junek who, as I learnt from my former colleagues, had done very well for himself in the few months since our last meeting. He had been among those officers who had decided that Mrs Pendelmanová's death had been suicide and cut short the investigation. He had been promoted to inspector and, despite the odd complaint about his unscrupulous methods, had managed to insinuate himself into the Superintendent's confidence.

As I entered Junek's office, with mixed feelings in my heart and Mrs Pendelmanová's raincoat over my arm, he greeted me with a jolly laugh like an old friend. Behind the bonhomie, I knew, lurked falsehood, but I was grateful for the cordial reception none the less. Unlike him I was in no mood for laughter. Having spent over two months in a fruitless search for work I was virtually broke and even owed money to my landlady – a disgrace considering how little she charged for my room. Perhaps I could have taught history in a grammar school, but I baulked at the thought of confronting a class of unruly louts; besides, it would have meant waiting for a vacancy. I had a vague promise of a job at the City Archive, but not until after New Year, and it was by no means certain they would take me with neither a degree nor the state examination. Drop-out history student, discharged policeman . . . I could hardly have concocted a worse CV. What other skills could I offer? An intimate knowledge of Prague demolition sites?

Junek, whose mind was clearly on other things, merely remarked that I had always attracted bad luck. He went on to assure me that, as far as the Pendelmanová case was concerned, he didn't believe I had anything to do with it (though there had been suspicions in some quarters), a belief now vindicated by the official police verdict of suicide. He then asked me about the Zahir case. I gave him a rough account of the frantic ringing in the empty church and my discovery of the body crudely lashed to the bell's clapper. Junek listened distractedly, interrupting his chain-smoking only to make the occasional note in his jotting pad. The telephone rang. No sooner had he put the receiver to his ear than he shot me a sharp look and quickly averted his eyes. Whoever it was, I realized, was talking about me. He hung up and said he would be back in a minute. He was away for half an hour, during which time I was able to observe his young colleague doing battle on his computer screen with a fearsome fanged monster that, with fiendish cunning, outwitted and enslaved him.

When Inspector Junek returned his mood was noticeably worse. Flopping into his armchair he tapped a cigarette irritably from its pack and lit up. Then, after a brief hesitation and with barely concealed distaste, he began reading out my statement. When he got to the end he informed me, without looking up and in the same bored tone, that the Chief was waiting to see me. I wanted to ask if he meant Superintendent Olejar, but he had already turned away, so I got up and walked out.

In the corridor it took me a moment to get my bearings and find my way to the main stairs. I climbed up to the fifth floor and found myself outside the office to which I had been told never to return. Well, here I was again. I took a deep breath and knocked. Before I could even lower my hand an unfriendly voice – not that of the Superintendent – boomed, 'Come in!' As my other hand grasped the handle the door flew open as if by magic, and I was confronted by a carrot-coloured head and a grating voice ordering me to step inside.

In the middle of the room stood Olejar, open-mouthed, his hands arrested in an indeterminate gesture, with an expression that doubtless reflected my own surprise. In his hand he clutched a satin handkerchief. When he realized who it was his jaw snapped shut and with a forced smile he gave me a welcoming nod. His manner suggested that of a visitor rather than the boss: that role clearly belonged to the man standing behind him, who was none other than the giant I had observed in the street. He leant lightly on the oak desk, his powerful fingers – each almost as thick as my wrist – toying with a single red rose which he somehow succeeded in not damaging. Without his coat and hat, which now hung on the stand by the door, he was still enormous though no longer of superhuman proportions. Apart from his restless fingers and strange eyes, which studied me with a curious though not discourteous expression, he was quite immobile. Suddenly I was standing right in front of him. How I got there I had no idea – perhaps it was the force of his gaze that pulled me into the room. I heard the door close behind me.

I could not keep my eyes off the big man. He might have been about fifty or possibly sixty – or perhaps only a little over forty. To my surprise the crown of his skull, whose bony prominence could have been fashioned by Rodin's chisel, was perfectly bald, whereas the lower part of his head was covered with a dense growth that reached down to his collar at the back, merging at his ears into a full beard. Above his thin upper lip the beard was trimmed, so that the wide mouth and full, angular lower lip were plainly visible. When closed, his lips made me think of a long deep wrinkle – a mirror counterpart to the actual, and equally striking, double furrow that traversed the sloping forehead just above the eyebrows. The eyes, too, were angular. Their green irises stared out through two oblong apertures like two pieces of jade set into the perfectly immobile mask that served him as a face, from the very centre of which projected a broad, short nose, hooked like the beak of a raptor. The head was unusually symmetrical and looked as if it had been cast in bronze or moulded in extreme heat like some rare annealed glass.

He was dressed in a dark-grey suit, carefully tailored to make him look slimmer, with a high-collared white shirt and loose crimson tie. On its knot sparkled a blue gem – probably a sapphire – set in a silver pin. This small yet striking and doubtless very costly ornament testified to the eccentric and lavish tastes of its owner, as did his light-tan summer shoes, perforated at the instep, which added an almost dashing touch to his otherwise conservative attire.

Needless to say I did not take in all these details at once. Meanwhile the Superintendent had recovered his aplomb and was explaining in a rasping voice that he had just been telling his guest about me, so all that remained was to introduce him. Whereupon he uttered the words 'Matthias Gmünd.'

The giant stepped forward and held out his hand. It was as heavy as stone, but the grip was surprisingly gentle, and there was something reassuring in its warmth. In that instant the hand spoke to me. 'You're safe with me,' I heard it say.

'And this is my companion,' said Gmünd with a nod to the door, 'Raymond Prunslik.' I turned and held out my hand to the curious midget who had let me in. Bounding forward, he slapped my palm with a vigour that made me jump. With a laugh and an awkward convolution of his hips he muttered, 'We'll get on grand, I'm sure. In the army they called me Raygun. But, to you, plain Mr Prunslik.'

'Švach,' I mumbled, endeavouring, as I forced my wretched surname past my lips, not to betray my conviction that the man was not only physically but mentally unhinged. I assumed there was something wrong with his hip joints: even when his legs were straight the upper part of his body leant sharply to the left and his round little belly jutted out like a pregnant woman's. His whole weight rested on his left leg, so that as he stepped forward to introduce himself he had literally to bend over backwards to disconnect his right hip, shift his weight to his right leg and thus reverse his stance. He held his hands clasped in front of him in a coy gesture of self-mocking modesty. His air of physical vulnerability was to some extent offset by the padded shoulders on his jacket and an eye-catching bright-red tie with a symmetrical pattern of snarling yellow heads, which I assumed were those of lions.

However, Prunslik's most remarkable feature was his flame-like shock of hair that in the street I had mistaken for a red cap. Indeed, it resembled a flame not only in colour but in shape: cut short at the nape, long on top of his head and brushed up into a constantly bobbing crest. His eyes were of a translucent blue reminiscent of stained glass, his nose straight and lightly freckled like a child's and his mobile mouth forever twisting into some new grimace. As with Gmünd, it was hard to guess his age, but he must have been several years younger than his companion.

'Take a seat, er . . . constable,' began Olejar with some hesitation, indicating a chair. 'And you, too, gentlemen.' He was ill at ease and struggling to conceal it. Sweat glistened on his forehead.

I sat down and looked out through the Venetian blinds that stretched the length of one wall. The office was above the level of the surrounding rooftops and faced north-west, so the blinds were hardly necessary. Then I remembered Olejar's ears and guessed why he probably preferred this dim light. Through the window I could make out the mighty spire of St Stephen's, that gem of Bohemian neo-Gothic whose ring of decorative turrets – eight at the base and four halfway up – is such a striking feature. The tower itself rises sheer from the front façade of the church, directly over the west door. At its very tip the spire is crowned with the royal diadem, a reminder that this parish church was founded by the monarch himself. Now, after a recent shower, it sparkled brilliantly above the city. From my vantage point I could see two of the clocks on the four-sided tower. One showed three fifteen, the other eleven fifty-five.

'It may surprise you to learn that Mr Gmünd is a member of the nobility,' the Superintendent went on, still far from confidently. 'A knight, in fact. Of what city did you say?'

'Lübeck,' replied Gmünd.

'Lübeck. He is also descended from a family of Czech aristocrats . . .'

'I am a scion of the house of Hazemburg,' continued Gmünd, turning to me. 'A once eminent family that almost died out in the seventeenth century. But not entirely. Its last branch, the Úštěk Hazemburgs, were still flourishing a hundred and fifty years ago.'

'Now I'll put on my policeman's hat,' interrupted Olejar, 'and point out that the Knight has all his paperwork in order, all legally authenticated. So we can believe implicitly what he says about his background. His pedigree and title are proven historical facts. It's a very ancient family. Quite remarkable.'

I glanced at Gmünd. He seemed bored, as if none of this concerned him. Clearly he did not relish Olejar's introduction – and even less his tone.

'Mr Gmünd is not a Czech citizen,' Olejar went on, propping his elbows on the desk, hands clasped in front of his face as if in prayer.

'It's a shame you weren't here last time . . . constable. He was telling me about his childhood during the German occupation and how he and his parents escaped to England, at considerable risk, after the communist takeover in 1948. That's right, isn't it?'

Gmünd gave an imperceptible nod.

'A few years ago, soon after the . . . changes,' – Olejar shifted uncomfortably in his seat – 'Mr Gmünd returned to this country. He made no claim to his parents' property, a very laudable decision in my view. In any case, he would have found all the litigation most distasteful and probably ended up leaving the country again, this time for good.' Olejar's expression suggested that this outcome would have suited him very well. 'And, if I may say so, it would be a shame if he were to fall out with us.'

The diminutive Prunslik, who for the last few minutes had been swinging his legs about impatiently on his chair, occasionally kicking Olejar's desk, now poked a finger into his ear, worked it vigorously to and fro and made a show of looking at his watch.

The Superintendent noticed and was not pleased. With an apprehensive glance at Gmünd he continued, 'Bear with me, gentlemen. The Knight was received by the Mayor, who I am told was very satisfied with their discussion. Mr Gmünd, you see, is something of a patron. His great love is Prague and our district in particular. He wants to help. He's interested in the New Town's old churches and what's left of the Carolingian buildings and would like to contribute to their renovation. He's working with the City Institute of Architecture and the conservation people. Everyone – or almost everyone – thinks he's an absolute godsend. City Hall asked us to provide Mr Gmünd with an escort on his visits to various selected buildings, as the law requires. The administrators of these buildings would, of course, grant him access – but not the unlimited access he needs and certainly not to sites containing valuable works of art. So we've been asked to help.'

He turned enquiringly to Gmünd, who, seemingly aware of what this was leading up to, nodded his approval.

'But things aren't always as straightforward as they are here in the commissariat or in City Hall. The church authorities haven't exactly welcomed Mr Gmünd with open arms. In fact they've already crossed swords over one church . . . what was it, that place on Na Slupi? Our Lady on the Lawn, was it? Whatever you say, I'm no expert. The Knight offered to pay for the costly repair work but on one condition: that the church be reconsecrated as a Catholic place of worship. They wouldn't hear of it.'

'A few years ago a Catholic priest was attacked there and maimed for life,' explained Gmünd, his voice devoid of expression. 'Since then the church has been considered deconsecrated. It was leased to the Orthodox Church. I've nothing against that, but it seems to me they're evading the issue. Evil must be resisted.' These last words he uttered with a smile, perhaps to avoid sounding sententious.

'Father Florian,' I whispered, shocked to hear of him again and in such strange circumstances.

'Yes, I remember it well,' the Superintendent broke in again. 'The Knight was against leasing the church. It was built for Catholics, he said, and should remain theirs as long as it stands. That's right, isn't it? I expect both parties will come to an agreement sooner or later, but at the moment the question is still unsettled. I might as well tell you, the clergy have their own vested interests in this, and unlike City Hall don't want Mr Gmünd to be involved in any way in the renovation of the New Town churches. They seem to be afraid of him. I must confess I find some of his plans rather radical – I mean radically reactionary – though, as I said, I'm no expert, and it's not up to me anyway. But I'm sure he'll tell you about them himself. By the way, didn't you study at a seminary for a while? Or am I mistaken?'

Gmünd and Prunslik turned to me with interest – the former with a slightly raised eyebrow, the latter with a malicious grin. I felt my cheeks burning. Obviously some of my nicknames had come to the Superintendent's attention.

'I'm afraid you are,' I stammered. 'I never considered any such thing.' Gmünd turned away, while Prunslik continued to relish my embarrassment.

'I *am* sorry. I must've got it wrong,' said Olejar mildly. It was a tone I had not heard during our previous meetings. Could this be Gmünd's influence? Out of the corner of my eye I studied the massive figure. There was about him an aura of authority but also of vague and indefinable menace. Yes, since that first friendly handshake a change had come over him. Little wonder the church authorities are wary, I thought. The only person who was unperturbed by this strange individual, or at least pretended to be, was Prunslik. I decided that I would be another. And at that moment there rang out a peal of mocking laughter that no one heard but me.

'But to get back to why you're here,' continued the Superintendent. 'These gentlemen need a police escort if they are to enter properties that are normally kept closed. The Mayor told me they were a veritable boon to the community – yes, those were his very words – and instructed me to give them every possible assistance. The problem is, I can't spare my best men. I offered them what I could – I was even prepared to take a couple of detectives off some ongoing investigations, but Mr Gmünd didn't want us to make any sacrifices. And you know who he suggested? You.'

Not surprisingly his words rather took me aback. I couldn't help casting a suspicious look at Gmünd and Prunslik. This they were clearly expecting, for both men laughed and exchanged glances.

'They won't tell me how they heard about you,' he went on. 'To tell the truth, it's a complete mystery to me. Of course I had to say no. I pointed out to the Knight that you are no longer in the police, since you were instrumental – albeit indirectly – in someone's death. I don't recall you ever brimming over with initiative; in fact you never excelled in any way. I offered the gentlemen Inspector Junek, but they wouldn't hear of it. They wanted you and wouldn't take no for an answer. Our negotiations were on the point of collapse. The Mayor again intervened, arguing it was in the public interest. What was I to do? I couldn't ignore my responsibilities as a senior police officer, even if I wanted to. Then Mr Gmünd came up with the idea of getting one of our own men to work alongside you. Once again I had to explain that you were no longer in the police and even when you were – I'm sorry, but I had to say this – you were never one of our more reliable officers, as I'm sure even you will admit. The Knight then hinted that he knew something about the Pendelmanová case and gave me some valuable information . . . But we're not here today to discuss that. What I wanted to say is this: let us assume, for the . . .' Olejar seemed to run out of breath. He clapped his hand to his temples. Then, with a violent shudder, he grabbed his handkerchief, clenched it in his fist and sank his teeth into it.

'I see you are in pain,' observed Gmünd, 'so allow me to finish the story myself.' He flashed the Superintendent a curious little smile in which sympathy was mingled with contempt. Then he turned and looked at me intently. 'I believe your presence at the scene of the criminal assault in St Apollinaris' Church was no accident. Neither was your failure to protect the life of that old woman. There was a suspicion that her death may have had something to do with her husband's political career. Has such a possibility been eliminated? And what about Zahir? Wouldn't it be worth having a look at his political past?'

'Of course, that already occurred to me,' replied Olejar. 'One crime might throw light on the other. It's the best method – that's why we always try to solve several cases simultaneously. My men are already checking Zahir's past.' He spoke more quietly now, holding his head to one side like a swimmer shaking water out of his ear. The pain still grated in his voice. 'I have complied with the Knight's wishes and promised to try and persuade you to help him in his work.'

'What kind of work?'

'Special duties. You will accompany these gentlemen whenever they need you on their walks around Prague.'

'Is that all?'

'Yes. Isn't that enough for you?'

'If it's enough for you, then, of course, I accept – and very gladly. But on one condition, if I may: that I get my job back in the police.'

'Isn't that asking a bit much? Well, we'll see. I won't make any promises. Meanwhile you can be grateful we're offering you this. As I understand it, the job will be for about six months. We can't pay you, of course, but luckily Mr Gmünd is more than happy to do so. We'll give you a special ID card for plainclothes duties. You'll mainly be covering the Upper New Town – near where the two murders took place. There are a couple of buildings Mr Gmünd is particularly interested in and wants to visit regularly. All your movements will be detailed in two reports: one will be written by you, the other by one of our people. If you acquit yourself well I'll give your request my consideration.'

'I'll do my best.'

'I'm sure you will. But don't do anything rash, all right? Now I'll let you meet the person you'll be working with.'

He reached for the telephone and mumbled a few words into the receiver. Moments later the door opened and a woman's voice announced itself.

'Let me introduce you,' said Olejar. 'Mr Švach, our former comrade-in-arms. Miss Bělská, Special Duties Section.'

I turned to see a policewoman dressed in a uniform that was obviously too small for her. She was about my age and quite pretty, though not strikingly so. But she had beautiful dark hair, tied at the nape in a regulation ponytail, and large very dark eyes that somehow didn't go with the rest of her, as if she had borrowed them from someone else. She stepped forward with outstretched hand and smiled. Two dimples appeared in her full cheeks. In that moment the uniform became a costume, a girl's fashion fad. I remembered having had a similar feeling about my own uniform – that I didn't belong in it. But a second later the dimples vanished and she was a policewoman again. Her handshake was formal, the hand withdrawn before I had a chance to grasp it, the skin rougher than I had expected. Pretty, though, I found myself thinking – just a bit on the plump side. I couldn't help noticing her breasts and stomach straining at her blouse, and her thighs tightly encased in her trousers. I quickly looked away. This was exactly the kind of unprofessional conduct Olejar would pounce on.

'She's one of our best people. Best student in her year at Police Academy. Has the makings of a top-notch officer.'

Olejar turned to the visitors to make the introductions, starting, naturally, with Gmünd. But before he could make a move Prunslik had slipped past him, seized the girl's hand and planted on it a slobbery kiss. As he did so he lifted his left leg and ran his instep down his right calf, a sight so comical that I let out a snort of unseemly laughter. The girl shot an enquiring glance at Olejar who, concealed behind Gmünd's back, simply shrugged. On hearing his master's name Prunslik leapt to one side and, with a series of jerks, indicated to Gmünd that it was now his turn. The big man took a step forward, bowed slightly and handed her the rose. He seemed to have been holding the flower in readiness with exactly this in mind, which rather gave the lie to the authenticity of the introductions I had just witnessed and gave me further cause for suspicion. Again, the girl looked across at the Superintendent. He nodded. Seeing this, Prunslik began nodding violently in manic imitation. Then he cocked his head to one side, poked a finger in his ear and grimaced.

The girl coolly shook Gmünd's hand and took the rose without batting an eyelid. I could not help noticing how utterly self-assured she was. But what if things were not as they seemed? What if this were not the first time she had met this grotesque pair?

We sat down again, the Superintendent pulling up a chair for Miss Bělská as he began explaining her duties. In a somewhat nasal voice she assured him she understood everything and had no questions. I couldn't resist sneaking a look at her in profile: a strong neck bulging over the shirt collar, a clear complexion, a rather heavy chin and fairly full lips – though not as pronounced as the features around her mouth and cheeks. Her nose was slightly upturned, her forehead smooth, her eyebrows long and black. It's her body that lets her down, I thought. Pity.

Gmünd began explaining his immediate plans to Olejar, as if he were the only other person in the room. The policewoman twirled the rose pensively between her fingers, occasionally glancing up at me with dreamy eyes. Prunslik eyed her lasciviously while I pretended to look out of the window. I couldn't stop thinking about her mouth. That first smile had revealed a row of little teeth and beyond them a black cavern. It was a mouth that could keep silence.

Suddenly she looked at me squarely and said, 'I think I know you. I've heard about you. Not very nice things, actually, but I didn't believe them. Giving you the sack like that was a mean trick. Anyway, I'm glad you're back.'

I was completely thrown. Gmünd was still talking quietly to Olejar, while Prunslik watched us in amusement. She noticed my embarrassment but sailed on regardless.

'I'm glad we'll be working together. You're the first person I've met who goes to church with a pair of binoculars. By the way, what's your first name?'

Still perplexed by the fact that she knew of me, I shook my head, then changed it to a nod. 'Um . . .' I stammered. 'You can call me . . . Would you mind just calling me . . .'

But she cut in, 'I feel the same about my own name, actually. Rozeta. Awful, isn't it? And yours must be Květoslav, right?' She tapped my forehead lightly with Gmünd's rose: a medieval token of favour.

She knew my name but didn't find me ridiculous! I could have jumped for joy.

With some effort I snapped out of my reverie. Something had made Gmünd laugh, and he was now leaning back in his chair examining the ceiling. Prunslik, for some reason best known to himself, was crouched behind the Superintendent who, one hand at his throat, the other gripping the top of his head, stood looking out of the window. Suddenly there came spurting out of his right ear a thick, pitch-black fluid. Prunslik pulled a grotesque face, rolled his eyes, and turned off an imaginary tap at his own ear. Rozeta sprang to her feet and opened her mouth to speak. Quick as a flash the midget put a finger to his crooked lips, fixing her with a cold blue stare that stopped her in mid-step and froze her to the floor. She looked back at Olejar, whose head was now shaking uncontrollably as if in a fit of colic. The foul discharge from his ear dripped on to the shoulder of his jacket. Then the attack passed. Suddenly aware of the situation, he looked round at us in alarm and strode out of the room.

Gmünd was still staring at the ceiling as if nothing had happened. Prunslik giggled. He tried to cover it with a cough, though not well enough to prevent it being heard by the departing Olejar. Rozeta seemed on the point of telling him to shut up but thought better of it and followed her boss out without a word. I remained in my seat, intent on the pounding of my heart, which for some inexplicable reason both wanted and did not want to go running after her.

8

There's the church
And there's the steeple
Open the doors
And there's the people.

Nursery rhyme

We met in the metro. Gmünd arrived alone. When I asked where his companion was he told me not to worry, no doubt he was sleeping in after a wakeful night in his hotel room. I looked around to see if Rozeta was on her way. Our meeting had been fixed for six o'clock. Gmünd pulled a silver watch and chain from his waistcoat pocket, flipped it open, then immediately snapped it shut. 'Time we were off,' he said. 'Rozeta is going straight to St Stephen's.'

We went up the steps and found ourselves in that extraordinary stage set called Wenceslas Square. The yellowish flares of the streetlights glowed indistinctly in the flying spray. Black night, locked in mortal combat with dawn, was already striped with red and beating a retreat. Water dripped off the great bronze statue into the filthy gutters, while the taxis' windscreen wipers kept a remorseless count of the last minutes of darkness. A mean place in mean times.

Gmünd was in a foul mood. In the square he kept his sullen face hidden behind his coat collar, looking neither right nor left, as if wishing he were somewhere else. For a long time we walked in silence, so his question was all the more unexpected.

'Do you know when the Prague pedestrian died?'

'I'm sorry?'

'That once famous figure, the Prague Man in the Street? Now to be found only in literature.'

'I'm afraid I don't know what figure you're referring to.'

'I don't suppose you do. Well, the Prague pedestrian died the day the Magistrale cut the city in two. Since then, only nostalgic fools go anywhere on foot – you, me, Rozeta, Raymond, a few others. We risk our lives, but we don't give up. Other people protect themselves in automobiles, and can you blame them? Instinct of self-preservation. They're terrified of being run over.

'Do you know which place in Prague I like least?' he went on, after I had declined to share his umbrella, which in his enormous hand seemed like a child's paper parasol. 'This. Wenceslas Square, as they now call it. The square of St Václav. What used to be the Horse Market.'

'I don't enjoy coming here either. Why do you suppose that is?'

'It lacks the vertical dimension.'

'What about the Museum?'

'A tea-chest! With a bright bonnet stuck on top of it to distract attention from its hideousness. A neo-Renaissance barn! Schulz's travesty of a classical temple! They'd have done better to keep the old Horse Gate. At least it was honest – like all the old buildings. But anything of any value they flattened. There used to be a house here called U Lhotků. It had a beautiful tower, but now it's gone, vanished. Same as U Císařských and U Žlutických, on the corner of Jindřišská and Vodičková. And next to them stood another tower, built in the sixteenth century, with a view of the whole city. This box of a museum can't measure up to them, however huge it is. It's quite the wrong shape, which is why it can't dominate the square the way it should. But those towers they demolished formed a natural focus midway up the Horse Market, which Lilienkron once described as the most magnificent square in the world, no doubt partly because of those towers. The original plan was to keep them, but then in the early twentieth century they put up a couple of so-called "palaces" right next to them – great sprawling blocks riddled with arcades like an Emmental cheese – which completely overshadowed them and made them look like sentry-boxes. What would a tower look like right beside a great colossus like that? A beggar on the steps of a bank.'

'I've heard they're going to build a glass tower at the bottom of the square, at Můstek.'

'God forbid! The architects of the twentieth century have no humility, and their punishment is impotence. But when I spoke about the vertical I was thinking of something else. As you can see, Wenceslas Square is long and narrow – half a mile long, in fact – and I admit it does at least fulfil the function of a Greek agora. But, incredibly, there isn't a single church here! Our Lady of the Snows is just a stone's throw away, but you can't see it from the square, not even if you dislocate your neck. You can't see St Jindřich's either, let alone Holy Cross on Na Příkopě – the most overlooked church in Prague. Out of sight, out of mind. I'm not surprised Prague has gone to the dogs in the last hundred years. An ugly city breeds ugly people.'

I turned to him in amazement. Here was a man I hardly knew speaking aloud my own thoughts! Either I had chanced upon a kindred spirit or he knew more about me than I realized and was making fun of me. His face, however, was hidden from view behind his hat brim and turned-up collar.

I looked at the pedestrians around us. The sight of so many pallid vampire-like faces bearing down on us, only to step feebly aside to let us pass, filled me with revulsion. Even at that early hour we were accosted by pimps, and other shady characters sidled up to Gmünd with offers to change money. We crossed the end of Krakovská and Ve Smečkách. The streetlamps struggled to penetrate the mist and persistent drizzle so that the approaching faces loomed out of the darkness like the lining through a threadbare coat. The cars were still of no definable colour, appearing either dark or light with nothing in between. The hour for colour had yet to come.

'I'm sorry,' said Gmünd, his voice now calmer. 'Excuse my churlishness. I'm not used to getting up so early – I prefer to sleep in. But today I need to be in the church at sunrise. I want to observe something I couldn't see later in the day – how the first rays of the sun fall into different parts of the building, how the light plays on the carvings and pictures, on the pillars and flagstones. Don't expect anything too spectacular. The windows are all of plain glass. But once I get permission I intend to replace it with copies of the original stained glass. The windows are rather narrow, so it was always a bit dingy inside, which makes what light there is all the more precious. We must choose strong colours but not too dark.'

'And don't you mind that there'll be nobody around to appreciate your lighting effects? There are no services this early in the morning.'

'Not at all. Just because you or I are not in a church doesn't mean it's deserted. It is my belief that a church is never empty. Anyway, things may change. The glass will be in those windows for at least fifty years. We won't live that long, but the windows will.'

'You seem very sure about that.'

'To tell the truth I'm not. That's why I have to be all the more single-minded. I have to convince myself that my efforts are worth while. A church is the Lord's dwelling-place: it should always remain the way it was the day it was built. If it used to have stained-glass windows, then it's our duty to restore it to its original condition and not to reason why.'

'Even if no one ever uses the church?'

'Even then.'

We turned into Štěpánská Ulice. I tried to think of a way of changing the subject, as our conversation was beginning to oppress me. As if reading my thoughts, the Knight struck out on a new tack.

'My Hazemburg ancestors were and always had been Catholics. They came from Úštěk, a little place in a forgotten corner of Bohemia. In around 1360 Václav Hazemburg got into a dispute with the Berks of Dubá over some land. He fought three battles and lost them all. Two of his castles were razed to the ground. Wounded and much reduced in circumstances, he moved to Prague with his two sons and bought several houses in the New Town. He offered his services to the King, accompanied him on his foreign tours and was for many years one of his most trusted advisers. And then the King, just a year before his death, had him executed. The whole country was shocked. Historians have never discovered why our family suffered this cruel blow. There is no doubt that the Emperor was behind it – he was in the habit of punishing people but was not vindictive and never bore a grudge against their children. So he never touched Václav's sons' property. That we lost much later, during the Utraquist rampages.[1] Our houses were burnt down, and those who survived escaped with their last remaining possessions to Lübeck in Germany. There they remained for a long time. Some time in the seventeenth century my ancestor Heinrich Hazemburg, who was a councillor, saved the city from destruction by uncovering an arson plot, and he was rewarded with a hereditary knighthood. That was when we stopped using our old coat-of-arms and began calling ourselves Knights of Lübeck.'

I pointed out that I was also from the same part of Bohemia – a fellow northerner, in a manner of speaking. Gmünd said he knew that already. He had evidently found out everything about me. But how? And why? My questions would have to wait. This job meant a lot to me, and I didn't want to risk losing it.

We had been walking briskly up Štěpánská, and soon, little by little with each step we took, the church came into view.

'Until the 1860s we did fairly well. By that time we had close ties with the Gmünds in Denmark – I have ancestors there as well. One branch of the family remained in Lübeck; another returned to Bohemia. That was the first Hazemburg homecoming. As you have no doubt guessed, those are the people I am descended from. Wilhelm Friedrich Gmünd, who came to Prague in 1865 with his wife, children, brother and sisters, was my great-great-grandfather. He owned nothing here, but he was not short of money. Like his ancestor he bought a house in the New Town. It was called U Pekelských – Hell House.'

'I know the name. Wasn't it on Žitná?'

'That's right. Another victim of the clearance. A city is like a woman: she needs to be protected. But no one protected Prague in her hour of need. The evil came from within, from the city council itself. Like a cancer. No one ever ruined Prague as comprehensively as they did: not the marauding Swedes or Bavarians; not the Prussian bombardment, not even the great fires in the Old Town and Jewish Quarter. My great-grandfather Peter Gmünd fought to save his house, but where his forefathers had prevailed he failed. He was forcibly evicted and the building was demolished. In its place they put up an oversized apartment block totally at odds with the medieval spirit of the city. Peter Gmünd was a building engineer and worked with the neo-Gothic architect Josef Mocker.[2] Like him, he was a purist who believed that every building has a right to look the way it was when it was built; alterations carried out in later centuries must go. He moved to the growing suburb of Karlín, to a new house of his own design in Krakovská Ulice, now called Sokolovská. Here he had no objection to the new tenements, since they stood on the old Spital Fields where there had never been anything except a few wooden barns and, on the far side of the wood, the Invalidovna Hospital. Great-grandfather even went as far as to say that the architecture of Karlín was "moral" since it did not displace any existing buildings. From his windows he had a view of the newly built neo-Romanesque church of Saints Cyril and Methodius, a sight that gave him some comfort.

'In 1948 my parents escaped to England, taking me with them. We were the last members of the Czech branch of the family. I learnt English quickly, but my mother and father insisted I also keep up my native language. At university I started studying architecture, but it wasn't a good choice: I couldn't stand the sight of those iron skeletons wrapped in concrete. At about that time my father got in touch with our distant relatives in Lübeck – the descendents of the ones who had remained in Germany a hundred years earlier – and they invited us to visit them. They had managed to escape the old ill luck of the Hazemburgs and had become prosperous businessmen. None of their menfolk had been killed during the war, since the family had supplied the Wehrmacht with canned fish and were therefore exempt from military service. After the war they lost everything through reparations, but within ten years they had got it all back again. They were interested in the family's history and genealogy and were eager to learn how the Czech side had fared. They were fascinated by the similarities between us: my father, they said, had the typical Gmünd look, while I was a true Hazemburg. When they showed me a portrait of Heinrich – the one who was knighted – even I had to admit there was a certain likeness. They invited us to stay on in Lübeck. My parents declined, but I accepted. I joined the family firm and eventually became managing director. At the moment I'm on voluntary leave. Selling tinned sardines is all very well, but I have other fish to fry.'

'You're a successful man,' I said. 'Do you have a family?'

He did not reply. By now we had crossed Žitná and were in front of the church. There was still little sign of daylight and none at all of Rozeta.

'Come on. We can at least walk round the outside.' Gmünd set off briskly up Na Rybníčku, the lane leading up past the church. My curiosity finally got the better of me, and I asked him why he was telling me his family history.

'Earlier on you seemed rather sceptical,' he replied. 'I must know I have your confidence.'

'Did you gain Olejar's confidence in the same way? Did you tell him what you've just told me?'

'Yes, in a condensed form. He knows no more than what I have told you.'

'What do you think of him?'

'I think he's a poor blighter. His illness has made him into a tough cop but not a terribly good one.'

'It's made him vulnerable, too. I'm sure he doesn't want people to know about his condition.'

'Exactly. He's in a bad way. People could exploit his illness – and other things as well.'

'Do you really think he's in such a bad way? I mean as regards his health?'

'He's in a bad way as regards everything.' Suddenly Gmünd stopped and turned to me. 'Do you see what I see?'

I looked around. The traffic on Žitná and Ječná was now no more than a distant hum. Out of the gloom at the end of the lane rose a majestic pile of stone, tapering to a pointed silhouette against the paling November sky. To our left reared another mass of masonry, its head held high above a stooping body: the bell-tower.

'I've been coming here for years,' I said, 'usually on Saturday evenings when there's no one else about. If you forget about the surrounding houses it feels as if you're in one of the most ancient places in the city.'

I had let myself get carried away, perhaps more than I should have. Gmünd, too, I noticed, was moved. He gave me a curious wide-eyed look and smiled with something approaching satisfaction.

'The stone,' he intoned in an oddly hollow voice. 'At moments such as this, doesn't it seem to grow? How does it strike you?'

'I'm not sure I know what you mean,' I mumbled, unnerved by the strange look on his face and those all-devouring eyes.

'Don't you get that feeling?' His voice was calmer now. 'Take that late Gothic bell-tower you've just been admiring. It was built in 1600 as a modest auxiliary belfry. In 1601 a rumour went around Prague that the tower had grown, of its own accord, by several feet. This went on for a number of years. The same thing had happened in 1367, after St Stephen's was completed. And when the Great Tower was finished in the fifteenth century it also kept on growing, as if dissatisfied with its allotted dimensions. Then they hemmed it in with all these stupid apartment blocks, and it shrank again. But now it's grown once more – look, it really has. And over there, that's where the Chapel of All Saints used to be. The original roof was extremely steep and high – twice as high as the walls that supported it – similar to the bell-tower roof, in fact. And on the very top there was a lantern. Just imagine it. The chapel was octagonal in shape, like Karlov Church, but its proportions were more subtle. Like Karlov it used to have a steep-pitched roof, which was also observed to grow a couple of feet higher every year. A few hundred years later, when fashions sadly changed, it was given a domed roof – as was Karlov, of course. It looked absurd, like a cheese-bell. Immediately afterwards the walls began to crumble and disintegrate, and the whole building nearly collapsed. I believe this was a direct result of that totally unsuitable new roof. In the eighteenth century the chapel was deconsecrated by imperial decree and was used as a store. In the mid nineteenth century the roof fell in, killing one person and crippling another, and the chapel was demolished. Why? As punishment for a crime committed by someone else. Karlov still stands – a magnificent building. They've been repairing it for years. Such a shame no one has thought of giving it back its original roof. No one except me, that is. You'll see – one day I'll replace that ludicrous tin hat with a proper pitched roof.'

'I see you're a purist, like Mocker. You and I have similar tastes. Though I doubt you'll have much success with your plans for Karlov Church. Prague has grown accustomed to its three domes. Besides, I'm not convinced that every church must have a spire or tower.'

'That's not what I'm saying. You tell me the people of Prague have got used to Karlov. But they don't even know about it, because they can't see it! Ask anyone in Prague the way to the Church of the Virgin Mary and Charles the Great, and I bet you'll draw a blank. I don't absolutely insist on pointed spires. But to every building its own. Look at the rotunda over there, St Longine's. Yes, it's in a shocking state, and most tourists probably wouldn't give it a second look. Still, there's nothing about it that spoils its Romanesque style. Even the lantern-light suits it. A rotunda with a steep pitched roof would look too hostile, like a Saracen tent. Ah – look at those ravens circling above its roof. Why are there six of them? Why are they flying in such regular circles? And what do you think they're saying? Doesn't it sound like "Nevermore"?'

I looked up to where he was pointing. Sure enough, some crow-like birds were flying above the rotunda of St Longine. Their glossy black plumage glinted in the now unmistakable first light of dawn. It would never have occurred to me to count them, but since Gmünd had mentioned a figure I now tried. Five? Eight? No, he was right: there were six. I was surprised how good his eyesight was. Slowly, silently, they floated over the little round tower. Now and then one would settle on the sloping roof only to take off again a moment later. And suddenly there were not six but seven! Quickly I counted again. Yes, there were seven ravens. The seventh must have been hidden in the bell-tower and joined the others while we were counting. Then they flew off. Gmünd had an almost smug look on his face, like a conjuror who has pulled off a difficult trick.

'Tradition has it that in the thirteenth century St Longine's was the parish church of the long-vanished village of Rybník. I'd say we were now standing in the middle of the village green. But the building is older than that; it was dedicated to St Longine only much later. In pre-Christian times it's thought pagan rituals were enacted here.'

'The ravens certainly had a pagan look about them,' I joked.

'It's a short step from paganism to Christianity. Unfortunately, the reverse is also true. I expect you've heard the story of the bell of St Stephen's. It was called Lochmar after the bell founder who cast it: Lochmayer. Lochmayer was a good Catholic, but he lived in a bad century. The Hussites – who, like the Catholics, tolerated no faith but their own – heard about his views and had him executed in the Cattle Market. As he laid his head on the block he heard the bell of St Stephen's ring a death-knell and realized it was bidding him farewell. So instead of forgiving his executioner he called down a curse on his own bell. Even though it was not directed at them, the anathema alarmed the Hussites, who decided to reserve a special task for Lochmar: it would toll disasters – fires and approaching storms. For years it served this purpose well. Then, one day in the mid sixteenth century, a boy climbed the tower and began frantically ringing the bell, though no danger threatened the city. It could be heard as far as the Cattle Market. But before the citizens had time to congregate the ringing stopped as suddenly as it had begun. They found the boy lying at the foot of the tower with a shattered skull. Legend has it that Lochmar hurled him to his death.'

'For ringing the bell without good reason?'

'Possibly. Or maybe it simply killed him on a whim. Bells can be unpredictable. Doesn't it remind you of anything? A church, a bell . . . a man.'

'I suppose you mean the Zahir case?'

'It is rather a nice coincidence, don't you think?'

'Who told you about it?'

'Guess. The poor fellow could have ended up at the bottom of the tower with a broken neck, too. St Apollinaris' is high enough. If the rope had broken . . . or if you hadn't saved him in the nick of time. Olejar appreciates what you did, by the way. Don't be taken in by his cool manner. He may yet pardon you. It all depends on how well you do your job for me.' He gave me an ironic smile. 'Incidentally, I went to see Zahir in hospital. He's making a good recovery and hopes to be back at work soon. Tough little chap. Ingenious, too. He told me he's having a car made with pedals you operate with your hands. It'll take at least six weeks for his tendon to grow back, and he doesn't want to wait that long. And before I forget: he wants to meet you and thank you personally. Says he's got something for you.'

'A gold watch?'

'Some proposition, I think. He seems to trust you more than he does the police. Talking of the police . . .' He looked round. A woman in police uniform was walking quickly towards us across the main road. 'There's Rozeta. Come on.' And off he marched, with me hard on his heels. Suddenly it was daylight. As we hurried past the Branberg Chapel on one side of the church, I glimpsed the grinning face of a cherub.

Gmünd said nothing to Rozeta about her late arrival, which I suspected had been prearranged. The girl took a bunch of keys from her pocket and offered them to Gmünd, but he shook his head and she handed them to me. She then led me not to the main front door of the church or the side entrance into the north aisle but to a small door towards the back, almost at the presbytery. I approached it, keys in hand. All three locks (one ancient, two modern Yale-type ones) slid back smoothly. I placed my hand on the knob and pushed. The door swung open without resistance, almost of its own accord. Inside, instead of the dungeon-like chill I was expecting the temperature was no lower than outside. The air was musty and smelt faintly of incense. It was quite dark. I turned round. Gmünd and Rozeta were standing quietly side by side, as if waiting for something. Though I couldn't see their eyes I was sure they were watching me intently and noting my hesitancy and lack of resolve. Steeling my nerves, I took a step or two into the darkness. Then another. Suddenly my hand touched a second door, larger than the first. Finding no light switch, I groped around until I found the lock and inserted the fourth key. The door sprang open a few inches, admitting a dim light. I stepped into a small room – the sacristy. Rozeta and Gmünd followed me inside. From there another door took me into a side aisle of the church.

I was still in almost total darkness, but the presbytery and nave were dimly illuminated by a greyish light filtering through the small hexagonal panes of the heavily leaded windows. The high altar was adorned with flowers that glowed bright in the penumbra – the only 'play of light' worthy of any notice. Gmünd would be disappointed.

But where was he? There was no sign of him. He must still be in the sacristy with Rozeta. There was nothing I specially wanted to see in the church, so I turned back to rejoin them. Suddenly I stopped dead. A woman's voice cried out, echoing through the whole church. It was not Rozeta's.

It seemed to be calling out a name. Yes, there it was again – someone's name, I was sure of it. I made a dash for the nearest pew and ducked behind it. Again the name rang out, clearer this time but still not clear enough. I crept along to the end of the pew and slipped behind the confessional, from where I was able to peer around the church. The voice, louder now, had a hollow, plaintive ring, as if it were issuing from the depths of the earth. Then, at last, I saw a figure standing by a pillar next to the sacristy near where I had come in, blocking my way out. Yes, it was a woman, her pale silhouette outlined against the dark void of the north aisle. Again the name rang out. It was a voice deranged with grief and loss, a voice that knew it fell on deaf ears and had long since turned in on itself. It was the voice of despair.

I listened, not moving a muscle, ready to run for it if anyone else appeared. But the woman and I were alone, she standing by the pillar with her back to me, I crouching behind the confessional. Apart from the woman's cries the silence was total. Then I had an idea – something I'd seen in a film when I was a kid. I slipped my hand into my pocket and found a five-crown piece. That should do the trick. I threw the coin as far as I could towards the south aisle, in the direction of the Kornel Chapel, in the hope of diverting her attention. A hammer striking an anvil could not have made more noise. The sound rang out on the flagstones, leapt up the great pillars, bounced off the vaulted roof and echoed round the organ-loft, reverberating like a bell long after the coin had rolled to rest.

The woman did not react.

'Simon!' wailed the voice into the dwindling echo.

This time I heard it plainly.

I mustered all my courage and came out from my hiding-place. One step . . . two steps . . . three. Now I could make out what she was wearing: a long beige cloak with a white hood. Nine . . . ten . . . eleven. The slender figure was standing with lowered head, her hands clasped in front of her. Twelve . . . thirteen. 'Madam . . .' The word came out feebly. What was shaking more, my voice or my knees? My mind flashed back to another morning not so long ago and the woman I met outside St Apollinaris' Church. 'Madam, can you hear me?' Still no reaction. I took another step, now trying to move round her in the hope of seeing her face. But she turned so that her back was still facing me. I moved the other way; again she turned her back. It was quite extraordinary: she didn't want to show her face! This way and that she turned, like a weathervane. Could it be Rozeta having a joke at my expense? Impossible. The voice, the slender figure – they were not Rozeta's.

A chill ran down my spine. I touched my forehead: it was cold with sweat. The woman stood quite motionless, with not even a tremor in her hunched shoulders. Suddenly I knew what I had to do. There was nothing stopping me from running to the open sacristy door and out of the church. Yes, that's what I would do. Instead, quite involuntarily, I put out my hand and touched the draped shoulder. Except it wasn't a shoulder. It was a pillar.

A pillar? No, a tree. Whatever made me think it was a pillar? And what was that under my feet? The flagstones were gone: instead the ground around me was covered in grass. A lawn? Inside a church? It was unbelievable. I looked up: no windows, no ceiling, just white clouds high above and beyond them a brilliant blue sky – too bright for eyes expecting the subtle shadows of a Gothic ceiling. I looked about me. I was standing in the middle of a dismal little field full of strange flowers, some of iron, others of stone: a graveyard. Near by, leaning over me, stood the church I was supposed to be inside, its apse jutting into the jumble of stone crosses. Beyond the graveyard fence I could make out part of a garden, with flowerbeds, a large ornate greenhouse like a huge transparent tent and several fruit trees through whose bare branches loomed the black outlines of the presbytery windows.

Right at my feet was a grave with an iron cross. Fixed to it, some distance above the ground, was a rusty plate bearing an inscription, the letters corroded beyond legibility. Yet I was sure I knew what it said and can still recall every word: 'Hearken to a sorry wonder – Lochmar threw my son Simon from the window . . .'

My head spinning, I collapsed on to the crumbling gravestone.

'You're talking in your sleep, my friend. I thought you were praying.' Someone was standing over me. Someone else slapped my face. A giant with a gentle voice; a girl with questioning eyes.

I was sitting on the church floor, propped against a pillar in the north aisle near the sacristy door. There was a roaring in my temples and a violent churning in my stomach. 'It's the stale air,' said Rozeta, thrusting a bag of sweets under my nose. 'You took just a few steps, then staggered and fell over. You might have done yourself an injury if it hadn't been for this pillar. You slid down it as gracefully as a Hollywood heroine. Do you suffer from low blood pressure?'

'Where were you? I was looking for you.'

'We were behind you. But not close enough to catch you when you passed out.'

'You can't have been. I was alone here for ages.'

'What were you dreaming about?'

'I want to know why you stayed outside. You planned this, didn't you?'

They exchanged a curious half-smile.

'We were right behind you, honestly,' said Gmünd. 'I'm sorry I didn't catch you when you fell. It happened so quickly.' Despite his show of contrition, he was clearly rather enjoying himself.

'You mean you didn't see her?'

Again they exchanged looks.

'You've been dreaming,' said Gmünd. He looked like a man at a funeral – hat in one hand, cane and umbrella in the other. Rozeta, too, unusually for a policewoman, had removed her cap.

'And such a fascinating dream!' continued Gmünd. '"Hearken to a sorry wonder – Lochmar threw my son Simon from the window." That's as far as you got. It goes on: "And wounded a mother's heart with grievous woe." That's the whole epitaph. It was written three hundred years ago on the grave of the boy who fell from the tower – the one I was telling you about. You must have read it somewhere – I certainly don't recall quoting it to you. Of course, there used to be a graveyard here behind the church. There was a garden as well, but over the years it went to seed and ended up as pasture. It must have been a bucolic sight – St Stephen's, the bell-tower, Longine's and All Saints, with sheep grazing among them and all around nothing but fields. A charming spot. Then the graveyard was abandoned, too, and all that was left of the garden were a few trees.'

I gave him a sceptical look, but he had already turned away and was walking towards the high altar. Rozeta popped a sweet into her mouth and went off in the opposite direction. I struggled to my feet. I was angry – angry with myself and angry that Rozeta accepted my weakness as a matter of course. As did Gmünd. At this rate he'd soon want to be rid of me.

'Mocker!' he boomed, and the name reverberated around the walls. 'Where would I be without him?' He was standing at the altar pointing up at the windows. 'Just look at that tracery! And those Gothic ogival windows in the nave! Do you know what those Baroque vandals put there before Mocker restored the place? Round windows!'

'I must admit,' I mumbled, anxious to agree, 'I'm none too fond of the Baroque myself.'

'Baroque is the silliest of styles. Can you imagine anything more hideous? Only functionalism and all the other half-baked "-isms" of the twentieth century. I don't object to Baroque buildings as such, but what a brass nerve those seventeenth-century architects had to tamper with the glories of Gothic! I suppose the occasional onion roof may not be out of place in a Czech village – in fact it was the first indigenous architectural element in Bohemia – but otherwise beware of the Baroque! It can be insidious, pernicious. For our towns the over-elaborate ground plans and decoration and domes of the Baroque spelt disaster. The Gothic pitched roof, the most characteristic feature of medieval European architecture, was thrown overboard for the sake of a bunch of onions! I believe in the beauty of simplicity. No amount of complexity can ever surpass it. The Renaissance built on to that tradition, organically. Yes, I admit the Great Tower of St Vitus', which for years I regarded as an eyesore, is not without aesthetic merit, for all its audacity. But if you look at the cathedral as a whole, including the tower which was supposed to be knocked down but never was, you can't help seeing something blasphemous about it. It glories not in God but in itself.'

'Compared with the Baroque churches it's certainly a beautiful building.'

'You don't have to convince me of that. I know I tend to try to win people over to my side, even when they're already on it. What do you think, Rozeta? Do I have any success?'

'What about that crackpot Prunslik?' she replied, countering question with question. 'I thought he was your servant, but he doesn't seem to take much interest in your work.'

'He's not my servant. He's a free man and can do exactly as he chooses. Yes, he's a bit mad, as you've noticed.' Gmünd shielded his eyes against the morning light. I tried to follow his gaze and guessed he was studying the tracery in the windows. He took out a notebook and began making a sketch.

'His name – Raymond,' Rozeta went on. 'Isn't it English?'

'Your name is not exactly Czech.'

'My father wanted to call me Růžena – Rose – but my mother fancied something more exotic.'

'I've known Raymond for years,' said Gmünd. 'We were at school together. He was the first fellow Czech I met in England, though in those days he knew precious little about Czechoslovakia. I was in my last year when he was in his first. I couldn't stand the way the other boys bullied him, just because God had made him different from them. So I took him under my wing and we became friends. He's half-English, the son of a Czech émigré who fled the Nazis. He was born soon after the war. His mother came from a family of impoverished aristocrats somewhere in Lancashire. In fact he claims both his parents were blue-blooded, though I'd take that with a pinch of salt if I were you. Anyway, it's all the same to me.'

'Is he your employee?'

'In a manner of speaking.'

'What does he do for you?'

'Various things. Legwork mostly. Dealing with all the red tape. I don't have time for that.'

I could see he was getting tired of the conversation. He looked at his watch and raised a finger. At that moment the church clock struck eight.

'To get back to Josef Mocker, he gave the tower a new roof and knocked through the west façade to put in that big Gothic window. A hundred and twenty years ago the people of Prague were wiser than they are today: they could tell a decent architect when they saw one. Sadly, the same could not be said of the city councillors, who were just as blinkered as they are today and at the time were already thinking about pulling down the Jewish Quarter. Nowadays people tend to dismiss purism, but the cult of the new can only lead to crisis – witness the current fashion for jumbling up all sorts of different styles. Of course, Mocker can be accused of being over-ornate – an approach better suited to French cathedrals than Bohemian parish churches – but that's a mere peccadillo when you set it against all he did for the Gothic Revival.'

Gmünd strode off down the south aisle, his cane tapping on the flagstones. As he passed the three altars he paused and contemplated them with distaste. 'Revolting. That must go. Look at St Gregory there – he's supposed to be suffering, not pouting. And that ghastly Pietà – did you ever see anything so tasteless? And just look at that Rococo altar – the Virgin Mary of St Stephen's.'

'I like it,' Rozeta said defiantly.

'Well, I don't. It's a wart on the perfect complexion of a Gothic church. All falsity and pretension! I'm glad someone stole the picture of Rosalie by that overrated dauber Škřeta. As far as I'm concerned they can help themselves to the whole damn lot, chubby cherubs and all. As long as they don't take the church.'

'They can't very well walk off with the church,' said Rozeta. 'Or the chapels and altars.'

'No, they must leave them to me,' replied Gmünd, calming down a little. His indignation had made him breathless. 'I'll chuck the whole lot out,' he added, mopping his face.

'They'll never let you do that,' said Rozeta, rather sharply. 'Actually, not even I agree with you. There must be a better way of going about it.'

Gmünd's demeanour changed abruptly. With a frown of irritation – less at his own outburst than at Rozeta's contrariness – he consulted his watch again and announced curtly that it was time we were going. Slipping his notebook and pencil back in his pocket, he walked back to the pew where he had left his hat, which he gave a perfunctory brush to remove the dust. I secretly admired the way Rozeta was able to contradict the Knight without any of the nastiness I might have expected from a policewoman. Once again, I felt there was something false about her uniform: it seemed like a fancy-dress costume or a mask whose purpose is to conceal.

I stole a sidelong glance at her ample figure straining at the seams of the black fabric. That the uniform did not suit her was perfectly obvious. But now I became aware of something else: her body didn't suit her either – and least of all those chubby cheeks straight out of a Baroque altarpiece. The dimples that appeared every time she smiled were certainly real enough. But the face itself, equally certainly, did not belong to her.

Catching my eye, she scowled and quickly looked away. Surely she wasn't embarrassed? This was the end of the twentieth century, after all, when women made a point of showing off their bodies. But that's what it looked like: she wanted to conceal everything about her that was feminine.

I followed Gmünd towards the exit, but as soon as he had disappeared into the sacristy I turned back to Rozeta. She had stopped beside the second pillar in the south aisle and was stooping to pick something off the floor.

'Guess what I've found,' she called out. 'Someone's dropped a five-crown piece.'

On the way out she tossed the coin into a tin bowl for donations.

'Nevermore,' cawed a raven as it swooped over the rotunda roof. Now I understood what it meant: 'You cannot escape from yourself.' My terrifying experience in St Stephen's Church had confirmed my fears: the thing I had been fleeing for years would remain with me all my life.

9

What say of it? What say of conscience grim,
That spectre in my path?

W. Chamberlayne

Lilac is the loveliest of flowers. Or at least the second loveliest – for what can surpass the rose? Or perhaps the third, since between rose and lilac must come the peony. The massed florets of lilac in a clear-glass vase take my breath away; so do full-blown roses an hour before their petals start to drop, and peonies caught in the first rays of sun glancing through an eastern window. When I say lilac I mean pre-1945 lilac, before its scent was tainted by the stink of gunpowder and diesel fumes, before history was displaced by politics. But how can we think all that away? The same ignominious fate befell carnations: to adorn the grey suits of important men; to welcome them at international airports; to bedeck the platforms of their congresses. The VIP flower. And when the vases run out there are always bottles. Even red roses are treated no better, yet somehow they survive without dropping their petals. Like the medieval garden, the rose garden is a place for contemplation. There let me sit and pretend the twentieth century never happened.

The flowers on the high altar of St Stephen's had been white lilac. It only came back to me the day I went to visit Mr Zahir in hospital, though at the time I barely gave it a second thought. After all, they could have been artificial or imported from Holland or Brazil. But why had they been there? And for whom?

Zahir was a stout, vigorous man in his early forties who contrived to look elegant and well-groomed even in his striped pyjamas and powder-blue dressing-gown. He had paid extra for a single room in the hospital on Charles Square, with a shower, television and even a balcony, from where he had a view of the bare trees in the hospital grounds and the spire of St Catherine's. The room was overflowing with masses of cut flowers that immediately made one forget this was a hospital. Most were yellow and yellow-and-red tulips, almost tastelessly perfect with their long, straight stems and large identical heads. Something in their fastidiousness, in their obsession with breeding, gave them a foolish look: silly flowers for silly people. The patient nodded vaguely in their direction and said he had no idea who had sent them. Propped up on a pile of pillows, he was sitting up in bed peeling oranges, his swarthy complexion contrasting with the bright colours around him. On the bedclothes beside him was a tray of fruit, half hidden under a growing pile of peel. I saw grapes and apples as well as a greenish fruit with fleshy spikes that I did not recognize. Over this cornucopia Zahir reached out a sticky hand for me to shake; then, following my curious gaze, he offered me one of the spiky balls. I thanked him and declined. He told me to take a seat. The only two chairs in the room were occupied by flowers – in vases, plastic cups and even glass laboratory beakers. Under the chairs I noticed a neat row of variously coloured and labelled bottles, all of them full. Having nowhere to sit I leant against a desk that obviously didn't belong in the room. Zahir explained that his colleagues had brought it over from his office.

'They must think very highly of you,' I said.

'They know I'd be stuck without it – as stuck as I am without legs.' Grinning, he pulled back the bedclothes to reveal his right leg. It was bandaged from toe to knee with a bulky dressing bulging around the ankle.

'Is it healing well?'

'Oh, with me everything heals well!' He gave a forced laugh and popped a grape into his mouth. He had an unpleasant habit of speaking with his mouth full. 'What with all these vitamins, you know . . . It's the women bring all this – the fruit and liqueurs. But not the flowers. God knows who they're from. Maybe a secret admirer.'

'They must have cost a pretty packet,' I said, surveying his little Eden.

'But *she* has never been to see me,' he complained. 'That's the sort of visit I could do with – it would perk me up no end. Well, at least the others drop in. See that key over there? I can even lock the door.'

I had no interest in his private life and found his boasting offensive. With distaste I studied his bristling moustache. It reminded me of a cat's whiskers. In fact his whole head had something of a cat about it – a well-fed, crafty tomcat. Seeing my disapproving look, he winked knowingly.

'There's no need to look like a squeezed lemon,' he chuckled. 'You're right, of course. It's a tiresome business, especially with this kind of injury. A sprained Achilles tendon hurts like hell, even if you don't move from the waist down. And my ribs . . . But they tell me it's nothing compared with what I'll have to suffer when I come off the painkillers and start physiotherapy.'

'But you can walk a little, can't you?' I said, indicating a pair of crutches leaning against the wall.

'If I really have to I can get about on one leg. But it's no fun, I can tell you. They had to cut out the ruptured blood vessels and sew up the tendon and calf muscle. In fact it was such a mess they had to operate twice. And, of course, after a few weeks the tendon starts to atrophy, which means I'll have to spend the next six months doing special exercises – that's the worst of it. I'm due to attend a big architecture symposium in Ljubljana in December, and I plan to be there whatever happens.'

'I'm sure you will. It could have been much worse. You realize what could have happened to you? There's a lot of power in a big bell once it gets swinging – as we know from certain cases in the past . . .'

I stopped short. This was hardly the right moment for the story of Lochmar.

'I know what you mean.' Zahir waved his arms in the air and began talking so fast I could barely follow him. 'And I'm terribly grateful to you. The doctors said a couple of minutes longer and the tendon would have snapped completely and left me lame for life. So I want to say thank you, Mr Švach, thank you so much. That's why I was hoping you'd come to see me. The CID were here, you know, to interrogate the victim – including Superintendent Olejar himself. When I asked him about you he mentioned vaguely that you'd "blotted your copy-book" – something political, I gather. Well, show me the man who hasn't cosied up to the big boys at some time or another. And why not if it's the only way of winning the odd public contract? I'm no angel myself. No, don't tell me – you're different, of course you are. Anyway, Olejar said you'd been hired by that crank Gmünd – with the connivance of the CID apparently. My guess is they gave him one of their own men so they could keep tabs on him. Gmünd doesn't need you all the time. I don't know what he's paying you, but I'll be happy to pay you a second salary – and don't tell me the extra wouldn't come in handy. At least you could buy yourself a new coat.'

I glanced at the crumpled raincoat Mrs Pendelmanová had given me, which I'd slung over the back of a chair, and found myself recalling her unhappy fate and my part in it.

'Am I to understand,' I said, 'that you wish to employ me as some kind of bodyguard? If so, I should tell you the police once gave me a similar task and I made a complete botch of it. I'm not cut out for that kind of work.'

He shrugged. Yes, he knew about the Pendelmanová affair. 'You might even find some link between the assault on me and your own sorry story. Wouldn't that tempt you? It might help you get back into Olejar's good books. Everybody knows it wasn't suicide.'

I couldn't believe my ears. 'Did Olejar tell you something?'

'He had to. I'm entitled to police protection, but I refused. I'd much rather hire you. You've already saved my neck once, and, being the superstitious old gypsy woman I am, I want to make sure it gets saved again.'

'So you're afraid they'll attack you again?'

'I'm certain they will. Olejar told me old Mrs P. had first received threats – which was why you were sent to protect her. Well, the same thing happened to me. Except I didn't take them seriously – not until they actually grabbed me.'

'How did they threaten you? With a cobblestone, too?' Fool! But the word had already slipped out. I felt like kicking myself. Some detective I'd make! For every fact I gleaned I gave two away.

'A cobblestone? So that's what it was. Break her window, did they?' He gave me a shrewd look, evidently pleased to have got so much out of me.

'Yes. Look, I only want to know if they threatened you in the same way.'

'No. About a month ago I received a letter. Then a week later another. They're both in Olejar's desk.'

'So the Superintendent knew you were in danger?'

'No. I didn't tell my wife to give them to him until later, when I was already here. Now he's trying to puzzle out whether there's any link between me and Mrs Pendelmanová.'

'What was in those letters?'

'I'll tell you if you agree to give me protection.'

'Are you bargaining with me?'

'Good Lord, no! I'm indebted to you as it is. I want to know how I stand, that's all. Just because a man's lucky enough to escape death once doesn't mean he'll be lucky the next time. I have to insure myself.'

'Very well. Call me whenever you need me. But Gmünd must have precedence.'

'I can live with that. So, about those letters. The strange thing about them was that they weren't actually written. They were drawn. Just a lot of lines, like rather crude meaningless doodles. But I sensed there was something evil about them. There must have been, otherwise why didn't I simply throw them away?'

'What made you think someone was threatening you?'

'In one of them there was a picture of me. In among the mass of squiggles I suddenly saw myself – my curly mop, my fat face – framed in what looked like a window, maybe a car window. It was definitely me.'

'What if it was just someone's idea of a joke? Your children perhaps.'

'It's possible. But if you saw the drawings you'd agree they were deliberately meant to look like the work of a child. I'm a professional draughtsman, so I know a bit about drawing. I could produce a similar result by using my left hand and holding the pencil the way you hold a wooden spoon to mix a cake. I've tried it.'

'What was the second picture of?'

'Houses. Peculiar, ugly houses without roofs. And some people standing outside – five or six of them, maybe more.'

'Without roofs? I wonder why?'

'I don't expect you to interpret them. We'll leave that to the CID. Anyway, the Superintendent won't let you see them. He's put one of his own men on to the case – a mean-looking bloke in a leather jacket. Some whizzkid, apparently. To me he just seemed like a conceited idiot.'

'Was his name Junek?'

'I don't remember. Possibly. So you know him, do you? Well, if it is him you'd better watch your step. I reckon he's up to something, and it's not the sort of thing a policeman should be up to.'

'I suppose you could say he was a sort of friend of mine,' I said, without much conviction.

He looked at me doubtfully. 'If I were you I'd have as little to do with Junek as possible.'

I considered this for a moment. Olejar had to be desperate if the only person he could put on to the case apart from his blue-eyed boy Junek was a nobody like me. He wanted it to look as if I was working for Gmünd but had a hunch I could be useful to him, too. To be on the safe side he teamed me up with Rozeta, who may have been told to follow a lead I knew nothing about. Even the offer to work for Zahir might have been Olejar's idea – though, of course, I was supposed to think the engineer was operating behind his back. At any rate, the Superintendent would be taking the anonymous drawings seriously. Or was I reading too much into it?

'The police see a connection between the threatening mail and the assault. What exactly happened?'

'I don't know much more about it than you do. Early that morning I was woken up by the telephone. It was my boss – at least that's who he said he was. His voice did sound a bit different – kind of hoarse – but I put that down to a cold or a hangover. He told me to come over at once: they'd found a vital mistake in the plans for the new housing estate we were just finalizing. Or maybe he said "fatal mistake" – I couldn't quite catch it. I got dressed, ran downstairs and crossed the front garden to the garage. The moment I opened the garage door someone put a sack over my head and bundled me into a car. I tried to shout for help, but they'd dowsed the sack with something – it stank of meths – and that was the last thing I remember.'

'Was it still dark?'

'It was just getting light.'

'And you didn't see anyone?'

'No.'

'When did you come round?'

'Not until I was in the tower, though of course I had no idea where I was. I still had the sack over my head. What brought me to my senses was a terrible pain in my lower leg. First they made the hole, which was painful enough. But when they pushed the rope through it, between the tendon and the bone, it became quite unbearable. I passed out again. I have a faint recollection of swinging and banging against the wall. By then they'd removed the sack and my hands were free – for all the good that did me. I covered my head and face with my hands and prepared to meet my maker, dimly aware that I was ringing my own death-knell. Again I lost consciousness. When I came round the din had stopped and I was alone in the bell-tower, swinging to and fro in eerie silence: I was stone deaf! Then someone caught hold of me. I turned my head and beheld my saving angel. There you were, grappling my legs and mouthing inaudible orders. Then everything went blank again.'

'Do you think they wanted to kill you?'

'What do *you* think?'

'It looked more like a warning – a final warning.'

'Yes, I think you're right. They managed to give me concussion and a couple of broken ribs, but if they'd really wanted to bump me off they could have done so ten times over. They had plenty of time.'

'But what was their motive? What have they got against you?'

'That was the first thing Olejar and Junek asked. I have no idea. Envy? Revenge? It could have been the people who used to own our villa, which we got back from the state under the restitution programme after a bitter struggle in the courts. That's Junek's pet theory, though it seems a bit far-fetched to me.'

'The kidnappers set a trap, and you fell right into it. They knew you would. They know how much your work means to you.'

'That's exactly what the Superintendent said. He thought it might be someone from a rival firm of architects.'

'And is there such a firm?'

'What a question! I can think of at least thirty – and that's only in Prague and only the bigger ones. There's plenty of competition out there. We'd be killing each other all the time if there weren't laws against it. But who wants to spend the rest of their life behind bars?'

'Did your firm ever win a contract that had been promised to someone else?'

'Again, you're not the first person to ask that. I'm afraid the answer is no. We haven't pipped any of our competitors to the post like that – at least not in the last year or so. We've been working on that new housing development I mentioned, but so have other firms. No one would dare mess with such a big consortium.'

'How about your employees? Do you get on well with them?'

'Very well. I'm good at dealing with people. You want to know the secret? Praise and flattery. Always works like a charm.'

'You mentioned your girlfriends. Are any of them married?'

He seemed impressed. 'I see where you're heading,' he said. 'Almost all of them are married. You know, that never occurred to your friends in the CID. On the other hand, they came up with something that hasn't occurred to you. There are things you don't know. Two other people have been getting threatening letters.'

'Who?'

'I wish I knew. Junek and Olejar talked about them when they were here. They said they should have police protection, too, after what happened to me.'

'Why didn't Olejar tell me?'

'Doesn't trust you, I suppose. He talked about the Bělská girl as well – the one who's working with you. What a backside, eh? It's the pride of the Prague police. As a matter of fact, she did come here once to see me, but sadly I wasn't feeling quite up to it. She's bound to know more about those two. I've told you all I know.'

With surprising agility he leapt out of bed, reached for his crutches and propelled himself to the table. Selecting a bottle, he invited me to open it and drink to our future collaboration. The brandy (which he served in plastic cups) quickly put me in that strange mood that always precedes a lapse of judgement. I told Zahir about my failed career as a student and listened while he related his numerous successes as an architect. He then returned to the subject of Rozeta, demanding to know everything about her. His intentions were transparent, and this infuriated me – perhaps because my own thoughts about her were so utterly different. I didn't want to find out anything about her. I had no right to. Zahir poured me another brandy, which I hardly touched. Misconstruing my sulkiness, he grinned and told me that if I had designs on Rozeta myself I should say so and he'd give me a clear field.

That really wound me up. 'Designs? What designs?' I snapped, snatching up my coat. As I made for the door I told him to give me a call if he needed me. He was about to stop me when the door flew open and a young woman sailed in, nearly knocking me over. She was attractive in a rather obvious way: thick red hair, wide mouth and a figure that gushed and cascaded over itself like a Baroque fountain. She rushed over to Zahir and threw her arms round his neck, dropping a bunch of bananas in the process. Not the wife, I thought, and made a hasty exit. As I closed the door behind me I heard shrieks of laughter. Automatically I put my hands in my pockets – or tried to. The lining hung limply at my thighs: I'd put my coat on inside out.

For several days my telephone was silent. No calls from Gmünd or Zahir, not even from Olejar. Outside, the rain came down steadily out of a leaden November sky, and in the flats opposite the lights stayed on all day. I had caught a cold, no doubt in the church, and was now confined to my little room in Prosek with a sore throat, a runny nose and a throbbing in my ears. Installed by my reading lamp, I tried to immerse myself in Pekař's history of the Hussite Movement, in particular his chapter on Želivský's sacking of the New Town,[1] which sent shivers down my spine. Or was I simply feverish?

The rain was relentless. Even a trip to the corner shop was impossible without an umbrella. Anything more ambitious – say, a walk to Ďáblice Wood – was quite out of the question. Anyway, I had no umbrella. And my sleuth's raincoat proved as waterproof as a sieve.

I decided to spend more time tending my exotic plants, but they lived their own lives and apart from occasional watering didn't really need me at all – except for the vine I'd found by a wall near Botič brook, which for several days now had been looking poorly. Its yellowing tendrils were losing their grip on the lattice they had so eagerly embraced and white spots flecked its limp leaves, which lay on the soil as lifeless as a stillborn babe. I made the sign of the cross over it, unwilling to throw it out until it was completely dead.

When I had not set foot outside the house for several days Mrs Frýdová started worrying. She probably sensed I was overwrought;

certainly she can't have failed to notice the tense, anxious look of a man who lies awake all night and wakes from an uneasy sleep at noon. Towards the end of the week, on the Friday, as I lay uselessly in bed staring weary-eyed at the white ceiling, she came into my room carrying an armful of books. They were some of her favourites, she said, and might be of some help – though it might be robbing Peter to pay Paul, as it were. The books landed with a thud on the table, and Mrs Frýdová left the room.

Raising myself with an effort, I reached out and picked up the volume on top of the pile. It was Horace Walpole's *The Castle of Otranto*. I smiled. Opening it at random I began to read but soon turned back to the beginning. That was in the morning. Then there was a knock at the door and my landlady brought in my supper. I'd had the light on all day and lost all sense of time. Outside it was pitch dark. I looked at my bedside clock: seven forty-five. I had finished the *The Castle of Otranto*. I ate my supper and cast a curious eye over the other books: *The Old English Baron* by Clara Reeve; *The Mysteries of Udolpho* by Ann Radcliffe; *The Angel of the Odd* by Edgar Allan Poe; E.T.A. Hoffmann's *Sandman*; Eichendorff's *Autumn Sorcery*; and more besides.

Those books cured me. It would be an exaggeration to say that by Sunday I was as fit as a fiddle, but I was certainly more in tune with myself. The Peter-and-Paul remedy had worked. I got dressed and set off for the New Town, which I had missed during my illness. On Charles Square I went into the Black Brewery, a seedy bar where I occasionally had lunch. I ordered a grog and headed for the cleanest-looking of the stand-up formica tables, where an old man was bent over a plate of soup. As I sipped noisily at the scalding drink I casually glanced up at his face. It was my old teacher Mr Netřesk.

He smiled, wondering if I would recognize him, and we greeted each other like old friends – I the more effusively, since I longed for someone to talk to and could not have wished for better company. Finding it odd that he should be here alone at lunchtime on a Sunday, I asked after his wife. He laughed and said I hadn't changed a bit since my schooldays. He then explained, with a sheepish self-deprecating smile, that he had a five-month-old daughter and sometimes had to escape to the bar when he could no longer stand the noise at home. The old man's embarrassment was touching. His wife was a vegetarian, he went on, and didn't mind if he – an incorrigible carnivore – went out for a solid Czech meal now and then.

I studied his face for signs of ageing, but he hardly looked a day older than when I had last seen him. The eyes were alert behind their thick glasses, the cheeks ruddy, the uneven teeth stained yellowish by tobacco – a sure sign they were his own. As if reading my thoughts, he assured me that his marriage was a success and his wife quite contented. She had known who she was marrying: a lifelong bachelor who was unlikely to change his ways in old age. People took them for grandfather and granddaughter, he added with another laugh, and his daughter for his great-granddaughter. He invited me to his home so I could see for myself just how successful such a bizarre domestic set-up could be. I accepted without hesitation.

He took me to an unassuming apartment block in Václavská, where we took the lift to the third floor. The two-roomed flat looked out on to a back yard, which Netřesk said he didn't mind because it got the morning sun.

My meeting with Mrs Netřesk was rather embarrassing. First her husband took me through to the kitchen, where floral drapes covered the lower half of the windows, expecting to find her there. She was not. Neither was she in the adjoining living-room. He called her name. A voice replied from the bedroom. Mr Netřesk signalled to me to go in, warning me with a finger to his lips not to wake the baby.

The heavy curtains were drawn, and the old teacher's poor eyesight had deceived him: the baby was not asleep. Mrs Netřesk sat in an old-fashioned wing-chair beside the unmade bed feeding her child. Judging by her expression she was debating whether to ask her husband to wait until she had finished or put down the happily sucking child. It was a beautiful sight – but not one meant for my eyes. The mother gave me a nervous smile and said she would shake hands with me in a minute. I tried to look relaxed.

Netřesk seemed even more flustered than I. He told me to keep his wife company while he made a cup of coffee, leaving me to manage as best I might. I would much rather have joined him in the kitchen and left mother and child alone at such a private moment, but that would have looked like running away. So I sat down on the edge of the bed.

The room was quiet save for the sucking of the infant. I was glad of the semi-darkness. My cheeks were burning, and I felt sorry for Mrs Netřesk for having been placed in such a situation. I looked at her out of the corner of my eye. She was smiling encouragingly at the baby as if there was no one else in the room, which somehow made it easier for me to talk. I told her I remembered her as a schoolgirl. She seemed unsurprised but said she had no recollection of me: she had only ever noticed the older boys and hadn't bothered with the 'youngsters'. Immediately realizing how ridiculous this must sound in view of her husband's age, she lapsed into awkward silence, which I attempted to fill by asking which teachers she had had and reminiscing about my own. Since we'd been at school together, she said, why didn't I call her Lucie? I told her my name – both names – and was surprised how easily I uttered them. I thought of Rozeta and thanked her silently.

More than once I stole a glance at Lucie's breasts, which shone in the darkened room like two round lamps, drawing the eye with almost violent insistence. Though surprisingly small, their heaviness left no room for doubt that they belonged to a nursing mother. The white skin was shot through with small, bluish veins. She detached the child's mouth from her right breast and held it against her left.

Where the baby had been sucking a white droplet appeared. As I watched it grew into a fat drop, but still it clung fast. From the kitchen came the whistle of the boiling kettle and clink of cups. As if listening, the child stopped sucking and raised a podgy hand to the free nipple. The drop of milk slid down its fingers.

A second drop appeared, and I forced myself to look away. Raising my eyes to Lucie's face I was shocked to find her gazing at me with an expression of pure pity. She knew exactly what I was suffering, sensed my burning throat and parched mouth. What she next did took me quite by surprise. Without taking her eyes off me she gently shifted the baby on to her right hip to make room for me beside her. I don't know what came over me, but before I could stop myself I had lowered myself on to the soft pile of the carpet and, as if in a trance, crawled the few feet to her chair. As my hands found her thighs I felt her hand in my hair. The unimaginable had happened: I was being caressed by a beautiful woman. Her image shimmered indistinctly before my eyes. The only thing I could see clearly was a creamy bead in the centre of a dark circle. A warm hand at the nape of my neck gently pressed my face against her soft body. This is all that matters, whispered a silent voice. Do what you have to – you won't regret it. Only this moment matters. But I failed to grasp it. Slowly, I turned my head towards the child. I could feel its faint breath on my lips. Then I looked into its eyes. The fear I saw there made me start back in alarm. As I did so my cheek brushed Lucie's nipple. It left a sharp, burning pain, as if someone had scratched me.

From just outside the door came the sound of a cup being stirred. In a flash I was on my feet and standing by the window surveying the grimy yard through the parted curtains. I could see nothing but a vague grey haze. I blinked. Gradually the outlines of buildings came into focus.

I heard Netřesk enter the room. He put down the tray and told his wife he had made her a camomile tea. She thanked him and said he'd forgotten to ask whether I took sugar. I said I didn't, which was a lie, and raised my hand to my cheek to wipe away the drop of milk from Lucie's breast. It's bound to be sweet, I thought, but didn't dare lick my fingers. I gulped my coffee much too fast, burning my mouth, then said I really had to be going, as I had work to do. Mr Netřesk suggested we go out for a beer some time and asked for my phone number, which I gave him. Out on the landing, after he had quietly closed the door behind me, I put my fingers to my lips and sucked them greedily. But my scalded tongue, the clumsy fool, could taste no trace of mother's milk.

10

All roads lead uphill
To the cemetery.

Oldřich Mikulášek

The next week started badly.

I was awoken at seven o'clock sharp by my old enemy the alarm clock. Moments later the phone rang. Experience had taught me that early-morning bells generally heralded disaster, as they had in Mrs Pendelmanová's flat or in the church on Větrov Hill. As I picked up the receiver in the hall, still half-asleep, Mrs Frýdová poked her head round the bedroom door. It was a woman calling. She did not identify herself, but I recognized Rozeta's voice. She said something about Vyšehrad. I was to go over at once to the Congress Centre. I'd find out what it was about when I got there. Then she hung up.

Mrs Frýdová, obviously miffed at not having got to the phone first, asked me what had happened. When I failed to reply she took umbrage and shut herself in the kitchen, which was her way of telling me I wasn't going to get any breakfast. For some time now I'd had the feeling that my presence in the flat was increasingly irksome to her.

I took a bus to Holešovice, then the metro to Vyšehrad. It took forty minutes. I ran up the steps on to the paved terrace outside the Congress Centre and immediately headed for the two metal flagpoles that had once proudly proclaimed Communist Party congresses. Around the two grey wooden-topped poles with their gilded spikes – designed by Josip Plečnik for a courtyard in Prague Castle – a small throng of people had gathered. Among them I could make out Junek and Rozeta, both in plainclothes. Rozeta spotted me and waved, then tilted back her head to stare at something above her, thus adopting the same comical posture as the people around her. A man in a cap who happened to be walking past also looked up. He stopped, and his mouth broke into a grin. I followed his gaze to the top of the poles and beheld a strange sight: some joker had stuck two socks on them. This made them look like the legs of an upside-down giant, the hefty thighs embedded in the concrete terrace, then tapering up to the skinny ankles and stockinged feet. Was this why they'd called me – simply to witness a grotesque piece of vandalism?

I said hello to Rozeta. Junek, however – radio in one hand, binoculars in the other – was too preoccupied to even notice me. They both looked pale and far more serious than the other onlookers. Two nervous-looking young policemen were hanging about near by, apparently unable to decide whether they should send the crowd home. Craning my neck, I looked up at the mast-tops again and saw to my amazement that the socks were wearing shoes. Each shoe pointed in a different direction and rocked slightly in the morning breeze, as if the giant were wiggling its toes. It seemed extraordinary that they hadn't already fallen off. Sitting on one of the shoes, which pointed along Nusle Bridge to Karlov, was a reddish-looking pigeon pecking at some muck on its sole. It blinked down at us conspiratorially, wondering, perhaps, whether to throw us a titbit.

Hopeful of some explanation I turned to Rozeta, but her eyes were still fixed on the mastheads. At the same moment there was a sudden gust of wind. 'Watch out!' she shouted, quickly stretching out her arms and stepping back. Instinctively I also took a step backwards. One of the socks thudded on to the stone paving as heavily as a well-stuffed Christmas stocking and broke in two. One piece was blue and quite long, the other black and much shorter. The second –

the shoe the pigeon had been feeding on a moment earlier – bounced off into a clump of dwarf cypresses in a nearby concrete tub. The first – a human leg clad in denim, which I had thought was an enormous sock – lay where it had landed at the foot of the pole.

The man with the cap recognized it first. He doubled up and vomited. The young constables exchange a quick glance and began telling people to leave. Many of them didn't wait to be told. Junek barked an order, and an officer ran over to his car to fetch a roll of blue-and-white tape. Within minutes the area was cordoned off. Rozeta led away the man who had been sick and left him in the care of a well-dressed fellow in a dark suit and trenchcoat, who produced a flask from his breast pocket and administered first aid.

I could have done with a drop of the stuff myself. Squatting down beside the severed limb I stared in fascination at the patch of pale skin visible below the turned-up bottom of the jeans. I couldn't bring myself to look at the other end, about halfway up the thigh, where the material had been ripped off. Junek was shouting at someone over his crackling handset – it appeared that the coroner was refusing to come to the scene of the crime – while Rozeta attempted to revive a young woman who had fainted. Steeling my nerves, I went to look for the shoe. I soon found it among the shrubs and took it over to Junek, who was still arguing with the pathologist. He snatched at it distractedly and held it up to his other ear as if it were a telephone receiver: this was a man used to taking two calls at once. Realizing his error, and without interrupting his conversation, he thrust his face threateningly in mine. Zahir had been right about his nasty streak. I backed off, gesticulating at the filthy shoe to try to stop him putting it in his jacket pocket. But he already had. I went back to the disembodied leg and this time forced myself to examine the ghastly wound. There was no sign of blood on it. My first thought was that it had all dripped down the side of the pole, but a quick upward glance confirmed this was not the case. That meant that the blood must have drained out of the victim while he was still on the ground. In the flesh beside the broken femur – yes, the leg had been broken off, not cut – was the hole where it had been impaled on the masthead, its round outline held in shape by the rigid muscle.

The second leg still hung triumphantly atop the Congress Centre flagpole, its black shoe pointing over the Nusle valley towards Na Slupi. A platform crane was called in to get it down, which took almost an hour. Both limbs had been detached from the body in the same way – not neatly severed but broken and wrenched off. The pathologist, in view of the size of the shoes and hairiness of the skin, pronounced them to be the legs of a man. Before taking them away for detailed forensic examination he asked where the body was, as it was unthinkable that a man could lose his legs in this manner and survive. But a thorough search of the surrounding area revealed nothing.

Shortly after ten o'clock the Superintendent arrived. He looked haggard, dejected, barely capable of taking any kind of decision. As on that previous occasion in the office he seemed to have been caught off-guard. He held a silk handkerchief to his right ear and shook his bald head, on which was perched a natty Hollywood gangster's hat.

His first question was whether the legs were those of Zahir. Rozeta replied tartly that he was definitely still in one piece, since she had just telephoned him at the hospital and he had invited her to his bedside to see for herself that all his vital organs were in order. I was secretly incensed by his impudence. Junek, too, reacted angrily, though not for the same reason. When he snapped at Rozeta that she shouldn't have told Zahir about the legs, she shrugged and said she had had to warn him in case he suffered the same fate.

To avert further argument I pointed out that the legs could belong to one of the other people who had received threatening letters. Junek asked who the hell had told me about them. So I told him: Zahir. Zahir was a con man and a womanizer, he shouted, and one day he'd get his come-uppance, adding that somewhere behind the Zahir case you could bet there was a woman. At this point Olejar stepped forward and, after examining his handkerchief and replacing it in his pocket, said I might as well know who the other two were. Their names were Rehoř and Barnabáš. The CID had been trying to contact them all morning, but Barnabáš wasn't answering the phone and Rehoř was away on business.

Junek went off somewhere – to the Congress Centre lobby, I guessed – to compile a list of potential witnesses from among the night staff. Olejar said he was going back to the office and told Rozeta to get in touch with Rehoř and Barnabáš as soon as possible, so they could be eliminated as possible victims. Rozeta got into her car and started the engine. Then, seeing me running towards her, she wound down the window. I asked what Rehoř and Barnabáš did for a living. The engine spluttered and fell silent. Her reply, and the strange look in her eyes, took me by surprise. 'I think you know that already.'

She was right. I was convinced that Rehoř and Barnabáš were either architects or building engineers.

Before she drove off Rozeta said she had a message for me. Gmünd, she said, with a quick glance around to make sure no one was within earshot, would be waiting for me at two o'clock outside the Church of the Annunciation on Na Slupi. I said in that case I'd no doubt see her there as well. She nodded. Then, as if she'd just remembered, she pulled a bunch of keys from her pocket and handed them through the car window.

'The church,' she smiled. 'I picked them up yesterday.'

To my surprise she added that Gmünd and I were to go to the church alone. She would join us later.

'But that's not allowed!' I objected, realizing at once the absurdity of the situation – a civilian reminding a policewoman of police rules. 'Not allowed?' she repeated, almost curtly. 'Olejar isn't allowed to find out, that's all. On no account.'

I asked her what pressing engagement was keeping her from joining us – after all, she would be on duty.

'None of your business.' She started the car and drove off.

I was at the Church of the Annunciation – or Our Lady on the Lawn, as it is sometimes called – well before the appointed time. As I walked down Albertov I screwed up my eyes against the sun, which after a fortnight of sleet and drizzle hung low over Vyšehrad like a late golden apple. I passed a group of students from the nearby medical faculty, but otherwise the streets were silent and deserted. From Na Slupi came the clang of a tram's bell. Further off, a train rattled over Výtoň Bridge.

I looked up at the spire of the church I had once visited so regularly. I had often thought it would have made the perfect sanctuary for writers, with its octagonal minaret-like tower tapering like a sharpened pencil to a black tip. When it was built in the fourteenth century pencils were not yet in use, but the architect's humility before the Lord of creation and creativity was evident in the whole conception of the church. Today the spire seemed even higher than usual, though I could not say why.

The keys Rozeta had given me jangled in my pocket. Weighing them in my palm I had a feeling of power, as if the door they belonged to would lead me not merely into a Gothic church but into the Temple of Knowledge itself. I glanced up the street towards Charles Square, where I could just make out, beyond the roofs of St Elizabeth Hospital and the spires of St John on the Rock and the chestnut trees in the botanical gardens, the dark outline of Faust House. All morning I'd been trying to make sense of Rozeta's behaviour. Why had she been so touchy, yet so cool and matter-of-fact in the face of what was obviously a vicious practical joke by a demented murderer? I now realized that I, too, had not allowed myself to admit the full horror of the incident. Why was I suddenly so insensitive? After all, I was very far from the hard-headed cop I had once aspired to be. Maybe it was simply my instinct of self-preservation. Why let something so ghastly – two legs torn off someone's body and put on display instead of the national flag – cast a shadow over your life? In the past it might have served as a warning. But in this day and age? In such violent times what's a bit of leg-pulling? A leg on a flagpole: of course it's tragic, but it's also comic. People like a bit of gallows humour these days. What's the alternative? Laugh and you survive; despair and you go under.

But does laughter make us any the wiser? Do we see more clearly through tears of mirth or tears of misery?

I glanced at my watch: two fifteen. I looked up and down Na Slupi and set off for a second time along Albertov, Votočkova and Horská, around the Servite Convent. Still no sign of Gmünd. I found a phone box and called his hotel. The receptionist told me Mr Gmünd was not in his room. It occurred to me to ask her whether he had spent the previous night at the hotel. Would that be wise? I did anyway. But before the question was out of my mouth she slammed down the phone.

Returning to the church, I went up to the main entrance under the spire and tried the door. It was locked. I took out the keys. They fitted. One after another the locks slid open, noiselessly and without protest. I looked round for Gmünd one last time, then went in.

Inside it was light and warm. The first thing that struck my eye was a pillar: a plain round stone pier nearly thirty feet high set on a massive plinth, branching out at the top into rib vaulting that arched a good fifteen feet higher to join the keel moulding that divided the two naves. No wonder the church had so captivated Balbín, for whom it represented the essence of Czech architecture.[1] And what more fitting symbol than a pillar, I thought, supporting as it does not only itself but the whole structure, while protecting all those who enter the building? The stonework – the vaulting, the walls between the windows and the pier itself – was covered in limewash, giving an impression of cleanliness and immaculacy that made one forget the desecrations of the past. In the late fourteenth century the interior – as in all Gothic churches – was a blaze of colour: the ceiling blue and gold; the windows yellow, green and red. There were even oriental motifs, designs brought back by crusaders from Damascus, Jerusalem or Antioch that here found new expression in countless variations. The ribs of the vaulting were striped silver and vermilion; gilded petals gleamed in the emerald fluting of the great arch that divided the nave from the chancel. Whichever way it turned, the eye of the medieval worshipper, eager for manifestations of the Father, Son and Holy Ghost, beheld fantastically intertwined floral motifs – symbols of eternal life; a long-vanished feast for the eyes.

I walked over to the pier, which caught the light from the windows in such an extraordinary way that it seemed to light the space itself, like a giant neon tube. Its sheer simplicity and lack of ornament made an odd contrast with the rest of the interior: a plain stone pillar of no definite architectural style that could have been designed by some pre-medieval functionalist. I scratched the plaster with a key in the hope of finding a splash of red beneath the whitewash. For it is said that in pagan times, before the church was built, the pillar had been the site of sacrificial rituals and was still red with the blood of animal and human victims – the tithe exacted by an insatiable deity. Later, when they came with crosses and holy water, they thought it prudent not to clean the pillar but, instead, to pin it down with the weight of a roof. Like Atlas in the Greek myth, the only way to render it harmless was to ensure it was perpetually burdened.

I ran my fingers over the surface, looking for indentations that might have been caused by a sharp knife. Nothing. It was as if the tissue of the ancient pillar had grown over the wounds. I pressed my palm against the stone. As I did so I felt a distinct movement. The pillar, immovable for centuries, was shaking.

Suddenly I heard distant footsteps and turned in fright. But there was no one – only that same feeling I had had in St Stephen's and St Apollinaris'. The pulpit was palpably empty, the organ loft eerily still. All that disturbed the majestic immobility of the chancel were a few specks of dust stirred up by my own footsteps. I was quite alone in the midst of that ethereal beauty. The sounds must have come from outside.

A hundred and fifty years ago the church and nearby monastery were given over to the local lunatic asylum. Ironically enough, it was this that saved it from rack and ruin, since it was reconsecrated soon afterwards. The pious of Prague were granted access once a year. Prior to that, the monastery had been a school for army cadets, who had brought their girls here and indulged in shameless orgies where once holy mass had been said. Some things never change, and the barbarity of soldiers is one of them.

The army moved into the Servite Monastery on Na Slupi at the turn of the eighteenth century, after it was closed down by order of Joseph II. The gunners and cadets of the Kinsky and Kallenberg regiments treated the place like conquered enemy territory. Nothing was sacrosanct. They took whatever they could, including the organ pipes, which they melted down, mixed with lead and made into musket balls. But that was nothing compared with what had happened in the autumn of 1420 when Hussite forces turned this house of God into a gun emplacement from which they shelled Vyšehrad.

I dropped to my knees beside the pier and pressed my forehead against it. I had an urgent impulse to pray, to beg forgiveness. The words formed in my mind, but they stuck in my throat. How could I ask the stone to pardon deeds done by people I knew almost nothing about? Tears of pity blurred my vision. But instead of rolling down my cheeks they splashed straight on to the flagstones: drops of rain from an overcast soul.

Then I saw the star. A small, bright, golden star falling to the ground. Then another . . . and another . . . then a whole burst of stars at once. I picked one up and examined it: a soft strip of gold, hammered wafer-thin by a craftsman's delicate fingers. Then another piece landed beside me, this time not golden but a deep sky-blue, as large as the palm of my hand yet light as a feather. I looked up. One by one, stars were peeling off the painted ceiling and floating to the floor in eddies of gold, leaving pale star-shaped patches on the night sky. Once more I felt a tremor shake the ancient pillar, stronger than before. High above, the perforated canopy shuddered and rumbled as if it were about to collapse on top of me.

Suddenly the place was bedlam. People appeared out of nowhere and dashed about frantically, apparently making some kind of preparations. Then the walls cracked as if under the impact of a giant hammer. There was a shattering of glass. Flakes of plaster fell off the ceiling, landing like bluish snow on the soldiers' helmets. One man had a star on his helmet, gleaming red like a portent of disaster, and a chalice emblazoned across his chest. He charged past me, almost knocking me over, then stopped at the altar and turned round to face the church, holding some kind of shiny stick which he pointed towards the middle window of the chancel. I realized it was a sword. Another man rushed up and started shouting, but in the deafening din I could not even make out the language, let alone the words – though from his furious tone I guessed he was swearing. The first man reacted by raising his sword in the air and looking about him as if deciding what to do. From somewhere a voice called out, 'Over here!' The man with the star and the chalice ran to the epistle side of the chancel, stopped under the middle window and again raised his sword. The other man rushed out of the church. What was going on? A game of medieval musical chairs? Meanwhile the rumbling noise had risen to a thunderous roar and now seemed to be coming from outside the north aisle. Suddenly, with an almighty crash, the wall behind me was blown wide open.

Some massive object appeared in the gaping hole. When the dust settled I saw it was an iron-clad war engine, pointed at one end like the prow of a battleship. From it was suspended an iron battering ram in the form of a clenched fist, larger than a human head and white with plaster and rubble. The fearsome juggernaut was being wheeled into the church be ten sturdy men – great hulking fellows dressed in faded smocks and homespun tights – each gripping a leather strap attached to the shafts. Slowly they turned the monster round and the ram slid out of view behind its bulk. In its place a long, black barrel now glinted above the men's heads. It looked like a giant musket, a sort of fifteenth-century arquebus but much bigger than anything I had ever read about in contemporary accounts. The men hauled the machine over to where the man with the star was standing beneath the chancel window and gave it a mighty heave. The window shattered, and fragments of stone tracery fell to the ground outside like so many dice. There was no doubt where the barrel of the gun was aiming: straight at Vyšehrad.

A hook was made fast to the parapet. Someone shouted an order, and a young boy, no more than ten years old, leapt up on to the engine, bent to pick something up and, nimble as a monkey, shinned up the to the end of the barrel and installed himself in the narrow aperture of the window. Someone else threw him a metal rod, with which he cleaned the barrel and rammed down the powder. In his hand I glimpsed a shiny lead ball, about the size of an orange, before it disappeared into the muzzle. By the time it thudded into the breech the boy had already jumped down from his perch. A bare-headed man in a green tunic and high boots climbed on to one of the wooden wheels and held a torch to the fuse. There was a deafening explosion that shook the whole building. A few bricks, dislodged from the vault above the nave, crashed to the floor. Before everything was obscured by a cloud of grey dust I noticed that the force of the recoil had split the wall just in front of the gun, which now stood impassively awaiting a new charge. The men looked up at the ceiling apprehensively. Shaken to its foundations, violated, the church clung to its mighty pillar. I put my hands over my ears and shut my eyes tight.

When I opened them again Prunslik was standing over me. A small leather-bound notebook with gilt edges dangled on a gold chain from his hand. It was exactly the same as the one I had seen Gmünd use. Seeing my bewildered expression he quickly slipped the notebook into his trouser pocket. As he did so the ornate hilt of a small dagger flashed briefly from under his jacket. He buckled at the hips, first to the left then to the right, and screwed his mouth into a vicious grin. 'Well I never!' he crowed. 'What's our learned lithophile been up to this time? More bad dreams, eh? Something on your conscience? Bless you!'

It was the dense plaster dust that had made me sneeze, but now I saw no trace of it. All was as it should be: the window-panes were intact, the walls as stable and solid as ever.

'Didn't you hear anything?' I mumbled, still half-dazed.

'I heard you sneeze, yes. And before that you were jabbering away to yourself. In fact I took the liberty of making a few notes.

Dreams are my speciality, you know. I've always been a great fan of old Sigmund, what with being a bit on the short side. I could take you to pieces like a rusty alarm clock! You'd be amazed at the horrors I'd bring to light. People always are.'

I got to my feet and brushed some non-existent dust off my trousers. I looked at my watch. It was four fifteen – at least an hour and a half later than I expected.

'Where's Gmünd?' I asked.

'Busy. I've come instead. Aren't you glad to see me?' With long, awkward strides he began pacing off the width of the great arch above the altar. He reminded me of a small knock-kneed bird – maybe a sandpiper or dunlin – though the pointed tuft on his crown gave him more the look of a lapwing.

'What do you think you're doing?' I blurted out.

'Matthias and I are planning a few improvements. Just you wait. This here, for example. It used to look very different.'

He had stopped in front of the carved neo-Gothic pulpit. 'Grüber put back a lot of the original Gothic features. Superb piece of work, isn't it?' I presumed he meant the pulpit, though he seemed to be pointing at himself. 'But he never finished the job. We're going to put in new pews – copies of the ones that were here when the church was consecrated in 1385, the year the roof was completed. What a sight that must have been! What a magnificent occasion! Pity we weren't there. But then neither was the Emperor Charles. Václav IV was out of town, too, at Točník Castle. You told me a few things about it yourself. History is made up of little scraps of half-remembered dreams, and each one is incredibly precious.' He hopped up to me and went on with a wink, 'That Roza's a bit of all right, isn't she?'

'What's she got to do with it?' I snapped. 'Look, whatever you're insinuating I'd rather you didn't.'

'Insinuating? Who do you take me for? I don't mince words. I just open my beak and Caw! Caw! Caw! Do you like my tie?'

My gaze shifted from Prunslik's manic features to the gaudy

yellow confection at his throat, which was covered in dozens of grinning cartoon lions. I raised a quizzical eyebrow.

'I see the penny's not dropping too well today,' he cackled, skipping around me in crazy circles. With his blue suit and orange topknot he looked like a flickering gas flame. 'A good kick sometimes helps.'

Suddenly he stopped his jinking and became perfectly serious.

'See that boss up there?' he said, indicating the ceiling.

I followed his gaze. At the apex of the ribbed ceiling was a boss bearing a coat-of-arms. On it was a lion rampant.

'Poor thing,' he said. 'Imagine how the King of Beasts must have felt when they stuck that stupid onion on the tower! The ignominy of it! Thank goodness they called in Grüber.'

'Are you talking about the nineteenth-century Gothic reconstruction?'

'Of course I am. He wants to see you, by the way. And it was a request, not an order. He doesn't give orders.'

'Who? Gmünd?'

'You won't regret it. We really are a bit slow on the uptake today, aren't we? Are you listening to me at all?' He held his head in my face like a burning match. 'Something on your mind? Don't tell me you're in love! Yes, it has to be you, apparently – no one else will do. I mean Gmünd, not Rozeta, though I'm sure you'd go running to her at the drop of a garter. The Count seems to like you more than me. I can't think what you've done to deserve it, but never mind. He'll give you the once-over . . . check the old form, you know. Then he'll either give you a bollocking or pay you an advance so you can kick your heels for doing sweet damn-all.'

'For what? Can't you talk sense for once? Am I to understand he wants me to go to his hotel?'

'Spot on!'

'I'm sorry, I can't do that. I don't know if you've heard, but last night there was another murder . . . well, another assault. Except this time it was fatal. The police are still trying to identify the victim. They may need me. I'll go and see Gmünd some other time.'

'Typical police – always the last to find out.'

'You know something then?'

'Not a lot, so don't get excited. It was one of the blokes the police were supposed to be protecting. But of course they didn't.'

'Barnabáš?'

'You get them mixed up, too, I see. Barnabáš, Rehoř . . . Rehoř, Barnabáš. I think it was Rehoř, but don't quote me on that. His wife thought he was away on business. Until they showed her the shoes, that is. Apparently she passed out on the spot.'

'I hope they broke it to her gently. It must have been a terrible shock.'

'Better than showing her his hairy legs.'

'You have an unusual sense of humour, Mr Prunslik.'

'Thank you.'

'Did the police by any chance mention a cobblestone? Did anyone break Barnabáš' window?'

'I see you're a proper little Maigret . . . except we're talking about Rehoř. Actually I couldn't care less about cobblestones – just so as you know. And you may as well know this, too: they've found the crane used by those villains – may they sizzle in hell!'

'Crane? They used a crane?'

'Yes, a platform crane. An old Tatra – one of those big orange contraptions you sometimes see around town fixing the streetlamps. Nowadays they're museum pieces. And guess where it was: in the park on Cattle Market – or Charles Square, as they say these days. No one gave it a second look. The police probably thought it was there to pick the bloody chestnuts. Then someone noticed it didn't have any number plates.'

'What made them think it had anything to do with the murder?'

'How should I know? No one knows for sure. But it does look a bit suspicious, and if you put two and two together . . . The ignition key was left lying on the driver's seat. No fingerprints, of course. No one would be that stupid.'

'Of course not.'

'Of course not.' Prunslik rubbed his hands and wagged his head excitedly. 'But it's pretty damn suspicious, isn't it? Can you imagine a truck driver buffing up his cab every time he leaves it – steering-wheel, gear lever, everything? Or maybe it was some sensitive soul who drives in kid gloves and keeps his cab smelling nice with one of those little cardboard trees?'

He bared his yellow fangs in triumph. I supposed he had a point.

'No plates,' he went on. 'And no chassis number or engine number either. They'd been burnt off with acid and covered over with orange paint, the same colour as the rest of the vehicle. It's even got orange wheels. Not a pretty sight – certainly not for someone of your aesthetic sensibility. I heard that back in the seventies when half the streets in Prague were dug up those things used to drive along the pavements.'

'I'm not from Prague. But surely only a madman would cover his tracks so thoroughly as to arouse suspicion?'

'That's what I say: he must be a nutter. Olejar isn't quite as stupid as he looks – I always said he had more between his ears than that gunge that comes out of them – and he wasn't fooled by the absence of clues. And there's something else.'

'What?'

'The direction the crane was facing. It was parked at an odd angle across the grass, for no obvious reason. But if you look straight ahead through the windscreen it's actually pointing at the flagpoles on Vyšehrad, where you found those legs this morning. And do you know what lies exactly halfway along that line from Charles Square to Vyšehrad?'

'I have no idea.'

'I'll give you three guesses – but only one word each.'

'Look, just stop fooling around and tell me.'

'Saint . . .'

'Saint?'

'Apollinaris.'

'That's a very . . . interesting observation. But not terribly helpful. What I'd like to know is what the police have done with that crane. I want to take a look at it myself. I might discover something.'

'Don't be absurd! Talk about shutting the stable door . . . They couldn't get the thing started, so the traffic cops decided to leave it there and tow it away tomorrow. But no one thought of guarding it. Fancy the police letting someone swipe that monster from right under their noses! Olejar refuses to talk about it and says no one's to mention it to the press. You'd have thought he'd have been more careful, wouldn't you?'

He giggled, and fixed me with one crystal-clear, crystal-hard blue eye.

'Or would you?'

11

Could I revive within me
Her symphony and song,
To such a deep delight 'twould win me,
That with music loud and long,
I would build that dome in air,
That sunny dome!

Samuel Taylor Coleridge

It took us ten minutes to walk to the Bouvines Hotel in Na Zderaze. The light was fading fast and a cold wind had sprung up. In Charles Square the rush-hour traffic had come to a standstill. The shop windows in Wenceslas Arcade were bright with plastic Christmas trees and coloured streamers.

Prunslik didn't talk much. And what he did say, even concerning Matthias Gmünd, was not particularly civil. In a would-be confiding gesture he took me by the arm and confessed in a breathy whisper that actually he didn't think much of his employer, though one shouldn't bite the hand that feeds. A failed architect, Gmünd was obsessed with the Middle Ages and dismissed out of hand the art of all subsequent periods. Having inherited a fantastic fortune he was now in a position to put some of his madcap schemes into practice.

I begged to differ. I knew something about Gmünd's family history and was sure he was acting on the noblest of motives.

Prunslik shrugged and said I was too young and gullible and couldn't tell when people were making fun of me. He was right – at that moment I didn't know which of them to disbelieve most, Gmünd or Prunslik himself. Lowering his voice again, he opined that Matthias was a complete crank who had decided to call himself Gmünd after some famous medieval architect. And didn't I think Matthias had a very odd head? Before I could reply, he said he thought it looked as if it had been stuck on to his neck upside down.

Again I had to disagree, though I did find myself suppressing a smile. At our first meeting I, too, had had the feeling there was something peculiar about Gmünd's head. 'Not only that,' Prunslik went on, 'he's so absent-minded he sometimes puts it on the wrong way round in the morning – back to front as well as upside down – with his chin pointing up and his face turned backwards, a bit like Lot's wife. When he's like that it's best to keep out of his way and wait until he sorts himself out. One day he'll turn into a pillar of salt . . . and finally into a lump of rock, a big motionless boulder. Maybe then he'll be happy.' The midget gave a brief laugh then lapsed into gloom. 'Being with Matthias Gmünd is no tea-party, I can tell you. Sometimes I have the feeling he wants to put right all the mistakes of history . . .' He checked himself before adding in a dismal voice the strange words, '. . . All his *own* mistakes. But why did he have to choose this country? Why the Czechs? Why *me*? It's as if he were Fate itself.'

We walked the rest of the way in silence.

The Hotel Bouvines is a low two-storey building situated at the top of a street that used to be called Little Charles Square, near the site of the ancient Crusaders' church of St Peter and St Paul (originally Romanesque in style, then Gothic, then, inevitably, Baroque and finally, since it was knocked down, in no style at all) and the Chapel of the Holy Sepulchre (also long vanished), and where once stood, in the pre-Christian settlement of Zderaz, an ancient smithy steeped in folklore. It is a cheerless place. The next street is called Na Zbořenci – 'On the Ruins' – a name that sends shivers up my spine every time I hear it. Matthias Gmünd certainly had a well-developed sense of historical topography; in fact he could hardly have picked a better place to stay. At the time of these events (that is, six months ago) the building was a typical *fin-de-siècle* stucco pile that had recently been converted into a hotel, though not having a restaurant it probably escaped the notice of the casual passer-by. Discreet and unassuming, it looked much the same as hundreds of *pensions* in cities throughout Western Europe. What set this one apart, however, was a central tower that rose one floor higher than the roof. Visible only from the upper windows of the surrounding apartment blocks, it provided the only clue that the building actually dated from the Gothic period. Until then I had never known of its existence.

We passed the reception desk, walked up to the first floor and knocked on the door of Room Six. A voice told us to come in. We entered a spacious hall with various doors leading off. Beyond it was a comfortable sitting-room where most of the décor – carpet, wallpaper and furniture – was white or off-white. But the first and most striking thing I noticed were the flowers. Wherever I looked – on the floor, on the table and sideboard, on the window-sill – were vases of clear crystal or greyish porcelain, all full of flowers: dahlias and asters in giddy profusion; pearly pink marigolds; and, gleaming though the shaggy heads of chrysanthemums, great starbursts of delicately flecked lilies. Most of all, however, my hungry eyes feasted on the roses: dazzling white roses in every stage of bloom, the heavy, bulbous vases in which they stood contrasting starkly with their petals as soft as Chinese silk.

Only one thing marred this visual banquet. In a semi-circular alcove at the far end of the room stood a tall black-glazed Chinese vase, intricately decorated with a writhing green-scaled dragon. Crammed into it were around thirty stalks of pampas grass, their pallid plumes smooth as a bridal gown and cool as a shroud. There was something scary and brazenly provocative about the way they poked their long, bent stems at me, quite spoiling the otherwise magnificent display of more congenial blooms. I was convinced they were carnivorous and fed on choice morsels of human flesh.

Something else struck me as odd. The air was heavy with a sweetish scent that did not come from the flowers. My first thought was incense. But there was some other fragrance in it, too, something bittersweet and slightly acrid – not unlike herbal tobacco or some other dried plant used for smoking.

'In your honour.' My intoxicated senses were suddenly aware of Gmünd thrusting his right hand at me, while with his left he indicated the room with a sweeping gesture. As he rose from his armchair (where he had been reading an English newspaper) his body appeared to take up at least half the room, which was by no means small. The Knight of Lübeck was dressed in a dark-green open-necked shirt, a brown corduroy waistcoat and black trousers with a narrow grey stripe. On his feet he wore casual moccasins, and a half-smoked cigar smouldered in his hand. He looked a bit like a bearded Winston Churchill.

He asked me to sit down and told Prunslik he would not be needing him. But the little fellow appeared not to hear and installed himself on the window-sill among the pots of rampant tuberose, his arms folded across his chest. When the room attendant brought in a tray of hors d'oeuvres and a carafe of red wine, he ordered a brandy.

On the tray were hot fresh rolls, a fist-sized ball of butter, a selection of cold meats that included slivers of roast beef folded into rosebuds, yellow Appenzell cheese and runny Normandy Brie (both, to judge by the smell, the genuine article), avocado, asparagus, olives, gherkins and prunes, as well as that strange spiky fruit I had seen Zahir eating, which Gmünd referred to as a 'durian' and recommended I try.

While I dithered over what to put on my plate I was aware that he was watching me closely, as was his companion. I began with a small piece of hard cheese and an olive. As I withdrew with my prize to the sofa Prunslik burst out laughing from his perch and tossed Gmünd a coin, which the giant caught with surprising dexterity and slipped into his pocket. He, too, seemed amused. I did not know whether to laugh at a joke I neither shared nor understood, or pretend not to notice and get on with my supper.

'Please excuse us,' said Gmünd. 'As I'm sure you realize, we had a little bet. Raymond said you'd be hungry after your visit to the church and go for the meat. I knew you'd be tempted by the meat but guessed you'd pick something more modest.'

'Do I strike you as modest?'

'Yes. You are by nature timid, and your upbringing has reinforced that trait. You always need to be asked twice. Go on – help yourself to whatever you fancy. Or perhaps you'd prefer something different? I can get some fish sent up from the restaurant by the river – they do excellent trout. I often go there. Order anything you like. It's what they expect at the Bouvines.'

'No, this is quite sufficient. I'm just not used to such a spread.' Bolstering my courage with a good gulp of wine, I helped myself to some diced chicken in dill sauce and a few thin slices of meat. Not until my mouth was crammed with food did I realize how improper my behaviour must have seemed – like a poor relation stuffing himself at the table of a rich and successful uncle. I forced myself to chew more slowly. The twinkle in my host's emerald eyes told me what I already sensed: he knew exactly what was going through my mind.

'I understand, Květoslav,' he said quietly. 'I used to suffer from shyness, too. I had to work hard to lose it, even superficially. After all, one can't change the way one is. But I asked you here so that we could talk about you. You know quite enough about me already.'

'If you ask me point blank like that,' I said, 'you won't learn a thing. I get tongue-tied when people ask me direct questions. I wouldn't know where to begin.' In my embarrassment I bit off an enormous chunk of roll and found myself having to cover my mouth with my hand as I chewed my way through it. The effort brought tears to my eyes.

Gmünd looked away tactfully, cast his eye over the newspaper on the table beside him and relit his cigar. Without looking up he said, 'Begin wherever you like. You could start by telling us about that old man you met in the bar yesterday.'

The roll stuck in my throat.

'Raymond was walking past and happened to see you,' he added by way of explanation, apparently unaware of my consternation.

'With my little eye I see . . . Tweedledum and Tweedledee!' mocked a bleating voice from the window.

Gmünd smiled indulgently. 'Don't mind him,' he said. 'He's an orphan. He's jealous of all my friends.'

There was a crash as Prunslik knocked a pot of tuberoses off the window-sill. Gmünd did not react. A second pot fell to the floor.

A long silence followed. When it became unbearable I slowly began to speak. First I talked about Netřesk. I did not mention the embarrassing visit to his flat, recalling instead my schooldays in Mladá Boleslav and the favourite teacher who shared my passion for history and praised my famous 'story boards' on the classroom wall. At some point I realized I was no longer talking about my school but my family. My voice at once faltered, and it was only with great difficulty that I kept myself from stuttering.

Prunslik, still on the window-sill with a glass of brandy on his knee, seized on the brief hiatus: '*Aber wo haben Sie Ihr Herz verloren*?'

'I'm sorry?' I said. 'Where did I lose my heart? You mean what place is most dear to me?'

'I mean what wench,' he growled. Again that cold blue stare.

Gmünd turned to him without a word. I could not see his eyes, but he must have looked daggers at the little scamp, who at once fell silent and launched instead into a bizarre charade. Closing his eyes, he balanced his glass on his head and produced from his pocket three little balls – blue, green and red – which he then proceeded to juggle with his left hand, still with his eyes tight shut. His right index finger, meanwhile, poked around in his nose. Clearly he had taken offence.

Gmünd shrugged his shoulders apologetically. 'Raymond is not the soul of discretion, I'm afraid. He was no doubt hoping you'd tell us about all the girls you knew at school. He doesn't have much luck with the ladies himself, so he takes a vicarious interest in these things. The last time we visited Zahir in hospital all they talked about was women. That man makes no secret of his conquests.'

A gentler tone had crept into his voice, and I felt more inclined to trust him. Still, I was surprised at my own words: 'I don't have any secrets. Whenever I fell in love it was always with the wrong person. Besides, I was so ashamed of my name that I never made the first move.'

'You've really suffered on account of that name of yours, haven't you? It's strange. I wonder if perhaps you don't blame your name for all the bad things that have ever happened to you.'

'Perhaps I do. The awful thing is not being able to do anything about it. You're given a name and that's it – you're stuck with it for ever.'

'Yes. It's rather like being born in the wrong century and slowly coming to hate the age you live in. You're stuck with that, too. All you can do is dream about times long past or those yet to come.'

'I agree. It's just as awful.'

'Tell me, have you ever considered getting married? Having children?'

'If I did it would only be to prove I'm not suited to it. Or maybe I simply haven't met the right woman.'

'Take my advice: don't be in a hurry. As long as you're working for me try not to think about women at all.'

'Why not?'

'It would only distract you. You're going to be learning a lot of interesting things, many of them of a confidential nature, and I don't want you discussing them with anyone else – not even inadvertently. Women make excellent spies, but they're bad listeners. I'll tell you something that happened to me yesterday, something so extraordinary it beggars belief. Yet I'm absolutely sure that my wife – if I had one – would think it perfectly normal.'

'There must be exceptions. Anyway, are you quite sure there is no woman in your life? The other day I noticed the way Rozeta was looking at you. I would count myself lucky if any woman looked at me like that.'

'Like what?'

'Admiringly. Devotedly. She couldn't take her eyes off you.'

'Really? I never noticed. How nice of her. Perhaps I ought to start courting her.' He gave a bitter laugh.

Suddenly I wished he would shut up. I wanted to tell that blasé man-of-the-world, who never let anything ruffle his sleek plumage, that some men would give ten years of their life for a single smile from a woman like Rozeta. But I kept silent, astonished at the pounding of my own heart.

No doubt reading my thoughts again, Gmünd gave me an enquiring look and replenished my glass. 'Calm down, old chap. You shouldn't take everything people say seriously. When it comes to telling the truth, I'd say you were the Knight, not me. You must learn not to attach the same importance to everything you hear. After all, even you have on occasion doubted my word. Is that not so?'

Remembering what Prunslik had told me on the way to the hotel I glanced towards the window, where the little freak was curled up on the sill fast asleep. I looked Gmünd straight in the eye and shook my head.

'You haven't? I feel honoured. But if you do ever think I'm not telling the truth you must say so. No shilly-shallying! I enjoy a good frank discussion.

'Anyway, about what happened yesterday. Since some of my clothes are at the cleaners, including my overcoat – without which I feel quite naked – I went out for my usual evening stroll without it. I'd been restless all afternoon. I dislike Sundays at the best of times, but yesterday I felt particularly uneasy. I had a feeling – a kind of strange, nagging intuition – that something was going to happen to you. Nothing fatal, not an accident or anything – but something dangerous none the less, dangerous to your soul. By late afternoon the feeling had became so intense that I simply had to get out of doors in spite of the miserable weather.

'Not having my coat, I decided just to walk round the square and come straight back. It's only a couple of hundred yards from here. I left the hotel shortly after supper, at around half-past seven. I know the Cattle Market like the back of my hand. You can never tire of a beautiful place like that. And if you shut your eyes and let Time take you by the hand, you can meet those who lived there before you: Jakub Kuchta the cooper, Jakub Kacíř, Dimuta the fishwife, Jakub Pastuška, Michal Hrbek, Frenclín of Kamenice, Řehák the tanner, Mikuláš the ironmonger, old Petr Kolovrat – to name just a few of the honest folk who owned houses there in the fourteenth century. We'd all love to meet them, wouldn't we?

'But to get back to my strange experience last night. There were few cars about, and the streetlights glowed like sulphur in the damp air. A biting north wind sprang up, worse than any February frost, and chilled me to the bone. But it did blow away the foreboding that had plagued me all afternoon. It also brought something with it: a kind of hallucination.

'As I was walking up Resslova towards the square, past the Church of Cyril and Methodius, a strange thing happened. I could have sworn I heard the sound of horses' hooves behind me, faintly at first, then ever more distinctly, and more than once actually looked over my shoulder expecting to see a carriage full of tourists determined to see the city sights even on this bleak autumn evening. But apart from a few speeding cars the street was deserted. Then all went quiet, which was even stranger considering how early it was. I entered the park through the pedestrian subway then headed slightly left over the grass towards the New Town Hall. It was then that I caught sight of a cluster of lights through the trees in the direction of St Ignatius' Church: small orange lights, quite unlike the street-lighting, that seemed to shiver in the cold and send a faint, flickering message to anyone who happened to notice them. Candles! I went closer to investigate, assuming this must be some commemorative event connected with November 1989. The flames wavered slightly but otherwise remained motionless. No one was holding them – they were much too high off the ground. And how did they stay alight in the strong wind? Perhaps they were shielded in some way. Yes, that must be the answer.

'I made my way through the bushes, past the statue of Eliška Krásnohorská, and came out on to the pavement. I couldn't believe my eyes. At first I had thought the lights were on the south side of the park, but I now saw they were suspended high above the road in front of St Ignatius' Church – right over the intersection where Resslova turns into Ječná. They were very high up – about a hundred feet, I reckoned – and arranged in a regular pattern. There was no one else about to corroborate this strange apparition. Was it a figment of my imagination? Now and then a car sped by underneath, quite unconcerned. Drivers never notice anything. They don't have a clue what's going on around them.

'Again I heard the sound of hooves and at the same moment realized what those ghostly lights reminded me of: the inside of a church. If you joined all the points of light together they would trace the noble interior of a magnificent sacred building! Just imagine, in the middle of the square! As far as I know the only great building ever to have stood on that spot was the Chapel of Corpus Christi, which in the fourteenth and fifteenth centuries was one of the great churches of Central Europe.'

I didn't know much about the Chapel of Corpus Christi. Now I was aware only of a vague sense of regret, a feeling that came over me every time I read about that mysterious church demolished in the late eighteenth century. But something about Gmünd's story disturbed me even more. Years ago, when studying for my examinations, I had read about a similar vision in the Cattle Market (it must have been in some old diaries or memoirs) witnessed by a well-known nobleman; Jiří Vilém of Chudenice, I think it was. No, Vilém Slavata of Košumberk – that was the one. I told Gmünd at once. He was impressed. Clutching at his beard in excitement, he begged me to tell him everything I knew.

'There's not much to tell,' I said. 'As far as I remember the nobleman wasn't even born when the incident took place, which I think was in the early 1570s. He first heard about it from his nurse, then from elderly New Town burghers who claimed to have witnessed it first hand. Some no doubt embellished the story a little, but all agreed that one summer's day a strong wind suddenly got up and without warning a large company of cavalry rode into the square. Apart from the clatter of hooves on the cobbles, they said, there was not a sound to be heard. At first people took no particular notice; but when an enormous carriage appeared at the corner by Emmaus and ploughed its way (for it had no wheels) towards the Chapel of Corpus Christi their hair truly stood on end. Most terrifying of all were the guards that rode beside it. They were mounted on huge horses and were themselves so tall they could easily see into the first-floor windows – or could have done had they had heads. Four headless knights – in broad daylight! Some people who saw them fainted on the spot and never fully recovered their wits. The phantom procession then vanished as quickly as it had appeared.'

'I never heard that before,' said Gmünd, tugging thoughtfully at his beard. 'Even if it isn't true it's still a marvellous story. But I'm sure the author of those memoirs didn't make it up. And the knights were riding towards Corpus Christi, you say? Amazing. That would mean . . .' He stopped short, then looked at me and said in a much more cheerful tone, 'You see how useful you are? I was right. You're just the man we need.'

I objected that I was not even a university graduate and, in fact, knew nothing at all. But his words gave me a thrill of pleasure, and so did what he said next.

'Who cares about degrees? What matters to me is that you know a damn sight more than those chaps in the history departments – thank God you didn't end up there! Oh, I'm sure they know a great deal about particular events – what happened when and so forth – but I doubt if any of them could match my story with one as good as yours. Their history is dead; ours is living. Here we are, having a simple unscholarly chat about the past – we're *living* the past! What does it matter if a few facts escape us or if we don't have all the answers? The important thing is the *feeling* it arouses in us.'

Was he saying this only for my sake? Was he leading up to something? What was his game? These were the questions that flashed though my mind as he fixed me with his steady, vaguely expectant gaze. What did he want of me? His next words only added to my perplexity.

'Don't say anything to Olejar about our conversation. He needn't know anything that's not absolutely essential. If he knew the half of my plans for the Heptecclesion I'm sure he'd be far less cooperative. He has his own objectives, some of them questionable to say the least. I heard something about a corruption scandal. Do you know anything about it?'

I shook my head. My attention had been arrested by the word Heptecclesion, tossed casually into the conversation as if it were a household name too commonplace to merit explanation. I had no idea what the term might refer to, but under Gmünd's watchful, angular eyes I tried to look as if I knew all about it – though not, of course, about the corruption scandal. But what he said next took my breath away.

'Raymond can tap any telephone he likes using a computer. The other day when we were in Olejar's office he was called away, and Raymond took the opportunity to tamper with his phone – don't ask me what he did or how. He then listened in on a few calls and made a fascinating discovery: the Superintendent is being blackmailed.'

'*Was* being blackmailed,' came a voice from the window-sill. Far from being asleep, Prunslik had been following every word.

'No names were mentioned, but it wasn't hard to work out who the blackmailer is.'

'*Was*,' corrected Prunslik.

An idea dawned on me.

'Come on, you must have some idea,' Gmünd prompted me. 'An architect . . . someone who's been working for years at the city planning office.'

'The man who was murdered last night! Barnabáš. Wasn't that the name?'

'No. Rehoř.'

'And you think . . . I suppose the Superintendent *might* be capable of something like that, but why would he choose such a brutal and roundabout method? It would be out of character.'

Yet all of a sudden I was convinced that the nightmare haunting the architects of Prague was none other than the police chief himself. He knew they were up to something and was blackmailing them! But instead of exposing them to scandal, he simply murdered anyone who refused to pay up and displayed their body in public as a warning to the others.

Or was it the other way round? Maybe Rehoř and Pendelmanová had had something on Olejar so he'd had to silence them. Maybe he had an accomplice; a cold-blooded killer like Junek, for example, who hid his sadistic impulses under a policeman's uniform.

'It's Olejar!' I blurted out. 'He killed Mrs Pendelmanová! He lured her out of the house when I was asleep then strangled her and hanged her from the bridge!'

For the first time I saw Gmünd look genuinely surprised. He turned to Prunslik, who was staring at me sceptically, then let his eyes drift somewhere over my head and said, 'But didn't the police think the motive was political? Revenge for some back-stabbing by old Pendelman?'

I was undeterred. 'I think you're on the wrong track. We know Mrs Pendelmanová worked for the city council. What if she was in the planning department? She was a qualified architect. She may have taken bribes for approving projects that should never have seen the light of day, and Olejar found out. Using the same methods that Mr Prunslik here employs.'

Again they exchanged looks, but nothing was going to stop me now.

'He deliberately entrusted me with keeping an eye on Mrs Pendelmanová because he knew I wasn't up to the job. I'm not surprised he wanted to hush the whole thing up. And even if the truth had come out he would still have had his cover. That's why he got Junek involved, an exemplary officer who always looks after his own interests – the perfect contrast to a duffer like me. He had to show that the police had competent law enforcement officers, too. The bunglers had to be flushed out. I reckon the two of them are in it together.'

'What you say is not without interest. You may even be on to something,' said Gmünd quietly. 'But if I were you I'd keep my suspicions to myself until I was quite sure. Forgive me for saying so, but so far this is nothing but speculation. I advise caution. In other words, keep your mouth shut. If you are right and Olejar finds out, he'll make short work of you. Mincemeat, I'd say.'

I wanted to object but held my tongue. He was right. For a moment he gave me a contemplative, slightly amused look. Then he went on, 'Of course, you could put your hypothesis to some use. Tell him your theory about Mrs Pendelmanová – that the motive for her murder might be linked to her work, to which she was very committed. That is, if she really did have any say in issuing building permits. In that case Olejar would have nothing to hide. Make it look as if he was the one who made the connection with this last murder, then watch his reaction. After that we can talk it over again. By then we may know a bit more.'

I said I would try. The food, I was surprised to see, had disappeared – into my stomach. I had polished off the lot. I had no recollection of having enjoyed it; in fact, distracted by Gmünd's baleful gaze, I'd been quite unaware of what I'd been eating. I drained my glass. Suddenly my eyelids were heavy with fatigue. I didn't want to think about Rehoř's murder or my hallucination in the church on Na Slupi. All I longed for was a long, dreamless sleep. My legs would hardly carry me to the door, but I tried not to let it show.

Prunslik accompanied me down to the lobby. After his nap on the window-sill he was perkier than ever. When I held out my hand to say goodnight he went on tiptoe and hissed into my face, 'Some goings-on, eh, Mr K? Old Nick alone knows where it'll all end up.' What with the unaccustomed food and the disturbing implications of our conversation, I was too exhausted to object to his odd turns of phrase. Actually I was getting used to them. I was getting used to everything.

12

The whole city lies extinct
– Prague is a barren grave.

Karel Hynek Mácha

As I awoke from a mercifully oblivious sleep the events of the previous day came back to hit me like a boomerang. I winced even before the pain struck: it was a pattern I knew only too well.

I staggered into the bathroom. The food I'd had at Gmünd's still lay heavy on my stomach. As I studied my ravaged face in the mirror purple circles swam before my eyes. I shouldn't have had so much wine. I thought of the legs on the flagpoles and nearly threw up.

At breakfast Mrs Frýdová took one look at me, went to the sink without a word and poured a large glass of water into which she dropped a soluble aspirin. She obviously thought I'd spent the evening at the pub, and I had not the slightest intention of putting her right. At any moment she would start lecturing me about the shocking state I was in – though I hardly needed her to tell me that. She had recently taken to nagging me again: I should get a proper job, I should stop wandering around the town. Especially *at night*, she added significantly. No wonder I was in such a bad way. Part of me secretly prayed she would turn me out on to the street.

I went to my room to telephone Olejar. As I dialled the number my eye fell on the vine I had found in Karlov. The days when it had thrived in my care had long gone: now it looked completely withered. I made a mental note to chuck it in the dustbin when I went out, pot and all. Of course, I forgot immediately.

Olejar told me tetchily that he had no time to talk. When I said I had something important to tell him about the Pendelmanová case he became even more irritated, then muttered something about coming to see him at the end of the week. I asked whether Friday morning would suit him or would he prefer the afternoon, but in reply I heard only a purring sound: he had hung up. I was disappointed he hadn't shown more interest in my enterprise. No sooner had I put down the phone than it rang again. It was Zahir. He was planning a bit of fieldwork, he said, and if I was free he would like me to accompany him. I was delighted: the thought of spending another day alone was beginning to oppress me. I resolved not to let his constant chatter get on my nerves and actually found myself looking forward to his company. I gave him my address, and he said he would pick me up in his car.

He arrived fifteen minutes early and kept his hand on the horn until I looked out of the window. Without getting out of the car he signalled to me to come down. Mrs Frýdová, who was leaning out of the window in the next room, declared that she wouldn't dream of getting into a car with a man who drew attention to himself so ostentatiously. She was a shrewd judge of character.

I found the passenger seat of Zahir's sports car none too comfortable. Despite my best efforts to hide the fact, he could tell I was nervous and saw how tightly I held on to the door handle. I was amazed at how confidently he manipulated the three metal levers fitted on to the left side of the steering column – clutch, brake and accelerator – and asked if he'd had to take a special driving test. In theory, yes, he said. But he hadn't bothered.

As we raced down the long, sweeping arc of the dual carriageway towards Holešovice Bridge I silently imagined the various forms of violent death that would inevitably befall us were we to hit another vehicle or skid off the road. Mind you, I have such thoughts every time I travel by car, which is no doubt why I have never been tempted to get a driving licence. It takes a certain courage to assume responsibility for a lethal four-wheeled weapon; visions of mangled bodies trapped inside tangles of shiny scrap-metal – or the bloody spectre of a dead child that I failed to see in time – ensured I remained a coward.

As soon as we reached the bridge we got stuck in a traffic jam. With a sigh of relief I let go of the door handle, which I had been gripping so tightly my knuckles had gone white. Zahir lit a cigarette and opened the window, drumming his fingers impatiently on the wheel between quick, hungry puffs of nicotine. Serves you right, I thought with satisfaction, for putting people's lives at risk. I took a sidelong look at his profile: his features were European, but his dark complexion and curly black hair, thinning slightly above his forehead, suggested he was of mixed blood. I had suspected as much when I first heard his name; now, studying his prominent nose and small black eyes at close quarters, I was sure of it. I was just wondering how to ask him about his origins without seeming rude when he began telling me himself.

His father had been an aviation engineer who came to Prague from his native Azerbaijan in the 1950s to train on Czechoslovak light aircraft. He met a Czech girl and, after a hasty marriage, they had a child. She, however, had no desire to move to Central Asia. Divorce followed and with it an alimony settlement. Though he never mentioned the fact to his wife, he was a devout Muslim and couldn't wait to return home. He came from an old and affluent family who had got even richer under the communists. His grandfather had been a senior apparatchik who had known Stalin personally. Stalin, the family story went, had been on the point of eliminating him when his plans were stymied by his own demise. In the event it was Zahir's father who died, when the jet he was piloting crashed into a desert. But, thanks to the grandfather, who knew his grandson only from photographs, the money kept arriving, and the boy was able to complete his education.

I asked Zahir if he shared his father's religious beliefs. Perhaps his being a Muslim might account for the threatening letters – though this theory could hardly apply to Pendelmanová, Rehoř and Barnabáš.

These speculations were quickly dispelled by Zahir himself: the only things he believed in were beautiful women, fast cars and well-designed buildings.

The traffic had slowed to a crawl. People on the pavement overtook us. Only the ever-growing swarm of cyclists and messengers on mopeds made any kind of headway. Trapped by low pressure, a cloud of toxic smog hung over the Magistrale and swirled around the deluded pedestrians, who were no doubt smugly congratulating themselves on having left their cars at home. It was nine thirty by the time we reached the junction of Žitná and Sokolská. Zahir parked the car in Hálková Ulice.

We were going to photograph a dilapidated house on a huge demolition site in V Tůních, the last survivor of a row of buildings dating from the mid eighteenth century. It had no owner, and without the protection of the conservation authorities it would have been demolished long ago. Now, Zahir told me confidentially, its days were numbered as a result of years of deliberate neglect. The same fate had befallen dozens of buildings of historical and architectural value, both in Prague and other Czech towns. With the advent of capitalism there was no shortage of investors, but their only interest was in acquiring building plots. So they sat back and waited for wind and weather to do their work, and before long the building would be declared unsafe and condemned. In this case that would be within the next few months, he said, adding that he had already designed a high-rise office block – or 'business centre', as he called it – for the site. The sound of that repellent phrase filled my heart with dread. I thought of St Stephen's, just a stone's throw away. Would it not be overshadowed by this new temple of Mammon? Would it not be starved of light and air? And what about the bell-tower? And poor little Longine?

But all was not lost. Not yet.

I left Zahir hopping around on one leg with his camera, lugging his tripod from one spot to another, and went for a stroll in Na Rybníčku. The quiet little street and, above all, the silent grandeur of St Stephen's reposing on its gentle slope below me calmed my nerves. I was aware of the distant snarl of traffic caught in the jaws of Ječná and Žitná, but here I was out of harm's way. For a moment I even had the feeling I was in the countryside, in a strange landscape full of apartment blocks. I would not have been surprised to hear a cock crow.

Suddenly, with a renewed sense of dread, I realized that apart from canned music, electrical appliances and the engines of cars and construction equipment I would never hear anything again. I thought, too, of the things I would never see again: a thousand spires rising above steep red roofs; the myriad secret nooks and narrow doors and tiny windows of old town houses; stone buttresses and wooden supports leaning over winding alleys; curiously shaped cowls atop white chimneystacks. This was no longer the town I knew, the only town in which I felt truly at home, the town I would have fought to the death to protect despite my innate cowardice. A town I could depend on and which could depend on me. A town where I could join a guild and work as a brewer or tanner or in the timber yard down by the river. My only wish would be to keep things as they were; my only prayer that the city, and my home in it, be spared from flood and fire and foreign occupation – and from destruction at the hands of my own people.

Long ago, on a high rock above the Vltava where archaeologists are still uncovering the crumbling remains of foundations and cellars in the parks of Vyšehrad, there once stood a castle and a town. The town was very large (a thousand years ago perhaps the largest in the world) and could rightly be called a holy city, since it contained more places of worship in relation to its population than any other. These included the Basilica of St Lawrence, the Chapel of Mary Magdalene, the Rotunda of St John the Evangelist, the chapels of St Hippolytus, St Peter and the Holy Cross, the Rotunda of St Margaret, the Church of the Decapitation of John the Baptist, the Church of St Peter and St Paul and the little chapel of St Clement where King Václav was baptized. They even had their own Chapel of Corpus Christi. Alongside the sacred buildings stood the many-towered palaces of the secular rulers, with the dwellings of the ordinary townsfolk clustered around them. Beyond the city wall, on the leeward side because of the noise and smell, smiths and tanners and butchers plied their trade. Close by was the massive Charles Gate with its ten spires – a beautiful fortress-like structure that in the fourteenth century was rivalled only by the Swine Gate in the New Town. Fifteen breweries ensured that the good folk of Vyšehrad had strength enough for work and prayer. The rocky, uneven terrain, full of hollows and gullies and countless streams, was interconnected by as many as 160 stone and wooden bridges. On the site of the modern cemetery, now the resting place of the nation's great and good, there once 'balanced on the wind' the hanging gardens of Libuše[1] – an Arcadian grove full of pagan temples set about with standing stones that symbolized fertility. Near by, where today there is a volleyball court, was Libuše's legendary labyrinth. Into this orchard of apple trees, planted in concentric rings and pruned into narrow green alleys, the unwary would be lured by the odour of blossom and ripe fruit. But only the cleverest, who could answer a question posed by the terrifying statue of the priestess in the heart of the maze, ever found their way out. The rest were condemned to remain inside the labyrinth as the priestess's servants. In addition to its gates, the town was protected by two huge towers. One was black, octagonal and early Romanesque in style, with six-foot-thick walls pierced here and there by small double-arched windows and surmounted by forbidding battlements. The other was a rectangular keep of white marble – a dazzling novelty, even though it had stood on the cliff-top above the river since time immemorial. It had not a single window and was thus as dark within as it was light without: to reach the battlements its garrison had to clamber up the wooden scaffolding and ladders by torchlight. At the bottom of the tower was a deep and ancient well – so deep, it was said, that it reached all the way down through the solid rock to far below the level of the river. And right beside this shaft the Modern Age, in its infinite folly, has cut a tunnel for cars and trams. Who gave us the right to drive through that holy rock? The engineers and navvies had more luck than sense: the well remained miraculously undamaged.

Legend has it that at its bottom lies Princess Libuše on a golden couch, awaiting the day when she will redeem her nation. Here the rock is said to reach down below the riverbed to a depth seven times that of its visible portion. No one has ever fathomed the black pool below Vyšehrad – no one has a plumb-line long enough. Somewhere at the bottom of the pool lies the altar of St Peter and St Paul, infamously cast into its depths by a gang of Calixtine cut-throats. Whoever pulls it out, the legend goes, will become master of all Bohemia.

The people of Vyšehrad devised a fitting revenge: if ever they caught Jan Žižka, the one-eyed bandit of Tabor, they would hurl him down the well, then board it over and use the makeshift table for a splendid feast.[2] But things turned out differently. The royalist forces could not hold Vyšehrad against the Hussites. The dead were left lying where they had fallen, since the Hussite clerics forbade the burying of enemies. A storm of religious fundamentalism swept through the town, leaving behind only the battered remains of the old provostry, the Church of St Peter and St Paul and parts of the city wall. The only building to survive intact to this day – and that only by a stroke of luck, after nineteenth-century plans to build a road through it were dropped – is St Martin's Rotunda, a monument to the Atlantis of central Europe that was Vyšehrad. Vyšehrad: a bright pearl hanging over Prague, the like of which the world has never seen. *Ein anderes Paradies an der anderen Seite: da habe ich mein Herz verloren*, Herr Prunslik. Prague's great vertical, her pathway to the stars. Prague was lovelier than Babylon, more magnificent than Rome.

Yet verticals point down as well as up. Our lack of respect for our ancestors' creativity has been staggering, and now, having perfected the art of destruction, we are paying the price. Most of all we like to start from scratch with a green field and cover it with concrete. Simple, quick, functional: that is the modern mantra. We have an insatiable desire to kill the past, an ineradicable instinct to destroy what others have created. Jan Žižka, the executioner's axe that dealt the deathblow to Czech piety and humility, was the embodiment of the very worst kind of Czech boorishness, the terrifying epitome of an Asiatic brutality and barbarity that spelt disaster and ignominy for our nation. Sixty decades later we are still struggling with his bloody legacy. His razing of Vyšehrad, the gem of Romanesque Europe, can only be likened to the Prague Clearances of the late nineteenth and early twentieth centuries. Yet even if he had never lived, his bloodthirsty sidekick Želivský, a terrorist in a priest's frock, would have managed well enough with his pack of rabid wolves from the Bohemian backwoods. Had it not been for their raids on the city (and to this day we name streets and squares after them), many of Prague's finest buildings, even some that survived long afterwards, would surely still be standing: the Church of St John on Na Bojišti, St Lazarus on Charles Square, Wenceslas Palace on Na Zderaze and the nearby Augustinian monastery, Swine Gate, Mountain Gate, Painters' Tower, St Wenceslas' Baths, the picturesque Podskalí district, Peter's Quarter and possibly even the whole Jewish Quarter, that magic maze from which no man emerged unchanged. We might even have the Chapel of Corpus Christi, since the double-dealing Utraquists also played their part in changing the course of history. All this was destroyed, directly or indirectly, by the Hussite movement – the great Czech Cultural Revolution.

A blind nation with blind leaders. No wonder we lost our way.

Blind men laid waste this venerable city because they could not see its beauty. Where was their humility before God? Was it not His children, their own forebears, who built these wonders? The querulous Huss would never have burnt at the stake had he not been so proud, so driven by his Messiah complex, so determined to die a martyr. Sooner or later he would have struck a deal with the Catholic establishment, a Compactate that was not besmirched with Czech blood.[3] The atrocities committed by extremist sects would never have happened, Czechs would not have taken up arms against Czechs, the flower of the nation would not have fallen to the rabble's scythe, there would have been no revolutionary orgy of killing and destruction, no defeat at White Mountain, no decimation of the Czech nobility.[4] But happen they did. And all because of the alarmist ravings of a fanatic who terrorized the masses with his visions of

Armageddon, lighting a fire that in the end consumed not only him but the entire country.

If I were King of Bohemia (or, even better, Queen, since women are less inclined than men to hazard their all for the sake of an idea), I would announce a nationwide Stay of Demolition whereby it would become a crime, punishable by confiscation of all the offender's property, to destroy any building within one hundred years of a demolition order being approved. People would then think more about posterity. New buildings would appear only gradually. The integrity of our towns would be preserved. Each new stone laid would be the result of generations of deliberation. Then, I believe, our streets would not be awash with trivial trash, waiting like rivers to be flushed clean by a hundred-year flood. A walk through the city's medieval streets, whether in the Old Town or the New, would then be a pleasant and calming experience. Their colonnades and gateways and projecting buttresses would deter the high-speed, armour-plated limousines that now make them a death trap, and banish them to the dreary asphalt of the motorways where they belong and where, for all I care, they could all smash each other to smithereens in a mass pile-up. The city is suited to the leisurely gait of pedestrians and the unhurried rumble of iron-rimmed wooden wheels clattering over cobbles and potholes.

We must go back.

Imagine a house, an old, stooping house, damp and covered in soot. Inside the arched gateway is a covered yard with a black earthen floor – as black as the cellar below, which is itself as deep as a well. The building has tall twin gables and a slightly sagging roof, with leaky wooden gutters and a chimney as slender as a bulrush. For windows it has keyholes with tiny panes of mica and coloured glass set into cracked timber frames. Its threshold is an ancient millstone worn smooth by innumerable feet. The stench of urine hangs in the damp air, inside and out. In the yard fowls peck in the mud under the ever-laden washing line.

Imagine, too, a street, a crooked, winding or at least curving street, as narrow as a footpath in a sandstone gully, as dark as the depths of a rock pool. (Yes, that is beauty – but a beauty only visible to those of us who are worthy of it, for whom the phrase 'avant garde' is meaningless and 'new' is a dirty word.) That is how Prague once was and how she should have remained for all time. That was the wish of her founders, and no one had the right to change her. It is my wish, too, trapped as I am in this vilest of ages when men insensitive to beauty think they can play God with their dictates about utility and straight lines; in this age of the Magistrale, that butcher's knife slicing the city's heart in two.

By now the morning was gone and the sun lost in a cloud of smog. It could have been midday, one o'clock, maybe even later. I found myself standing beneath the spire of St Catherine's, only a short walk away from St Stephen's, but had no recollection of how I got there. Did I approach the church from below, via Lípová or Ke Karlovu; or from above, down Kateřinská? I will never know. I gazed up at the white campanile: square at the bottom, octagonal from halfway up and topped with a long dark steeple – similar, in fact, to the spires of two other Carolingian churches, the Annunciation on Na Slupi and St Apollinaris' on Větrov. The churches have another thing in common: the fate of their religious foundations – at least in one period. In the latter part of the eighteenth century Joseph II, that acme of enlightenment, dissolved the Convent of St Catherine and turned it into an army training school. The young men trashed the place so comprehensively that when the school eventually closed it was only fit for habitation by the insane. So, like the Servite Monastery on Na Slupi and the asylum near St Appolinaris', it became a home for lunatics, open to the public just one day in the year. To me there is a certain logic in it: where godliness ends, madness begins.

Bestia triumphans. No lunatic asylum did as much harm to the Gothic religious buildings of Prague as did the Hussite armies. The diabolical din of their hooves shook every stone in the churches of Vyšehrad. Of St Catherine's in the New Town only the spire survived. I will say nothing of the bulbous belfry, a kind of oriental folly, that one of the Dientzenhofers[5] stuck on top of it in the eighteenth century; or of the other horrible little church tucked out of sight behind a colonnaded portico. A church no one can see! That was a Baroque speciality – there are several such Cinderellas hidden away in corners of the city.

Even the graceful Gothic tower was lucky to survive, after fire destroyed much of the church in May 1420. And when the word got about among the Taborite women that the Augustinian nuns of St Catherine's called themselves Brides of Christ, they swooped on the church like so many demented vixens thirsting for blood. For once divine retribution was swift: such was the violence of their assault that the west wall of the building collapsed, burying twenty-seven of the Hussite harpies. Their menfolk ran to their aid, but, fearing that the tower itself would come crashing down on their ridiculous helmets and nasty little shields, those valiant warriors of the Lord calmly left their wives to die under the rubble. Oh, they knew all about violence, those Hussites hordes. But charity? Compassion? Chivalry? Not in their book. The ideals of the High Middle Ages meant nothing to them. Not since the Vandals entered the Eternal City had Europe seen such barbarity.

Early evening, late November. Against the white wall of the church, behind a hawthorn bush, I spied a dark figure. A two-headed figure – rocking in the regular rhythm of illicit pleasure. I crept up to the nearest tree and knelt at its foot as if it were an altar. I counted to ten then peeked out briefly from behind the trunk. The couple was locked in an embrace, writhing this way and that like an angry dragon. The man wore an old-fashioned hat; the woman's dark hair fell down her back. I knew at once who they were, those secret lovers in an empty churchyard. My only thought was to get away unnoticed. But not quite yet . . . There was something odd about the couple's movements, something unnatural. I couldn't resist taking another look – and becoming that most pathetic of things: a voyeur.

It was a strange love-making. The man had his right side turned towards me, the woman her left. She sat astride him rocking to and fro, her skirt spread wide over his enormous lap. Her fleshy legs pumped up and down in the darkness . . . up and down . . . up and down. Her face was set in a frown of concentration – the look of someone determined to seize an elusive pleasure. Gmünd, in contrast, seemed quite detached, like a man working out in the gym or, given the ease with which he lifted and lowered the woman's bulky body, a fairground strongman showing off with fake dumbbells. The whole thing was fake. I glimpsed a flash of white thigh; then the woman pushed her face into the man's shoulder and they both laughed. After a slight pause they resumed their lascivious movements. This time she put her arms round his neck and wrapped her legs around him, no longer rocking up and down but rubbing herself against him. I felt both aroused and ashamed – one part of me longing to watch the performance to the end, another telling me to respect their privacy. Shame was the stronger. I turned away and tiptoed towards the gate. But before I reached it I stopped dead and almost screamed. Lurking behind the last tree was a satyr-like dwarf – a little Priapus standing guard for his master. He flashed me a lecherous grin, and I caught the glint of his rodent's teeth and wicked sky-blue eyes. But already I was racing for the gate. As I passed him I could have sworn his fly-buttons were open.

I didn't stop until I reached the junction by St Stephen's. I waited for the lights, then hurried on to Hálkova Ulice. As I passed the church I noticed some graffiti on the north wall that had appeared since our last visit. The blue-and-white hieroglyphs screamed their angry message to the world, while Stephen maintained the dignified silence of the humiliated and scorned.

Zahir wasn't in Hálkova. He wasn't in V Tůních either. He had gone home, taking his camera and car with him. Or perhaps he hadn't. Perhaps someone had taken him off somewhere and killed him.

The first phone box I found was in a subway on Wenceslas Square. With trembling hands I dialled the number. As I listened to the ringing tone I had a vivid picture of Zahir lying in a deserted cellar with a smashed skull. The longer the telephone rang, the more my fantasy turned to certainty.

13

> What is this fear I feel?
> What will become of me?
> I will see the unseen
> When once I cross the threshold.
>
> Karl Kraus

In children the ability to wonder is a sign of curiosity; in adults it is a sign of childishness. I shall never cease to wonder, not even on my deathbed. I will be amazed I am lying there at all, amazed that I have not disappeared off the face of the earth long ago along with the victims of the terrible Prague conspiracy which, in the confines of my strange incarceration, I am relating on these pages.

Zahir was alive. On Thursday evening I had a call from Olejar. My first thought was that he was going to tell me Zahir had been murdered. When I casually asked after him it immediately became clear that the two men had just been speaking together. I was so overwhelmed with relief that I had to sit down. Apparently Zahir wasn't even angry with me. The Superintendent was only calling to put off our meeting. His voice was insistent and confident – the voice of a man used to commanding an army of subordinates – but there was a note of anxiety in it. As I listened, my visions of him as a homicidal psychopath haunted by his past began to fade. A senior police officer who has more to hide than an ear infection and won't admit the error of his ways – perhaps. But a ruthless killer? Surely not. Not poor old Olejar, whose guilty conscience oozed out of his ears for all to see. I asked if the CID had come up with anything new but was careful not to mention the threatening letters. He said Rehoř's legless body was still unaccounted for, but that he had a new case involving two youths who had been missing since Tuesday. I stifled a laugh and said I hoped the police would soon find them. Not all crimes are violent, he said, almost affably; sometimes all you have to do is put out a nationwide missing-persons alert. We postponed our meeting until Monday.

Once again the empty days yawned before me, and time was heavy on my hands. I felt the investigations into the two New Town murders were proceeding intolerably slowly; but then I reflected that most serious cases took a long time to clear up and my impatience was probably down to lack of experience. I tried not to think about the possibility that someone might be trying to obstruct those investigations deliberately.

The next day the phone didn't ring once. Mrs Frýdová had gone out. After breakfast I returned to my room thinking I would finally throw out the withered vine from the slopes above the Botič brook. But as I bent to pick it up I saw to my amazement several small white shoots, each no bigger than a pinhead, poking out of the twisted brown stem. Having made sure they were not spots of mould, which I had at first taken them for, I carefully watered the plant. Then, since I had nothing better to do, I spent the morning reading. Mrs Frýdová returned and made lunch, but I had no appetite for conversation and grew increasingly restless. Outside a cold winter sun had come out – the kind of sun I love – so I decided to go downtown and take a stroll around Vyšehrad. Perhaps I would find something the police had missed.

My tram was just passing the Church of the Annunciation when I saw Lucie Netřesková pushing a pram across the street. I got off at the next stop and, after a slight hesitation, walked back towards Albertov.

I soon caught her up. The baby was asleep. When I asked if I could accompany her for a while she seemed pleased. We walked slowly round the church and old convent garden. She did most of the talking, while I listened and studied her profile. She had medium-length fair hair with an unusual silvery tint. I wondered if she dyed it, but it was sparkling and sleek right down to the roots in her central parting. Her skin was pale and dryish-looking, without wrinkles except on her forehead. Every time something captured her interest (as happened several times during our talk) three horizontal furrows – the lower two deeper, the top one hardly noticeable – appeared above her eyes, only to vanish an instant later. Her eyes were not blue, as I had thought that day in the darkened room, but grey. I was attracted by their soft, gentle expression, which I sensed was not only for the benefit of her child. Everything I said seemed genuinely to interest her and was immediately reflected on her eloquent forehead. In Lucie's presence I grew calmer. She gave me confidence.

As we walked together along Albertov she told me she had no friends in Prague and spent most of her time at home. She didn't dare take the baby too far in the pram – in fact this was the furthest they had even been. She had been hoping to go to the botanical garden, but it had been shut.

The baby woke up and scowled at me uncertainly. Then, seeing its mother, it gave her a toothless smile and flapped its arms. Lucie lifted the child out of the pram, bedding bag and all, and held it in her arms. For a while I pushed the pram myself. It felt very odd, I had to admit, and a tiny bit embarrassing. I tried to see myself from the outside, as I appeared to others. Would people think I was the child's father? What a pathetic delusion! I saw no father. In the empty pram I saw a phantom child being pushed along by a man with sweaty palms. I was both man and child. I was pushing myself.

The pram felt heavy and cumbersome and difficult to manoeuvre, and the presence of the baby unnerved me. Wishing I had never embarked on this conversation, I began talking about my days as a police constable in the New Town, a district of which I was very fond and to which I would always return. Lucie listened attentively, or appeared to, so I began expounding my pet theme. These days, I told the poor girl, the people of Prague are living on top of ruins, on a rubbish tip in Švejk's backyard, adding with a wry smile that just along the road there was a street called On the Ruins, which in my opinion wouldn't be a bad name for the whole city. I liked Albertov because it had never been heavily built up. Here you could still find something of the original, now vanished atmosphere of old Prague.

I was interrupted by a sudden burst of crying from the baby. Clinging to her mother in fear, the little girl was staring wide-eyed at the pale blue façade of the Hlava Institute of Pathology, which we were just passing. Nothing Lucie did could reassure her. Thinking she might be suffering from teething pains I took out a packet of chewing-gum and dangled it in front of her eyes. It worked. She immediately stopped crying and reached out for the bright paper wrapper. Her mother snatched the child away, remarking irritably that that was the kind of silly joke her husband liked to play. I hadn't meant it as a joke, of course, and the comparison with the septuagenarian Netřesk rankled. Still, I put the gum back in my pocket. The baby began its bawling again.

Lucie suggested we turn back towards the church, and I said I would go with them at least some of the way. As I spoke I happened to glance up in the direction the child had been looking . . . and stopped dead. In a large upper-storey window in the curved north wing of the building was a woman's face. Rozeta was staring down at me. She looked different – not like the Rozeta I knew. But it was her all right. She was visible from the waist up and wearing a dark hooded garment with what looked like a silver band across her bosom. Her face was pale and thin, with none of its usual fullness; her cheeks were sunken, her nose bony and sharp, her jaw clenched in pain (or perhaps plain fatigue). Her lips were drawn in and barely visible, while the upper half of her face was dominated by the long black slits of her lacklustre almond eyes. The figure stood quite motionless, as severe as a Greek goddess: a caricature of Rozeta created for my benefit by some practical joker. No wonder the child had been scared.

I turned to Lucie, but she had disappeared. Plucking up my courage I crossed the street and looked back at the window. Rozeta was still there, glaring down at me with a look of stony rage that made me cower in alarm. She seemed to be following my every step, but mechanically, as if her body was being turned by some unseen agency. The thought was intolerable. Throwing caution to the wind I hurried back over the street and crossed the grass to the front door. I turned the big brass knob, slipped inside and closed the door behind me. On my right was a makeshift concierge's booth, but there was no one in it. I looked around the lobby.

The building had mercifully been spared the full rigours of functionalism – that pernicious product of the twentieth century that has done so much to suppress human individuality and the diversity of our manmade habitat. The result was a happy compromise between utility and beauty: the acceptable face of functionalism. I had often walked past the Hlava Institute; and every time my eyes had lingered with pleasure on the pale blue sweep of its neo-classical façade, its large divided windows and the delightfully redundant row of little arches under the eaves of its flat roof. It is my firm belief that decoration, more than anything else, makes a house into a truly human habitation. A badger doesn't know that its home is no more than a hole in the ground, so its sett is built on purely practical principles. This functional approach is fine for such a simple dwelling. But can't our architects do better than badgers?

The ceiling is supported by a Doric colonnade serene in its austerity. In the middle of the hall there is a fountain and beyond it a monumental triple staircase with a stone balustrade. Set into the polished floor is a decorative mosaic, its colours iridescent in the dull glow of heavy iron lamps. Yes, the twentieth century has also produced beauty.

I stood in silent wonder. All that disturbed the perfect peace was my own heartbeat – a tap of tiny drumsticks in my ear.

I made my way up the stairs. At the top I turned left then right and found myself looking into a large lecture hall. The auditorium was so steeply raked that the lectern seemed in danger of being engulfed by an avalanche of oak benches and brass rails. There was still not a soul about. I was on the point of closing the door when I noticed something scrawled on the board in red chalk. From that distance I couldn't make it out, so I took a few steps down the aisle and read 'Diss. Rm. 3'. Diss. as in dissecting?

There were altogether five dissection rooms, all of them located in an arc-shaped wing with large glass windows facing out towards Větrov and Karlov. In the past I had often taken a detour from my beat and scrambled down the steep thorn-covered bank to peer into those laboratories of death, curious to see what kind of gruesome operations went on in them. But each time the long heavy curtains had been drawn. Alongside the building were a few hutches where experimental animals were kept. One winter's morning, from up near St Apollinaris', I had heard a blood-curdling squeal rend the freezing air and imagined white-coated professors larding a pig with long scalpels and grilling it over Bunsen burners: an academic exercise in slaughter.

It took me some time to locate the curving corridor that led to the dissection rooms. On the way I met only one person – a heavily bearded man in a white coat with gold-rimmed glasses and a pot-belly. I was sure I had seen him before – but where? Lost in his own scientific thoughts, he scurried past me without looking up. From a room on the left came the sound of laughter: a woman's voice but not Rozeta's. The third door on the right was painted glossy white, with a small black '3' at eye-level. I knocked cautiously. Silence. I pressed down the handle. It felt slightly sticky but yielded easily.

At first sight the room seemed to break all laws of perspective. I quickly realized this was because it was wider at the far end, where the windows were. It reminded me of a white coffin with the head end made of glass. I went in. The heavy curtains were open. In the middle of the room stood the dissecting table. It was irregular in shape, with indentations around its rim as if someone had been taking bites out of it. Their purpose, I guessed, was to afford better access to whatever was being dissected.

There on the table, under the glare of a surgical lamp, was a horse – a not very large brown horse, lying perfectly motionless. I could see its mane, its left flank, its extended neck and part of its head. Its glassy, unseeing eye stared into vacancy. Its hooves were covered in bandages of some coarse material, but even so I could make out their curious pointed shape. Steeling my nerves, I inched towards the table. A clean incision, pulled slightly apart in the middle, ran the length of its flank. I caught a glimpse of pink flesh, yellow fat and a black encrustation of blood. I edged a step closer. Now, in the bright overhead light, I could see the whole of the animal's head and, projecting from the centre of its forehead, a long tapering horn. I stretched out my hand and touched its rough surface. It felt as warm as a living body. But weren't unicorns supposed to be white?

Suddenly the window shattered. Something crashed on to the floor in front of me and flew off into a corner. I dived under the dissecting table. My first though was: This is it; I'm going to get shot. There was no way I could reach the door. A cold wind blew through the jagged, gaping hole in the glass. Of course, a stone! Not a bullet. From my hiding place I peered out through the window and tried to work out exactly where it had come from. All I could see was a grey retaining wall and above it a bank of bushes, their branches swaying gently in the wind. There was no sudden movement, no sign of anyone running from the scene.

The stone had come to rest under a washbasin at the back of the room. I crawled over the floor to retrieve it, thinking to examine it under the surgical light. I didn't need to. My fingers had already told me what it was: six regular sides, smooth, slightly crystalline . . . and with pale green veins. A cobblestone. A warning from the street.

No doubt you are asking what all this means. I can give you no immediate answer, let alone a direct one. No doubt you suspect me of deliberately leaving some things unexplained. You may be right – up to a point. But if I am keeping you guessing it is because I want you to grope for the truth, just as I had to grope for the truth. I want you to feel the same uncertainty, the same anxiety, the same fear that I felt. Without them you will never attain knowledge, as I did. So if you really are a seeker after truth you would do well to keep close behind me in this labyrinth of words.

I left the institute, as I had entered it, unobserved. Retracing my steps to the church I found Lucie sitting on a bench outside. With one hand she was rocking the pram; in the other she held an open book. I was sure she had been waiting for me.

By now I was feeling a little calmer. I went up to her and asked what she was reading.

She raised her pretty grey eyes. A Gothic novel, she said, and asked where I'd been all this time. I told her I had dropped into the institute to see a friend. She got up, straightened her skirt and put her book in the pram. Before we moved on I glanced at its cover: it was Horace Walpole's *The Castle of Otranto*. There was a bookmark in it near the end.

'That's a coincidence!' I exclaimed. 'I read that only recently. How are you enjoying it?'

'I liked the beginning very much, then it got weirder and weirder. I just hope all the mysteries get cleared up in the end.'

'You may be in for a disappointment. I must say I found it wonderfully graphic, though there's very little logic to the story. Do you know Clara Reeve?'

'No.'

'She was a great admirer of Walpole's. But like you she didn't much care for all those mysterious groans and apparitions, people stepping out of pictures and chains clanking in dungeons. Walpole doesn't doubt their reality for a moment, so the reader has no choice but to take it all on board – or chuck the book in the bin. Reeve refused to do either. In her *Old English Baron* – a kind of variation on *The Castle of Otranto* – there's no shortage of mysteries either. But being a child of the Enlightenment she tones them down to an acceptable level. All her spooky apparitions and supernatural phenomena are eventually explained.'

'Does it work, do you think?'

'If the success of the book is anything to go by – yes. But tell me: when you were little did *you* like stories about sensible children? Walpole was a Romantic with a wonderfully anarchic love of the incongruous. Reading his novel is like a trip through a haunted castle at a fairground. At first you laugh – then suddenly fear whizzes out of the dark like an arrow and hits you in the back of the neck. And there it stays for the rest of the ride. Reeve wouldn't let that happen. She loves order. Walpole revelled in chaos, but she detested it.'

'So was she more of a coward?'

'It depends on your point of view. A love of order is the result of a fear of disorder.'

'That's not the case with you, obviously. So you prefer Walpole?'

'Yes. But it's not that simple. The modern reader finds his scenes of would-be hair-raising horror quite ludicrous – as when the statue of the good Duke Alfonso has a nosebleed. Pretty silly, isn't it? A statue in need of a handkerchief! But there are some scenes in *The Castle of Otranto* that really do make your hair stand on end.'

'I should say so! What did you find most horrifying?'

'The suffering of innocent people.'

'Me too. That's why I don't watch TV or read the papers.'

'A gigantic black-plumed helmet drops out of nowhere into the castle courtyard. But instead of flattening the diabolical Manfred – the one person in the story who deserves it – it kills his son Conrad, a sickly youth who has to pay for his father's sins. Manfred himself outlives the lot of them and in the end even manages to kill his own daughter Matilda, the most likeable character in the book . . .'

'Thanks a lot for telling me. Now I can save myself the bother of finishing it. But aren't you missing the point? Manfred *is* punished: for the rest of his life he's tormented by guilt.' She glanced down anxiously at the sleeping baby and rearranged its blanket.

'Sorry, I let myself get carried away. Do finish it – it's worth it. Basically it's a very truthful book. Just look at all the innocent suffering in the world today. *The Castle of Otranto* is a true reflection of reality at the end of the twentieth century. Like life itself, it raises more questions than it answers. Which has some bearing on whether I prefer Walpole or Reeve. Ideally I'd choose something in between: a story with a rational, logical conclusion that satisfies the rationally minded reader but with some extra, inexplicable element to support my conviction that some things in life simply cannot be understood. The world is as inexplicable as a Gothic novel.

'Imagine if Walpole were writing today. Would he find modern Prague terrifying enough? I mean in the Romantic sense of the word. Would he rise to the challenge? Or would he fashionably follow the likes of Josef Svátek and Gustav Mejrink and write about the 'magical Prague' of Rudolph II? Would he have anything to say about the modern world? Would he make his characters suffer for the sins of their fathers? Would his villains be punished by implacable ghosts? Whatever he wrote about, he'd be more concerned with questions than answers. He'd locate his settings and characters in our cybernetics-obsessed civilization, but you can bet they'd be the most bizarre and mysterious places and people you could possibly imagine. Mind you, he'd have no lack of types to choose from – just look around our university campuses.'

Lucie stopped and looked about her. 'Where are we?'

We'd walked almost as far as Nusle Theatre and were standing by the railing above Botič Brook, but I'd been so engrossed in conversation that I hadn't even noticed. Lucie smiled. Perhaps she found my enthusiasm for ghost stories amusing. There was something maternal in her smile that went straight to my heart. For a moment I envied her child.

'You say that nowadays there are still more questions than answers,' she went on. 'I'm not so sure. What about coincidences? Couldn't they be answers to questions that were always there but no one ever asked? We met by chance today. And the first time we met was chance, too – when you just happened to bump into my husband in town.'

'You mean this walk we're having could be the answer to a question that was hanging in the air, waiting to be answered?'

No sooner were the words out of my mouth than I realized their implication: the question was about me, Netřesk and Lucie herself. I felt my cheeks flush. But Lucie didn't notice; she had turned away and was leaning over the railing. My eyes involuntarily traced the curves of her body. There was something coquettish about the way she stood – nothing obvious but noticeable none the less. To my surprise I noted that I was slightly aroused. But I am not a man capable of exploiting that kind of situation, a fact that had been painfully obvious at our last meeting. I felt sorry for her – and for myself.

But the attraction was there. I leant against the railing at her side, so close that our elbows touched. She didn't move. But out of the corner of my eye I thought I glimpsed three little lines of apprehension furrow her brow. Or had I imagined it? I hung my head and gazed into the muddy stream below.

'Can a walk be an answer?' she said suddenly. It took me a second to realize she was resuming our conversation. 'Possibly. Or it may just be a mistake. Hey, look at that thing in the water, down there by the bridge. How on earth did it get there? Do you suppose someone dropped it? Or maybe a thief panicked and dumped it there deliberately.'

I saw the object she was pointing at and guessed that it, too, might be the answer to a question no one had asked.

I walked Lucie to the tram-stop. As I helped her up with the pram her wrist, probably unintentionally, brushed lightly against mine. I watched the tram disappear, then went back to the bridge and climbed down a rusty ladder into the cold murky water. Knee deep, I waded towards the metal object protruding above the surface and yanked it out – it had got wedged in the stones on the bottom. It was a large bow-saw. The blue-painted frame was unchipped and the blade, though broken, bore no sign of rust.

You don't throw away a new saw just because it has a broken blade.

The teeth were large and seemed to have been bent deliberately and filed into jagged, vicious-looking claws. If you cut a log with a saw like that I could imagine what it would look like. It would look as if it had been torn apart.

It had been a curious sort of day (like most of my days now), and it had a curious epilogue. I took the saw back to the flat in Prosek, planning to hand it in to the forensic people at the earliest opportunity so that they could examine it for traces of blood. Carefully I dried it and wrapped it in newspaper. Then I washed, got into my pyjamas and, without putting on the light, climbed into bed, content in the knowledge that I had something new for Olejar. Just as I was dozing off I remembered that I hadn't watered my beloved plants, so, dragging myself out of my warm cocoon, I switched on the light and picked up the watering can. I dropped it again the moment I looked up. From the convoluting stem of the Karlov vine, on which I had recently seen those first green shoots, had sprouted a dense growth of hairy white fibres, some nearly two feet long. They shot out profusely in every direction, looking for all the world like the beard of a crazy old man.

14

Sever
The cord, shed the scale. Only
The fool, fixed in his folly, may think
He can turn the wheel on which he turns.

T.S. Eliot

On Monday I rose early. Mrs Frýdová, who had been up since six watching television, was delighted and promptly made me a breakfast of bacon and no fewer than three scrambled eggs. As she placed this royal dish before me she said I was looking much brighter this morning and assumed this was because I had found a job. I didn't have the heart to disillusion her and merely mumbled, through a mouthful of bread, something about a possible opening somewhere. Outside, a dirty yellow-grey day was dawning: we were in for snow. The thermometer on the window hovered around zero.

In fact the snow started on the television screen. Mrs Frýdová bashed the set a couple of times, but the blizzard only got worse. Eventually she turned it off and sat down at the table facing me. She asked what I'd been up to recently. I muttered some excuse and went off to my room, but she came after me. Bedding lay scattered about on the furniture and the air was stale and fuggy. But what caught my landlady's eye were three books I'd left open on my little desk. Rather presumptuously, I thought, she went straight over and picked them up: *Chronicles of Royal Prague*, *Prague Tales and Legends* and *The Speaking Architecture of the City of Prague*. She raised a disapproving eyebrow and said she hoped I wasn't thinking of going back to that stupid college. I assured her that it hadn't even crossed my mind. Then, reaching under the bed for the saw, I told her rather abruptly that I had urgent business at the police station. At this she blinked in surprise and backed out of the room. She had not noticed the hideous vine.

I couldn't wait to get out of the flat, so left unnecessarily early and decided to go into town on foot. The grey blocks of flats were still asleep, the bushes huddled in their frozen patches of garden, and even my own footsteps barely disturbed the silence of the pavements. The main road, in contrast, was loud with traffic. Now and then I glimpsed a pale smudge of human face through a gleaming windscreen. I felt like an alien in this city of somnambulists hurtling into oblivion. I was different, unique: a solitary pedestrian – a hitch-hiker, a vagrant. After a while I even felt a sinful thrill of complacency as the umpteenth bus roared past me and I tried to see myself through the eyes of those pale faces trapped inside it: a lone Indian in a tattered poncho, bow-saw slung over his shoulder, heading for the woods. The man is obviously moving, but compared with the speeding cars he appears stationary, as if for some reason he's only pretending to walk. Another idle loafer, thinks one of the pale shadows. Surely he's not expecting anyone to join him? Who would dare? Not with Time baying at our heels, snapping its deadly jaws. Time always catches the slowest first, the laggards who can't keep up – who can't *escape*. It lures them into its labyrinth, disorients them, then sets them off in another direction: backwards.

I'd been half hoping to see Rozeta at the police HQ, but when I entered Olejar's spacious office just before ten o'clock I found him alone. Without taking his eyes off his computer screen he waved me into a seat. Beyond the half-open blinds of the huge windows fat flakes of snow fell out of a greenish sky. A thin covering of white lay on the pavements; by noon it would be gone. The tower of St Stephen's loomed through the leaden mist.

I removed the saw from its wrapping of newspaper and, knocking it deliberately against the metal frame of my chair to attract Olejar's attention, placed it on my knees.

His reaction to my find was less enthusiastic than I had hoped, but he was at least interested enough to send it to the laboratory for forensic tests. When it had been taken away he handed me a few photographs.

'The first arrived on Thursday, the second on Friday. And the last one just a few minutes ago.'

I studied them closely. The prints were very dark, with here and there a lighter, reddish area. In the first I could make out very little except what looked like a patch of dusty ground, a few scraps of rubbish and three or four stones or pebbles – it was hard to tell how big they were. Behind them was dirty wall, its flaky rendering painted light brown or ochre. The second picture was a little lighter. It showed the same place, but the camera had been moved slightly to the right. The two stones at the left-hand edge of the first photograph were no longer visible, but on the right a blue shape had appeared. The pictures had been taken at night or late in the evening, without flash. The third photograph showed the area even further to the right. There were more blue shapes, now in the background. Most strikingly, there was a kind of long nebulous streak, though the photograph was so underlit it was impossible even to guess what it was. It didn't help that, like the others, this one was also out of focus. At the very edge of the picture was a fuzzy white object with a curved edge, partly obliterated by a black stain. It took up about a sixth of the height of the photograph.

I shrugged. 'I expect it's another warning, this time meant for you. They're biding their time, waiting for you to lose your nerve – which is exactly what they want. You're bound to get some more – tomorrow, the day after. Sooner or later they'll tell you what they want.'

'I've never had anything like this before, not in my whole career,' said Olejar. 'There's something fishy about it. It's almost as if . . . Of course, it could just be some harmless nutter having a little joke at my expense. Like that old man who called us last week – Tuesday, I think it was. He told the girl on the switchboard he'd "lost a diadem", so she put the call through to us as a case of theft. It turned out that the item in question had not been lost by him personally but by all of us, or some such nonsense. Then he said something about "looking at it, but it wasn't there" and went on to complain about all the shady-looking characters he saw from his window these days, whereas he never saw a policeman from one year to the next.'

'He said he was looking at something that wasn't there? A diadem?'

'Yes. Of course, they didn't take him seriously, but they took down his name and address. He insisted on that. They asked him to come down to the station, but he said he never went out. Lives quite near here apparently.'

I offered to go and see him myself. The Superintendent had no objection; in fact I had the impression he had been expecting it. He was probably glad not to have to waste his own men's time on such a trivial matter. I took the piece of paper with the name and address and put it in my pocket.

At last I could tell Olejar about the hypothesis at which Gmünd and I had arrived. He listened attentively, his eyes narrowed in concentration. When I had finished he called through to his secretary and asked her to bring him the Pendelmanová file. We waited in silence. Olejar stood looking out of the window cleaning his ears with a rolled-up handkerchief. When the girl came in with the file he quickly leafed through it before handing it to me. I was clearly meant to feel extremely honoured.

I opened the file. There it was, on the very first page: Engineer Milada Pendelmanová had been working for the city council for nearly thirty years . . . in the planning department.

'You see, I was right!' I burst out, unable to conceal my satisfaction. 'It's not about politics. It's about architecture.'

'Motive?' Olejar peered through a cloud of cigarette smoke with a wily, sceptical expression.

'That we have yet to discover. But we can be pretty sure Rehoř and Pendelmanová were killed by the same person – obviously an unbalanced and highly dangerous individual with a penchant for theatrical effects. And between the two murders he nearly succeeded in maiming Zahir as well. That was another of his little dramas.'

'Do you really think one person could have done all that alone? Think of the practical obstacles: the high fence on Nusle Bridge, the narrow steps up the tower of St Apollinaris', the flagpoles at Vyšehrad . . .'

'You're forgetting he had a mobile crane.'

'I know he had a mobile crane, for God's sake. But how do you account for the fact that none of the victims put up a fight? Well, I'm sure the old lady wasn't too much trouble. But what about Zahir – who, incidentally, also gave us a description of the kidnapping? What about Rehoř? He was a pretty big bloke. Where is he now? All his family got to bury was a pair of legs.'

'So there must have been several of them. A terrorist cell . . . or maybe a sectarian gang. Or both.'

Olejar considered this. 'You may be right. But in that case why didn't they claim responsibility for the murders? No, that's not how terrorists operate. Anyway, I'm going to have those cobblestones examined again – the ones Pendelmanová and Rehoř were threatened with – as well the letter sent to Zahir.'

I knew it! Rehoř had also been on the receiving end of a cobblestone. I thought of the one thrown at me, now safe in my desk drawer. I had intended to keep quiet about the incident at the Hlava Institute, but now I came out with the whole story. Not quite the whole story: I didn't mention Rozeta's face at the window, and, of course, I didn't breathe a word about the animal on the dissecting table. I simply said that I had gone there to see a friend; the criminals had been following me and decided it was a good opportunity to give me a bit of a scare.

Olejar's face grew increasingly sombre until finally he exploded.

He forbade me to carry out any more investigations off my own bat and asked why the devil I hadn't told him at once, on the Friday. Then, in a more placatory tone, he asked me to bring the stone in so they could compare it with the others. The last thing he wanted, he added, staring fixedly out of the window, was my death on his conscience.

His concern seemed genuine enough. Or did it, too, contain a coded threat?

It was nearly midday when he rose to his feet and invited me to lunch in the canteen. I accepted. I ordered a vegetarian dish and pea soup. The girl behind the counter took it into her head to fill my plate to the very brim, much to the amusement of her assistant, and I couldn't avoid slopping a couple of spoonfuls on the tray. Olejar raised a mildly disapproving eyebrow at my choice, having decided to give the soup a miss. He ordered two large lagers and took out his wallet to pay – for both of us. As he did so he knocked a foaming glass of lager against my tray, and I very nearly dropped it on the floor, lunch and all. By now there was almost as much soup on the tray as in the plate. From the kitchen wafted clouds of steam saturated with the smell of stewed meat, garlic and ginger.

There wasn't a free table in sight. I felt every head in the room turn to watch my unsteady progress across the slippery polished floor and got so nervous that the overladen tray began shaking in my hands. The clink of cutlery fell silent at my approach, and even after I had passed I could feel mocking eyes bore into my back. Everything became a blur; my head was reeling. Then, to cap it all, my nose started bleeding. I felt humiliated, trapped.

I tilted my head but not fast enough. The warm rivulet tickled my upper lip, and a few drops splashed into my soup, leaving three small slicks on its viscous surface. My eyes watering from the steam of cooking, I stood in the middle of the canteen trying to blink back my tears. Then I caught sight of the Superintendent, who had found an empty table at the other end of the room and was waving at me, and realized to my intense relief that apart from him nobody seemed to have noticed me. There were no mocking faces. With a more confident step I made my way between the tables.

Suddenly I got such a shock I nearly dropped my tray again. Sitting alone at a table on the far right of the room, near the conveyor for dirty dishes, was Rozeta. I would have dearly liked to join her but couldn't face the embarrassment of exposing my wayward nose to her critical gaze. I was amazed at how different she looked. There was no trace of the emaciated face I had seen at the window of the Hlava Institute. Instead, I saw full cheeks, a plump neck bulging over her collar and fleshy shoulders straining at the black jacket of her uniform. What one might call a strapping lass, in fact. How could anyone put on so much weight in such a short time? Her clothes seemed to be holding her in like a straitjacket. A policewoman imprisoned in her own uniform; a woman imprisoned in her own body. In front of her she had three empty plates (one of them a soup plate), and three bowls – one nearly empty, the other two (one of vanilla pudding with raspberry sauce and cream) still full. I passed her table as she was finishing off one bowl, just in time to see her push it aside and reach for another. She looked unhappy. I forced myself to keep walking.

Against the babble of voices the conveyor squeaked and rattled as it bore its freight of dirty plates into the bowels of the kitchen, and I imagined all those disgusting leftovers ending up in Rozeta's insatiable mouth. I quickly turned away towards the windows on the left of the room, hoping that the sight of the pale empty sky would calm my nerves. Instead I saw a flock of ravens.

Over lunch Olejar spoke about the boys who had gone missing the previous week. They were both seventeen, the police had learnt from their parents, and attended a modern languages-oriented secondary school where they were considered average pupils. They had recently become close friends, regularly visiting each other's homes or going out to concerts. The obvious explanation for their disappearance was that they had decided to run away from home. Their parents, however, thought this unlikely: there was no trouble or conflict in either of the families other than the usual petty disagreements. The police therefore assumed the boys had gone off on some secret trip, possibly abroad, without telling their parents. This theory was somewhat weakened by the fact that they had not taken any personal belongings with them – not even their passports – though at least they had been wearing warm outdoor clothes. One of them told his mother he was taking his skateboard down to the Laterna Magica Theatre, where there was a big paved yard he and his pals often practised in, and promised to be home by midnight. The police still favoured the secret trip theory. Olejar recalled that not long ago Amsterdam had been a popular destination.

I pointed out that those were the days when drugs weren't so readily available in Prague. He waved aside my objection and said he was well aware of that. But the police at least had to make it look as if they had something to go on, whereas they actually didn't have a clue. They had hoped the boys were simply partying somewhere and would turn up after the weekend. But they didn't. I now realized it had been wrong of me to make light of their disappearance.

While we were having our coffee a big fellow in a white coat sat down at our table and began furiously attacking a slice of tough beef. He had rather greasy black hair with an odd metallic sheen and an old-fashioned but meticulously trimmed moustache, slightly turned up at the tips. On his nose balanced a pince-nez which, in combination with the white coat, should have lent him an air of stern authority. The effect, however, was spoilt by his otherwise scruffy appearance and a strong smell of sweat. He looked as if he had stepped out of a nineteenth-century daguerreotype.

I was sure I had seen him before. As he chewed on his beef he, too, glanced across at me as if in recognition, though with little sign of pleasure. Olejar introduced him as Dr Trug, a forensic pathologist and lecturer in anatomy at the university. Suddenly I remembered: I had seen him not once but twice. The first time was last Monday at the Congress Centre, when he had made such a fuss about the murdered Rehoř's legs; the second was on Friday in the corridor of the Hlava Institute. Was he the mysterious dissector of unicorns?

By now he, too, had placed me – being observant was part of his job, as it was of mine. He immediately asked me what I'd been doing at the institute on Friday afternoon. I could hardly tell him I'd gone there to see a friend, since he was sure to know everyone in the place. Instead, I gave him a cool, level look and said I had been following up a clue but could say no more as the case was still under investigation. The Superintendent frowned and without a word took out his handkerchief and held it to his right ear. Trug simply shrugged. His next question almost made me choke on my coffee. Did my clue have anything to do with the broken window in the dissection room? I shot a look at Olejar. His head, half hidden behind the satin handkerchief, shook almost imperceptibly. I said I didn't know anything about a broken window.

As Trug ate he told us, not without relish, about the tests for blood carried out on the saw blade. The results had been positive. I smiled in satisfaction. Olejar, for once a model of reticence, merely nodded and gave me an acknowledging look that redoubled my satisfaction. But in his smile I also sensed a gentle mocking of my childish delight. Noting my smug expression, the doctor immediately turned away and addressed all further conversation to the Superintendent. He said he was pleased we were pleased but was afraid he had to disappoint us: he had taken the liberty of testing the blood sample from the saw against a sample from the severed legs – at least he had tried to. But the metal blade had been so corroded by the chemicals in the scummy water of the Botič that more detailed analysis had not been possible. Neither the blood group nor the age of the sample could be determined.

In the afternoon I went to see the old man who had telephoned the police. He lived close by in Lípová, near the corner of Ječná. Across the road the tower of St Stephen's stood tall against the darkening sky.

The man, whose name was Václavek, refused to let me in as I didn't have an ID badge. When I suggested he call the police station to verify my identity there was no reaction. He had left the door on the chain so that we had to speak through a narrow chink. I couldn't see his face properly but glimpsed the pink gleam of a bald scalp, a crooked nose, watery eyes with bags under them and a scrawny, wrinkled neck. He was not at all forthcoming, merely repeating that he had told the police everything already. 'With these very eyes' he had seen that 'the crown was not there'. Someone had stolen it and then put it back again. He refused to say any more and would have shut the door on me had I not wedged my foot in it. I tried to pin him down: if he hadn't seen the 'crown' what had he seen? Nothing, he repeated stubbornly. I then asked whether the 'crown' was the same as the 'diadem' he'd mentioned to the police, whereupon he stamped hard on my foot. I instantly withdrew it – more as a reflex action than in pain. Somehow my shoe caught on the old man's slipper and pulled it out through the crack. The door slammed shut. I rang the bell several times, but it was clear that my interview with the witness of the disappearing crown that 'belonged to us all' was over. I hung the slipper on the doorknob, cursing Olejar for sending me on a mission that would have stumped even the most accomplished of detectives.

As I had predicted, the snow soon melted, but it remained bitterly cold. I looked forward to being back in my snug little room at Mrs Frýdová's, curled up with my books on the woolly carpet. Had I known what was awaiting me I would have been in less of a hurry to return.

The moment I set foot in the flat Mrs Frýdová informed me that the keys I had just opened the door with were to be returned to her at the end of the month. She was trembling with rage; but in her eyes there was also fear. Fighting a rising sense of dread, I calmly asked her to explain. We went into the small sitting-room (which I now rarely entered) and sat down. Above the television, with its crocheted cover of roses and pomegranates, hung a black wooden crucifix.

Her voice shaking with anger, Mrs Frýdová pointed towards the door of my room and ordered me to 'in God's name get rid of that thing'. I said I didn't know what she was talking about. She screamed something about a diabolical plant and crossed herself. Presuming she meant the vine I laughed and said if that was the only thing she had against me I would throw it out right away. She shook her head and kept on shaking it even when I offered her another five hundred crowns rent. Now she was insulted and became even more adamant. She said I would never make anything of my life because I couldn't stick at anything: I'd dropped out of college; I couldn't even hold down a job in the police force. I told her the police had already taken me back on probation and I was working for other people, too. But she wouldn't listen. For months, she went on, she hadn't said a word, only prayed for me. But witchcraft? That was going too far. She'd been nourishing a viper in her bosom. For all she knew she would end up in little pieces under the floorboards.

Her words hurt and angered me. But at the same time I felt a wild, despairing laughter well up inside me at the absurdity of it all. Criminals were threatening to kill me, my boss thought I was an incompetent idiot, and now my landlady was scared to death of me! I told her she was imagining things and shouldn't judge other people's behaviour by her own.

Until then I had always thought of her as a kindly, if somewhat eccentric, little person and would never have dreamt of deliberately saying anything to hurt her. But over the years some kind of unconscious resentment against her must have built up in me. Her hateful outburst had hurt, and like a fool I hit back.

I tried to apologize, but it was too late. My riposte had cut her to the quick. Suddenly Mrs Frýdová had become a pitiful old woman. She stared at me with her myopic eyes, her breath laboured, her bony fingers pressed against her wrinkled neck. Then it all came pouring out. That plant, she said, was evil. Yesterday morning it had been no more than a withered vine, but this afternoon, when she had gone in to open my window, she had nearly had a heart attack. Its tendrils had reached out at her like the tentacles of some monstrous octopus – no, I mustn't interrupt – she knew where the plant had come from and should have intervened at once, the moment I had brought it into the house. I had found it on the slopes below Karlov, hadn't I? – a place well known in the past for wicked goings-on (fornication, murder, every kind of mortal sin), a place where witches held sabbaths and rode about on black goats with green eyes. And wherever these unspeakable things were done there sprang up horrid hairy vines – a punishment from God for the city's iniquity. The Lord forbid they should ever bear grapes. If they did they would swell up and burst, hatching little devils that would infest the whole town with plague and destroy every living thing in it.

What could I say? Without a word I stood up and went through to my room. The first thing I saw was the flower pot festooned with strange white fronds. They did indeed reach down to the floor and were by no means a pretty sight, but they certainly did not reach out like tentacles or threaten my life in any other way. I went over to examine them more closely in the fading light from the window and saw that, in fact, they did not belong to the vine at all, which was obviously dead. Though attached to it, they were clearly some kind of parasitic growth, similar to ergot and possibly just as poisonous – a fungus or mould. I sniffed and got a whiff of penicillin. But it was I who had killed the plant by transplanting a living piece of the Middle Ages into the moribund environment of a council flat. Romantic intentions usually come to a sorry end.

I packed up my belongings, which filled two suitcases and a rucksack. There were too many books to take all at once, so I told Mrs Frýdová I would have them picked up by the end of the week. By now she had calmed down a little and even reminded me that she wasn't throwing me out but giving me a month's notice. After all, where would I go? She wasn't the sort of person to turn a tenant out on to the street.

As I packed I thought about where to go. First I'd try Netřesk, then Gmünd. I dialled my old teacher's number but hung up as soon as I heard the ringing tone. How could I possibly sleep on a camp-bed in the sitting-room or the kitchen with Lucie talking and moving about in the next room? How long could such a situation last? How would it inevitably end?

I called the Hotel Bouvines and got through at once. But before I could say anything a voice announced that for technical reasons the train departures information service was temporarily unavailable, and whoever it was hung up. I had no doubt it was Prunslik. Preparing a few choice expletives I dialled the number again. But this time Gmünd himself answered.

I explained the situation. Without a moment's hesitation he told me to come to his apartment, where I could stay for as long as I was working for him. In the meantime he and Raymond would keep a look-out for a permanent place for me.

I could not even thank him – partly because I was lost for words and partly because I didn't want him to hear my voice choking with emotion.

My farewell to Mrs Frýdová was anything but long drawn out. I tried to shake her hand, but since in my other hand I was holding the accursed hairy plant she leapt back in fright and shut herself in the living-room, and the arrangements concerning the removal of my books were finalized through the closed door. It wasn't worth asking her to return any of my rent – November was nearly over and I hadn't yet paid for December. That bill would await me elsewhere.

I left the keys on the shoe-rack in the hall. As I pulled the door to behind me I heard her shouted promise: she would pray for me.

The vine I had rashly transplanted from its home in the New Town to inhospitable Prosek had wrought a fitting vengeance: now I, too, was homeless. Downstairs I dropped it in the rubbish bin. The clang of the metal lid closing over it echoed round the housing estate like a cry for help. I was free.

15

I am free as a stone
That lands where it falls,
I am free as a man
That has pledged his word.

Richard Weiner

Twice on my way to the hotel I tripped on a cobblestone. The sodium street lighting flickered into life, its feeble orange glow gradually brightening to white. The number three tram had been diverted, so I had to get off at Myslíková. As I crossed the road I stumbled and fell. One of my suitcases flew open, spewing a jumble of clothes and paperbacks over the tramlines. I had almost got everything back in the case (apart from a broken mirror) when I was nearly killed by a large white car that hurtled out of the gloom, horn blaring, and grazed me with its metal wing. I watched it retreat: a mortal foe whose weapon had miraculously missed its mark. Down by the river the big square windows of the Manes Gallery shone into the night like giant television screens. Inside, shadowy figures holding glasses moved about in the yellow light. An exhibition opening, presumably: a social occasion for the select few; a beguiling dumb-show for the uninitiated outside.

Strangely, the Hotel Bouvines was in darkness. On entering, however, I saw one small lamp in the reception booth and beside it a head bent over a book. Before I could even introduce myself the receptionist greeted me by name and said he knew all about me. Reaching behind him for a key, he explained that Mr Gmünd had been called away on urgent business, but I was to go on up regardless and make myself at home. Mine was the blue room.

He locked the glass door of the reception booth and hung on it a card with the words BACK SOON. Picking up my cases, he apologized that the lift was out of order – Mr Gmünd's great weight had been too much for the steel cables. It took me a moment to realize this was meant as a joke – a joke in poor taste, I thought, given the distinguished nature of his guest. We climbed the stairs in silence. At Gmünd's door he put down my luggage and stood waiting. I told him I would no longer be requiring his services, and he walked away without a murmur. A man of few words, thank goodness. It would have been awkward had he asked for a tip.

Gmünd's apartment was pleasantly warm without being hot. At first all I could see in the darkness was the little orange light of the heating thermostat flashing in the hallway, where I eventually found a light switch. Three double electric candelabras lit up, casting a soft glow over the cream walls. I dragged the two suitcases under the coat stand and placed the rucksack on top of them. There was no sign of Gmünd's coat and cane. The only indication that someone lived here was an umbrella propped in the corner of the hall. Everything was clean and tidy, the muted green carpet spotless. There were no shoes in sight, which struck me as odd: a rich fellow like Gmünd was unlikely to be short of footwear. He probably kept them in the three small cupboards on the wall opposite. My fingers itched to open them, but I resisted the temptation.

Four doors opened off the hall: two on the left, one on the right and one straight ahead. As far as I recalled from my previous visit, the door opposite led into the sitting-room where Gmünd had received me. I tried the first door on the left, hoping it would be the blue room. But as I opened it I started back in surprise: before me was a long narrow passage, apparently running parallel to the main hotel corridor on the other side of the thick wall. The house had once been a fortified residence consisting of a central tower with galleries running round it. Gradually, in the course of the seventeenth and eighteenth centuries, more comfortable rooms had been built on around it and the galleries had become corridors. As the building had slowly evolved it was quite possible that a few pockets of unused space had remained – spaces with no obvious purpose, like this passage. It was five or six yards long, and at the far end there was a closed door. It was uncomfortably narrow, no wider than a man's shoulders. Even more disturbing was the dark red of the walls.

I turned to the second door on the left of the hall and peered inside. Only a boxroom. No, a darkroom! It was a tiny space, just big enough for one person. On a metal-legged table stood a photographic enlarger wrapped in a large plastic bag. Metal shelves contained polythene trays, a few light bulbs, two timers and stacks of yellow, red and grey cardboard boxes which I guessed were full of photographic paper; and mounted on the wall was a small but unusually deep enamel sink, shaped more like a rectangular bucket than a basin – no doubt specially designed for darkroom use – and over it a brass tap projecting from the wall. Above the shelves, just below the ceiling, was a small extractor fan. A chair had been pulled up to the table.

Quietly I closed the door again and approached what I was sure was Gmünd's sitting-room. I looked inside. It was just as I remembered. A shaft of light fell across the deep-pile white carpet, the springy softness of which pampered my feet even through the soles of my light shoes. In the semi-darkness beyond I made out the coffee-table at which I had been served supper and, at the back of the room, beside the dark mass of the fireplace, a drinks trolley. The curtains were drawn. I almost decided to wait for my host here in these congenial surroundings but thought better of it. I did not want him to think I was not even capable of moving into a room that had been put at my disposal. Prunslik would never let me hear the end of it.

I tried the last of the doors, the one on the right of the hall, and found what I had half expected and hoped to find: a toilet. Even this little room held a few surprises. The seat on the gleaming white porcelain bowl consisted of three sections. The lower one was very large and made of some rare hardwood, possibly mahogany. Above it was a second much smaller seat, of the kind one might fit temporarily for the use of a young child. This was made of a lighter-coloured wood – walnut, at a guess. The two seats were covered by a small lid even lighter in colour and inlaid with the same two darker woods in a checkerboard pattern. On one side of the bowl, set into the wall, was a radio; on the other was a glass-fronted medicine cabinet full of coloured glass bottles and tiny metal canisters.

I returned to the hall and decided to try the first door again, in the hope of finding the blue room at the end of the narrow passage. With some trepidation I stepped into the darkness – there was no electric light, which suggested it might once have been used as a clothes cupboard, though I could see no hooks or hanger rails. The walls and low ceiling were covered in some kind of red fabric that was soft to the touch and, as far as I could tell, seamless.

I thought that two or three steps would take me to the other end of the passage. In fact it was more like ten. The further I went the more confined the space became, until I had to not only turn sideways but stoop, since the ceiling, too, grew lower. That was why the passage seemed so much shorter than it was: you expected the usual effect of perspective – lines converging to a vanishing point – but didn't reckon with the fact that the space actually tapered away from you.

Towards the far end the red walls were so close together I could barely squeeze through. Despite the soft fabric they were quite unyielding, and I began gasping for breath. I reached out my hand towards the tiny door, which was more like a hatchway. It had no handle, but about halfway up there was a keyhole. Let's hope it isn't locked, I thought, and leads to the blue room. If it doesn't, I'll have to go back and wait for my host in the sitting-room.

It was not locked but did offer some resistance. Maybe it was on a spring. I struggled through the opening and immediately fell headlong into the darkness. Groping around me, I realized I had landed on some steps. The hatchway, then, must be higher than the door at the other end, which meant that the floor in the red passage must slope up towards it. I had not noticed.

The hatch banged shut, leaving me in pitch darkness. I couldn't even see my hand in front of my eyes. But while the darkness was total, the same could not be said of the silence. From somewhere there came a faint humming sound. I got up and felt along the wall until I found a light switch.

The darkness was instantly transformed into a hall – the very same hall from which I had entered the red passage. My head spinning, I quickly reached for the switch again, this time to turn it off. It was like a bad dream: whichever way I turned, after a few steps I always ended up back where I had started.

I turned off the light, took a deep breath, and turned it on again. It was not the same hall but a different, though very similar one. The wall lights, the green carpet, the doors – these all looked the same. But there were differences. The coat stand was there in the corner next to me; but there was no umbrella. In the first hall there had been no steps like those I had fallen down. And here there was no door opening on to the hotel corridor. I leant against the wall beside the hatchway; it felt reassuringly solid. Right in the corner at the far end of the hall was another door recessed in an alcove. The wall at right-angles to mine, which led to the alcove, had two doors in it; so had the wall facing me. Counting the hatchway into the red passage, that made six doors altogether.

I decided to proceed anticlockwise, starting with the door in the alcove. I pushed it open and recognized to my amazement the white carpet and dim lighting of Gmünd's sitting-room. From where I had been sitting the other evening I had not noticed that the room, which in fact described a quarter-circle round the old tower, had this second exit.

I crossed to the second door on the left. It looked no different from the others, but something told me I ought to knock, even though I was sure the apartment was empty. The room was divided in two, the front part separated from the back by a semi-partition coming down from the ceiling, below which on either side hung heavy curtains of some brocade-like material shot through with glints of red and tied back with yellow tasselled cords. At the far end of the room, under a window that gave on to the hotel yard, stood a double bed with, I noted, a small pile of books on the bedside table. More books lay open on a desk just visible behind the curtains, their white pages catching what little light the window admitted. In the front part of the room, besides a card-table, two armchairs, an antique wardrobe and a glass-fronted cupboard crammed with yet more books, I made out the rectangular outline of a door in the wall to my left. There was a very faint odour of tobacco in the air. And I noticed something else. The strange humming noise – the only sound that broke the silence within these old walls and which now seemed more like a swishing or rustling – had grown perceptibly louder. Not daring to explore the room, which undoubtedly belonged to the Knight of Lübeck, I closed the door again – taking quite gratuitous care not to make a sound.

I moved to the next door and held my ear to it, as it seemed to me that this was where the swishing sound was coming from. I was right. But as I listened the sound suddenly stopped. Then I heard a faint clink, as of metal against metal. Could there be someone inside? There was a soft thud, a rustling noise . . . then silence.

Resisting the urge to run away, I placed my hand cautiously on the door handle. Through a crack came a shaft of light and a waft of warm, moist air heavy with a sweet scent like that of full-blown roses. I inched the door open, just a fraction, and saw a small room with four doors. The ones on the left and right were closed, while the door opposite, like the one where I was standing, stood ajar. I calculated that the one on the right must lead to Gmünd's bedroom. But it was the door facing me that seized my attention. Through it I could see part of a brightly lit bathroom: a washbasin with big brass taps; a section of mirror above it; an area of cream-coloured tiling with a delicate vein-like pattern; and, next to the basin, an enormous wooden tub from which rose a cloud of steam – not, as one might have supposed, to the ceiling but into the baldachin-like awning of some kind of Ottoman tent hung with heavy crimson-and-white striped drapes and trimmed with a long black fringe. The bathroom of the lady of the castle! What I had heard was running water.

Someone must have turned off the tap. Thinking that whoever it was would by now be in one of the side rooms, I was about to close the door when a naked woman suddenly appeared at the basin. She gazed thoughtfully into the mirror, slowly raised her hands and, holding a clasp at the ready in her teeth, gathered up her long dark hair behind her head. I wished the mirror was larger, as all I could see in it was one side of her face, from throat to forehead. I had an oblique side view of her heavy breasts, which were a shade lighter than her arms and which reminded me of ripe pears. I pressed my eye closer to the door, determined to commit to memory every movement of that superb body. Rozeta's body.

My gaze slid down her back to her buttocks. Apart from the occasional fatty dimple they were as smooth as silk. Where her hips merged into her ample thighs the flowing curve of her body was broken by a strange undergarment, very small and tight, that gleamed like burnished pewter.

Rozeta raised herself on tiptoe against the basin, and I heard the clash of metal on porcelain. At the same moment a small, oddly shaped padlock swung into view on her hip. It resembled a miniature coat-of-arms whose central motif was a tiny irregular keyhole. For a split-second I saw Rozeta's look of terror in the mirror. Then the bathroom door slammed shut.

I turned away and tried to find my bearings. The last remaining door was the one opposite the red corridor. That must take me to the blue room, surely. I had to decide quickly: at any moment Rozeta might come rushing out to see who had been spying on her. She might have a gun. I was sure she hadn't recognized me, but if I hung around a moment longer . . . I pushed open the door: another dark anteroom. I slipped inside and closed the door. By chance my elbow knocked against a light switch. I turned it on.

Here the arrangement was different. On the right was a bathroom, while facing me was a room so crammed with furniture, all piled in higgledy-piggledy, that it was hard to imagine there was any space left for a human occupant. It looked like a stage set. In the middle of room were two wardrobes standing back to back surrounded by an assortment of chairs, tables, stools and plant stands, as well as a slatted iron construction that I recognized as a medieval footwarmer, a battered upright piano and two life-sized classical plaster statues, each on a plinth. The headless male torso served as a clothes stand, its arms and shoulders festooned with waistcoats, jackets and topcoats. The female figure, which was without arms, had various colourful cravats and ties draped around its neck. The floor was strewn with clothes – some dirty, some clean and some brand new (there were several shirts still in their cellophane wrappers).

It was chaos but a habitable chaos none the less. I saw that the furniture had been positioned in such a way as to leave narrow aisles which allowed access to the back part of the room. There, I assumed, would be the bed.

No sooner had I turned back to the anteroom than I heard a door opening in the hall beyond. I knew it must be Rozeta – no doubt reassuring herself that the prying eye she had imagined at the bathroom door had indeed been an illusion.

I could not very well leave the anteroom, but if my calculations were correct the last door in the hall should lead to the same room as the last door here, that is, to the blue room. Pushing it open, I at last found myself in the place that for the coming days would be my home.

A worn grey carpet, a convertible sofa-bed with the stuffing coming out of it, turquoise curtains, a table with a Provençal tablecloth, a couple of landscape paintings of ponds and distant reed beds, a vulgar table-lamp shaped like a harebell: this was the blue room. Unattractive, cold, impersonal, cheerless – a typical hotel room, in fact. Yet, strange to say, the moment I closed the door behind me, leaving Rozeta, Gmünd and Prunslik to their fate in their eerily labyrinthine abode, I began to feel quite at home.

16

I watch you fall: the swiftest arrow
is not more terrible than you.

Richard Weiner

I went to sleep in my clothes on the couch and did not wake up until morning. During the night someone had brought in my luggage so I was able to change. I took a cold shower in the bathroom, which I discovered I was sharing with Prunslik. There was a note on the sitting-room table telling me that breakfast was being served downstairs.

The Bouvines did not provide cooked meals, but it did do an excellent breakfast. Of the three tables that were laid, two were unoccupied. At the third sat my host, in white shirt and scarlet waistcoat, with Rozeta and Prunslik on either side of him. Rozeta was in civilian clothes – a white blouse and brown skirt – while Prunslik wore his usual blue-grey suit. At the foot of the stairs I hesitated, wondering whether I should join them, but Gmünd quickly spotted me and beckoned me over with a welcoming smile.

After the waiter had taken my order of coffee and, on his recommendation, a soft-boiled egg served in a glass, I thanked Gmünd for letting me stay in his apartment despite the obvious inconvenience. I refrained from mentioning that I had nearly got lost in its maze-like ramifications. While he apologized for his absence – Raymond and he had had some matters to attend to and only got back shortly before dawn – I observed Rozeta out of the corner of my eye. She had not even said good morning and continued to sit in stony silence, sullenly chewing on small pieces of a dry roll that she crumbled on the tablecloth. Prunslik saw me watching her and explained with his usual malicious glee and thin, piercing voice that 'gorgeous here' was on another of her diets. She gave him a sharp look but said nothing. He had decided to join her out of solidarity, he explained, raising a glass of ruby port (his sole breakfast) in a mock toast. Unperturbed, Gmünd tucked into his scrambled egg, scooping it up with slices of thickly buttered brown bread.

Knowing even as I spoke that it was a mistake, I remarked in a conversational tone that I had had no idea Rozeta also lived in the apartment. I waited for a reaction and was not disappointed. Clenching her fist and crushing her roll to crumbs, she asked whatever had given me that idea.

I told her, not without irony, that it had simply occurred to me as a possibility and, of course, I could be mistaken. Perhaps like myself she was merely a temporary guest. She told me to mind my own business. 'I hope you're old enough to find your own bathroom,' she added.

At that point Gmünd, who had no idea what was going on but sensed Rozeta's tacit reproach, changed the subject and enquired how I had slept in my new quarters, whereupon I described, much to Prunslik's amusement, the circuitous route I had taken to the blue room. All three were intrigued to learn that I had not reached the second hall via the door in the alcove but along the padded red passage that used to be a clothes cupboard. No comment was made, but meaningful glances were exchanged. I made no mention of the other rooms I had inspected nor, of course, of the bathroom. I asked which of them had given up their room for me. Gmünd brushed my question aside with some remark about it not being the first time he and Prunslik had had to muck in together . . . Suddenly checking himself, he asked me not to tell the Superintendent that we were all living under the same roof. At the mention of Olejar's name Prunslik leapt to his feet and shook his head like a wet dog. His laugh sliced the air like a rusty knife.

Gmünd then wrote me a cheque for an amount far in excess of any sum I might have dared request for my services. Part of it, I knew, was hush money, but I gratefully accepted all the same. I even accepted Prunslik's offer of a glass of port. The dark red liquid splashed into the glass like spurting blood. I drank to the health of all three of them and made a point of favouring Rozeta with a little bow. She smiled absently, avoiding my look, and I saw the sadness in her eyes. The potent wine soon calmed my troubled mind.

Olejar was having a bad day. His face was a picture of misery as he paced up and down the office with long nervous strides, a handkerchief pressed to one ear and a cordless phone to the other. He was shouting something about results from the lab, so I guessed he was talking to Trug, who had obviously not yet analysed them. It was not until after two further phone calls and some emergency aural irrigation (at the sight of which I felt quite faint) that he registered my presence. He seemed surprised to see me sitting there in the leather armchair in the corner of the room from where I had been watching him expectantly for the past half-hour. Without a word he picked something up off his desk and brought it over to me. It was a photograph – the fourth of the series he had shown me the other day. The image was indistinct but its subject clear enough.

The dusty ground was the same as in the other shots, but this time the camera had been moved further to the right and the picture was better lit and sharper – all too sharp, in fact. In the foreground was a body. It was a male body and evidently lifeless. But it was not that of Rehoř, since it had legs. These projected obliquely towards the camera, with the trunk and head receding beyond them. The corpse's shoes and trousers – trainers and faded jeans – were clearly visible at the left edge of the picture. A strong light must have been placed close to the subject, probably just out of frame. To judge by its brightness, height and narrow beam, I guessed it might be a car headlamp. The dead person's face was only dimly discernible in the shadowy background, but even so I could tell at once it was that of a very young man.

His dark checked shirt, which was unbuttoned, contrasted strongly with the brightly illuminated skin. His trousers had been pulled down to reveal a flat, preternaturally white abdomen that called to mind a dead fish – or, more precisely, a fish that has just been caught and gutted: a deep cut ran all the way from the breastbone to the pubic area. As with Rehoř's legs there was no blood visible. But this time the incision was clean and straight, only widening to a hole just below the navel. There, in the black cavity of the boy's belly, glinted some metal object – perhaps the knife used to disembowel him. I had no doubt he had been murdered: one doesn't conduct an autopsy on a fully dressed corpse.

Only then, once I had absorbed the ghastly scene in the foreground, did I notice the shadowy form of the second victim in the darkness beyond. Next to it, propped against the wall (definitely the same yellowish, flaking wall as in the previous pictures, with the same blue patch or streak) was a large black circular object with a few golden specks gleaming on its rim. Two things about it struck me as odd. The first was the colour of the reflections, since the light in the foreground was pure white with no hint of yellow. The second was that, apart from those five or six bright points, the dark mass of the circle seemed to swallow up every particle of light. In front of it, its wrists tied to the outside of the ring, lay a crumpled doll-like figure, its head lolling on its chest. The face was hidden, but hanging out of its mouth was some kind of elongated cylinder, not unlike a cigar, clearly visible against the pale blue of its T-shirt. The tight trousers, apart from several dark stains on the thighs, were of exactly the same light-blue colour as the T-shirt, which made it look as though the figure was wearing close-fitting washed-out overalls. Could it be a kind of uniform?

As I stared at the gruesome image I experienced an almost inhuman detachment, without a glimmer of compassion. Perhaps, I thought, I am a crime victim myself. Perhaps I, too, have been disembowelled and emptied of all feeling. Perhaps I have also been forced into skin-tight overalls that separate me from real life. Was it possible?

Surely not. What stopped me from being overwhelmed by pity for those two boys was the morbid beauty of the picture. It was like a scene from a play, a publicity shot displayed outside a theatre. Yes, that was it: this wasn't so much a representation of real death as a clever piece of *mise-en-scène*. All would be explained in the dénouement, maybe even the two severed legs fluttering in the wind above Vyšehrad or the body of an old woman hanging from Nusle Bridge, pirouetting slowly in that same wind. But could that alone excuse my alarming lack of empathy?

In a curious way what Olejar said next implied that it could.

'Let's not read too much into the photos yet. I know no more than you, but I hope that'll change as soon as I get the enlargements. Now, I've got news for you. Did you know Rehoř was sent a threatening letter, too, like the one Zahir got? And we think Mrs Pendelmanová as well. Neither of them mentioned it, so it came as a bit of a surprise. But when Barnabáš told us last week that he'd received a similar letter Junek immediately had all Rehoř's personal effects sifted through. They found it in his desk. It was too late to check the contents of Mrs P's bureau – she had no heir and the new owner of the flat had thrown all her stuff out. For all we know she might have had several warnings. Quite possibly she didn't have a clue what they were about and put them straight in the bin.'

'When we last spoke I told you I thought both victims might be involved in architecture in some way. Have you considered this theory?'

'Don't tell me you think you're the first to come up with that one,' he growled. 'We've been working on it for some time.'

I didn't argue and let him carry on. But underneath my expression of eager interest I was chuckling quietly to myself.

'It's a vital clue. We're keeping an even closer watch on Zahir and Barnabáš. Neither of them is aware of having done anything to earn them death threats or even of having any enemies. And they're being pretty uncooperative. A pair of conceited idiots, if you ask me – each as bad as the other. Barnabáš is a big shot in the construction business and one of the most influential architects in Prague. He refuses to talk to my men, even though his life is in danger, and won't let them inside his house – some posh place he built himself above Bertramka on the other side of the river. Do you know where they have to watch the house from? A summer house in the garden! Keeping track of Zahir is no easier. He's not quite so bloody-minded, but he spends every night at a different woman's place so it's impossible to keep tabs on him.'

I nodded at the photograph. 'And these two? Where do they fit in?'

'What makes you think they have to fit in?'

'You're handling the case personally. You could have delegated. After all, you're busy hunting down a psychopathic killer who's terrorizing the city. I just put two and two together.'

'Very astute. Yes, I had a sort of intuition I should look into this one myself. There was also the fact that the photos were sent to me and arrived one at a time.'

'I'm sure you're right. And there's another thing: the other day I was saying how theatrical the two New Town murders were, not to mention the assault on Zahir. And now this. Those photos are just the same – in the way the scene was set up, even the way they were delivered to you. Suppose there's more to them than can be seen with the naked eye? They're all a bit fuzzy and blurred . . .'

He cut me short. 'Do you take me for a fool? Here, take a look at this.'

He tapped at his computer and all four photographs came up side by side across the full width of the screen. Olejar zoomed in on various portions of the pictures, enlarging them several times. But the images became overexposed and polarized until all I could see was a mass of square dots that hurt my eyes.

'You're on the right track,' said the Superintendent, his voice calmer now. 'But I'm a step ahead of you. As in most such cases, computers are a fat lot of good. But there are still the good old-fashioned processing methods, aren't there? The minute I got this I called Trug and told him to get them done by lunchtime. He said he was up to his eyes and couldn't it wait until tomorrow, but I twisted his arm a little. I have ways of making people cooperate. He used to be a surgeon, you know, and a big fish on the local party committee. One day he was doing a routine operation on some foreign diplomat when his hand slipped. The diplomat died. Luckily for Trug there were no international repercussions, but it was the end of his career as a surgeon. That's when he became a pathologist. At the time the whole thing was hushed up and even now it's considered bad form to mention it. So not a word, if you don't mind. Trug returned the originals just before you arrived, and I'm expecting him back any minute with the blow-ups. It's only a long shot, of course, but at least he'll have been sweating blood over it.' With a thin mirthless smile he added, more to himself than to me, 'Woe betide the bastard if he gives me any lip.'

Any further remarks concerning the absent Trug were rendered superfluous by the arrival of the doctor himself, who burst into the office and handed the Superintendent a bundle of papers. His hair was awry, his beard bristled, and beads of sweat stood out on his furrowed brow and pockmarked nose. Judging by his clothes – corduroy trousers and tweed jacket – Olejar had called him away just as he was about to give a lecture.

'Best I can do,' the pathologist grunted in lieu of a greeting. After a brief fit of coughing he pulled a crumpled packet of cigarettes from his pocket and, without asking permission, lit up and began exhaling quick jerky puffs of malodorous smoke. On the packet, which he had left lying on the desk, was a short name in Cyrillic script. When he eventually noticed that I was present he screwed up his nose in disgust, as if I, not he, were the one who stank. Perhaps he was bothered by my lily-of-the-valley aftershave. For my part, I was equally displeased to see him. Trug may not have had a leaking ear like Olejar, but I found him quite repellent.

The prints were fanned out across the desk like playing cards. They were still wet and reeked of chemicals – I got a whiff of ammonia, formaldehyde and what I thought was hyoscine – or at least something that produced a bitter taste in my saliva. But that was nothing compared with the horror that assailed my eyes. An evil spell, it seemed, had revealed the meaning of the pictures all too clearly. They had acquired a three-dimensionality that gave one the sense of looking below the surface of reality. Olejar and I stared at them in dread and disbelief, while behind us the diabolical doctor breathed brimstone down our necks.

From Trug's enlargements it was still not possible to identify the black circle on its grey, blue-streaked background. Now it looked more like a hoop propped up against the wall. It seemed to be wrapped in black paper, with here and there a patch of gold showing through. Attached to it were some kind of decorative spikes jutting out at an angle towards the camera lens; and tied to the spikes were the slender arms of the corpse, which sat slumped against the wall inside the ring. The sheer blue overalls we had noted in the earlier prints had disappeared: the deceased was wearing nothing more than his own skin. Hanging from his mouth was a small aluminium can.

Trug had managed to sharpen up the body in the foreground, so that now we could make out the individual scratches and bruises around the navel and on the chest and throat. We also had a clearer view of the face: smooth, calm and pitifully young. Sixteen? Seventeen? But above all the eye was drawn, inevitably, to the ghastly wound in the abdomen and especially the point where it sagged open. Here the skin bulged unnaturally, particularly on the left side of the belly. From the dark centre of the wound protruded a shiny metal object, some kind of short rod or spindle with a rounded knob-like head covered in some unidentifiable greenish substance.

My head reeling from the sight of the two dead bodies and the stink of Russian tobacco, I got up and went to the windows that took up a whole wall of the Superintendent's office. Having at last found one that could be opened, I leant out and drew in a lungful of Prague air, which after Trug's cigarette seemed like a breath of paradise. As I did so the clock of St Stephen's began striking noon. Drawn by the sound, my eyes alighted on the sheer stone of the tower with its sparkling golden ornament – the royal crown. Suddenly I understood what the photograph was telling us.

17

They died hideously, cheated by death:
caught up in a mesh of ghastly screams
(their own screams)

Richard Weiner

A north-westerly wind accompanied by frequent showers gradually dispersed the thick morning mist. What had become of the brave autumn colours? The chestnut trees in the Cattle Market (that is, Charles Square), with nothing more to lose, bared themselves to the inclement weather with stoical calm. For nearly a month drifts of decaying leaves had transformed the place into a vast neglected graveyard. Now, as November drew to a close, an army of the homeless and unemployed, belatedly recruited by a lethargic city council already looking forward to hibernation, was sweeping every last corner of the park, exposing to public view expanses of anaemic grass and mould-reeking earth. Only in the surrounding streets a few last yellow leaves remained, scattered over the paving-stones like golden coins from the purse of some ghostly dawn rider. The profligate colour of the scene enchanted me: the vivid leaves, the sweepers' luminous jackets shining in the mist like fireflies, as if some midsummer night's assembly had sent them forth to bring the people of Prague a little autumn cheer.

Even Resslova, normally a drab street, now had its share of colour. One morning a row of flashing orange lights appeared on the road, fenced in with red-and-white tape. No one knew why. The traffic at first slowed to a crawl, then to a stop-go jam, trying the patience of drivers and passengers trapped inside their cars. Not more traffic lights surely? But with only one lane open they had no choice but to wait their turn. I, on the other hand, was delighted: crossing this terrifyingly straight and lethally fast thoroughfare would now be child's play – as long as I remembered to hold a handkerchief over my face. Slow-moving vehicles may not kill as fast as those travelling at full speed. But in their quiet, indefatigable way they are equally effective.

When I opened the evening paper I found out why the street had been partially closed. A lorry laden with crates of fruit and flowers had broken through the road surface just opposite the church of St Cyril and St Methodius and sunk in up to its axle. The driver and his mate had jumped out at once. The driver had gone to put up a warning triangle, while his companion rushed off to call the emergency services from the nearby metro station. They were lucky. When the driver turned round the lorry was gone. His mate returned to find him, triangle in hand, gaping at a crater at his feet and laughing hysterically.

My hypothesis regarding the mysterious photographs sent to the Superintendent's office was never actually confirmed. Officially, the matter was considered closed; unofficially, the investigation quietly continued.

When I had been summoned to a meeting of CID officers working on the New Town murders and asked to explain my theory I was somewhat taken aback by their cool reaction. At first things seemed to be going well. Everyone listened and took me seriously, and when the Superintendent conceded I might be right the others agreed. Even the arch-sceptic Junek, the last person I would have expected to admit that any idea of mine could benefit the police, had to agree it was the only explanation that might give the investigation new impetus. What finally convinced him was an apparently insignificant but, as it turned out, crucial discovery made near the side entrance of St Stephen's Church, where a constable had found half a skateboard.

They might not regard it as proof, I said, but for me it certainly was. The dead bodies in the photographs were those of the two boys who had been missing for several days. They had been murdered for a mere trifle – a bit of naughtiness their parents would have sorted out by boxing their ears or docking their pocket money. The two young rebels' crime had been to spray their angry message on those hallowed walls. Desecration is a serious matter, usually punishable by a stiff fine; in this case, however, the culprit (the figure in the background of the photograph) had been stripped naked and covered with the same foul paint he had used to deface the church wall. He must have suffered terribly as the chemicals slowly starved his skin of oxygen. The empty aerosol had probably been rammed into his mouth while he was still alive. The other boy – the one who had left home with a skateboard under his arm – had no doubt been standing look-out for his friend. His punishment was less severe: a quick, less painful death. This was borne out by the look of unconcern on his face. Yet his corpse (the one in the foreground) had been mutilated no less horribly than his friend's: someone had slit open his belly and thrust half a skateboard into it – half, presumably, because there was no room for a whole one. What we had seen protruding from the wound was its steel axle and a green wheel. The half skateboard found at the church had wheels of the same colour.

To judge by the jagged edge of the break, the board had not been cut in two but simply smashed. For the murderers it served a dual purpose: as a deliberate clue and as a warning to other potential desecrators of the house of God – assuming, that is, the police decided to publicize the crime. The mysterious circle left beside the graffiti-smeared wall fulfilled a similar function. The crown symbolized the worldly power that had ordered the building of the church and stood guard over it to this day. That is why it had been removed from the tower. That is why it had been used to chastize those hands that had defiled a holy place they had no right to touch.

What terrible justice! But how on earth . . . ?

No, not that. The thought is too awful to contemplate.

If we remember how the previous murder was carried out, it is not hard to imagine how this elaborate piece of savagery was executed. We know the murderers had a platform crane at their disposal – it had at one point been one of the police's main clues. So when a second opportunity to use it suddenly presented itself they simply stole it again. The people of Prague are not known for their powers of observation – they notice almost nothing, in fact, except the chaotic mess at street level. Besides, walking with your head in the air admiring the façades and cornices and caryatids is a risky business, given the shocking state of the pavements. Little wonder that the only person to notice the disappearance of the diadem from St Stephen's tower was a pensioner who lived across the road. His testimony, which at the time had seemed like so much gibberish, now fitted precisely into our reconstruction of events.

But what was behind the murder of the two youngsters? Why the excessive brutality? One thing was clear: the common denominator of the New Town murders was their ostentatious theatricality. And a common motive. But what? Revenge? Punishment? A warning to others? All we knew was that the murders (and one attempted murder) had been conceived as aesthetic spectacles, and that they had all taken place near or inside New Town churches.

As I have said, my theory was well received. Junek blinked enthusiastically, puckering his lips slightly as if he had bitten on a slice of lemon and didn't want anyone to notice. The others, whom I knew only by sight, silently made notes. Rozeta raised one corner of her mouth as if to say she had some doubts regarding my sanity. When I had finished she raised the other corner and made a mute show of clapping. Then, with the tiniest of nods, she tapped her wristwatch with a fingernail. Surely she didn't want to talk to me alone? Rozeta – to me? My throat went dry, and by some strange trick all the moisture in my mouth was instantly transferred to my eyes. I couldn't speak. I couldn't even move. I was seized by vertigo. I leant back hard in my chair, gripping its arms with all my strength, but the office kept spinning round and round. The others sat as if nailed to their seats, quite unaware of my plight.

Olejar was beside himself with agitation. Moaning in pain, he applied a succession of clean handkerchiefs to his ears in a desperate effort to stem the well-nigh volcanic extrusion. Before he closed the meeting he asked me to stay behind. As soon as we were alone he asked if I would consider rejoining the police in the New Year. I said I'd think about it. My face was gave nothing away, but behind the deadpan mask I was jubilant.

Rozeta was waiting down in the street. She wore a light raincoat that concealed her plump body and a floral scarf tied rather unfashionably under her chin. I was flattered by her punctuality and apologized for keeping her waiting. I had to shout to make myself heard in the wind, which whisked my words away towards Karlov, rattled the street lights and buffeted us from all sides. We took refuge in a nearby bar, where we warmed our hands on glasses of hot grog.

'Why did you look at me like that?' she began in a surprisingly cold tone, very different from her manner a few minutes earlier. 'You were keeping something from them, weren't you? Tell me.'

'Me? It was you who were looking at me. Everything I know I've told them already. Is that why you wanted to see me – to pick my brains?'

'Don't be silly. I have something to tell you. You may be in danger, too. I'm afraid for you.'

'Really? That's the nicest thing anyone's ever said to me. Say it again.'

'I'm serious. Look, I don't know what kind of fantasies you have about me, but you might as well forget them. Don't get mixed up with me. You're the one who'll get hurt, not me. You seem to have quite the wrong idea about me. So don't raise your hopes – you'll only be disappointed.'

'Raise my hopes? They couldn't get much lower. I've been in this situation before and can't think of anything worse. Anyway, what if *you* get mixed up with *me*? I don't know the first thing about you. But there are some things about you that just don't add up.'

'Well, forget them. I'm not what matters.'

'What does matter then?'

'You said yourself you know nothing about me. Keep it that way. You wouldn't like what you found. I'm not beautiful. I'm not well educated. I'm not interesting.'

'Is that what you came to tell me? Well, I beg to differ – and you can take that as a compliment.'

'Don't talk rubbish. You're as bad as that oaf Zahir.'

'There's no need to get angry. Look, I've really no idea why we're here. I thought you were trying to ask me out – though I couldn't quite believe it. I don't know who you are or what to expect of you.'

'Forgive me. Forgive me even if nothing happens between us, which I hope it won't. I can't really explain . . . not at the moment. If anything does happen I won't be the one to prevent it. Just let it run its course and you won't come to any harm. Then in time you'll get used to it.'

'Let what run its course, for God's sake? What will I get used to?' I didn't have a clue what she was talking about, but whatever it was I didn't like the way she was saying it. I hadn't exactly been expecting a declaration of love – in fact I was relieved she hadn't come out with one. All the same I found her words irritating.

'I was in the same situation,' she went on. 'Just because I'm living at his place doesn't make me his maid or dogsbody. I owe him nothing, nor does he me. I make my own choices about how I live. That's the way it suits me, at least for now.'

'I'm not blaming you for anything. How could I? What concern is it . . . ?'

'Exactly. None whatsoever,' she cut in. I wanted to tell her there was some mistake, that I wouldn't dream of disapproving of her simply because she lived in Gmünd's apartment. But she didn't give me a chance. Her next question bowled me over.

'How long have you been spying on us?'

'Spying? Me?'

'Prunslik saw you in St Catherine's garden the other day when I was with Matthias.'

'Prunslik indeed! The little rat. I don't suppose you asked him what *he* was doing there?'

'I can handle Prunslik myself, thank you. And another thing: keep out of my bathroom.'

'I don't know my way round the hotel. I opened the door by accident.'

'It took you a long time to shut it again.'

'Did it? Perhaps. That Turkish tent over the bath . . . and the metal thing . . .'

'So you got a good look at me, did you?'

'I was stunned. It was all so . . . beautiful.'

'Well, don't go gossiping about it. I don't even know what to make of Matthias myself. I may be moving out tomorrow.'

'What for? What's going on between you?'

'I wouldn't tell you even if I knew. You'll find out in time – if I can last out, that is. And if you prove up to it.'

'Prove up to it? Up to what? Anyway, what's in it for me?'

'Finding yourself, at last. Isn't that enough? The way I found myself. Though perhaps . . . Matthias will help you, just as he helped me. I was in a terrible state. He helped me back on my feet.'

'"He brought me up also out of an horrible pit, out of the miry clay, and set my feet upon a rock, and established my goings." Psalm 40, if I remember rightly.'

Suddenly she leapt to her feet, flashed me an unexpectedly warm smile and was gone. Her grog (into which she had poured four sachets of sugar) remained untouched on the table. I drank it. Though it was, not surprisingly, cloyingly sweet, I enjoyed it more than my own. As I slurped noisily at the hot drink I turned over in my mind everything Rozeta had said. If her words contained some hidden meaning, on that afternoon it escaped me.

*

All through the first week of December I was in better spirits. Once again I resumed my walks around my favourite corners of the city, and once again the city enfolded me in her embrace, revealing her hidden nooks and, whenever I lingered in nostalgic contemplation, the secret stories of her glorious past. The air was clear and sharp with frost. A fresh fall of snow, longer-lasting than the first, transformed the raucous streets into quiet corridors leading into the unknown. Drab house fronts were transfigured and dim alleys miraculously illuminated as the gentle flakes fell from heaven on the undeserving people of Prague. A white quilt lay over the Gothic spires and Baroque domes of the city, transforming it into a child's picture book. The same quilt had covered Prague a hundred years ago – three hundred, six hundred years ago and earlier still. And beneath it life had gone on at the same leisurely pace – at the most, the speed of a sleigh.

The bodies of the two boys from St Stephen's had still not been found. The only shadow that darkened those luminous days was a phone call from Zahir. After congratulating me on my change of residence he informed me he would no longer be needing me, since he now had round-the-clock police protection. I was not to take it personally but look on the positive side: when I had been guarding him he had worried more about me than I had about him. But now it seemed that someone meant business: he had also been sent a cobblestone – yes, literally sent, by express mail. And, yes, it was green like the others.

Something else had arrived by the same post. Fear.

I told him my big news – that I would soon be back in uniform, so we might meet again sooner than he thought. Even over the phone I could hear he was slightly taken aback. I knew he didn't think much of me as a policeman, especially not after I lost him on our field trip together. He quickly went on to tell me that he now had a new assistant: Rozeta. I didn't say anything. He asked me what I thought. Still I said nothing. I felt a sharp pain in my chest, as if someone were stitching me up with an electric sewing-machine. I told him I hoped he and Rozeta would get on well together, trying as I did so to imagine the expression on his face: a salacious grin, no doubt, plus a lot of winking and blinking. I shuddered. But my gloom at the idea of him and Rozeta wrapped in each other's arms was dispelled by the hilarious thought of how his jaw would drop the moment his groping hand encountered her iron underwear. Misconstruing my sudden laughter, he told me he had known from the start that she was the kind of woman who fell for men of experience. Anxious to change the subject, I asked whether, apart from the warning parcel, he had any other reason to fear for his safety. Somewhat guardedly he said he thought he was being followed, which was the real reason he wanted professional protection. I recommended Inspector Junek, even though I clearly remembered Zahir warning me against him. Again he misunderstood and thought I was trying to make him change his mind about employing Rozeta. Before he hung up he asked me to convey his regards to the Knight of Lübeck, giving the title ironic emphasis and stretching out the first vowel of the name so it sounded more like *Liebe*. Did he suspect there were any strange goings-on between them? As a parting shot he jabbered some nonsense about there being plenty of fish in the sea and on no account was I to throw myself off Nusle Bridge – he could think of far more romantic places, such as Petřín Tower. I started to tell him he should look after himself rather than rely on the police, but my words, as always with Zahir, fell on deaf ears. The line was already dead.

Gmünd seemed genuinely pleased to hear I was back in favour with the police. Even Prunslik, when I met him in the hotel lobby, was all over me and pumped my hand as if his life depended on it. As usual I could not make head or tail of him. Old love never dies, he said: he always felt happier when I was around. Gmünd congratulated me in a more seemly fashion and invited me to dinner in some club or other, adding that before long he would throw a party in my honour.

He asked Olejar to let me stay in his employ for another week or two in the hope that the work he was engaged on might be expeditiously concluded. Every day we visited the New Town churches, most frequently St Stephen's and St Apollinaris'. While Gmünd made sketches, measurements and calculations I wandered from one altar to another – always with one eye on Rozeta, who acted as if I wasn't there.

Again I was struck by the curious word Heptecclesion, which Gmünd was using more and more frequently without ever once telling me what he meant by it. At first I had been too shy to ask, and now it was too late. I guessed he must be talking about some foreign city whose architecture he found inspiring. Of course I thought of Quinque Ecclesiae, the old name for the Hungarian town of Pécs. So I was all the more surprised to discover that the Heptecclesion referred to some place in Bohemia, in fact, in Prague itself. The only similar name I had ever heard was Five Churches Square in Prague's Malá Strana and Five Churches House on the street of the same name. But the name had long fallen into disuse, no doubt because it had always been a misnomer: there had never been that number of churches in the cramped, dark quarter below the castle at the foot of Hradčany. Every time Gmünd talked about the Heptecclesion I longed to learn more about that mysterious place. Gradually the various pieces fell into place. The Heptecclesion must, on the one hand, refer to certain churches in Prague New Town that had all been built by order of King Charles IV (either replacing existing Romanesque churches or on new sites) and, on the other, to the district bounded by the axes connecting those churches. I realized to my amazement that it corresponded almost exactly to my favourite part of the city. But, frustratingly, I was unable to determine precisely which churches were included. There was nothing extraordinary about the Church of the Annunciation on Na Slupi, for example, with its unremarkable location and dubious Eastern liturgy. Yet it held a remarkable fascination for Gmünd and had an important place in his plans – as important as far bigger churches such as Emmaus or Karlov, to which, for some reason, he had never taken me. I was also sure that Stephen's and Apollinaris' had to be part of the Heptecclesion but was less certain about St Catherine's, which, unlike the others, had not been rebuilt in the eighteenth century (its Gothic tower alone had been spared) and only 're-Gothicized' in the nineteenth. But even if it were on Gmünd's list, that still only made six. What could the seventh be? St Henry's? Or maybe St Martin's? And what about St Peter's or Our Lady of the Snows or St Václav's in Na Zderaz? With their magnificent Gothic style – of which, thanks to Gmünd, I was now totally enamoured – they must surely all qualify for a place on his A-list. Their only fault seemed to be their location, which did not fit into his magic pattern.

On one occasion he said with a sigh, 'Don't think I don't care about St Peter's or St Lazarus'. I find them quite fascinating – and the whole district around them. But we must know our own limitations.'

Yes, I thought, I know my limitations. For the time being I would not try to discover the seventh church of the Upper New Town in Prague – Gmünd's magic mountain.

18

Here let us stand, close by the cathedral.
Here let us wait.
Are we drawn by danger?
Is it the knowledge of safety,
that draws our feet towards the cathedral?

T.S. Eliot

Dwarf-like, we stood under the colossal dome of Karlov Church, our heads lifted in wonder. Gmünd held his hat in one hand, his cane in the other. It was bitterly cold, and I blew into my cupped hands to warm them. The light slanted down from the tall windows, catching our vaporous breath as it floated up to the stars on the ceiling. The ecstasy on the Knight's face as he gazed up at the fresh gold-and-blue paint and new lighting was unfeigned, unlike my polite enthusiasm, though this was by no means the first time he had seen them. Today, for some reason, the mandatory second minder had been dispensed with. Gmünd and I were alone.

I had not been in the Church of the Virgin Mary and Charles the Great (to give it its full name) for several years. Now I felt as if I had stepped back into the past, to the time when it was newly built. Where I remembered darkness, now all was light; where the plaster had been flaking and patched with mould, now I saw clean, solid walls aglow with carmine and gold. Gmünd had decided to retain the golden pattern on its red ground, arguing that it corresponded to the original Gothic decoration; but the star-studded canopy in the severies of the vaulting was of his own devising – the huge eight-pointed star of the dome dated from the sixteenth century when nocturnal skies were no longer in vogue. The vaulting was similar in concept to the original (but never realized) plans, differing only in its geometrical complexity and, in particular, its unusually low pitch, which made it look as if it rested effortlessly on the slender pillars and supports. Gmünd had polished this Carolingian gem into a thing of dazzling beauty. For once he had departed from the puritan taste that he had so often invoked to curse the architects of the Renaissance and Baroque and demolish, at least with words, their vulgar monstrosities.

My views did not always concur. Since my arrival at the Hotel Bouvines we had become sufficiently close to be able to have differences of opinion without putting our friendship at risk. Now, too, standing right under the central boss of the vault, I objected that it would be a shame to do away with decorative features such as the statues, the blind windows and the famous Holy Steps.

But Gmünd was adamant. He couldn't stand the sight of them – one sentiment, at least, that he shared with that barbaric innovator Joseph II, who in 1786 had the church deconsecrated and turned into an infirmary for the incurably sick. He detested the emperor even more than he did the Dientzenhofers, whose sins against Czech architecture were in his view irredeemable, and prophesied that one day the country would have a better ruler with better taste.[1]

'I doubt it,' I retorted. 'As far as I know this church was due to be given a Gothic makeover in the early twentieth century, but the city fathers were against it. People have got used to all those pudgy cherubs and outsize altars and onion towers. There's no point in trying to recreate its original Gothic look. You'd be losing more than you'd gain.'

'Look up there!' he bellowed in reply. 'Look how the ribs of that vaulting intersect, like comets trailing arcs of light! Don't you see? It is not for us to ask where they come from, and of their ultimate purpose we may only dream. Comets are untouchable, beyond the reach of man. And is it not the same with Gothic churches? My mission is to protect them.'

I couldn't suppress a smile.

He tore his eyes away from the intricate web of stone and gave me a hard, level look. 'What are you expecting me to say? That my methods are less than honourable?'

'I'd never make so bold . . .'

'I don't want to keep anything from you. But I'm honestly not sure you're mature enough to face up to certain truths. I'm sorry, but I don't yet feel I can trust you completely. I may tell you some time. Or maybe never. But question me no further. Instead, try to answer some of my questions.'

'If I can, very gladly. I am in your debt, remember.'

'That's not the point. I'm not an extortionist! You are not obliged to me in any way, understand? No one is obliged to me – at least not yet. I really mean it. If Prunslik implied anything of the sort, ignore him. This is not a business transaction. Anything I ask of you I ask as a favour, from a friend.'

'You've no idea how dearly I would like to repay you for giving me a roof over my head. But as you know my abilities are negligible. And I'm a hopeless policeman.'

'I'm not asking anything like that of you. As for your abilities, I daresay I know more about them than you do yourself.'

We had reached the pews and now sat down on one of them – Gmünd on the very end, on account of his great bulk.

'I'm more interested in your knowledge of history,' he went on. 'You did study history, didn't you?'

'Yes. But I got sick of it.'

'What, even of the Middle Ages? I thought that was your favourite period.'

'Oh yes, I was fascinated by medieval history. But not the way it was taught at university. I never cared which kings ruled when or who they plotted against and how they punished them. And I still don't care. I always thirsted for a different kind of knowledge.'

'What kind of knowledge?'

'I wanted to know about everyday life. I wanted to be transported back to the Prague of the sixteenth century or the thirteenth century or the eleventh. I wanted to know what ordinary people had for lunch – aldermen and artisans and tailors and soldiers and innkeepers and market traders and the rest of them. Not only that, I wanted to talk to them and find out what they thought, what they dreamt about, what were their hopes and fears and joys. None of my teachers ever understood what I was after. Well, there was one, yes – when I was still at grammar school. But he abandoned me.'

'And your parents? Didn't they encourage these interests?'

'They couldn't get their heads round the idea of someone wanting to root about in the past instead of trying to cope with the present. But when I applied for university they didn't try to stop me. They just shrugged their shoulders. Maybe if . . . But that doesn't matter now. By that time they'd been separated for years.'

'That must have been very hard for you. Still, I don't think you needed much encouragement from them, did you? Why on earth did you give up your studies?'

'I couldn't see a way forward. It all seemed so meaningless. But I'd rather not talk about it. That's all in the past, too.'

'Meaningless, you say. Yet, unless I'm mistaken, the past – the great romantic past – still means a great deal to you.'

'You're right. I never gave up my love of the past, and maybe that was my undoing. After all, what's the point in this day and age?'

'Now you're confusing me. I know it's not easy for you, but could you at least try and tell me why you say that? It may help me – and you did say you wanted to help.'

'I don't know. Maybe . . . I suppose it was the usual escapism of a child dissatisfied with his home life and his parents' endless arguments. "Dissatisfied" is hardly the word. Maybe I should say . . . Well, imagine my situation: I hated what I saw around me – the present –

and the future only filled me with dread. I saw no hope. I needed a safe place, a harbour where my thoughts could escape from the sharp rocks of anxiety and the deadly undertow of despair. I craved solitude and found it among the ruins of medieval castles. There, every doubt had long been settled, every story concluded. Or almost: there was still room for the imagination. I spent many hours in those ruins and always contrived to be alone. Once I waited all afternoon for a family to finish their picnic so that I could have the whole place to myself. Another time I entered an area that was out of bounds – there was a military airfield near by – in order to explore a tumbledown fort. I knew that if someone caught me I'd be expelled from school at the very least. Or I might get shot by a sentry. No one caught me, but my mother gave me a terrible scolding. She said I was like a stray dog and was sure to come to a bad end. She was probably right.'

'Now don't start feeling sorry for yourself. You're not that badly off. Anyway, tell me what you got to up in those old castles.'

'Nothing very exciting, I'm afraid. I wasn't looking for treasure or ghosts or anything. That kind of shallow sensationalism never appealed to me. Though having said that, I must say I did see and hear and experience some quite extraordinary things. But I doubt if I can describe them properly. I'd probably sound like some crackpot spiritualist.'

'Let me be the judge of that.'

'As I said, I still don't really understand. All I can do is give you an example. One day, when I was fourteen or fifteen, I set off for Trosky Castle. My plan was to approach it from the steep south side, which meant climbing up the rock just below the two towers. At first I followed an easy path that led up through the woods. As it grew steeper I had to use a stick to keep my balance. Soon I was looking for handholds on roots and stones, and in the end the path petered out altogether. At this point the trees gave way to a sheer wall of fissured rock on top of which I could see the higher of the two towers. I knew that by carrying on I'd be risking life and limb. What I did not realize, however, was that I would also be risking my sanity.

'The moment I placed my hands on the hard, reassuringly familiar rock, which was pleasantly warm from the sun, a strange thing happened. All of a sudden a freezing wind sprang up, buffeting my back and howling about my ears. Within seconds my joints were numb with cold, and as the first drops of rain hit the back of my neck a chill gripped my heart.

'Had it not been for the warm rock under my hands I might have abandoned the whole enterprise. I climbed a few feet, but finding no handholds or footholds I was forced to go back and look for another route. Suddenly I heard a voice. I looked up and was astonished to see a young woman in a red dress leaning over the top of the wall that ran between the two towers, which are called the Virgin and the Witch. She was pointing into the distance and shouting excitedly – not to me, as I first thought, but apparently to someone behind her. Though I could hear her voice quite clearly I was unable to make out the individual words and had no idea who she was talking to. For an instant I thought she might be a guide but immediately dismissed the idea when I realized that the wall, over which spilled her cascade of golden hair and flowing scarlet sleeves, now looked quite different from the one I knew: it was higher, more solid and much, much newer. I inched myself a little way along a ledge and reached up with my left hand towards a stone in the base of the wall – a rough-hewn block with a shallow indentation in the middle. The moment I touched it there was an explosion of noise inside my head, a shrill cacophony of pain and rage and grief.'

'Voices?'

'Everything imaginable. Dogs barking, horses whinnying, children laughing, youths jeering, the angry shouts of men and merry chatter of women and croaking voices of the old, the wheezing of the dying and booming of the death-knell. And there was the clatter of horseshoes and crack of whips, cattle lowing, pigs grunting, the splash of water, howls of anguish, the rhythmical rattle of some simple machine, the beating of anvils and clank of armour and, at intervals, the peal of bugles and din of battle, each time different yet always the same. Despite the clamour lesser sounds could still be heard: a rustle of silk, a cat purring and, trembling like a spider's web in unimaginable darkness, a litany of whispers. I put my hands over my ears, but it had little effect. Only then did I realize that my eyes were tight shut. I opened them and again saw the girl, this time looking down at me with an alarmed expression. She shouted something, but her words were drowned out by the deafening noise from the wall. Then she pointed to some spot below me. I looked down and was surprised to see a narrow path I must have missed on my way up. It led along the foot of the wall above the steep drop, through a tangle of brambles and up to one of the towers – the more squat of the two – where I could make out a small door. The path was so narrow I was sure I would lose my footing if I tried to climb up it. But that is just what I did, emboldened by the thought of the girl looking down at me, who was more beautiful than any woman I had ever beheld in my short life. There was something imploring in her expression that urged me into action. At that moment I was capable of anything.

'As I had feared, scrambling down to the path proved extremely difficult. My foot slipped on a wet rock, and I tumbled headlong into the brambles. Instantly, the din in my head stopped. I had not fallen far, and, apart from a grazed hand, a scratched neck and a painful bang on the ribs, I was unhurt. I picked myself up, took stock of my wounds and ran like a hare. I never once looked back. As I reached the trees the rain suddenly stopped, as if at a command. Above me the sky was a clear, cloudless blue.'

'A remarkable and disturbing experience,' said Gmünd thoughtfully, running his fingers through his beard. 'Revealing, too. No doubt you've had others like it?'

'Yes.'

'Tell me, how does this church affect you? Don't you feel you could have a similar experience here? Right now, for example?'

'I don't know. I have no control over when these states come over me – they're rare these days, but I used to have them regularly. Don't think I enjoy them. On the contrary, I find it very hard to get back into everyday life and carry on as normal – and doubly hard when this reality is so dull and impoverished compared with that other world. I'd rather stay there, I don't mind telling you, and never come back. But I can't. What I want or don't want is immaterial.'

'Dull and impoverished, you say? Lift up your head! Look at that ceiling again and feast your eyes on my stars! That's wealth for you – wealth you can touch!'

'What you say only proves my point,' I went on gloomily. 'The only way to raise ourselves above the misery of this world is to keep looking upwards. Upwards – or backwards.'

'You're a man after my own heart, Květoslav. We must look up or look back. Those are the only two ways of surviving these desolate times at the end of the Modern Age – and ideally we should do both at once. And now it's my turn to be honest with you. All my life I've been looking for someone like you. Only you can answer the questions we have . . .'

There was a passion and urgency in his voice that put me on my guard. Instinctively I backed away along the pew.

'We? Who is we?'

'Oh . . . me, Raymond . . . People who want to find out more about the past so that . . .'

'So that what?'

'So that it may once again become the present.'

'That's a strange thing to want. I'm not much of a historian, you know. The things I'm interested in are hardly the stuff of academic research. What interests me is *being* in the past – the past as here-and-now, the present moment of an age long gone, at least for us, but which from a cosmic point of view is still with us. Is that what you mean? Here is the sort of thing – among a thousand others – that interests me: what flashes through the mind of the cooper Kryštof Nápravník as he steps out of his home on Nekázanka, Golden Cross House, on the twenty-fifth of October 1411 and, strolling down towards the Příkop, discovers in his pouch a strange squarish object he could swear was not there when he dressed this morning. Now what kind of history book would you find that in?'

'None. You are interested in things that have no historical foundation. The truth of your story, however remarkable, cannot be substantiated with hard facts.'

'Precisely. Any historian would dismiss it as banal. That's why I had to get away from university. There's nothing I detest more than facts. Facts constrain me. They tie my hands and oppress me. They crush my will to live.'

'That's exactly what I meant. We need you. And we'll pay you handsomely.'

I laughed. 'I'm flattered by your good opinion. But I still don't know what you want of me.'

'As you must have noticed I tend to avoid giving direct answers – partly because I don't wish to alarm you but also because I know you yourself are not overly fond of straight talking. So I will answer you with another question.' Extricating himself from the pew, Gmünd walked over to the pulpit side of the nave and stood resting his hand on the wall, just below the point where the rib vaulting fanned out majestically into a delicate web of intertwined floral motifs. He turned to me and continued, 'Do you know who built this church?'

'It was begun by Matthias, wasn't it? Your namesake.'

'Matthias of Arras? Possibly. We don't know for sure.'

'How about Peter Parler of Gmünd, your other namesake? His name appears most frequently in connection with Karlov.'

'As far as I know, work on the building was well under way by the time he arrived in Prague. If he was in charge of it, then only as a supervisor executing another master builder's plans.'

'There's another name that crops up: a certain Bohuslav Staněk, who is said to have made a pact with the Devil. He succeeded in putting up this amazing dome, but when it was finished no one dared take down the scaffolding in case it couldn't support its own weight. The Devil suggested he burn the scaffolding, which he did. When it collapsed Staněk thought the entire ceiling had come down with it and leapt into the flames. He'd pledged his soul to Old Nick anyway, so it didn't much matter.'

'Is there any truth in it?'

'How should I know?'

'You really have no idea?'

'Pardon me if I sound insolent, but are making fun of me?'

'Absolutely not.' His tone was suddenly serious. 'You seem to know very little about yourself. Don't worry, I won't rush you into anything. Now come with me.'

His face gave nothing away as he beckoned me over. He still inspired my trust, just as he had at our first meeting. But once again I realized it was a trust mingled with fear: fear of the irresistible force of his personality.

The big man's gesture was cordial and friendly enough, but in his large moist eyes I read only one word: command.

I got up and walked over to him. At that moment I became aware of a movement high up above the main entrance. On the narrow gallery, from where a single door opened on to an inaccessible wall covered with frescoes, one of the statues had noiselessly risen to its feet. But it was not one of the foursome that had always occupied that space – the Virgin Mary, Elizabeth, Joseph and Zacharias. This was a fifth statue that had slipped in among the others, apparently looking for a good vantage point from which to look down into the nave and chancel. As I watched, it shook the dust off its robes, climbed over the balustrade and – to the astonishment of the wooden figures, of which I was now one – slid down a fluted Ionic column and landed on the stone floor right beside Gmünd. Its fluttering hair, brushed up into bushy tuft, barely reached up to the big man's chest.

My head was spinning, and I reached out to steady myself. Catching the Knight's hand I fell back against the cool stone wall, safe in the grip of that huge leonine paw.

19

Take down the clocks!
The hour strikes in my heart.

Karl Kraus

I was the very model of immobility. Suspended in space, I breasted the air in a motionless leap. Far below, the little ones shrank from me in terror. They knew I couldn't hurt them since I was fixed immovably to my allotted spot; but still they ran crying behind their mothers' skirts, and this provided me with a little modest entertainment. Years later I would be punished for it, when hooligans in green hats and clerical garb toppled me from my perch, smashed me to smithereens and used me as ammunition for their wheeled catapults adorned with that brutal emblem of fratricide – the black banner with the crimson chalice. Their faith was false. That is why they were mortally afraid of us, my brothers and me. That is why they destroyed us.

All that now remains of me are stories – stories intelligible only to those who are able and willing to listen.

I was part of a system of supports and buttresses and had a vitally important task: to drain water off the roof. Without me the roof would have caved in and the church would have been flooded.

It flowed into me from behind and spouted out in front – a strange occupation, you may say, but I was proud of it. I spewed my water further than any of my stone brethren, of whom I was by far the ugliest.

Since my head and body projected far out into the void, I felt giddy whenever I looked down and so preferred to keep my eyes fixed straight ahead. (Looking up was no less frightening – that is a gift granted to the worthy few – though I could have if I'd wanted to. Don't believe those liars who tell you I couldn't.) Behind me rose a great spire, with two smaller ones on either side: a constant reminder to the city of where it should direct its gaze.

I was responsible for the central section of the north-west side of the roof. The water was fed to me via a stone gutter built into the cornice surmounting the yellow rendered walls. Sometimes a few drops from the south-west side found their way to me. These I gladly accepted and spouted forth in a graceful arc, as prescribed by the French custom.

Yet, however much I rolled my eyes, I never managed to see what I myself looked like. Perhaps it was just as well, for if my two closest neighbours were anything to go by I was anything but handsome. Like them, I guessed I had an elongated body with a spiny dragon-like mane, stunted paws held close to my chest and a pointed tail curling into a diabolical figure six. What I did see were the tips of two long curved horns thrusting out above my upturned snout and a pair of mean fangs protruding from my muzzle.

On that particular morning the rain fell in torrents. The icy water rushed through me, chilling my throat and palate before spurting out of my mouth in an unbroken stream. But the cloud was high, and through the silver skeins of rain I could still see far into the distance. Hearing anything was not so easy, however, thanks to the constant banging of carpenters' hammers and masons' chisels under the roof behind me, which had been going on since cockcrow. On the grass far below knelt a workman chipping away at a large block of dressed stone, one of thousands destined for the new monastery being built next to the church. So engrossed was he in his task that the rest of the world ceased to exist. Seeing this, God devised a punishment. But not for him.

Beyond the lovely orchards on Větrník Hill, where my curious gaze had been fixed for as long as I could remember, they had resumed work on the church. Though it was older than ours it had never had a roof. Now, as it neared completion, the gallows-like jibs of two huge revolving cranes, one slightly shorter than the other, were never still from dawn to dusk – except, of course, on Sundays.

But on that Thursday morning, just as the crowds of labourers and artisans began pouring on to the site, they stopped. At the same moment a herald rode up on a chestnut stallion, bearing a banner with some bold device. Standing in his stirrups, he waved his arm in a grand declamatory fashion. I could not hear his words, but as he spoke there was a sudden commotion around him. Masons, joiners and steeplejacks dashed hither and thither. Some found clean clothes to change into, while others began scrubbing themselves clean in vats of water hastily brought up from the Botič. But there was no time. The herald leapt nimbly from his mount and knelt on the ground with bowed head. As he did so the dark shadow of a horse and rider appeared on the ochre wall of the presbytery, coming round the church from the south-west side. All at once the figure came into view at the foot of the tower and rode on past the first three buttresses of the half-roofed nave. The rider was tall in stature, though with an ungainly stoop. From his shoulders hung a long, heavy dark-green cloak with a dull sheen, probably of velvet. On his head he wore a wide band of silver fox fur that covered most of his hair, which was more grey than brown. He seemed not to notice the throng of workers, who reluctantly stepped aside to make way for the big slow-stepping steed then, suddenly turning pale, prostrated themselves on the dewy turf. The rider looked up – a movement that clearly caused him pain, as his whole body was twisted to one side. A man threw himself to his knees before the horse and clasped his hands together. I recognized him as the master of their masons' guild – and of ours – a stout little fellow all in black with a black hat. He seemed agitated and – if I was not mistaken – contrite as he addressed the rider. The latter appeared to dismiss his pleas with a condescending wave of his hand. The master put his face to the ground in supplication.

Suddenly the hunchback was surrounded by a group of knights

in bright-hued tunics, and for a while he was lost to view. Then out of the throng a horse's head appeared, followed a moment later by a fox-fur band and the rider's furious face. He was heading straight towards me – straight towards our church. No one dared follow him.

A motley caravan was assembling around St Apollinaris', comprised partly of mounted knights, partly of horses either laden with baggage, among which were several red, blue and white litters, or harnessed to carts and wagons of all sizes piled high with equipage. Meanwhile, the rider spurred on his steed and, unperturbed by the bewildered looks from the crowd around the church, cantered off along the path above the orchards and vineyards that fell away steeply to the new Servite Convent on Na Slupi, the pride of the city's carpenters. At one point he reined in his horse and cocked his head to listen – perhaps to the rhythmical hammering from inside our church borne across the slopes on the wind. Then, with renewed intent, he put his horse to a gallop.

The stonecutter directly below me, who had been toiling away since dawn, had seen none of this. The rider came up behind him, looked over his shoulder with a smile on his scarred face and slowly, with a practised yet careful movement, eased his boots out of the stirrups, dismounted and took a few halting steps – he had a pronounced limp. The stonecutter was still unaware of his presence. At that moment the horse whinnied. The man looked up . . . and his mallet came down squarely on his thumb. A murmur went through the crowd on the hill opposite. The stooping figure chuckled. Then, pausing once more to listen to the sounds coming from within the church, he pulled off his fox-fur hat and limped towards the portal.

What took place inside I do not know. The hammering stopped, and moments later the hunchback rushed out again, crimson-faced and hatless, his lameness apparently forgotten. With youthful agility he vaulted on to his horse, but instead of sitting up he remained slumped in the saddle, his face contorted with pain. Then he drove his golden spurs into the animal's flanks and galloped off down the hill through the vineyard like a man possessed, whereupon the company of knights at St Apollinaris' stirred into action like a swarm of wasps and set out to meet him. Meanwhile, the wagons made their way towards the new, less steep road that led down the slope from the chapter house.

The following morning three men – a nobleman and two masons who had been working on our church – were hanged from the crane that stood just a dozen rods distant from us. Even the stonecutter below me looked up from his work and wrung his hands at the sorry spectacle. When it was over he gave a loud sigh, and in the heavy silence I distinctly heard him say, 'Unhappy the master who punishes his most faithful servants!'

'Go on!'

He was bending over me, crushing my shoulders in a bear-like grip. His whole body was shaking, his muscular arms jerking in nervous spasms, his breath rapid and irregular, his huge mouth twisted in a grimace of extreme agitation. Such was his rage I feared he might throttle me or dash my head on the floor. Most terrible of all were his eyes: in contrast to the tension and passion that pulsed through his body, they remained as cold and hard as stone – two lethal shards of jade poised in the sling of his wrath.

'Speak! Tell me more! You talked about a roof. So there was already a roof on the church! What were those people doing there? Why were they punished? Who was that nobleman?'

'What . . . what do you want of me? What do you want me to tell you?'

'Don't you remember? The church being built opposite St Apollinaris' was Karlov, of course. And the man on horseback? He was the long arm of God . . . the instrument of divine will.'

'I had a fit . . . I feel terrible. Leave me alone, I beg you. I know nothing. I don't know what you want me to say.'

'Impossible! You're lying!' Gmünd thundered. 'You know perfectly well why he was executed, whereas I can only guess. The shameful injustice of it! Him of all people! Oh, I could weep! Can there ever have been a more tragic misunderstanding?'

'If I've been rambling I apologize. It's these fits that come over me – I've had them since I was a child. Please, just leave me alone.'

'You'll get no more out of him,' came a voice behind him. It was Prunslik.

Gmünd released his grip. Slowly I pulled myself up and straightened my crumpled coat. Still looking daggers at me, the titan took a step back. Then with a weary shrug he said, 'I'm sorry. I forgot myself. I got carried away by your story. It's amazing to think you know about those gargoyles.'

'About what?'

'The Karlov gargoyles. You see, they were only there for a short time before the Hussite hordes destroyed them. Being superstitious, the soldiers found those wonderful monsters absolutely terrifying. So they started shooting at them – dragon, demon, wild beast, human sinner . . . every one. All they had to do was break them off. Gravity did the rest. On hitting the ground they smashed into a thousand pieces, which our courageous Calixtins were careful to bury in five different places, to prevent their arch-rivals from discovering them and taking revenge.'

'I don't know anything about it. I want to go home. I'm not well.'

'Wait! Come up into the roof with us, and it will all come back to you. You won't regret it – I shall reward you well.'

'I doubt I'll be able to tell you anything. I'm exhausted. If you want I can accompany you – but not up to the roof, please. Don't ask that of me. I'm terrified of heights. Besides, it's not allowed. And why isn't there anyone from the police with you today?'

Slipping past him, I ran to the exit and pulled at the heavy door. As it swung to behind me I heard Gmünd's booming voice telling me to be on duty tomorrow at the same time. For once I felt like refusing, but at that moment all I wanted was my bed in the blue room at the Hotel Bouvines – a bed I owed to the largesse of my admirable benefactor.

*

The hole in Resslova Ulice – a gaping wound in the body of a city already crying out to the overcast heavens – was beginning to attract attention. Passers-by paused to peer into it, some tossing in a coin and listening to gauge how deep it was. Motorists wondered how long they would have to endure delays in the Charles Square area. Anyone bold enough to slip under the outer cordon and approach the second circle of tape at the edge of the crater was immediately aware of a powerful bittersweet smell that poisoned the surrounding air. In the cool depths of the pit the fruit decayed slowly, so it was some days before the process of decomposition reached its peak. By then the stench was overwhelming: the rotten mangoes, oranges and peaches, mixed with the putrefying irises, freesias and cyclamens made a noxious cocktail.

All attempts to salvage the buried lorry not only failed but increased the risk of further subsidence. The day after the accident a team of geologists and archaeologists was called in to carry out an underground survey. They discovered a series of caverns extending under a narrow strip of land from the site of the old church and monastery of St Charles Borromaeus and the Church of St Václav right down to the Monastery of Emmaus at the south end of Charles Square. The evening papers, sensing a good scandal, devoted entire pages to the affair, describing the cavities as prehistoric caves that had been converted into cellars some time during the Middle Ages and then, after the general dissolution of churches and monasteries in the eighteenth century, entirely forgotten.

The week wore on, and the hole continued to emit its noisome fumes. Some speleologists descended on ropes to explore its depths and returned from the underworld with news that astonished the people of Prague and their lawfully elected representatives. Under the three churches named in the papers they found a huge crypt, about two hundred yards long, thirty yards wide and several storeys deep, containing at least three hundred bricked-in cells. They were unable to discover what lay concealed inside those miniature vaults sealed in eternal darkness. The historians and archaeologists, however, agreed that it was probably a vast underground burial site and ossuary used by monks of the Order of the Cross from the Monastery of St Peter and St Paul and their brothers from the Benedictine foundation at Emmaus. Expecting to uncover a mass of priceless human remains, artefacts and other historical data, they called for a thorough investigation of the crypt.

But the Roads Department would not hear of it. The safety of dozens if not hundreds of pedestrians and motorists was at risk, they argued, since the entire west side of Charles Square might subside at any moment, and a fate similar to that of the fruit lorry could befall any number of buildings in the vicinity, including several belonging to the Czech Technical University. The safety of the public was paramount, they claimed, backing up their case with various apocalyptic scenarios. They called for a solution that was both speedy and effective – one that would solve the problem of road subsidence once and for all. The best and quickest remedy, they decided, was to forget about excavation and fill in all the underground cavities with concrete.

One group of architects protested at this crude and drastic measure, suspecting it had been pushed through by the so-called 'concrete lobby'. Another, an architects' cooperative, suggested a more gradualist and sensitive approach: give the archaeologists time to exhume the bodies and recover any valuable artefacts, then, assuming the cellars were not found to be of any great historical value (in which case they would be protected by law anyway), convert the space into a large underground car-park that would be equipped with heat collectors to exploit the thermal springs known to exist below the site.

One of the most vocal proponents of this second scheme was none other than Peter Zahir. I was quite taken aback to see his name among the signatories to an open letter addressed to the council, which also appeared in the press, calling for a rational approach. I was even more surprised to read, in a later evening edition, that the advocates of the more drastic 'concrete' plan had chosen as their leader the elusive Barnabáš.

I took the side of the moderates, since their proposal did not rule out possible further measures and was open to amendment. No doubt I was also influenced by the fact that I knew Zahir personally. I even considered telephoning him and offering my support but was prevented from doing so by Superintendent Olejar. The day after that painful visit to Karlov he summoned me to his office and told me I was to work with Inspector Junek on a new assignment: protecting Barnabáš. I was nonplussed. Interrupting him in mid-sentence, I told him I could not accept the job since I disagreed with Barnabáš' views, adding in an access of self-criticism that my own incompetence had already cost one human life. I also told him how I had lost Zahir that day near St Stephen's, even admitting, to press home my point, that he had fired me soon afterwards.

I might have known it was useless to argue with a cop like Olejar. He wouldn't take no for an answer, said my moonlighting for Zahir was no concern of his, and as for the Pendelmanová case I must be aware that it had never been closed, just deferred, so I shouldn't lose any sleep on that account. I was to stay in Prague, await instructions and be available for any further assignments. The Superintendent promised to fix me up with a room at the police hostel by the end of the month. He filled in a chit entitling me to pick up a two-way radio from the police store; then, after giving me a penetrating look, he added a pistol, a holster and twenty rounds of ammunition. Faced with such trust, which I was sure I did not deserve, I finally acquiesced.

The pistol was large and heavy, and the fat leather holster dug unpleasantly into my ribs. When I went to the store to collect it (together with the two-way radio and an identity badge) I felt like a little boy planning a game of cops-and-robbers. Fortunately the telltale bulge was safely concealed by the overcoat I'd inherited from old Pendelman. I had carried a firearm before, but it had been far smaller and less dangerous-looking. I had worn it on the back of my belt and hardly been aware of it – much less of the possibility of actually using it. But this chunky brute never let me forget its ominous presence.

I tried out the radio and heard Junek's voice. Even over the crackle and static I could tell he was less than delighted to be working with me again. As usual, he complained, no one had told him anything until the last minute. How we were going to operate as a team he could not imagine. I'm sure he would have slammed down the receiver if his radio had had one to slam. With a silent prayer that it would never ring, I slipped my own device into my pocket.

Events had held me up, and I was going to be late for my meeting with Gmünd. All the same, I decided to take a detour via Albertov, which meant that instead of ten minutes it would take me forty-five. Was I just being contrary? Or was it simply the fact that it had started to snow – the third fall this autumn?

Passing the Church of the Annunciation I turned into Horská Ulice, then wandered among the various departments of the Faculty of Medicine and Natural Sciences. Once or twice I paused to listen to the wind, blowing now from the north, now from the west with a fearsome roar, as if the purist architects of the early twentieth century had fitted their buildings with an ingenious apparatus for amplifying all the moans and groans produced inside them. Seeking shelter from the blizzard, I headed towards the Purkyně Institute with its rotunda-like wing that always reminded me of an oratory. As it came into view I stopped and stared. In striking contrast with the blanket of white covering the conical roof, sills and pavement, the five large windows on the first floor and ten smaller ones above them had been completely blacked out with dark drapes, transforming the rotunda into a kind of black lighthouse. A lighthouse with no light – a fitting symbol for a blind science that dares to probe into the mystery of life. I had no idea what kind of rituals were enacted behind those sightless windows but recalled with a shudder another temple dedicated to other scientific deities (its blue plaster walls now lost in flurries of snowflakes) and, quickening my pace, made for the foot of the Albertov Steps.

I had not gone far, however, before I stopped in my tracks. Just beyond the junction of Albertov and Votočkova, under the gnarled fingers of a weeping willow overhanging the pavement, stood a little old lady in a long coat, with large spectacles and a brown shopping bag. She was peering intently through the fence at a flower bed in the garden of experimental biology. A single glance sufficed to tell me what it was that had so caught her attention. Poking through the snow were the spikes of some strange spadiciform plant. Their stems – from the base right up to the cluster of unsightly half-eaten fruit at their crown – were yellowy-orange tinged with blue. The snow between the plants had been trampled down. Some tracks – hoofprints of a kind I had never seen before – led towards the fence. They were similar to those of a horse, that is to say not cloven, though noticeably smaller. Oddest of all, instead of the rounded front of a horse's hoof, these tapered to an ogive-shaped arch. Luckily the hooves were not shod. What kind of luck would such a horseshoe bring?

20

> We do not know very much of the future
> Except that from generation to generation
> The same things happen again and again.
> Men learn little from others' experience.
>
> T.S. Eliot

He was leaning against the door frame in the church porch, neither inside nor out, smoking. As I walked up he opened the door for me and threw his cigar into the snow. I thought he looked unusually penitent.

'I'm glad you've come . . . and didn't let yesterday scare you off.' The heavy door of Karlov Church had swung shut behind us. 'I owe you an apology. It was quite inexcusable, losing my self-control like that. You have every right to think the worst of me.'

'I think no such thing, but I must say you did rather frighten me.' We were walking down the octagonal nave – it was far too cold to sit.

'I feel ashamed mainly for your sake. You will have noticed that I am a man of some vanity, who prides himself on his ability to win people over without recourse to threats or violence. But this was a matter of tremendous importance to me. I'd give anything to find out the truth. Yet you refused to tell me.'

'You almost strangled me. I wouldn't have been much use to you as a corpse.'

'Don't remind me, please. And forgive me. I'm even sorrier than you are, believe me.'

'I would have forgiven you yesterday, but as far as I know you didn't come home all night. To the hotel, I mean.'

'Raymond and I were on one of our regular field trips. Do I look tired? If I do it's your fault. It was you who prompted us to take action. Things are moving forward.'

'What do you mean?'

'Do you remember what you told me yesterday? There, beside that pillar?'

'Only very vaguely. You don't mean to say it's been of some use to you? It was probably a lot of nonsense. I've no idea what I said.'

'You may be right there: you *have no idea* how important you are to us.'

'Us? Why the plural again? Do you mean you and Prunslik?'

'Essentially, yes. And possibly someone else. I'll explain some other time.'

'How do you know I didn't make it all up? You're obviously fascinated by this church and its history. I might have decided to exploit the situation for my own gain. For money, say.'

'Or the roof over your head.'

'Of course. I am very much indebted to you. Rambling on about the past of various New Town churches would be a way of showing my gratitude – though perhaps not the most obvious one. But I remember that day in St Stephen's you had the same look on your face. And that other time in the Annunciation, when I came over all peculiar and started spouting gibberish, Prunslik stopped playing the fool for once and wrote down every word I said.'

'I admit you might have had a motive for deceiving us. But I know you well enough to say you're no con man.'

'I can't imagine what makes you so sure of that.'

'There are still a lot of things you cannot imagine. But don't let that worry you – all will be revealed in the fullness of time. As for whether your stories are true or not, what makes you think I have no means of verifying them? Not all of them, of course. But some at least.'

'You mean there is someone else you consult? Someone similarly afflicted?'

'I prefer the word *endowed*. But let's suppose there is such a person. We live in an age of information. Information is ten times more valuable if it is verified. Every ignoramus knows that – even journalists.'

'Who is your other source? Do I know him? Where do you keep him? In a cellar somewhere? In a stone tower?'

'Your sarcasm distresses me, Květoslav. I thought I had just convinced you that violence is not in my nature. Do I owe you another apology?'

'Of course not. But you can't blame me for wanting to be careful. You ask me for information. Can't I ask the same of you? You say violence is not in your nature. What *is* your nature? Who are you?'

'Let us say I am a servant.'

'You don't expect me to believe that! You're a very influential man and probably quite a powerful one, too. You are also highly persuasive and not averse to using disreputable methods. Forgive me for saying so, but I strongly suspect that for some time now you've been bribing officials in the Town Hall and maybe in the police, too. It's not a pleasant thing to say, but I have to say it.'

'Don't worry, you're right anyway. I really did buy a few people off. Only the weaklings, of course. Strong men can't be bought. They must be fooled.'

'I appreciate your frankness. And now it's my turn to be frank: I am disappointed in you.'

'Oh, come on! Surely you didn't have any illusions about us?'

'It may surprise you, but, yes, I did. Not about Prunslik, of course. He's a harmless crackpot – either that or a dangerous maniac. But until yesterday I had a higher opinion of you.'

'I'm sorry to hear that,' said Gmünd with a shrug, before adding with a mischievous grin, 'I realize you would like to know as much about me as possible, especially now you're back in the police. Know your man, as they say. I am a servant, as I told you. I serve. I can say no more than that.'

'Who do you serve?'

Gmünd was once again sombre. 'I understand your indignation and appreciate your idealism. But you must realize that I, too, have an ideal – even sinners have ideals. Mine is almost certainly unattainable, but as you will discover with your own eyes and ears – and perhaps to your own cost – I am doing everything in my power to get as close to it as possible.'

'You're a fanatic.'

'I don't take that as an insult.'

'Fanaticism is a very dangerous thing.'

'But are you sure you know it when you see it? I quite agree, though: fanaticism is dangerous. We must be on our guard against it. We must resist it whatever the cost. But that resistance can itself easily turn into fanaticism. Does it then remain a just cause? I believe it does.'

'Are you telling me that what you are doing is a kind of fanatical resistance against a certain world view?'

'In a way, yes. Though I fear people like Olejar might not see it like that.'

'So it's another case of the end justifying the means. The noblest of aims justify the basest of methods. You don't really believe that, do you?'

'If I didn't I wouldn't be doing this, would I? My adversary may call it baseness. I call it defending certain values. We'll never agree. I'm not a democrat. I don't have to agree with everybody.'

'You're not a democrat? Don't say that too loudly.'

'Why not? I thought it was back in fashion.'

'What are you then?'

'I told you. I'm a servant. Though you, Květoslav, may have a rather more romantic picture of me. The mysterious stranger and so on.'

'I must confess I do. Or did. I have a nasty feeling that particular illusion is beginning to crumble. "The mysterious stranger." It sounds like something out of a penny-dreadful. And so does your Heptecclesion. What is it exactly?'

'The Heptecclesion? Any one of a hundred different things.'

'The first being?'

'A state of mind.'

'What a cliché! I'd have expected better from you.'

'An apposite cliché, none the less.'

'And I'm supposed to get into that state of mind?'

'Put simply, yes.'

'So I'm to ignore my own common sense and join your side?'

He laughed. 'It's common sense that will guide you there. Sense . . . and sensibility. Wait and see. Though, in fact, a part of you is on our side already.'

'In that case you know more about me than I do myself. What if you're mistaken?'

'I am not mistaken.'

'What if I disappoint you?'

'Do you want to disappoint me?'

'Want to? How could I? But if I have no choice . . . Mr Gmünd, I owe you a lot. Yet there will come a time, whether I like it or not, when my conscience will rebel against you and your questionable schemes. I'm not looking forward to it. But I know it's bound to happen.'

'So do I. It will be an interesting contest.'

'And a dangerous one?'

'Probably. Aren't you attracted by danger?'

'Not in the least. I'm hardly a desperado.'

'So you're not coming up with me?'

'Up? Up where?'

'A place between Heaven and earth. I want you to go up into the roof with me, under the dome.'

'I will do no such thing. What on earth would I do up there?'

'The same as you did yesterday down here. You would look into those places . . . the places you sometimes visit. And talk about them. And I would listen.'

'No, I'm sorry. I've finished with all that. It makes me ill. Anyway, I'm afraid of heights.'

'Really? What about when you sprinted up to the top of St Apollinaris' bell-tower? Weren't you afraid then?'

'Who told you about that?'

'Olejar.'

'You weren't there yourself, by any chance? You or Prunslik?'

'Let's change the subject. You were asking about the Heptecclesion. I'm glad the word arouses your curiosity. That's a positive sign. What exactly would you like to know?'

'It refers to seven Gothic churches, right?'

'At the most simple level, yes. Seven Gothic churches.'

'The most important of which are Karlov and St Stephen's. Am I right?'

'Most important? I wouldn't say that. They are simply two-sevenths.'

'What about the others? Apollinaris', Emmaus, the Annunciation on Na Slupi . . . and St Catherine's.'

'Perfectly correct.'

'But the only original bit of St Catherine's is the tower! The rest is Baroque. What's St Catherine's got to do with your beloved Gothic?'

'A ghastly eyesore, isn't it?'

'Don't dodge the question. How can you count a tower as a whole church?'

'That bothers you, does it?'

'Of course it bothers me. It's no longer the building it was intended to be.'

'Well, that can be put to rights, can't it? You know yourself what the Church of the Annunciation looked like in the nineteenth century – and Apollinaris'. Not to mention these walls you see around you. What about Our Lady of the Snows? That was no more than a shell – just like Sázava Abbey today. St Catherine's still has a magnificent presbytery. All it needs is sensitive restoration in the Gothic style. If it was up to me I'd rebuild the nave as well. I certainly have no intention of depriving the city of any of its beautiful Gothic towers.'

'Neo-Gothic, you mean.'

'Don't be absurd! Half of St Vitus' is new, and who cares? It's the way Arras and Parler wanted it. What does it matter that the building was completed by our grandparents and not our distant ancestors? The important thing is to respect that first vision, that original intent. If we are not to belittle the achievements of our forefathers, if we are not to mock the age they lived in – without which ours would not exist – we must submit to their taste. We must have the humility to respect their wishes. We must go back. We must about-turn and fix our gaze on the past. Otherwise we perish.'

'With all due respect, isn't it a bit much to talk about perishing just because a few Gothic churches have been rebuilt as a result of changing tastes?'

'A bit much, you say? Listen, it started with the Renaissance, when a few impious individuals, instead of clasping their hands in prayer, had the audacity to hold them up to their eyes as a frame for viewing the world. But they forgot to look up to Heaven. They saw only what was right in front of them: their fellow men, in other words, with all their faults and follies, just as the Lord created them. Which is why their buildings are so unspeakable. Preposterous hovels for pompous fops whose only concern was how they looked in their new clothes – and how other people looked without theirs. Ugh! Doesn't it remind you of our own age? *Plus ça change . . .* In the Baroque, fashion at least paid lip service to modesty by attempting to conceal more than it revealed. But people remained as arrogant as ever – and worst of all were the architects. Wherever they saw an elegant Gothic tower they would cap it with a bulbous onion as crass and empty as their own heads. They knocked holes in ancient, hallowed walls to make room for their fancy windows. They had no right! You don't have to go far for an example of their vilest excesses. Just look at these ghastly oval windows, gaping like suppurating wounds in a sick man's body. Or consider the ground plans of Baroque buildings: the more absurdly elaborate they were, the more they were admired. Not satisfied with squares, circles, rectangles and octagons, they had to add ellipses and stars and horrible rounded corners. The kings of kitsch, that's what I call those Erlachs and Dienzenhofers. Charlatans, the lot of them!'

'I quite agree. We have exactly the same taste. But what about the seventh church? Which is it? St Martin's? St Henry's? St Peter's?'

'You really don't know?'

'How should I know? On several occasions you've talked about seven churches, and I keep following you around from one to another listening to how you plan to rebuild them. But so far I only know six of them.'

'Wouldn't it be better if you found out for yourself, Květoslav? That shouldn't be beyond you. You are a historian, after all.'

'A dropped-out historian.'

'Even better. You are not yet sated with knowledge.'

'Give me a lead.'

'A lead? Are you a dog?'

'A clue. I don't know what I am. Hardly a historian. Not a policeman either.'

'Dogs need masters.'

'So do I. But where can I find one?'

'Well, you're in a church. Your master is here.'

'Where? Where is he?'

'You asked for a clue – a *lead*. Here's one. Do you know Vincenc Morstadt's etchings of Prague? The Stag Moat at the castle, the old Chain Bridge, the views of Malá Strana?'

'Of course. Everyone knows them.'

'How about his picture of St Stephen's?'

'Wait a minute . . . that rings a bell. It's a view of the back of the church, isn't it? Of the presbytery.'

'Correct. As seen from the south-east. In my opinion it's one of Morstadt's most satisfying works. He wasn't quite an artist of European stature, but as historical documents his pictures are invaluable.

Most of his subjects don't get more than a rather superficial, postcardy treatment – I'm thinking of his Old Town Hall, Powder Tower, St Vitus' Cathedral and Charles Bridge. But that view of St Stephen's is different. It's not just the unusual angle. There's something indefinable about it, something inexplicable . . . as if it contained a mystery, even a secret. The church itself is not the most important thing in the picture: in the right foreground we can see the round chapel of St Longine; to its left is the square bell-tower; and on the far left the Chapel of All Saints. In the middle of the picture is a sort of horizontal beam with three planks resting on it – some kind of ramp perhaps. I've no idea why it's there, but it immediately gives the scene a whole new dimension – a feeling of domesticity, even of intimacy. It's as if you were looking into a family's backyard: at any moment father will come out with his hammer and start banging away at the planks.'

'Yes, as far as I remember it does seem more like a domestic scene.'

'The effect is heightened by four figures – a mother and child on the grass in front of the rotunda, a man with a hat and a woman standing a little way off by the chapel. Four people on a church green, with the suggestion of a graveyard behind them. That's not much by Morstadt's standards – his scenes are generally crowded with figures. But this is a different sort of space. The green behind St Stephen's, though still within the New Town walls, is depicted as a quasi-rural setting with an almost bucolic charm. The artist's virtuosity is evident in the way the buildings are arranged within the composition. This, combined with perspective, allows him to play with their heights and create a diagonal from the top left corner of the picture to the bottom right, thus adding depth to the space. In that lower right corner there is another, fifth building. It's very far away so it appears to be the smallest of all. Even so, its tall tower is clearly visible. A muddy path leads down to it, past St Longine's chapel, towards the north-west. And that building is . . . What do you think?'

'A tall tower . . . and the path leads north west, so . . . The only place that comes to mind is the New Town Hall on the Cattle Market.'

'Right!'

'But I'm looking for a church!'

'Don't be hasty, Květoslav, or you'll never follow my clues. By the way, I still haven't told what for me is the most beautiful thing about Morstadt's picture. It's not the skill with which he documented the condition of a particular set of buildings at a particular point in time. It's the sense of place, the way he rendered the surroundings of those sacred buildings: the greensward, the well-trodden path, the gardens with their picket fences, a scattering of low cottages. I repeat, *low* cottages. And out of this setting rise four superb buildings: chapel, rotunda, bell-tower and, dwarfing them all, the church itself. They are visible for miles around – both catching and captivating the eye. People who enter such buildings, or simply walk past them, cannot be bad. That beauty alone must banish the evil in them. Beauty has that power, believe me. What finer sight can there be than a church growing straight out of the green, the stone pushing forth from the ground where it has lain since time immemorial? A church like the Holy Spirit in the Old Town was lucky enough to keep its green apron (though its luck didn't extend to its tower, which some Baroque vandal disfigured with a Saracen turban). Only the architecture of the Middle Ages is great, Květoslav; only Gothic architecture is *moral*. Human morality and architectural morality go hand in hand. If life on earth is to be preserved we must never again allow our holy places to be overshadowed by the beastly boxes that pass as buildings in the temporal world, as was the fate of so many of our churches, including those you mention – St Martin's, St Peter's and St Henry's. A town that allows its churches to be hemmed in by banks and office blocks deserves to languish in the custody of speculators and bureaucrats! It is a crime to put such places next to the Lord's abode! It is a sin to play God and build higher than His spires!'

'It's not against the law.'

'Then I will change the law! God willing, I'll see to it that St Stephen's and the other churches once again enjoy the right they were granted by their founders: the right to reign supreme over the New Town of Prague.'

'So that's your clue, is it? I guessed St Stephen's was one of the Heptecclesion a long time ago.'

'Don't be childish, Květoslav. This isn't a game of twenty questions. Just think about what I've told you and you'll soon work out which the seventh church is. Now before I go I'll ask you one more time. Will you come up to the roof with me?'

'No, I can't. I'm sorry.'

'Are you afraid of me?'

'Yes . . . and of myself.'

'And nothing can overcome that fear? Not even curiosity?'

'I don't want to know what's up there. So please stop trying to persuade me.'

'Are you afraid of finding out something about yourself? But isn't that just what you need, Květoslav? To find yourself? Isn't it time you did?'

'Perhaps that's what I'm afraid of. Yes, I'm a coward. But it's a fear I know I'll never overcome.'

'That's a pity. Until we meet again, then.'

With that he left me.

21

Like faltering hooves
A death-knell tolled

Oldřich Mikulášek

In first two weeks of Advent the heavens opened. Torrents of dark brown sludge poured down Žitná and Ječná into Charles Square, inundating the park like a spring flood. Marooned in deep puddles, the black trunks of the acacias cast eerily distorted reflections in the almost continuous lake. A bank of sticky mud piled up against the shrubbery on the lower side of the park, creating two large ponds that made the area impassable for anyone not equipped with rubber boots. And still the rain came down in ever-thicker sheets, as if St Peter were trying to bring down the curtain on the shameful burlesque that was Prague at the close of the twentieth century.

The straight thoroughfare formed by Ječná and Resslova, where there was nothing to impede the flow, became a regular river. When the waters abated the hole in the road was revealed to be twice as large as it had been. Since the cellars were now flooded the putrid stench had become less overpowering, but the cones and tape marking off the scene of the accident, along with all the warning signs and flashing orange lights, had disappeared into the pit. Drivers approaching the spot had no idea of the danger ahead. Confronted suddenly with a gaping hole in the asphalt, they simply drove up on to the pavement and carried on. Before the police got round to closing the street an impatient taxi driver tried to beat the tailback by driving round the other side of the hole, over the pavement in front of the Church of Cyril and Methodius, and paid dearly for his impudence. Having just managed to squeeze his battered Volkswagen past the lip of the crater, the buffoon stopped to gesticulate triumphantly at the drivers stuck in the queue on the other side of the road, gloating all over his porcine countenance. At that moment the car dropped out of sight. In its place a geyser of brown water spewed out on to the road. Not only had the taxi disappeared, a section of pavement below the church had also been swallowed up by the insatiable hole. Part of the church wall had gone, too, leaving a three-foot gap in the brickwork – a handy niche for a small statue.

I learnt all this from Zahir, who at the time had been measuring the exact location of the hole with a team of surveyors. He sounded very gloomy over the phone, fearing that Barnabáš and his cronies would seize on the incident as further proof that their 'concrete' solution was the right one.

The next day the taxi was winched out by a fire service crane. It had not sunk in as far as the fruit lorry, its fall having been arrested by one of the cellar's Gothic arches. The car was full of water, but there was no sign of the driver. Either he had fallen out or managed to free himself, only to sink even deeper and drown in the murky depths. Now the whole street was closed in both directions to all but police and Roads Department vehicles.

Zahir and I met by the hole. I almost didn't recognize him. He looked even more miserable than he had sounded on the phone. He told me there had been a council meeting the night before, at which the 'quick-and-easy' option had been virtually approved. As he hobbled round the barrier on his crutches like a Gulf War veteran, I noticed that his black moustache, which normally bristled like a shoe-brush, now hung limply from his nose, looking as if it might drip on to his lapels at any moment.

'It's a punishment,' he muttered, turning on me his bloodshot sleepless eyes. 'A punishment for that housing estate. I knew something was going to happen. I've known it for years – felt it in my bones. The first punishment was when they crippled me. The second was when Rozeta slammed down the phone on me. No woman's ever treated me like that! But they haven't heard the last of me!'

I wasn't sure what these quixotic ramblings were all about and tried to reassure him by saying he would be walking normally again in a couple of months. I was surprised how distraught he seemed – more so than after the attempt on his life – at what was no more than a professional and personal setback. He obviously needed to talk, so we slowly made our way to Wenceslas Arcade and found a seat in a cheerless, overlit bar with large plate-glass windows in full view of all the passers-by. This didn't seem to bother Zahir, who at once launched into his story.

He began with Rozeta. One innocent phone call was all it had taken to antagonize her. He couldn't understand it – on the one occasion they had met she had been perfectly pleasant. Hoping to impress her, he had begun telling her about his work and made a point of repeating several times that he was an architect. She had asked tersely what buildings he had worked on. Caught off-guard, he had mentioned various projects he had been involved in. Without another word she had let out a peal of shrill, hysterical laughter and hung up. I said I also found her difficult to deal with – the lovely creature was as much a mystery to me as she was to him. The only person who knew how to handle her was the Knight of Lübeck, Matthias Gmünd. At that Zahir lapsed even deeper into melancholy. Then he took a big gulp of his drink and started to tell me about his past.

For years, he said, he and Barnabáš had been bitter rivals. But it had not always been so. Fifteen years ago they had been in the same firm, working with architects from other companies on various big housing projects. One day someone came up with a flawed design. The project went ahead, but some time after the building was finished people started dying. The design team responsible for the project had been covering for each other ever since. To this day no one had spoken out, even though they could no longer be sued thanks to the statute of limitation.

I found myself looking at a changed man. Gone was the charm, the confidence, the *savoir vivre*. Little had I suspected that Zahir's past held such a dark secret. Now, as he drained his fourth liqueur, he seemed more depressed than ever. I asked him to tell me more about that flawed design, and with a surprising lack of embarrassment he proceeded to do so.

The project in question had been an estate of prefabricated residential blocks in the suburb of Opatov. One of the architects had specified a new fire-retarding system using a material manufactured by a firm whose managing director was a friend of Barnabáš. It worked well enough, until after a while people in the block where this material had been used started dying of cancer. Many of them were children.

'That block's still standing,' he went on in an almost inaudible whisper, his eyes boring into the formica bar top. People were no longer dying there, since the fire-retarding material was by now more or less inert. But in the 1980s their experiment had cost the lives of nineteen people, eleven of them children. Plenty of people in the construction business knew of the affair but they were forbidden to talk about it. The conspiracy of silence included not only the culprits themselves but the officials who had approved the scheme. Some of them, Zahir hinted, I might even have known. In an attempt to salve their consciences the individuals concerned began avoiding the others, while taking every opportunity to blame them behind their backs. Barnabáš and Zahir were by no means the only two who came to resent each other. First they went their separate ways and found new jobs; then they started competing with each other. Zahir, the younger of the two, was more successful in terms of the number of commissions he won. Barnabáš, on the other hand, used his senior administrative position to gain power and influence. Both tried to forget about the faulty design and its consequences, as did all their co-perpetrators. For one of them the guilt was too much. One autumn evening in 1987 he walked off down the railway line beyond Smíchov station, lay down on the track under a striped eiderdown and fell asleep. He never woke up. A locomotive shunting back from the depot went right over him.

'That anonymous letter I got,' Zahir concluded his mournful monologue, 'is proof that someone out there knows. And that someone is out to get us.'

I recalled the anonymous letters with their childish drawings of unfinished houses without roofs. Now I understood. The houses were not missing anything. They did have roofs – strange roofs you couldn't draw. Flat roofs. Those little houses were prefabricated blocks of flats.

I accompanied the Knight of Lübeck on three more occasions. But something had changed. Gone was the feeling of trust and friendship; instead, the atmosphere between us became tense and oppressive. The cause of Gmünd's gloom was no longer the parlous state of the buildings we visited but my reluctance to fall into a trance and start talking – at least that is what I assumed. I took great care not to go too close to the ancient church walls and to touch only what was evidently new.

The Church of Emmaus, dedicated to the Holy Virgin and the Saints Jerome, Adalbert, Prokopios, Cyril and Methodius, was consecrated in 1372 in the presence of the Emperor Charles. The original Gothic building with its three naves and three choirs had long since lost the austere beauty of its intersecting verticals and horizontals, having throughout its long history been subjected to a series of painful alterations. The most lamentable of these was a thoroughgoing Baroque reconstruction in the seventeenth century, which added the two massive towers it had been lacking; these, however, were 'finished off' early the following century with a pair of pot-bellied kohlrabis that entirely ruined the masculine character of a building hitherto perfectly suited to the needs of the Croatian Benedictine monks who used it and gave it the look of a buxom fishwife calling down damnation upon the brothers' heads. Towards the end of the nineteenth century monks from Benedictbeuern attempted to give it back its Gothic appearance, but in a Bavarian rather than a native Bohemian style. With its two over-ornate spires and exaggeratedly high triangular gable, it now resembled at best a fortified city gate, at worst a superior covered market. In February 1945 it was bombed by Allied planes (one could hardly expect Americans to know the difference between a medieval church and an arms factory), and its present, rather provisional appearance – glass concrete gable; two curving crossed spires with gilded tips – is the result of the most recent renovation dating from the 1960s.

With the help of a professional photographer Gmünd compiled a pictorial documentation of the interior, in particular the presbytery windows and the mouldings on their jambs (concave rather than simply angled) which, alongside those of St Stephen's, St Apollinaris' and the Annunciation, are an example of High Gothic stonework at its most delicate. Never have function and ornament been so felicitously united; never has architecture attained such perfection.

At the end of my turn of duty I would often drop in at Emmaus and spend some time with Gmünd. The Superintendent's orders were that we should guard Barnabáš twelve hours a day each under the command of Inspector Junek. But since Junek didn't trust me he generally stayed on to keep a watchful eye on the architect with me. Having decided to work all the night shifts himself he got very little sleep and was in a constant state of exhaustion. He walked round like a zombie – a zombie with its finger on the trigger. I kept out his way as much as possible, marvelling from a safe distance at his pig-headed persistence and unshakeable belief in his abilities as a policeman. Twice I caught him taking a nap in our car near the hole in Resslova, which had now become a construction site. If Olejar had found out he would have fired him on the spot. I think he knew Junek was angling for his job, and dereliction of duty would have given him the perfect excuse to get rid of an over-ambitious subordinate. But he didn't find out, and events took a different turn.

On Wednesday morning, a week after the end of the December thaw, I was in the blue room at the hotel when the telephone rang. A man whose voice I did not recognize told me he had an urgent message from Olejar. I was to go to Resslova at once: Barnabáš was waiting for me at the pit, alone; Inspector Junek had been involved in a fight during the night and was now in hospital with head injuries. Olejar would send someone over within an hour, but as I lived closest I was to go there right away. I thought of that morning when I had been roused from my sleep by the doorbell in Mrs Pendelmanová's flat. Rude early morning awakenings were the kind of nasty surprise the twentieth century had taught us to expect.

Ten minutes later I was in Resslova. It was very cold, just a degree or two above zero. All around was silence. Even the wind, which for days had been battering the hotel windows, seemed to be holding its breath. The whole street was still closed and void of traffic, save for a cluster of dormant construction vehicles – mobile crane, mixer truck, roller, asphalt laying machine – parked by the steps of St Václav's Church. A red-and-white traffic cone had been placed, slightly askew, over the freshly asphalted hole. Beneath it, in the course of the last week, all those precious archaeological finds and tombs and mummified monks had been consigned to oblivion, lost for ever under a massive, impenetrable mesh of iron rods and girders filled with concrete. About twenty yards up the street towards the square stood a white Škoda. Though it was unmarked, I guessed from its plates it was a police car. There was no one at the wheel.

I expected Barnabáš to appear round the corner at any moment – after all, he was supposed to be waiting for me. The minutes ticked by. Everything seemed frozen in time: the scraps of paper and cigarette butts in the gutter; the few acacia leaves blown down from the park. I paced back and forth across the street, stopping frequently to look at my watch.

A sudden noise made me stop in mid-stride. At first I heard a faint rhythmical clanking accompanied by a rush of water. Then the sounds grew louder and began overlapping and reverberating in my head. I turned round in confusion, half expecting to see another flood pouring down Ječna towards the river. There was no water in sight, nor any sign of a water-driven machine.

But I certainly heard it. It was a quite distinctive sound – and definitely mechanical. A wooden wheel, perhaps? A water wheel? A mill? Two mills, by the sound of it. At least two.

Where on earth was it coming from? I clapped my frozen palms to my ears. I must be hallucinating. How could there possibly be a water-wheel anywhere near the Church of Cyril and Methodius? The closest there had ever been a mill to this spot was under the old water tower by the river, where the Manes building now stands. In the 1920s the dilapidated sixteenth-century structure had been pulled down to make way for the functionalist gallery. In a nice irony, this proved the salvation of the old stone tower, since the architect decided to incorporate it into his ultra-modern design. I could see them in my mind's eye: two mills under a single, high slate roof reaching halfway up the hundred and fifty-foot tower . . .

Suddenly the traffic cone moved. I blinked hard. Surely my eyes were playing tricks on me. But, no, it *had* moved. Before it had been leaning to the right. Now it was tilted to the left. What could have moved it? Certainly not the wind, as the air was perfectly still. Then as I looked it tipped back to its original position.

I went closer and knelt down on the fresh asphalt beside the red-and-white cone. On the white stripe was a crude child-like drawing of three little devils shaking their forks. And as I looked the whole cone started shaking. There was something inside it . . . something alive. I got down on my belly and peered through the crack under the red plastic base but could see nothing. The asphalt was pleasantly warm. For a split-second, as I lay there in the deserted street, I felt like closing my eyes and letting the blissful silence lull me to sleep.

Then the cone tilted again and I found myself looking into a pair of eyes. Hidden under that grotesque dunce's hat was a human face.

I leapt to my feet, grabbed the cone with both hands and pulled. There was a faint groan as the plastic slipped out of my grip. I took hold of it again, this time at the base, and tugged. In absurd moments we think of the most absurd things: I imagined myself as the old man in the fairy-tale struggling to pull up a turnip. But in my case the struggle was brief. The hat came off, revealing an even more fantastic tuber.

It was Barnabáš. He was buried up to the neck in concrete and asphalt and to all appearances still alive. His face looked like an overgrown tomato. It was scratched and scorched and covered in grey and black scabs of dried cement and tar. The poor fellow had lost consciousness and, to judge by his wheezing and gasping, was obviously suffocating. His bloodshot eyes rolled heavenwards. Pink saliva dribbled from his lacerated lips, from which escaped a few broken, delirious words: a talking turnip in a black cabbage-patch that stank of tar, wilted roses, rotten oranges and burnt flesh.

Remembering my walkie-talkie I pulled it out of my pocket and switched it on. But before I could speak I heard an angry screech of tyres. The white Škoda I'd thought was a police car sprang into motion like an irate iron beast and came hurtling straight at me. I realized at once it was a trap and I was about to be killed. But all I could do was stand rooted to the spot, paralysed by terror, with one final useless thought in my head: I wouldn't have time to reply to the angry 'What is it?' barking out of the radio. I might have answered Olejar with a single well-chosen word. It would have made a dramatic farewell.

Death, however, struck elsewhere. The car braked sharply a few yards in front of me, skidded off course and, its wheels blocked, glided gracefully over the asphalt. Though it was not travelling particularly fast, its front right wheel smacked into Barnabáš' head with the efficacy of a guillotine. With an ugly snapping sound it catapulted off down the street. Engine revving, the car sped after it for a few seconds before making an abrupt turn and disappearing into Dittrichova. I never even saw the driver.

I did not faint. I couldn't faint. I wouldn't allow it. But keeping quiet was another matter. Legs straddled, the walkie-talkie lying between my feet next to the bloody stump of Barnabáš' neck and my hands over my ears, I shouted 'No! No! No! No! No!' to shut out the maddening clatter of water-wheels from the long-defunct Šitkovský Mills. And I kept on shouting.

Then everything changed. Suddenly the street was swarming with black uniforms. Pushing its way through them was a grey overcoat and inside it a bald-headed man, heading straight towards me. He had two white handkerchiefs stuffed into his ears and was talking very animatedly – or so it appeared from his ferociously wagging tongue. Neither of us, it seemed, could hear a thing. I felt I should take my hands out of my pockets but discovered I couldn't: I was pressing them to my ears with all my strength. I removed them and the clattering stopped at once. Instead I heard Olejar's voice. He was saying something about Junek.

I said, 'Junek's in hospital. He got into a fight last night.'

'Are you out of your mind?' roared Olejar. 'Haven't you heard a word I've been saying? Who told you he was in hospital, for Christ's sake? He's lying in Barnabáš' living-room in a pool of blood. And there's a knife on the floor beside him – a long antique stiletto. It had gone in one ear and out the other.'

I felt an overwhelming sense of pity – not for Junek but for myself. I was sure his death would be added to my already considerable list of failures. I could kiss goodbye to the trust I had so recently and painstakingly managed to restore. I couldn't even remember more than half of the Škoda's registration number, even though I had seen it clearly. One short phone call was enough to verify that the three numbers I could recall did not match any vehicles used by the police. Another of my fatal mistakes.

In the afternoon Dr Trug, the pathologist, arrived on the scene, as he always did whenever there was some particularly delicate and disgusting matter to investigate. Barnabáš' head had bounced all the way down Resslova to the embankment where it had cannoned off one of the supports of Gehry's Dancing House like a football into a goal mouth – or, in this case, into the railings on the riverbank. There it had come to rest, stuck fast in a grille of cast-iron foliage. And there it remained until Trug extracted it with the aid of a surgical saw. You can see the round gap in the railings to this day.

That evening, finding myself alone again in the closed-off street, I remembered the mobile crane I had seen outside St Václav's Church – an orange Tatra of a type long since replaced by more modern and powerful machines. Why would road-menders need a crane? I ran down to the church and checked the parked vehicles: mixer truck, road-roller, asphalt layer . . . The crane had disappeared. I was quite sure it was the same one used by our homicidal maniac, first to hoist Rehoř's legs on to the Congress Centre flagpoles, then to remove the crown from the top of St Stephen's spire so that he could crucify a young vandal on it. It never even occurred to me to mention this to Olejar.

It was dark by the time I got back to the hotel. I thought about what the Superintendent had said before he left the scene of the murder. He had come looking for me on the embankment. His right ear was exuding so much black muck that he looked as if he had been tarred himself. This is what he said: 'What's more pathetic than a bodyguard who can't guard a client? A bodyguard who can't guard two clients. You're the very last thing the police needs. You may not realize this – or maybe you just refuse to see it or are playing some kind of double game – but it's really beginning to look as if all these murders have been committed on account of one person, though I still have no rational explanation for it. And do you know who I think that person is? Can't you guess? Ah, I see it may be dawning on you at last. I'm talking about the most incompetent policeman who ever lived – you.'

22

Livid in a lighting-bolt
Rears the ancient stoop
Of a velvet-black arch.

Richard Weiner

The police remained true to their tried-and-tested methods, and within no time they had a prime suspect. When I learnt who it was I didn't know whether to weep or laugh my head off, for it was none other than our friend Zahir. At first I dismissed the idea as preposterous. But then I had to admit it had a certain logic, however tenuous. I recalled our conversation in Wenceslas Arcade, when he spoke of the rivalry between himself and Barnabáš. What if he had been talking to other people, too, and letting slip more than he intended? He had taken to drinking quite heavily; in his cups he might easily have given himself away. It was not inconceivable. What if he had hated Rehoř and Mrs Pendelmanová as much as he hated Barnabáš? What if he had killed all three of them, safe in the knowledge that his damaged leg (a genuinely serious injury that I'd seen with my own eyes) would give him a watertight alibi? The victim of an attempted murder would be the last person they would suspect! He had inflicted the injury on himself! Anyone fanatical enough to judge his own and other people's sins as harshly as Zahir did might be capable of such a thing. All it would take for him to hang himself by the ankle from the bell of St Apollinaris' would be a biggish dose of self-loathing and a modicum of dexterity.

With perfect timing, Zahir left on his long-planned trip to Ljubljana, spurning the convenience of air travel in favour of his beloved car. He was due back in ten days. We were instructed not to talk about our suspicions. Similarly, Olejar forbade us to take any steps preliminary to making an arrest, dismissing as idiotic a suggestion to block his bank account. It was feared he might panic and decide not to come back.

Suddenly everyone was convinced he was the murderer. The team investigating the crimes (who were no longer on speaking terms with me) began to believe it almost as an article of faith. The architect's remark about my knowing some of those involved in the life-threatening construction project came back to haunt me: he hadn't actually said I knew them but *might have known* them, implying they were already dead. For a moment even I was tempted to see him as a half-crazed killer – until I realized there was no evidence against him. And what about the graffiti vandals – one spray-painted and asphyxiated, the other disembowelled with a skateboard? How did they fit in? Or the historical buildings? But I could hardly discuss the homicidal potential of Gothic churches with a superintendent of police.

Now that suspicion had fallen on Zahir and a case was being prepared against him, my suggestion to compare the green granite cobblestones became an irrelevance. Yet I was sure they all came from the same place. They were the same colour, size and shape – and all had delivered the same ominous message. I decided to bypass my superiors and go straight to Trug. He would surely agree to analyse the stones in his laboratory, if only because I had every intention of blackmailing him. I had a good idea who was behind the unicorn experiment and had no doubt he would have some trouble explaining it to the university authorities.

On the Monday following that fateful week, which saw the hole in Resslova filled in and the fate of the caverns under Charles Square irrevocably sealed, I once again had time on my hands. Olejar refused to have anything to do with me. Gmünd, too, no longer needed me. He seemed dejected, as if the light illuminating his smooth, *soigné* exterior had been extinguished or the thin crystal carapace that had hitherto protected him had shattered. He rarely slept in the hotel. I had not seen Prunslik for several days either. Yet as I wandered about the rambling Bouvines apartment late at night I had a feeling I was not alone. A heavy, sweetish fragrance wafted down the corridors, making my head spin and catching in my throat. I was unable to identify it, until one morning it hit me as I entered the sitting-room and I knew the stupefying smell must be that of burning opium. It seemed to be coming from Prunslik's room. More than once, feeling the need for company, I mustered my courage and knocked on his door. But there was never any answer, nor even the slightest sound: no hushed voices, no suspicious rustlings, no delirious laughter. I never dared try the handle.

Rozeta was often in my thoughts. I longed to unburden myself to her about my misunderstanding with the police and the cooling of my friendship with Matthias Gmünd. Twice I glimpsed her at breakfast, but each time she got up and left the moment I entered the room before I could even say good morning. After that she stopped coming down to breakfast. I tried to engineer chance encounters. I started getting up early, before six, and loitering in the empty corridors of that strange hotel. The one thing I did not do, since it was by now clear she was deliberately avoiding me, was knock on her door.

At last I found someone willing to lend a sympathetic ear and give me an absolution of sorts – my old teacher Netřesk. When I called on him unannounced after a sleepless night, he greeted me with an unfeigned delight I found very touching. I must have looked pretty wretched, because without further ado he asked me in, sat me down at the kitchen table and made me a strong cup of tea generously laced with rum. Then he sat down opposite me and asked what was troubling me. With an enormous sense of relief I embarked on a full and candid confession. The weak are easily led astray.

I related the whole story of the New Town murders, from start to finish, including details of the so far fruitless police investigation. As the words tumbled out I felt the blessed flow releasing all my pent-up anxiety and tension. I told him of my doubts about Zahir's guilt. I also told him of a suspicion that had long been germinating in my mind: that all the cases were in some mysterious way connected with my benefactor Matthias Gmünd.

I should not have been so hasty; it is always best to keep one's most secret thoughts to oneself. Netřesk, who until then had been listening with what seemed like rapt attention, winced on hearing the Knight's name. His face clouded, but otherwise he betrayed no emotion. Then, with a worried look directed somewhere over my shoulder, he asked what had given me such an idea. I turned my head and saw Lucie standing in the bedroom door, her forehead scored with three lines of questions marks. I guessed she had heard everything I had said, though she clearly had no idea what it was all about. In contrast, her elderly husband began acting like a frightened rabbit. His voice shaking with anger, he told her to leave us alone and go to see to her child. I could see she was hurt and wanted to leap to her defence. But I hesitated a fraction too long. The door closed, and Lucie was gone.

When he realized he would get nothing more out of me, Netřesk's manner cooled perceptibly. Drumming his fingers on the table, he glanced at his watch and said he had a meeting at the Historical Society so perhaps it was time we were off. I got the message and rose to leave. We went downstairs in silence and said a rather awkward goodbye in the street. Though I had nowhere particular to go we set off in opposite directions.

The air was full of a diffuse light that hurt my eyes and made everything seem out of focus. Head down, my gaze fixed on the pavement, I walked down Václavská as far as Moráň. From there it was but a few steps to Emmaus, to which I now found myself, a latter-day pilgrim, irresistibly drawn. As I stood outside the building I recalled the passage from St Luke from which the monastery takes its name: *And, behold, two of them went that same day to a village called Emmaus, which was from Jerusalem about threescore furlongs. And they talked together of all these things which had happened. And it came to pass, that, while they communed together and reasoned, Jesus himself drew near, and went with them. But their eyes were holden that they should not know him.*

I had a sudden feeling there was someone behind me. I whipped round, but there was not a soul in sight. The gnarled fingers of the chestnuts clawed at the alabaster mist. A pair of pigeons, oblivious to the ghosts of the past, huddled together for warmth on the church steps.

I wandered through the monastery precinct, cowering instinctively as I passed under the former offices of the Public Works Department, buildings sadly typical of the brash and bloated architecture of our time: three glass boxes, teetering precariously on chicken-like concrete legs, their functionalist vulgarity a permanent affront to the venerable church of St Jerome. Today the space is let to various munificent charity organizations; but that does not alter the fact that at some point somebody approved these monstrosities and somebody built them. Who could have sanctioned such a violation of Gothic Prague? Rehoř? Barnabáš? Pendelmanová?

In Vyšehradská Ulice I paused to look up at the presbytery and the black slots of those oddly Romanesque windows in the upper part of the choir. Above them, the slender Gothic flèche pierced the sky as it had done for six hundred years – a proud reminder of the most glorious epoch in the history of architecture. To make the roof timbers that support it the Emperor Charles sacrificed a whole forest; for the walls themselves he chose the finest grey sandstone – the same as was used in the bridge he had built between the Old Town and Malá Strana. How much stone must have gone into a church nearly fifty yards long?

I set off down Vyšehradská past St John on the Rock, the first of two Dientzenhofer churches in the vicinity. Though enjoying a good position, St John Nepomuk (as it is also called) is marred by its spires, which are set at a slight angle to each other and give the place an oddly disabled look. One would need a strong faith indeed to place one's trust in such a church. I walked down the steps from the Rock and carried on past the botanical garden and the second Dientzenhofer church, Our Lady of Seven Sorrows, an unassuming, easily overlooked building set into the façade of the St Elizabeth Convent. Further down the street, at Albertov, I could not resist pausing at the Gothic church on Na Slupi, whose simple beauty and clean lines contrasted refreshingly with those pitiful Baroque efforts. I let my gaze wander over the yellow stone walls, the compact square nave, the low choir. The place had a homely feel to it, like a village church set in some safe and tranquil landscape. All at once I was reminded of Father Florian but just as quickly dismissed him from my thoughts. I walked slowly round the building, as I had done not long ago with Lucie, savouring every moment, every step, unable to tear myself away. For a long while I feasted my eyes on the graceful form of Our Lady on the Lawn (as the Church of the Annunciation is also known) – a form only restored to her 130 years ago by the Gothic revivalist Bernard Grueber.

Then, in mid-step, I was assailed by doubt. What was the point of this endless wandering around, this self-indulgent ritual? And all at once I knew: subconsciously, I was bidding farewell to my beloved old buildings from a better, bygone age. Again I felt the presence of mocking eyes and cast a surreptitious glance around me. Again there was not a soul in sight. I looked up towards Větrov, where I could just make out the hunched almost human silhouette of St Apollinaris'. For a moment the dim, ghostly form seemed to sway to and fro, an effect I ascribed to the droplets of mist adhering to my lashes. Lured by its spell, I struck out up the hill.

It is not possible to walk right round St Apollinaris' Church, but since my route took me up the steps from Studničkova I had ample time to take in its southern aspect, that is, the side facing away from the town where the land falls steeply away. Reaching the top of the steps I skirted the vicarage garden and approached the church from the east, where I could not resist caressing the smooth plaster beneath the tall presbytery windows. This, I thought, was the only way to rebuild what the ravages of time and man had laid waste. This was the only permissible form of renovation. Josef Mocker, who a hundred years ago restored the building to its former glory, was indeed the greatest Czech architect of modern times, a worthy successor to Peter Parler and Matthew of Arras. He remains unsurpassed to this day.

Curiously, the plasterwork that only weeks before had been full of cockroach-ridden holes was now perfectly intact. Gone, too, were the patches of rising damp and moss at the base of the wall. The whole church was aglow with fresh vigour, shining in the milky haze as if charged with solar energy. Its spire seemed so high I could not even make out where it ended. Closing my eyes, I let Apollinaris enfold me in his strong fatherly arms.

From there I headed north up Viničná. Just before the end of the street, near St Catherine's, I entered a small iron gate into what used to be the convent garden.

It was here, in the shadow of the statuesque church tower, that I had chanced upon Gmünd and Rozeta and the ever-watchful Prunslik. Today I surprised no secret lovers, though I was sure plenty more amorous couples met in this quiet spot. The tower, however, kept a discreet and indulgent silence at this moral turpitude, no doubt painfully aware that it, too, was in permanent *flagrante delicto* with Dienztenhofer's unsightly bell-tower: a Gothic flute ravished by a Baroque kettledrum; a shameless spectacle devised by a perverse architect whose crass taste has been hailed as genius by the crass twentieth century.

In need of solace, I carried on down Lípová and, coming out on Ječná, was greeted by the reassuring sight of the glorious royal diadem atop St Stephen's spire. I walked slowly towards the church, noting with pleasure the irregularity of its solid, well-nourished form: the spiral staircase on the south side of the tower with its tiny chamfered windows; on the north, the great wedge of Renaissance steps; the mighty buttress jutting obliquely from the north corner; Mocker's elegant neo-Gothic windows; the tombs of Prague worthies set into the walls – all this recalled the days when life was worth living to the full and we could count on the Almighty for succour and support. I envied the knights who lay at rest here and resented the fact that not one of them had plucked me from the constellations of the unborn and seen fit to beget me. But I would have been equally happy with a father from the humbler ranks. Hunger and want in the blessed fourteenth century, Hussite outrages in the disastrous fifteenth, the vainglory of the Renaissance in the sixteenth, even the accursed Thirty Years War would have been preferable to this misery – a slow poisoning by over-indulgence in the toxic twentieth century.

I was distressed to see how shabby everything looked around the church: tenements with broken windows and peeling plaster, obviously empty; the pavement torn up but no indication that a gas main was about to be repaired. The ground seemed to have sunk, so that the church, rising out of the broken earth, appeared bigger, broader, mightier. The lights at the junction of Štěpánská and Žitná were not working, and a pointless wooden construction in the middle of the road further slowed the heavy flow of traffic. I had a sudden vision of this street also sinking into the bowels of the earth, taking with it a few more concrete-lovers. Then a shiver ran down my spine: by the wall where the murdered graffiti sprayers had been photographed lay a bunch of decomposing irises.

It was gone midday. The milky haze had evaporated to reveal a feeble sun ringed by shadow – a dirty smudge on an otherwise clean blue sky. As if eclipsed, the disc grew darker and darker: with twilight at one o'clock, it would be dark by four. It suddenly turned cold. I tried to shake off the gloom that had come over me outside St Stephen's by quickening my stride as I headed up Ječná and into Ke Karlovu. On the way I noticed that the Michna Summer Palace was closed.[1] It looked neglected and run down, in striking contrast to the tower of St Catherine's, which I was now able to observe from a different angle and a greater distance. Only the top three sections and the spire were visible over the top of the wall, but even so I could see clear signs of recent repairs that must have been done in the last few days: the roof was clad with new copper sheeting, the stonework gleamed white and the cornices, which a week ago had been chipped and crumbling, had been replaced with new neatly cut stone sections.

I hurried on, but not without looking back several times to admire the tower. So it was that more than once I tripped on some loose cobblestones that had been pulled out of the pavement and stacked into irregular pagoda-like piles. In the resulting holes puddles had formed, some of which had dried, leaving unsightly deposits of mud, sand and black filth. A typesetter's blocks scattered over the printing-room floor amid pools of ink, as if some censor had called 'Enough!' and made him start over again.

The road itself was even more pot-holed, and any cars intrepid enough to drive down the narrow street did so in a slow-motion, comically zigzag fashion. Beyond the junction with Wenzigova the surface deteriorated even further: in some places solid paving alternated with pools and ruts; in others it was reduced to a few jagged-shored islands of stone floating in a black mire. Wherever possible I jumped from one island to the next; failing that, I picked my way over the driest-looking mounds of mud.

When I reached the corner of the Medical School I saw the church. By this point there were very few wheel-marks on the road – it was almost as if they had been deliberately obliterated. Yet the road was obviously in regular use. Some tracks were clearly visible in the mud, but the impressions bore no sign of the tread of car tyres. Was the road used only by carts? I picked up one of the remaining cobblestones whose colour had caught my eye. It was neither grey nor white or red, like those used down in the town. This cube of quartz was veined with green. So this was the source of the stones that had smashed the architects' windows!

A slight sound, like a gasp of impatience, made me look up. Before me, in all its majesty, stood the Church of the Virgin Mary and Charles the Great at Karlov, the sixth church of the Prague Heptecclesion. The sun shone down almost vertically on its three copper domes, setting their lanterns and pepper-pot tops ablaze like the beacons of some mythical lighthouse. For the second time that day I had to close my eyes against the blinding, ethereal light. When I opened them again I saw Rozeta.

She was standing under the north portal, in exactly the same spot where I had recently seen Gmünd, and staring at me intently. She wore a long black robe and would have looked like a nun had her head not been uncovered. As it was, her hair fell over her thin, pale face on to her shoulders and chest. Her eyes were inscrutable, their total lack of expression so uncharacteristic it seemed to be deliberate, as did the savage set of her usually warm and welcoming lips. She had changed. She had become an unapproachable stranger – but a stranger I had seen once before. Yes, this was the woman who had stood at the window of the Hlava Institute. Her beauty struck fear into my heart.

Before I could call her name she was gone. I was sure she had disappeared inside the church, though now, with hindsight, I am not so certain. Perhaps she was still standing there and I simply failed to see her; perhaps it was I who was not there, standing outside the church; perhaps I was in some other place, in some other time. The sweet smell of incense floated on the freezing air, enticing me in through the open door. I knew it was a trap, and I walked into it willingly.

Out of the dazzling light I stepped straight into the gold-and-red penumbra of the unlit church, where only the eternal flame flickered in its crimson chalice over the high altar. A dim pinkish glow suffused the walls. On the galleries and altars the statues stood silent and still, awaiting a redeemer who would bring them back to life. A heavy fragrance hung in the air like a portent of evil.

Behind me I heard soft unhurried footsteps. I spun round, my heart pounding. The nave was empty. I walked towards the western tower whence the sound seemed to be coming. As I did so I had a *déjà vu*: Apollinaris' . . . steps . . . the man in the belfry. Instinctively I reached for my pistol in its shoulder holster. I did not release the safety catch: I would only shoot if my life was in immediate danger.

I went up to the first floor of the tower and peered into the organ loft. Nothing. I listened. Not a sound.

Very cautiously, I crept up the steps to the second floor, placing my feet noiselessly on the dusty treads. My right wrist was shaking. I gripped it tightly with my other hand, but still it shook. I swapped the pistol to my left hand, painfully aware that if I did have to use it I would probably end up shooting myself.

This time the bells were silent. There was no frantic ringing, no human spider swinging from a clapper. The small chamber below them was empty but by no means dark. A little light slanted through one of two small windows; the other had been walled up. In one corner lay some coils of rope and a pile folded sacks, and there were several planks propped up against the walls. Then I noticed a small iron door set into the wall about a foot from the floor. It reminded me of the door in the secret back passage of Gmünd's apartment, which was similarly awkward to get through. But this one had no steps.

The handle was quite high up, roughly level with my forehead. I grasped it and the door swung gently open towards me. Though it was rusty, a brief inspection confirmed that its hinges had been recently oiled. I raised my foot, hoisted myself into the gap and found myself looking into a circus ring.

Or at least that was my first impression. I remained squatting in the doorway, balanced precariously on the narrow stone sill. Below me yawned a black chasm, a tapering funnel of darkness that all but swallowed up the few rays of sulphurous light filtering through the lantern in the dome high above me and the tiny windows in the entablature around the top of the octagon. Near by I made out a second gaping hole and beyond that another. I looked the other way: two more black pits. Only one intrusive element spoilt the geometry of that perfect eight-sided perimeter: my own presence. In all there were eight dark funnels of dead, musty air, each divided from the next by a rounded ridge, like a mountain separating two valleys. Rising gently from the centre of this ghostly wreath was a masterfully built and perfectly circular dome, its ribs standing out like veins – a fantastic stone flower that glowed faintly as it thrust up into the darkness of that secret world. Here the din of the city was hushed to a bare murmur, the headlong rush of time slowed to the merest shuffle. Here, on the reverse side of the church vault, was a house of prayer as it might be seen by Him to whom all prayers are addressed. Above my head rose the rounded cupola – a baldachin to shelter a rare flower.

A shadow flitted across the far side of the dusky space: a flapping black cowl . . . wide, flowing sleeves. I took two faltering steps along the smooth ridge of the stone flower, which sloped gently away on either side. With my third, steadier step I felt my courage return. That, needless to say, was another mistake.

I called out Rozeta's name.

The gloom was instantly filled with a swarm of fluttering shadows, churning the air as they flew up towards the chinks of daylight above – a frenzied headlong flight like a scene from *Gargantua*. The dome reverberated like an old bell. Wing beat against wing in a blizzard of feathers.

In that moment of distraction fate dealt its blow. A soft, teasing blow – yet lethal none the less. Twice I staggered and caught my balance and would have avoided the awful fall had I not tripped on the hem of my infamous sleuth's mackintosh – that gift from a dead widow – and slid into the hole below me. The roof echoed with laughter.

My left elbow smashed against the brickwork as with my free hand I grappled desperately for a hold, my legs thrashing uselessly in the darkness. Slowly, absurdly, comically, I slithered down the convex incline as if on a child's chute until my feet came to rest on the narrow, firm, yet curiously soft bottom.

I was furious. Now I could have used my gun without a second thought. But where was it? I groped about in the confined space around my feet. I felt something solid and picked it up. It was a little bundle of bones and feathers, a desiccated body that crumbled between my fingers: a dead pigeon. Underfoot lay dozens, maybe hundreds like it. I was up to my knees in a birds' graveyard, no doubt the fullest and foulest of eight similar deposits under the dome. As my numbed senses returned, the stink of carrion caught in my throat and turned my stomach. With a huge effort of will I managed not to throw up – there was quite enough mess under my feet already. Is this what Gmünd had wanted to show me? Rotting corpses in a church roof? A charnel-house suspended between Heaven and earth?

I swore I would get my own back on Rozeta and cursed her with every name I could think of. They say anger is the best palliative to despair. But in my case it didn't work. I have always been an exception.

Floundering like a drowning kitten, I scraped my shoes against the curved face of the vault in the hope of finding a foothold and hauling myself out of the pit. It was useless. The arching stone ribs of the vault were as smooth and slippery as ice, while the newer brickwork between them, though rougher to the touch, afforded little better purchase. I tried straddling the narrow space, my back against the solid supporting wall, my legs against the vault, and managed to raise myself three or four feet. But the point where I had been standing before I was pushed off was still at least twice that distance above me, and as the rib arched away from me the gap widened. Not even a rock-climber could have got up that way. I had no choice but to lower myself back into the malodorous trench. Then an alarming thought struck me: supposing the old vault gave way under my weight and I came crashing down into the nave below? Supposing this is exactly what my captors had intended? I managed to control my anger, but it was immediately replaced by a paralysing tension around my spine. Panic surged through my gut and a deathly sweat dripped from my brow, stinging my eyes and mingling with my tears of impotence. How could I have been so stupid! I would rot to death here like a trapped pigeon.

And then, gleaming in the darkness, I saw Lucie's smiling face, as white as the porcelain face of a doll and just as small, with three wrinkles on the tiny forehead. It was a horrible sight – as if some African head-hunter had dried her skull and shrunk it to the size of a new-born baby's. I started back in fright, but there was nowhere to turn. Backing off as far as I could, I stared in fascination at the homunculus. It was quite motionless, its hair and body as pale as its face – a figurine sculpted in white stone. I stretched out my hand but could not reach it, which was strange since the width of the space at shoulder height was little more than an arm's length. And when my fingers finally touched it all they felt was a swirl of dust – as if the little figure kept wriggling out of my grasp. The body was curved like an 'S', with heavy hips and a protruding belly. I suddenly understood what I was looking at: a Gothic sculpture of the Mother of God. In the modelling of the face, of the arms and hands joined below the abdomen and the rich folds of the robe that completely covered the slender body, vertical lines predominated. A Gothic Madonna, pure and simple. The resemblance to Lucie was extraordinary and quite inexplicable. The Virgin's delicately fashioned face, with its closed eyes and serene smile, was clearly visible and seemed to glow in the faint light from above, while her body, shrouded in shadow, was barely discernible.

The Madonna was not alone. Close to my left hand, growing out of a stone block set into a brick bay in the vault, was a stone tree. Its leafless boughs, contorted like the limbs of a gouty old man, were laden with apples; yet the branches seemed untroubled by the weight of the fruit, which I now saw was shrivelled and crawling with worms. Fascinated, I leant forward to inspect one of them more closely – and immediately started back in alarm. The worm had a human head. As I watched, it thrust its horrible leering mouth at me, revealing rows of minute teeth.

Out of the corner of my eye I spotted another face sculpted from white stone, this one life-sized: a bald-headed glutton with pointed ears, flared nostrils and drooping, sensual eyelids, munching noisily and open-mouthed on some titbit. I peered inside the foul aperture, but all I could see was blackness. Or was it? There was a flash of something white and elongated and somehow familiar, something that had been placed in that vile maw for some evil purpose. Then I saw what it was: a miniature human arm reaching out imploringly before the mouth closed on it for ever. In the black cavern beyond shone a tiny human face. It was resigned to its death but horrified at the manner of it.

On top of the cannibal's head was a triangular object, set slightly askew, which at first I took to be a fool's cap, then a stylized Eye of God, before I finally recognized it for what it was: a simple geometrical device known since the Middle Ages. Enclosed in the triangle was a small naked human figure, its outstretched arms tied to the sides just below the right-angled apex, its legs fixed in place by the hypotenuse as if they were locked in the stocks. A hole gaped in the manikin's skinny chest: someone had ripped out his heart.

Near by on a three-legged stool sat a monk, his cowl drawn up over his head. He was bent over a sheet of paper or parchment, drawing, with one squinting eye fixed on the bald man-eater and the other on the crucified figure in the triangle. The face, just visible under the cowl, was not that of a man but of a lion. Its mouth was spread in a slight smile that puckered the skin on its snout.

Behind the lion in the cowl hung a plumb-line which I at first supposed was its tail. The weight was also carved out of stone, and instead of string the artist had used a length of wire. Sitting on the gently swinging plumb was a hunched dwarf – or possibly, judging by his little horns, a miniature devil. Seeing me, he hooted with lewd laughter and shifted his hairy haunches on his perch, perhaps so as to make me think that he was the cause of the plumb-line's oscillation.

The swinging weight led my gaze to another ghastly sight: a woman's agonized face, contorted by the throes of death. It was Rozeta. Stone rivulets of blood trickled down her chin from her twisted mouth. Her naked, fleshy body writhed under the hooves of a mighty beast with broad neck and powerful withers. I assumed it was a horse – a proud, untameable stallion – until I saw, growing out of its forehead above the demonic eyes that bulged like peeled eggs, a long, tapering horn with which it ripped open Rozeta's belly and gouged out her gory entrails with the ruthlessness of a butcher's knife.

I quickly averted my eyes to the Madonna, hoping her serene smile might restore my strength and composure. But the smile was gone. In its place was a ghastly grimace in which pleasure blended grotesquely with pain. Stone tears oozed from her half-closed eyes.

Her body, hitherto barely visible, was now in full view: her arms were flung back like the wings of an altarpiece to reveal her hollow torso, inside which sat the Infant Jesus on a throne of gold. The child was reaching out in supplication, yet with undiminished majesty and pride. 'Behold, all this I can do!' it seemed to say. Out of its head grew two tall, straight roses, inclined towards each other like the tips of a pair of draftsman's compasses intersecting at some invisible point. That point was the mother's stylized heart, plump and ruddy, from which glutinous drops of blood dribbled down the twin stems. The child, whose face seemed strangely familiar, cackled through its toothless gums, and there was madness in its wide staring eyes. Yes, I had seen that face before, long ago, long before I came to Prague. It was the face of a sad child I had once known, a child lost to life and the world. It was my own face.

I could stand no more. In a fit of rage I hurled myself at the ghoulish spectacle, fists and feet flailing. But all my knuckles encountered was the smooth, mercifully solid inner wall of the vault. I beat my head against it. All at once the funnel began rotating and I with it – anticlockwise, slowly at first, then faster and faster until it was spinning like a tornado. Centrifugal forces pinned me to the wall with relentless and invisible hands, while my legs bored into the ground like corkscrews. As the wildly gyrating funnel roared and thundered, a shining white ring appeared in the murky air. In my vertiginous state I could not tell whether it was merely an optical illusion or whether the whirlwind was turning into solid stone. I managed to detach my head from the wall and look into the centre of the circle. The last thing I saw was a terrifying toothed wheel, like the giant cog of a clock, and a hammer swinging first one way, then the other, as it struck an enormous quivering bell. Unfortunately I only saw it a split-second before it struck me. I was as glad of that blow as a dying man is glad of the *coup de grâce*. My suffering was at an end.

23

Clear the air! Clean the sky!
Wash the wind!
Take the stone from the stone
[...] And wash them!

T.S. Eliot

I had never seen such roses. They were the colour of fresh blood – a slow, viscous haemorrhage of living sap glistening with black pearls. The tight bunches of newly opened blooms filled three porcelain vases, one on the table, one on the desk and one by the window, beyond which was black night. A room full of flowers – in my honour, to be sure. Mauve asters mixed with scarlet dahlias in jars of garnet-tinted glass. A tall African hibiscus in an earthenware pot on the floor by the door. A profusion of purple carnations, with here and there a burst of flaming tulip. Instinctively, I looked into the alcove where on another occasion the ghost of a Chinese vase had appeared, bristling with dragons and pampas grass. In its place, uprooted and casually discarded on a small glass tray, was a wilting anthurium, its pale-yellow tongue lying limp on its crimson heart.

A whole room decked out in scarlet for my delectation. How dare they ingratiate themselves so shamelessly! And then I saw something else.

Gleaming dully among the flowers lay an ugly-looking iron

contraption, crudely yet cunningly wrought, that seemed to grin like the jaws of a snare.

Someone must have followed my baffled gaze. 'Chastity belt,' I heard a voice say.

It was indeed a chastity belt, and I had seen it before – fastened to a naked body. Now, abandoned and absurd, it revealed its primitive but perverse mechanism for all to see. I shuddered and closed my eyes, hoping against hope that when I opened them again I would at last be awake.

'You put on quite a show, I hear!' It was the same voice as before. 'Couldn't resist taking a peek at Rozeta, eh? Just had to see what she was up to? Itching to discover the hidden truth? You never did latch on, did you? Time is the father of Truth. Now Time has punished you.'

I knew that insolent tone. I decided not to react. The voice spoke again.

'Time is the father of Truth.'

There was no longer any point in feigning sleep. 'I don't understand.' My throat refused to let the words go, and it was all I could do to get them out. But from the answer that came back I knew they had not gone unheard.

'It's me, Raymond, and I'm talking to you. What I just told you ought to be carved into the vault of Karlov Church. Just mind no one catches you in the act.'

Alarmed that I might be alone with this madman, I cast my eyes cautiously around the room. Under me was a couch covered by a carmine Persian rug; above, a figure bending over me. Yes, it was Prunslik with that grating voice of his. I shut my eyes again and slowly sat up, cradling my head in my hands like a broken jug and afraid to let go in case it broke into a thousand pieces. I heard the unmistakable fizzing sound of a pill dissolving in water. At least someone knew how rotten I felt.

I opened my eyes again. There, not three feet in front of me, was the watchful, fleshy face of the Knight of Lübeck. He smiled.

'Prunslik didn't make that up, of course. A philosopher said it a long time ago. In an age younger than ours.'

'Older, you mean,' I croaked.

'Younger, Květoslav, younger. Time grows old, the same as we do. Only a halfwit could think up terms like "Modern Age", "New Age", "Young World" and suchlike idiocies. Only a lunatic could claim that the Late Stone Age *preceded* the Early Stone Age. As we know, the logic of language goes against the cosmic order. Language was invented by children – clever but conceited and self-important children who thought they were grown-ups and began measuring the universe with the yardstick of their own infinitesimal smallness. Was Time in 1382 older or younger than it is today? Historians would say it was older. Well, you're a historian. Do you agree? We call our ancestors grandfathers and great-grandfathers and picture them as old men. But has Time not grown older in the last six centuries since those golden days? Can Time grow younger? Of course it can't! Time is an old man tottering towards the grave – but the grave keeps eluding him. We are now entering the third millennium (by human reckoning anyway) – and I know I'm not alone in feeling that a twilight is descending on us: the twilight of humanity. Men have raised themselves above the gods; they have usurped the divinity and must now await retribution. That is only just. But others will appear and put things to rights. They are the emissaries of Time. They will halt the decline and arrest our fall.'

'I don't follow you,' I moaned. My skull was splintering.

'You don't follow me? But you know it all already. Be assured, the wise man knows everything without going anywhere; he recognizes all things before he has set eyes on them. When Lao Tse said that I'm sure he had someone like you in mind. We are grateful to you, Květoslav – myself, Raymond . . . and the other members of our society.'

'Society? I have no knowledge of any society.'

'Ah, but you have. Only it is buried deep in your subconscious, in that phenomenal intuition of yours. Rather ironic, isn't it? All those years of studying and reading and you still can't bring it to the surface. What you need is the right stone. But you haven't found it – not yet.'

'A stone, yes. I have always learnt more from stones than books. I'm glad you see it that way, too. Does that mean I'm not quite mad yet?'

'Is that what you're afraid of? How poignant. Don't you find that poignant, Raymond?'

Prunslik measured me with his cruel little eyes.

'Frightfully. Poor lamb. And just think, all that time he was thrashing away in that hole he fell into through his own clumsiness – with a little help from us – it never even occurred to him to stick his hand in the pocket of that filthy old mac and take out his walkie-talkie. I think we've won him over at last, sir.'

'I'm delighted to hear it. So can we assume you have joined our circle? The circle that binds us in a common cause? It's part of the insignia of our brotherhood, by the way: the hoop and the hammer.'

'I knew it!' I exclaimed. 'But isn't it rather ridiculous to play at being Freemasons in this day and age?'

Gmünd gave no sign of having heard.

'In the early 1370s the Emperor Charles had an inner circle of four loyal supporters and advisers, one of whom died as a result of a tragic misunderstanding. Shortly afterwards the Emperor himself died, and there was much debate as to the cause of his death. I am now convinced it was grief at the loss of that trusted friend. I'm sorry . . . I still find this difficult to talk about. I only found out recently – thanks to you. The three remaining counsellors then founded a brotherhood. They had various devout aims but chief among them was to build churches in Prague to the greater glory of God, as magnificent as those the emperor had endowed, and thus continue his work. The Chapel of Corpus Christi had been Charles's idea, but in his lifetime it never amounted to more than a wooden tower in the Cattle Market – a mere token of the splendid stone structure that was later to replace it. Most of his ideas suffered the same fate: only a handful actually came to fruition; the rest he took with him to the grave. Even so, we owe him an incalculable debt of gratitude. Were it not for the Emperor Charles you and I would not be here today. Neither would our city. And neither would the Brotherhood of Corpus Christi.'

'I might have guessed! Strasbourg Cathedral . . . Cologne . . . Batalha Abbey – they were all founded by Freemasons. Are you trying to tell me the Chapel of Corpus Christi was as well?'

'Oh no, we're not Masons. And we're only free within limits set by God, the sovereign, and the circle that is the sign of our order – an order that commits us to preserving the buildings erected by our forefathers.'

'You're talking about the conservation of historic monuments, I suppose. But who do you mean by the sovereign?'

'Well, I admit we have been rather short of sovereigns for a while. But that will change. As for conservation, you already have a good idea which churches I mean.'

'So far there are six.'

'Six? You don't imagine we would choose the number of the beast, do you?'

'I know there are seven in all. And now I know what the last one is. It's the non-existent Chapel of Corpus Christi.'

'Brilliant,' wheezed Prunslik and made a mock bow.

Gmünd was delighted. 'I knew you were with us!' he cried. 'I knew it from the very start. Now imagine this: a hammer suspended in a hoop, a dial and pointers, a clock and its pendulum: infinite Time and the instrument that divides it up into units intelligible to the finite life of Man. Haven't you seen these things before? In a dream, perhaps?'

'Yes. But it wasn't a dream. It was . . . something else.'

'It was your uncanny ability to see into the past. I have travelled the whole world in search of someone like you. Now I've found you, the best of them all, in the country of my ancestors – and not by chance, I'm sure.'

'But how on earth did you find me?'

'Rozeta helped. She had . . . a feeling. Like you, she has a gift. The dreams that surface in her body, and in yours, are the consequence of some kind of bodily deficiency – according to one medieval theory. They may be bad dreams, but they are truthful. Your secret sense enables you to distinguish between false hallucinations and manifestations of the truth, which reveals itself to you through words and pictures. Saint Augustine was familiar with such visions. Isidore of Seville also mentions them in his writings. There's nothing new under the sun.'

'The hammer and hoop – only a totalitarian regime would choose a sign like that.'

Gmünd sighed. 'My dear boy, you will have to get used to the fact that our brotherhood has never embraced the tenets of democracy. It has chosen the backward-leading path. Some superstitious folk would call it the path to hell. That is because they fear it. They think only in terms of progress and cannot conceive of any direction but forwards. In this they are sadly deceived. We must open their eyes.'

'And how does your brotherhood intend to do that? Shouldn't people be free to live as they please?'

'Free!' he thundered. 'What is freedom? An invisible ball and chain – that's why we are forever tripping up and falling flat on our faces. What I am proposing is a better life in a feudal state governed by a single elected ruler. Yes, let the plebs have their vote. If their master is shrewd and has what it takes, he'll make sure they vote for him – as the twentieth century has more than amply demonstrated. And another thing, just so that people know where they stand: secular power to the King, spiritual power to the Church . . . and absolute power to God.'

'Which church do you have in mind?'

'The universal church, naturally. Monarchy is a thousand times better than democracy. Democracy is dynamic. It feeds on perpetual growth of every conceivable and inconceivable kind; it lives on the cult of the new. Democracy is grotesque! It's obscene! It's against the natural order! Your loud-mouthed democracy with all its utilitarian platitudes about universal enlightenment and well-being has brought us to where we are today: the end of the era of Western Man. It's an end that's been long in the making. When did it all start? Was it when they scrapped the monasteries of Prague and turned them into madhouses? Was it when they paved the Horse Market with tombstones torn from the walls of the most sacred Chapel of Corpus Christi – with the blessing of that most enlightened of emperors, Joseph II? Is it any wonder that since that time the great square of St Václav has been cursed and turned into an open sewer vulgarly nicknamed *Václavák*? Such a name can only be the invention of the Antichrist. Joseph is also credited with the abolition of serfdom. Maybe that was a mistake. Or was he deliberately paving the way for two of the greatest tyrants of all time two and a half centuries later? A pair of vulgar commoners, each with a damaged ego and a grudge against the world! No one with a drop of nobility in their blood would have let such a thing happen. Noble blood would never have permitted anything as inhuman, as *anti*-human, as the last century. The twentieth century has shown once and for all that common people cannot govern.

'Decline is inevitable. Our task is to delay it. To arrest the downward slide. To freeze it in mid-fall. Monarchy gives us a measured, steady mode of life, a respect for old ways, a love of tradition. It gives us immutability, order, peace, calm . . . and Time – an ocean of Time. The finest moments in our history always coincided with a golden age of monarchy. Think of the fourteenth century or the nineteenth. How I wish I had your gift and could go back to those times whenever I wanted! You have no idea how bitterly I regret having been born so late – into this hell of electric instruments of torture!

'But I was going to tell you about the club we shall be receiving you into today. You'd better have some supper – it's going to be a long night.'

He looked at his watch and rapped his cane twice on the floor, which I took as a peremptory invitation to eat. I suddenly realized that after those interminable hours of imprisonment in the church loft I was aching with hunger.

The table groaned under a plethora of silver platters, ornate dishes and covered tureens full of the most amazing fare. Though the Knight's words had alarmed me, they had been delivered in such a suave and soothing manner that my appetite was in no way affected.

I knew that a full belly would lower my resistance – but was I not already past protesting?

While my mouth watered, the unaccustomed variety of the dishes before me urged me to caution. First, there was a strangely opaque jelly that smelled of fish, in which I indeed discovered some shreds of salmon. I did not care for it. My eye then fell on a dark, almost black paste mixed with pickled cabbage, with a whiff of cloves, thyme and wine vinegar. This, too, I tried. It was so sour I could not help grimacing. Prunslik, who was watching me like a hawk, found this most entertaining and was doubly delighted when I hesitated over the next dish. It contained three whole fish (some kind of white fish, I guessed) encased entirely in aspic, giving the impression that they were trapped under the surface of a frozen lake. They were surrounded by irregular rings of small orange balls which I decided were rowanberries. I dipped the tip of my knife into the transparent substance and licked it, only to find it was pork dripping. The fish instantly lost their allure. I quickly lifted the lid of a tureen placed discreetly at the edge of the table – and dropped it with an almighty clatter. And not without reason: staring up at me from a bed of onion sauce were the empty eye-sockets of a sheep's head, complete with curly yellow horns.

After a long hesitation that would have seemed indecent to any other host, but which Gmünd let pass with an indulgent smile, I selected, almost at random, a small sausage-shaped meatball, which I impaled on my fork, dipped in a dark purple sauce and popped into my mouth. It had a most curious taste. The red meat was not minced but roughly chopped and heavily spiced – I identified juniper, saffron and possibly calamus – dark, long-forgotten tastes from our ancestors' kitchens.

'I see it is not to your disliking,' said Gmünd encouragingly, despite the distaste written all over my face. 'You'll get used to it. That's a good sign. Soon you'll be eating this sort of thing every day. Well, perhaps not quite such feasts – then you'd spend half your time sleeping it off, and we can't afford to let you do that.' He gave a mirthless laugh.

'Go ahead, eat and drink whatever takes your fancy. The Château Landon is excellent. Allow Raymond to pour you a glass . . . Just look at that ruby-red sparkle!'

The wine was indeed exquisite. Resolved not to let it go to my head, I nodded my approval over the rim of the glass as Gmünd continued, 'Our brotherhood always enjoyed some affluence, although – and this will appeal to a democrat like you – anybody was entitled to join. We got off to a bad start when our four founding members were sadly reduced to three. Yet before long those three had gathered around them forty more brothers, increasing our number tenfold. Our patron was none less than the King and Emperor Václav II, which may explain why we were able to build the chapel in only eleven years, whereas some of the New Town churches took three, four or even five times longer to complete. A few unlucky ones, like Our Lady of the Snows, were never actually finished at all.

'The Gothic church of Corpus Christi was originally made of wood and only later rebuilt in stone. Its ground plan was an eight-pointed star or possibly a more complex but basically cruciform polygon, arranged around the axis formed by the west door and the presbytery. It had deep foundations in the form of a giant cogwheel, which is why we cannot be sure of the building's exact shape. It's not clear how many windows it had – five, six, maybe even seven, plus a possible light over the entrance. The Chapel of Corpus Christi was a place of astonishing beauty – a beauty I believe has never been surpassed. For centuries it made the Cattle Market the centre of the world. If you want an approximate picture of its extraordinary grace and grandeur imagine a combination of Karlov Church, the Star Summer Palace[1] and the monumental Royal Chapel in Aachen. Better still, don't think of any one particular building. Imagine instead a jagged skyline, a whole city bristling with spires and in its midst a dark cluster of vertical needles and cones gathered round a mighty square tower, like a flock around a shepherd.

'Our church was intended as a shrine for holy relics. Pilgrims flocked to it in their thousands – not only from this country but from

Brandenburg and Poland and all over Europe. Every good Christian wanted to gain merit and prestige by visiting the Chapel of the Most Sacred Body and Blood of the Lord and the Virgin Mary, as it was then called. On the holy days proclaimed by the emperor the Cattle Market would fill to overflowing, while the chapel towered like an immovable rock above the transient flux of humanity.

'The period that followed is one I detest, though it is no less famous. In the third year of the ill-fated fifteenth century our Brotherhood, voluntarily but unwisely, bequeathed the church to the university. Before long they were celebrating the so-called Utraquist liturgy there and even declaiming the shameful Compactates from its pulpit.'

'I know. They engraved them in gilt letters on tablets of stone, as if they were the Ten Commandments.'

'Dreadful. And then they had them set into the wall of the church. Utter sacrilege! Charles must have turned in his grave.'

'And I'm sure he turned again when Müntzer preached there.'[12]

'Ah, that Doubting Thomas! That querulous pantheist! That German Judas! Well said, Květoslav – my sentiments entirely! We speak the same language.' The Knight of Lübeck seized my right hand and shook it warmly, whereupon Prunslik sprang up and grabbed my left.

By now I was no longer surprised by his loony antics. 'So where was your Brotherhood at the end of the eighteenth century when the church was demolished and used for building material?'

For a moment I thought he was going to hit me. 'You've touched a raw nerve there, though it's a fair question. In the seventeenth century the Brotherhood had already become less active, but our nadir came during the Enlightenment – yes, that accursed age again. Ironically, it was a time when Masonic lodges were on the increase, but they were mainly concerned with different, totally useless activities, such as education.'

'You consider education to be useless?'

'Don't you? What good did it ever do? Where did it get us? To the Devil's own century, when the Reaper cut us down like so many ears of overripe wheat. Fifty million? Sixty? And still he wasn't satisfied. And all the while he hid his ghastly skull behind the smiling mask of a benevolent father promising to save this or that particular nation.'

'You, too, are a product of the twentieth century.'

'Every evil eventually destroys itself. But I played no part in the renewal of the Brotherhood – credit for that must go to my ancestors. My great-grandfather Peter Gmünd, as I have told you, was an architect. It may not surprise you to learn that he worked with Mocker and Wiehl on the reconstruction of several New Town churches in the Gothic style.'

'Were they also in the Brotherhood of Corpus Christi?'

'Yes. As were many others. And at the turn of the century the first women were admitted.'

'And Rozeta? I assume you got her to join. By the way, where is she?'

'You sound worried. Are you afraid for her safety?'

'Of course.'

'Do you love her?'

I did not reply. My eyes wandered towards the dying anthurium in the alcove and the iron object next to it.

Gmünd saw where I was looking and smiled mournfully. 'That chastity belt,' he said, lowering his voice, 'is as fake as Rozeta's mask. There is nothing mysterious about her secret. In fact it's rather banal . . . and terrible.' He crossed the room, picked up the device and ran his fingers over the teeth of its two serrated apertures. 'This is a copy, a product of the perverse tastes of the eighteenth century. The Middle Ages were not as cruel as is generally believed. That was a myth peddled by the Enlightenment, and, of course, our idiot historians fell for it. I bought this little item in an antique shop in England – some collector had sold it when he found out it wasn't a medieval torture instrument after all but an amusing trinket. There's lots of sham stuff like this around. Like the Iron Virgin of Nuremberg, who was said to extrude the blood of her lovers. She never did, of course: it was a fake, built to order some time in 1830.'

'So why was Rozeta wearing it?'

'Because of you. You have no experience of women. If you had, you would know they only let you catch them unawares when they want you to.'

'You mean she knew I'd look into her bathroom?'

'Sooner or later, yes. She wanted to let you know she was not available. But at the same time she had to arouse your desire.'

'Why, for heaven's sake?'

'For the sake of the Brotherhood. Don't forget it was she who spotted your remarkable gift. You turned up just in time. Originally her task was to corrupt the chief of police and get him to work for us, but you were a far more valuable catch. Olejar is a reliable plodder, but he has none of your talent. The more he slogs and sweats the further he gets from his goal. And if he does get on to our trail we can always stop him. You were right: he's easy to blackmail. That muck that comes out of his ears is his guilty conscience. But you were wrong about Barnabáš – he didn't know anything about the Superintendent's past. I do. One word from me and he's finished. Why do you suppose he let you work for me? He'd never have promoted you otherwise. You'd have been walking the same beat until you dropped.'

'And Rozeta? Why is she working for you?'

'You really want to know why she joined the Brotherhood of Corpus Christi? I'll tell you: Rozeta is not a real woman.'

'Nonsense!'

'She's a person of the female sex, of course, and a very beautiful one at that. But she cannot bear children. She has a badly scarred womb – the result of an operation she had when she was young.'

There was a crash. Prunslik had knocked over a vase of carnations. His face was as white as a sheet, his eyes wet with huge and improbable tears.

The Knight briefly raised an eyebrow and continued. 'A lot of people were affected. She was one of the lucky ones and will live to a ripe old age, God willing. Around twenty tears ago the case was the talk of the town – an open secret, you might say. Rozeta used to live with her mother in Holešovice. They had to move house when the metro was being built and were given a flat in a new prefab block in Opatov. The death block. Part of a minor architectural experiment . . .'

'Hold on, I've heard about that . . . some new fire-retarding technology, wasn't it? And she was one of the victims?'

Gmünd nodded silently. Another vase hit the floor – this one full of roses. The water at once soaked into the carpet, and splinters of glass caught in its deep pile. Prunslik was now eyeing some tulips that were still within his reach. As he put out his hand I ducked instinctively. But all he did was pull out a single bloom and sniff it. Then with one deft snap he bit off its head and swallowed it whole.

'As I said,' Gmünd went on, 'Rozeta had an operation to remove a malignant tumour on her womb. It saved her life. But the psychological shock was yet to come. She was an outstanding student and put all her youthful energy into passing her school-leaving exams and getting into university, where she hoped to study interpreting. She passed the exams and was accepted. That was when she had the nervous breakdown. Post-operative trauma – first latent, then more than manifest, followed by a long convalescence. She got over the worst of it, but ever since she's suffered from bulimia. When she joined the police she kept quiet about it.'

'What a sad story.'

'Have you heard it before?'

'No. But I did wonder how she was able to lose and gain weight so fast.'

'The attacks are so sudden and unpredictable. They leave her quite exhausted.'

'Where is she now? I'd like to see her . . . spend some time alone with her.'

'I think we can arrange that, can't we, Raymond?' He consulted his watch. 'Isn't it time we brought Květoslav and his secret love together?'

'Wait a minute,' I said, in a more assertive tone. 'Answer me one thing. Did you kill Mrs Pendelmanová?'

'What if I did?' His voice was firm, his face devoid of expression. 'She was in league with the biggest crooks around. For years she did all she could to destroy our holy city. She may have belonged to the gentler sex, but when it came to her work she was about as gentle as Attila the Hun. Our city is like a woman: persecuted by some, admired by others. But all want to win her favour, all want to conquer her – by fair means or foul. I, too, am her suitor, and I see the architects and builders and bureaucrats as my rivals. But, whereas they only want to exploit her, I kneel at her feet in awe and devotion as if she were the woman of my dreams.'

'And you won't let anyone stand in your way.'

'Does that surprise you? Rehoř and his ilk were responsible for bringing new roads into the city, which meant more cars, more tin trash on our streets. The same Rehoř also had a hand in building that concrete corridor over the Nusle Valley, though far better alternatives were available. One was a steel construction a bit like an Eiffel Tower lying on its side but widening out at either end. Another was like a two-tier Roman aqueduct supported by immensely high red-brick piers. The metro would have run on the lower level, with marvellous views from the train windows, while above it there was to have been a wide pedestrian thoroughfare and perhaps a road as well, though much more modest than the Magistrale – that venomous snake with its insatiable appetite for human flesh. Yes, the Brotherhood is going to be kept busy. By the way, did you notice how much better the church looks since we avenged the affront to its dignity?'

'You're referring to the Rehoř and Pendelmanová murders, I suppose. What about Barnabáš?'

'Another rogue, if ever there was one. Apart from building most of those rabbit-hutches on the Jižní Město housing estate – not to mention his involvement in the Opatov affair – he also approved the building of the Congress Centre (the Vyšehrad Hydra, I call it) and was instrumental in erecting that disgraceful menhir on Žižkov Hill – a suitably pagan monument to the modern Czech nation. There's not a view in Prague that hasn't been spoilt by Barnabáš' confounded concrete boxes. Thank God for the Hotel Bouvines – at least you can't see any high-rise blocks from there.'

'Unless you go up to the tower,' said Prunslik bitterly. 'From there you can see them all: Prosek, Háje, Jinonice, Černý Most – whichever way you look the Rehořs and Barnabášes and Zahirs and Pendelmanovás have left their mark on the horizon. Luckily the mark is not indelible.'

'Zahirs, you said. Does that mean . . . ?'

'Worried about him, are you?' asked Gmünd. 'Don't tell me you care what happens to Zahir. The police suspect him of murdering Barnabáš, so he might just slip out of our clutches and finish his days in the comfort of a prison cell. It wouldn't be the first time you've saved his neck.'

'St Apollinaris'! You set the whole thing up, didn't you?'

'That's how we operate. We let people walk into their own traps,' sniggered Prunslik.

I turned on him. 'So it was you in the bell-tower! How did you escape without my seeing you?'

'I waited until your Lordship saw fit to vacate the premises.' He cackled again, then went on to describe how he had climbed out on to the roof on the north side of the tower where, like a goblin hiding behind a chimney, he had been perfectly concealed.

I tried to picture how he had managed it and realized it might just be possible. Prunslik had been squatting there all the time, quietly laughing his head off.

'In a little under an hour your friend Zahir has a date with Rozeta,' said Gmünd, smiling broadly, 'in a restaurant just up the road in Vinohrady. He rang up from abroad to fix it. Quite an intriguing prospect, I'd say. Don't you want to rush to the rescue?'

'You mean she's going to . . . But first tell me one more thing. Why did you push me off the vault in the roof of Karlov Church?'

'Isn't it obvious? To make you finish telling the story you'd already tantalized us with. Forgive me, but I had to get it out of you. We could have tied you up and used force, but you'd only have struggled and ended up hurting yourself – or one of us. That was the last thing I wanted. Why are you looking so miserable? Because I tricked you? It was all in a good cause, believe me. And time was running out. If I'm not mistaken a certain lady has taken your fancy – and it's only a matter of time before she seduces you. Then you'll be no use to us whatsoever.'

'What do you mean? Are you telling me . . . ?'

'Precisely. Your miraculous powers depend on your remaining physically . . . untainted. Don't ask why. Just be thankful you have that gift.'

'So Rozeta is like me?'

'Yes, to some extent you are the same. But unlike you she does not have to renounce all pleasures of the flesh. Don't begrudge her that small consolation – her health is far worse than yours and her ability to see into the past much less acute. But don't worry, your time will come. When I no longer need your services I'll find you a good wife.'

'How about a nice widow?' whinnied Prunslik. 'I know someone – young, pretty. Her old man's still alive, but he's got one foot in the grave. Worth the wait, I reckon.'

'She had no right to deceive me.'

'Who? Rozeta? As the girl who bewitched you, no. As a victim of the Modern Age, yes. That small deception was a necessary part of her revenge. It's what the Brotherhood wants. I hope you will soon want it, too.'

'What did I say up there under the roof?'

'You weren't very coherent, but we got the facts we were after and they fitted the first part of your story. One morning in the year of our Lord 1377 Václav Hazemburg, a former governor of Úštěk and close confidant of the Emperor Charles, rode out to the newly built Augustinian monastery church, only recently dedicated to Charles the Great and the Virgin Mary, to supervise the carving of the ritual symbols of the so-called Brotherhood of St Charles, a society he had founded with three other noblemen. On that same morning, by a tragic quirk of fate, the emperor himself unexpectedly visited the church, though it was actually the turn of St Apollinaris' to be honoured with His Majesty's presence. On arriving at Karlov, however, he discovered two stonemasons and their master at work in the roof carving seven fearsome-looking monsters into the stone. Charles saw it as a desecration of the House of God, and the following morning he had the three men hanged. The emblems of the Brotherhood were crushed to dust, the entire roof was rebuilt and the church reconsecrated. The gargoyles alone survived – only to be smashed forty years later by the Hussites. All my life I've been looking into my family history in the hope of discovering why Václav Hazemburg lost the king's favour and consequently his life. Now at last I know, thanks to you and your miraculous powers of retrospective clairvoyance.

'From you I learnt it was all because of an unfortunate coincidence, a stupid misunderstanding. But such are the ways of history. Not even a monarch of Charles's perspicacity was infallible. The seven stone monsters enclosed in the hoop and hammer were meant to protect the church and six others like it. As you know, fantastic beasts on a Gothic cathedral usually have a very simple function – to drain water off the roof. In fact there was more to those grinning gorgons and scowling gryphons than mere functionality: they were believed to have protective powers.

'My ancestor was executed, the emperor was consumed with remorse and life went on. The three surviving members of the Brotherhood chose the chapel in the Cattle Market as their main church. From it they took their new name, and once again they had their emblems sculpted in stone under the roof. Thus it was, in the reign of Václav IV, that the Brotherhood of Corpus Christi came into being with the avowed purpose of protecting the churches of Prague New Town and punishing anyone who raised a hand against them.

'*Eye for eye, tooth for tooth, hand for hand, foot for foot, burning for burning, wound for wound, stripe for stripe*. It is high time we returned to the covenant that Moses made with the Lord. Is it not better to let a few incompetent and immoral architects and bureaucrats die rather than let them kill us? Is that not better than being slaughtered by a horde of motorized barbarians clutching steering-wheels instead of reins? Or choking to death on smoke in our own city? Well, isn't it better?'

He had finished. Now he waited for an answer.

I could not speak. I was paralysed with fear – of him, of the Brotherhood, of myself. Words crowded into my mouth yet I dared not let them escape. I closed my eyes and tried to swallow the words, but they stuck in my throat like fish bones. I was in agony. At last I coughed them up, spewing them out in an explosion of doubt and denial. But the words that came out were affirmative. Matthias Gmünd was right. I had finally found my teacher.

24

I walk.
My homeward steps indent the heavy soil.
And my one thought is this:
To walk with you, my one desire.

Richard Weiner

It felt like a march to the scaffold. The Knight of Lübeck strode at my side in silence, leading me in invisible chains. Prunslik walked behind us, whistling tunelessly. Perhaps he was watching my every move. Or perhaps I could have run for it and he'd have done nothing.

The full moon must have quarrelled with the night and gone into a sulk, for the sky was totally black. Only one in five streetlights seemed to be on, and I failed to recognize even places I knew well. I kept tripping on loose cobblestones and twice would have fallen had Gmünd not promptly seized my arm. He picked his way through the various hazards with remarkable assurance, as if he knew where to expect them. We met no one, and not a single car drove past – not surprisingly since the roads were by now barely roads. In the middle of one street – Kateřinská, probably – I saw a black cairn-like mound, higher than a man, and caught the smell of burning. Its walls, which were banked with earth, wood and leaves, glowed orange in the smoky gloom. I had no idea what it was for and did not dare ask, but something told me it was a charcoal kiln. My eyes smarted from the acrid fumes, but luckily the wind quickly dispersed them. Once I heard a distant screech of brakes and once, from beyond a dark apartment block, the brief wail of an ambulance. As we passed the police headquarters we felt the crunch of broken glass under our feet. A lot of broken glass. I looked up. Every window in the building was dark. The only light came from a torch burning in a bracket by the main entrance, which to my surprise stood wide open.

Within half an hour we were at Karlov. The Magistrale was silent. There was no sign of movement anywhere, not even on the pavements. The street lighting was not working – or had been turned off. Here and there a light shone in an upper window, but down in the street all was dark. I held my hand in front of my face and could just make out its pale outline; beyond it everything was lost in the clammy black void. Then, rising high above our heads, I saw the three domes of the church, like gold paper cut-outs against the faint green glow from the city below – a tourist's souvenir: 'Istanbul by night'. Soon it would again be graced with its three steeply pitched roofs that once towered three times higher than the walls themselves. And once again they would be visible from the castle.

Several people were standing around, apparently waiting, and stamping their feet in the cold. Now and then I caught the pale gleam of their faces, appearing and disappearing as they moved in the fickle light. In fact there was quite a crowd of them, and they seemed to be waiting for us. Someone came up to Gmünd, placed a hand on his elbow and took him to one side. I could see almost nothing but heard a muffled whisper and sounds of disagreement. It was the voice of a woman. She took a step towards me (or so I imagined) but was blocked by the bulky silhouette with the hat. There was more argument. Then the massive shadow let her past.

She came right up to me, so close I was able to make out her face. It was Rozeta – the other Rozeta. A slender young woman with elongated face, sunken cheeks and anxious eyes that were as black as the night behind her and made the whole face look like a white mask hanging in a black space. 'Into the church,' ordered the mask. 'Move.'

I moved. I saw the faint white smudge of her clenched hand and wondered what she was holding.

The fence around the church grounds had gone, as became clear to me the moment we entered the park at a point where I knew there had never been a gate. Under the presbytery wall, where a pair of torches flickered in iron holders, Rozeta told me to stop. I turned. In her hand was my pistol aimed straight at my face.

I was convinced she was about to pull the trigger. And she did. A loud metallic click broke the silence. I buckled at the knees and went down like a felled tree. But I was still alive. Rozeta bent over me and showed me her other hand. In it was a full clip of ammunition. She pushed it back into the gun and handed me the weapon. Then, taking me under the arm, she helped me to my feet.

'You saw me in the nude. I had to punish you.'

'But that was a trap!'

She gently touched my cheek. 'I know it wasn't your fault. If it had been, you'd be dying this evening along with Zahir. He should be here by now.'

My numbed hand felt the heat of the girl's body flowing into it from the butt of the pistol. I slipped it into my breast pocket where it warmed me like a lover's locket. Rozeta turned away and gazed at the dark mass of Nusle Bridge. For a moment her profile was lit up by headlights. I saw her gentle smile. The rest of her head was hidden by the hood of her long robe. Embroidered on its breast was a strange emblem: the sign of the hoop and hammer.

Two horizontal beams of light flooded the dark roadway at the end of the bridge revealing a truly theatrical scene. Standing on the stage in a semi-circle were forty or so anonymous figures, all dressed in the same manner as Rozeta, their heads hidden under hoods. Only a few of the conspirators' faces were visible. I picked out the bulky form of Gmünd, but there was no sign of his diminutive minion. I also noticed Mr Netřesk who, instead of watching the rapidly approaching vehicle like everyone else, was peering short-sightedly at the church with a wistful smile on his face, almost as if he hoped to see his former star pupil lurking in the shadows between its buttresses. Yet there was a furtive, guilty look about him: it was not the smile of a serene old man.

A little way off, scowling from under his hood, I caught sight of Dr Trug. He was staring straight at me, his face purple with apoplexy. Seeing my cursory wave he at once turned away and spat, then pushed back a capacious sleeve to consult his watch.

And there was someone else I recognized. Small head, down-turned mouth, enormous spectacles – it was the little old lady from St Apollinaris' who had been so outraged at the sight of coltsfoot on a girl's statue.

The car had now reached the end of the bridge and for a moment disappeared round a bend. Somewhere close by an engine spluttered noisily to life, and a moment later an orange behemoth lumbered out of the shadows on the far side of the road straight across the Magistrale. It was the platform crane. At first its cab seemed to be empty. Then I glimpsed a shock of flaming red hair at the window as the tiny driver battled with the controls.

Zahir always drove too fast. Now, unable to either brake or swerve, his car ended its journey at the precise point where the Heptecclesion began. The sound of the impact was barely audible – no more than a soft indescribable crunch, like a beer can crumpling in a fist. Everything went dark. Then the sky was pierced by a sudden flash . . . followed by darkness . . . another flash . . . and darkness again. Like a Ferris wheel come adrift from its moorings, the car cartwheeled slowly through the night sky – at first catapulting vertically over our heads, then curving into a slow lucent arc. I heard Rozeta laughing and clapping like a child at the circus. I could not bring myself to look at her face.

I knew what I had to do. I would run down the Albertov Steps, hide somewhere among the university buildings and telephone Olejar at the first opportunity. If anyone followed me I would shoot

– I had plenty of rounds. And if they caught me – well, I'd keep the last bullet for myself. Until then I would fight for my life. I would spare no one. I would pay them back for Zahir, whom they had just murdered before my very eyes; for Netřesk, whom they had inveigled into their bloody business; and for myself, whom they had abused for their own nefarious ends. And I would avenge Rozeta, whom they had turned from the unfortunate victim of a scientific experiment into a bloodthirsty monster. I knew exactly what I had to do. But I did not do it. This lovely, unhappy girl had saved my life. She had helped me escape. She had saved me from the madness that surely awaited me in this weird pre-Hussite brotherhood. How could I abandon her?

The car reaches the top of its trajectory, pauses in mid-air and starts to describe a second graceful parabola, this time downwards, before plummeting vertically on to the Magistrale. Meanwhile, as in a painting by Caspar David Friedrich, the pale clock-face of the moon emerges from the dark ruddy glow above the city and casts a ghostly light over the semicircle of the Brotherhood. Its gleaming orb resembles the iron bob of a pendulum about to come to rest – slowing down, shortening its oscillation, then stopping altogether. No, not quite: there is still a tiny tremor in it. We are all looking up. Nobody moves. I cannot even turn my head. The impossible has happened: Time has stopped and is waiting for a signal to move on.

Then, very gradually, the pendulum coaxes itself back into motion. And just before the giant painted dial slips behind its black veil something moves on its watery face. Is it a clock hand edging towards midnight or simply a random brushstroke drawn by an invisible hand? Suddenly it falters, goes limp, bends, droops . . . and slips back down the dial into an unknown realm of timelessness.

The girl in front of me stood still as a statue as she watched the spectacle. Suddenly her hood fell on to her shoulders, exposing a mass of dark hair. On her head shone a bright circlet of yellow flowers. I am a weak man, and the sight quite overwhelmed me. All I could do was step forward, lift those lustrous tresses and kiss the pale skin on the nape of her neck.

Through that pointed arch, drawn across the night sky by a somersaulting sports car, I caught a glimpse – as through a Gothic window – of a glorious world transfigured by God's blessing. And Rozeta was with me. In that terrifyingly beautiful, miraculously prolonged moment the heavens had mercy on me and I finally fell in love.

EPILOGUE

Why rush? Flight is in vain!
Faced with this wonder all haste dies.
The dying day opens its eyes
And time turns back again.

Karl Kraus

Praise be to God, the long cold winter is over. It lasted nearly seven centuries.

I spent the first six weeks of the New Year in bed with a fever. For some reason I had been moved to the red corridor of the Knight's apartment in the old Hotel Bouvines. Its upholstered walls afforded warmth and security and repaid me with soft caresses whenever I beat my head against them. During all that time somebody – usually Rozeta – fed and looked after me. I am still ashamed to think that every day she saw me in such a pitiful state. They say all I did was moan and wail, though most of the time I was aware of nothing. But winter finally came to an end, and one morning I walked out of the house like a man reborn.

Spring was slow in putting on her finery. Not until late April were the trees brushed with green, and only now, a month later, has the lilac burst into belated but all the more lavish bloom. As soon as I was strong enough I was moved from the Bouvines to my new home, where the first thing I saw from the window was their gleaming white clusters. How can one capture such beauty? Can one reach out and grasp it, put it in one's pocket or clasp it to one's breast? Ah, but beauty can be cruel, too, so merciless and immoral in its indifference. For hours on end I gaze at the blossoms from my window, savouring their distant fragrance, touching them in my imagination. I have great sprays of them brought up to my room, bury my face in the intoxicating cloudlets and secretly wish I could become one of the vases and let the flowers nourish my soul.

I now have a new name in addition to my old one. The seminary students have jokingly but good-naturedly taken to calling me Dalimil[1] in deference to my new role (born of necessity rather than choice, I admit) as chronicler of our little world. It's a job for a monk really, but since we do not yet have any monks the Master entrusted me with the task.

My windows in Faust House, which is at once my gaol, home and scriptorium, face north over the square. It is a good light for a painter. In the morning its cold fingers cleanse his mind and sight, etching on his retina perfect motifs for his clumsy hand to execute; in the evening it teases its way into his heart, tickling the organ that is the seat of sentiment.

My master, Matthias, continues to take me round the churches (albeit still blindfold and handcuffed) and is still eager to hear the voices that speak from within me. But his greatest thirst for knowledge was stilled under the roof of Karlov; since then he has merely been filling in the picture with more figures, buildings and landscapes. He knows that the canvas I am painting will never be – can never be – completed, so he does not call upon me as often as he used to. In fact this quite suits me, as I am kept very busy with the illuminations for the chronicle, for which I use a goose quill, oak-gall ink and an assortment of bright pigments. I am especially proud of my capitals, with their intertwining stems, leaves and flowers and, peeping out from among them, the occasional mythical beast. People come from all over town to admire my work. These are my people, and I am theirs. If some itinerant painter were to turn up here in search of commissions they would soon send him packing. Just look at this, K. Isn't it rather splendid? That gold! And look, if you turn the letter on its side it's like an M. Turn it the other way, to the left, and it's like a W. M for Mocker? W for Wohlmuth?[2] K for . . . ?

The Old Masters.

What I cannot put into words in the chronicle I express in my illuminations – and sometimes vice versa. I am in a privileged position, and for this I thank the Almighty, for it is from Him that I have my gift of retrospective clairvoyance and extraordinary awareness of times past. Without a knowledge of history we would drown in a mire of perplexity.

Our good lord and master Matthias quickly earned the sobriquet 'the Great'. At first we said it laughingly, but now we speak the words with the utmost respect and reverence. For not only is he his ancestors' most industrious disciple and a shining example to us all, he is the right hand of Providence itself. Soon after I recovered he said to me, 'You're not cut out for science or for a life of action. Why not try art?' – though that's not what we call it here. It was he who discovered my talent for painting, and in return I serve him faithfully. Besides, one day the Master will have no further use for my visionary gift, and I shall have to make a living on my own. Writing and drawing are the only trades for which I am suited, and none of the guilds would take me in as a journeyman. Whether they be potters, butchers, dyers, draymen, barbers, goldsmiths, saddlers, woodcutters, coopers, carpenters, tailors, armourers, water bailiffs, saltpetre-makers, bell founders, alchemists, tanners, inkers, dressmakers, fish-wives, soap-boilers, apothecaries, fish-salters, clothworkers or simple cottars – all guard their livelihoods jealously and brook no interlopers, even those who are prepared to buy their way in. This ensures they have a quiet life and are well provided for – indeed, some already own several houses. Time now moves at a slower pace. It is a goodly pace.

The biggest square in the world, which I survey with curious eyes from dawn to dusk, has been newly refurbished – by which I mean it has been rebuilt exactly as it was in the fourteenth century. The Upper New Town of Prague, alias the Heptecclesion, has triumphed over age-old human destructiveness: henceforward nothing here will change, and stone will rest on stone for ever more. As the Emperor Charles decreed, all buildings will soon be only of stone, with a single upper storey, wide eaves and vaulted cellars; some will have arcades, and all will have a long strip of garden at the back for growing vegetables. The layout of the streets will be more of a challenge. The experience of the recent past has shown that straight lines encourage drivers to behave like madmen and are the cause of many accidents. Our pre-Hussite brotherhood, unlike the rest of humanity, has learnt the lessons of history and decided to revert to the time-tested pattern of narrow twisting alleys, dark passageways and unexpected corners, thus obliging both riders and pedestrians to moderate their pace as a mark of respect for our city of stone.

I do not know how things are beyond the city gates – I have not yet ventured outside. The Heptecclesion is protected by stone ramparts with battlements and five fortified gates, the largest being the Swine Gate, whose pennants can be seen from every corner of our little world. Our walls cannot keep out the poisonous gases emitted by the unnatural means of transport still being used outside, but at least they put the fear of God into vandals and other barbarians. For their part, the folk outside complain of the stink from our middens and open sewers, so we sometimes sling a few barrowloads of the stuff down on them from the battlements. One of the first things we did was to get rid of the underground sewers and convert the tunnels into armouries and storerooms. In the event of a war with the Old Town – which I wager will come before the year is out – they will also provide us with an escape route to the river.

On the far side of the square, next to the Town Hall, stands the New Gate. Its mighty walls are topped with embattled parapets and nine turrets, each flying the colours of the Master. All those who pass under that Gothic arch cannot but feel its power, and once inside they are as meek as lambs.

Our soldiers have put up a pillory in front of the Town Hall. It is a most ingenious invention, guaranteed to bring the most recalcitrant of miscreants to their senses. There is even a waiting list of sinners. Next to the pillory stands the gallows – a hitherto unused deterrent.

We have suffered several raids. They drove through our square in their wheeled metal boxes terrifying our people. They also took photographs – those of them who did not have their little machines smashed to pieces on the spot. We even caught one of the scoundrels. He was given a good hiding and a few nights in the stocks. His diabolical vehicle was burnt at the stake. The metal parts were salvaged by smiths, who melted them down for swords and iron bars. And we had one tragic incident. One day (it was market day, so the small gate on Ječná was open) a car hurtled into the square, blinding shoppers with its headlights and terrifying them out of their wits. A child ran out in front of it and was killed outright. The culprit was on the point of driving off when a baker, known to one and all as Martin Houska, or Bun, ran out of the Saltery (a new building in the middle of the square) and whacked the car window with his long wooden peel, shattering it in a single blow. The murderous machine skidded to a halt and out staggered its driver, bloodied, groaning and unable to speak in consequence of a broken jaw. His audacity, however, was undiminished. He took out a revolver – an old-fashioned model but none the less effective – brandished it briefly in the air, then took aim at the baker and shot him in the chest. At once a hail of arrows rained down on the intruder from the tower of the Town Hall. One hit him in the shoulder; another pieced his flank. The townsfolk threw themselves upon him, and it is a wonder they did not batter him to death. Instead they dragged him over to the Town Hall and put him in the stocks. The next day they gouged out his eyes, since it was they that should have seen the child. The day after that they drove nails through his right foot, since it had operated the accelerator – that primitive weapon of the pagan past. And on the third day they cut off his hands with a butcher's cleaver, since they had held the wheel and were thus the real murderers. They say he bled to death. I did not see the incident myself, being occupied with other business at Emmaus; but the gruesome meting out of justice, with neither judge nor executioner, was witnessed by a sizeable crowd, among them several aldermen at the windows of the Town Hall, who dared not intervene. Martin the baker recovered, cured by a coltsfoot salve prepared by a herbalist – none other than the little old lady from the beginning of my tale – and was appointed Vice-Governor. Nor did the vehicle escape punishment: its tyres were slashed, its lights smashed, and its gear lever torn out and, together with the driver's hands, nailed to the outside of the New Gate as a warning to other devotees of twentieth-century life. Since then we have had no more trouble with automobiles.

Saturday is market day for fish, eggs and fruit. The meat market is on Thursdays. Costermongers and tinkers set out their stalls on fast days as well, but the aldermen generally turn a blind eye and punishment is rare. There is a brisk trade in livestock. Now that we have demolished all buildings on sites not designated by the Emperor Charles we have an abundance of new pasture. Vines have been planted beneath the city walls, and in the summer we shall harvest the first wheat from our little fields.

On Sundays I go to mass at the Church of Emmaus just across the road. Sometimes I also go to St Václav's, where the canon preaches a good sermon. Once a week Netřesk comes up for a game of backgammon. The physickers and apothecaries who live downstairs and keep the herb garden at the back say he won't last very long. And so, with one eye on the hourglass as we play, my old teacher prepares me for my life with Lucie, the young woman with the worried brow and the wry smile. It's very kind of him. I have promised him that when he departs this world I will be a good father to his daughter.

As befits a wife, Lucie only visits me in his company. When she looks at me with those clever grey eyes I see melancholy, astuteness, even a promise of tenderness and realize to my amazement that the only thing that troubles me about this beautiful woman – my earthly betrothed – is her availability. My heart aches.

She enjoys listening to me talk about the unicorn. Or is her interest only feigned? She has never set eyes on it, whereas I see it regularly, whether I want to or not. How blasé we become about our gifts! On silvery medieval nights, under a full moon undimmed by the glare of streetlamps, the unshod beast comes prowling under my window and raises its long slender horn in greeting. We understand each other. I know that once I am married the unicorn will disappear for ever. In the meantime, however, it continues to flatter my vanity with its visitations.

In the evenings, at the first call to rest, I lay down my quill or brush (I cannot work by the light of tapers or tallow lamps) and hasten to the window to look down at the darkening square, where Matthias the Great and his retinue can generally be seen inspecting the building works. Sometimes Rozeta is with him. And sometimes, when I'm lucky, she glances up at me with a little wave and that direct yet strangely blank look I have never ceased to marvel at. When I paint her I give her a transparent veil falling from her elaborate coiffure to her breast. Though I know her terrible secret the woman remains a mystery to me. I console myself with dreams of a black angel: when we are in purgatory together she will be my bride. But now she moves in higher circles.

Matthias, of course, enjoys the most exalted station. The Knight dresses very grandly in a loose-fitting scarlet robe. From his broad leather belt hangs the Ducal Sword inlaid with agate and moldavite. His consort wears long flowing gowns, blue or black in colour and richly bejewelled, with a low waist and wide sleeves and, about her neck, a fine golden chain hung with little bells. My own attire is modest: a coarse tunic, narrow hose and fashionably (though not immoderately) pointed boots. I know my place and am content in it.

I have immortalized Matthias and Rozeta in many of my illuminations, into which I often incorporate the elongated shapes of the church windows my master loves so much, embellishing them with elaborate floral motifs. I once painted them as Adam and Eve and even allowed myself a little joke at Mr Prunslik's expense (he is now our Lord Chamberlain, by the way) by portraying him as the Serpent. I have also depicted them as the Holy Family in the stable, with the Duke as Joseph and her Ladyship as Mary gazing adoringly on an infant that bears a striking likeness to yours truly. Yes, I know it was a sin. But I have confessed, and as a penance promised the priest I would design some new windows for Emmaus.

On clear evenings I like to watch the sunset. If I lean out of the window far enough I can just see the orange rays catching the little tower of Bouvines Palace, which still serves as the ducal residence. But already, twentyscore paces to the left, another tower can be seen above the rooftops: the castle of St Václav is rising again on the spot where it once stood. I eagerly await the day when its battlements flash in the setting sun and Lord Matthias invites me to his new home.

The sight that gladdens my heart most lies just beyond the large, artfully wrought stone fountain where tradesmen and housewives go to fill their pails and pitchers. For there, rising out of the ruins of the park like a phoenix from the ashes, is the Chapel of Corpus Christi – stone for stone as once it was. It will be the purest symbol of our changed age. The work is being directed by none other than Master Zahir. Yes, he survived his execution. Afterwards Matthias asked Rozeta to pardon him and, after a modest hesitation, she consented. The wily tomcat quickly adjusted to his new circumstances and now seems happy enough with his lot, though he will never walk again in any of his seven remaining lives. Four journeymen carry him around the building site on a litter and keep a constant eye on him. I did a painting of him too – see? – in the arms of a lovely odalisque.

While the chapel is under construction mass is celebrated in a wooden building near by that serves as a temporary shelter for the old altar from St Peter and St Paul's on Vyšehrad, recently salvaged from the riverbed by a team of our men led by the Master. His sacred right to rule has thus been reaffirmed. Already the faithful of Prague are flocking to the altar, and only last week the Bishop of Olomouc came to pay his devotions.

There is nothing new under the sun and never will be. Is it not time to return to a world that works? We believe in the old ways – ways that lead us back. Our friends in Písek, Kutná Hora, Úštěk, Český Dub, Sezimovo Ústí and Jindřichův Hradec are with us. Together, with the help of the Almighty, we shall bring the whole country back into the safe embrace of the Middle Ages. The Modern Age is at an end, glory be to God and our wise leader Matthias. Without them we would be doomed, together with the rest of humanity. At the eleventh hour they opened our inner eye and turned our vision back. Only with this vision can we await the apocalypse; only with this faith can we enter the new heavenly age, the beautiful and blessed fourteenth century.

NOTES

Chapter 4

1 Nusle Bridge is a massive concrete viaduct built in the 1960s. It carries a six-lane highway (the notorious Magistrale) and, running just below it, a railway line that forms part of the Prague metro network. It is a favourite place for suicides.

2 Klement Gottwald, first President of post-1948 Communist Czechoslovakia.

Chapter 6

1 The protagonist of Jaroslav Hašek's novel of the same name. Both loved and loathed by Czechs, he remains their archetypal antihero who survives by cunning, insolence and earthy common sense.

Chapter 8

1 The Utraquists maintained that the Eucharist should be administered 'in both kinds' (*sub utraque specie*), that is, as both bread and wine, and to all the congregation rather than only the clergy. They were also known as Calixtines, from their emblem the chalice.

2 Josef Mocker (1835–89) restored many Gothic buildings in Prague. Apart from St Stephen's, he also rebuilt the Church of St Peter and St Paul at Vyšehrad and played a major role in the completion of St Vitus' Cathedral.

Chapter 9

1 Jan Želivský (1380–1422), the radical priest who led the Hussite procession through the streets of Prague that led to the First Defenestration of Prague (1419) and, ultimately, to the Hussite Wars.

Chapter 10

1 Bohuslav Balbín (1621–88) was the outstanding Czech historian of his age.

Chapter 12

1 The princess of medieval Czech legend who is said to have stood on the rock of Vyšehrad and had a vision of the future glory of Prague.

2 Jan Žižka (*c.* 1360–1424), follower of Jan Hus; a brilliant general who managed to turn an army of ill-equipped peasants into an efficient fighting force against the Roman Catholic army. The name Žižka means 'one-eyed'.

3 The Basel Compactates (1433) marked the readmission into the Catholic Church of the moderate Hussites who, as a concession, were allowed to practise the Eucharist in both kinds (see note on the Utraquists). The Compactates were never recognized by the Vatican.

4 The Battle of White Mountain (*Bílá hora* in Czech); a turning-point in the Thirty Years War in Bohemia, when a Czech army was crushed by the Habsburg Ferdinand II and his allies. Subsequently twenty-seven noblemen and burghers were executed in Old Town Square, and many members of the Czech aristocracy fled the country.

5 A family of Baroque architects. The best known are Johann Dientzenhofer, his brother Christoph and his nephew Kilian Ignaz.

Chapter 22

1 The Michna Summer Palace, a stylish eighteenth-century villa built by Kilian Ignaz Dientzenhofer, now the Antonin Dvořák Museum. It is also known as the Villa America.

Chapter 23

1 In Czech, Letohrádek Hvězda; a Renaissance hunting lodge built in the form of a star. Once surrounded by forest, it is now within the city of Prague.

2 Thomas Müntzer (*c.* 1488–1525), German anti-Lutheran theologian and rebel leader.

Epilogue

1 Dalimil is credited with writing the earliest Czech chronicle, describing events up to around 1314.

2 Bonifaz Wohlmut (1510–79), German architect known especially for his work on St Vitus' Cathedral.